A
PARLIAMENT
for
OWLS

MARY REEVES BELL

For

Robert David Bell

TABLE OF CONTENTS

BOOK ONE

BOOK TWO

BOOK THREE

BOOK ONE

CHAPTER 1

SONGS FOR SIGHING

. . . thorns shall come up in her palaces, nettles and brambles in the fortresses
thereof: and it shall be a habitation of dragons, and a parliament for owls.

—*The Prophet Isaiah*

THERE WAS NOTHING ABOUT THE DAY TO SUGGEST THAT EVIL
was on the way. Ominous clouds did not cover the sky. Winds were not
blowing a gale. There was an ordinary weak spring sun doing little to
warm Raluca Moldovan as she stepped out of her family's courtyard onto a
muddy street in the remote Transylvanian village where she lived with her
parents and younger brother. The slight girl struggled to hold open a heavy
courtyard gate for a gaggle of noisy geese. They rushed past her, shattering the quiet with bad-tempered squawking, then took running bursts of
unsuccessful flight that quickly gave way to grazing for grubs in the grassy
verge. Raluca shut the gate, smiled at the foolish birds that behaved as
though they had escaped rather than been released, then she set off to pick
up her best friend for school.

Trailing a twig along the stucco-covered houses that lined the street,
Raluca tried to slow her naturally quick steps. Nadia was always late and
she hated waiting in her house. It smelled of dirty dishes, moldy walls,
and of the old woman who was no longer able to wash herself or clean the
miserable little space she shared with her granddaughter.

"Morning," Raluca called to the village shepherd who was gathering sheep from each courtyard on their way to pasture. The old man had been taking his dog, a flask of wine, and a loaf of bread (but no book of verse) to keep him company while grazing animals through long days of searing heat and biting cold for more years than he could remember. He would take the herd to common land around the village and return them home at dusk.

A vast chasm separated the people of Tirnova from modern times, with the exception of the recent arrival of the Internet. Each earthen-tiled roof held a satellite dish and free Internet access flowed from a government trying to drag its population into the twenty-first century. Watching *CSI Miami* did little to bridge a widening gap with the outside world. But it did make girls like Nadia who observed that world on television every night want very much to try it out.

Unlike her friend, Raluca didn't feel trapped by life in Tirnova. She liked the rhythm of it and cheerfully did chores in the garden, gathered eggs from the hen house, and when their big brown-and-white cow came through the courtyard gate at sunset Raluca often followed into the shed and talked to her father while he milked. Sitting on a wooden three-legged stool, bucket between his legs, the hard-working man listened to his daughter's stories while his rough hands moved quickly from udder to udder until the bucket was filled with warm foamy milk. A trio of cats waited nearby for the last squirts he always sent their way, then settled down to lick what they missed from whiskers and fur. Their soft purrs added to the night music in the courtyard.

Raluca shared the chores with Adrian, her younger brother. They fed the rabbits and pigeons that would become meat pies for Sunday dinner and a pen full of pigs eating their way toward certain slaughter at Easter or Christmas.

"You're late again," Raluca complained when Nadia finally emerged from her house.

"And what's up with the clothes and makeup? If your mother... "

"If my mother could see me," Nadia snapped. "If my mother could see me, she wouldn't let me out the door like this? Is that what you mean? Well, I don't have a mother anymore and my grandmother doesn't even know where she is most of the time — let alone what I'm wearing — so I can wear what I please. Which I will."

"Sorry, Nadia. I didn't mean it that way. Really."

Nadia's parents left two years ago to find work in Spain, promising to return and take her along for a good life out of Romania. But they never returned. And apart from the rare letter with small amounts of cash, which she spent on clothes and a new cell phone, Nadia tried not to think about her mother and father. It only fueled a growing anger in her that sometimes erupted at the wrong people.

Today, Nadia was wearing a short tight skirt, faux black leather boots, and a denim jacket not designed to keep out the morning chill. Her short-cropped hair was dyed bright red and piercings ringed both ear lobes.

"I said I'm sorry," Raluca insisted, getting a little tired of apologizing to her increasingly volatile friend. "It's just that you're so angry all the time," Raluca caught up with her and tugged on her sleeve. "Please tell me what's wrong."

Nadia stopped, turned around and glared.

"Wrong? Tell you what's wrong. You're my best friend and you have to ask what's wrong? Where've you been while my whole life's falling apart? Lost in your own happy little world — with your own happy little family, gathering your own stupid little eggs with a father who adores you, a mother that's always around taking care of you. Nobody is calling you Gypsy trash... oh never mind... you don't understand. Nobody understands."

Nadia saw the look on Raluca's face.

"I'm sorry. I didn't mean to take it out on you. None of the crap happening in my life is your fault. You know," she went on, trying not to sound so angry, "that old proverb your mother loves to quote... something like... 'don't run after the train that's left the station'."

Raluca was wishing she hadn't started this and replied, "I don't even know what that stupid proverb means, anyway."

"It means that I'm going to stop 'running after a train that's left the station' — my parents are gone and they're never coming back. There's nothing for me in this godforsaken place. For you either! Look at us! People in the rest of the world do not still use outdoor toilets, for one! I want out. I want out. I want out... " her voice trailed off. "I just want out."

An old woman sitting on an upended bucket splashing whitewash on the trunk of a spindly plum tree listened as the girls passed.

"Okay. Calm down," Raluca said. "Me too, one day. I guess. But right now we have to finish school. We're just kids."

"You might be a kid," Nadia snapped. "I don't have the option." As much as Nadia wanted to, she couldn't tell Raluca what was really on her mind. She couldn't tell her about the two men she'd met at the café yesterday. About their expensive clothes, and fancy car. Their very white teeth, soft hands, and clean fingernails. They didn't look like anyone Nadia had ever seen before in her whole life. Except on television. She still couldn't imagine why they had talked to her. Or bought her an orange Fanta and asked all kinds of friendly questions. Finally, someone was actually interested in her. She smiled at the thought.

"Okay. You're right. I'm wrong," Raluca said. "I know it's hard living alone with just your Baba for company but you're always welcome at our house. In fact, my Dad offered to paint your trees this weekend. Adrian will come too. It'll be fun."

"See," Nadia shouted dramatically, "that's what I mean! Painting tree trunks in spring is not fun. It's stupid."

"Even if Adrian comes along? He has a crush on you, you know."

Raluca's brother Adrian was going to be handsome. Someday.

"Oh please, Adi is such a baby!" She was striding off down the street again, aware that she might not see Raluca or Adi or her Baba again for a long time.

"Adi is exactly one year younger than we are," Raluca reminded her. "And thirteen is not a baby."

"Well, tell your dad and Adi thanks but no thanks. I won't be painting my trees this year."

The spring ritual of whitewashing the trunks of plum trees planted along the roadways of villages throughout Romania had gone on unchanged for centuries, through wars, revolutions, communism, and modernity. Like everything else in Tirnova, Nadia hated it.

I am getting out, she thought with each step. *I am getting out of this place that never changes. No more lonely nights spent in a dark and miserable room with Baba. I will become the smart girl who got out,* she told herself as she watched her best friend enter the school building a few steps ahead of her. "You have always been first at everything," Nadia muttered under her breath. "Until now."

Five hours later when the closing bell rang, the sun was high and hot. Raluca glanced up at a mother stork standing on skinny legs working twigs into a vast nest atop the electric pole outside the school; the storks, at least, were putting the arrival of new technologies to good use.

"Why don't you come do homework with me this afternoon?" Raluca asked, hoping her friend was in a better mood. "Mom made your favorite. Walnut cake. Please come, Nadia."

"I'm going to the café," she answered. "Why don't you come with me for a change?"

It was an ongoing argument. Raluca rolled her eyes, "For the same reason I never go with you. I'm saving my money for something useful

— not wasting it at the café. There's no one there but a bunch of creepy old men sitting around drinking beer anyway."

Not the ones I met yesterday, Nadia thought.

Then she screamed. A long, high-pitched shriek that shattered the morning quiet.

"See, that's what I mean — this place makes me sick."

"It's only a dead pig!" Raluca laughed as a farmer pulling a flatbed cart came around the corner toward them. Blood was spraying from the pig's nearly severed head as it bounced along independently of its body over the rough road.

"It's not the first dead pig you've ever seen, and I guess you eat pork like the rest of us."

Raluca couldn't help laughing at her friend.

"Well, I don't have to watch it bleeding all over the bleeding street, do I? I'm sick to death of this place."

A few minutes later Raluca hesitated at Nadia's door, wondering why her friend merely waved without the usual "see you tomorrow". She wondered, but not for long. Raluca was sorry for her friend, but Nadia's moods were getting on her nerves and she rushed up the street happy to be going home. Alone.

Later that afternoon, while Raluca was eating walnut cake and telling her mother about the day, Nadia was spreading tasteless, artificially-bright yellow margarine on a piece of stale bread left over from breakfast, and watching jittery images on the television screen. Sound off. Usually Nadia wanted her grandmother to wake up and keep her company. Even babbling nonsense. Not today.

With a small handheld mirror, Nadia checked her outfit one last time. Front and back. Short black skirt, red tights; lacy low-cut white camisole, and her new denim jacket. She pushed her tiny breasts up without noticeable effect, teased her hair, sprayed it again, pulled on her black boots — confident now that she looked at least sixteen.

She checked and double-checked to make sure her cell phone was charged and safely zipped inside the pocket of her purse, then looked around the miserable room. Nadia gently shook the mound of dirty blankets covering her grandmother.

"Baba," she whispered. "I have to go away for a while. There's bread and zacusca for your dinner and Raluca will come by sometimes and look after you until I get back."

A slight movement and muffled sound came from under the covers; it startled Nadia and she backed away from the bed, whispering: "I love you, Baba. I promise to come back... with money to fix our house, I'll come back and take care of you. I promise."

It didn't occur to Nadia, until much later, that this was exactly what her parents said the day they slipped out that same door with promises they didn't keep.

Geese and ducks scattered as she ran down the street, skipping over bird droppings and mud puddles without looking back.

The men were there. Sitting at the outside table again, just as they had promised. Trying to look cool, calm, and sixteen, Nadia approached with a swagger. Empty espresso cups and scattered sugar granules littered the red plastic tablecloth. The men smiled, white teeth gleaming.

She ducked her head under the big Coca-Cola umbrella, stumbling on a crack in the uneven cement floor. One of the men reached over to steady her chair, brushing her arm with his gold bracelet.

"So, is your friend interested in getting out of this place and starting the good life with you?" he asked.

"We can get her a good job too, probably working for the same family with you in Sweden."

"She's interested," Nadia lied, wishing the men would offer her Fanta like they did yesterday.

"Of course she's interested," the man went on. "Who wouldn't want out of here? Not only is this place nowhere — it isn't even on the way *to* nowhere."

Laughing at the locals was something Nadia did all the time, so she was surprised to find that the sneers of these strangers made her uncomfortable.

"You are a very clever girl to get out of all of this. God, why would anyone live in this dump?"

Something in her face alerted the men that they didn't want to go too far until they were actually in the vehicle. Some of the girls were not, they knew, as dim as they first appeared. It was time to go.

They stood.

The first thing Nadia noticed about the interior of the car was the beautiful smell of fine leather. It was like nothing she had ever known, yet somehow it was exactly as she had always imagined.

The second thing she noticed, as the door of the plush SUV with tinted windows closed and automatically locked, was that something was terribly wrong.

Sun glinted off the metal of Nadia's cell phone and caught the shepherd's eye as he took the animals to pasture the following morning. He pushed the tiny buttons with his thick fingers, mildly amused by the strange beeping sounds, then stuffed it in an inner pocket and followed the animals to a high pasture, where he took a drink from his flask of wine before laying down in the grass to join them in a nap.

Ever alert to all known dangers, the old man slept through the first muffled ringing of the phone. The second time it woke him. Irritated now, and already slightly inebriated, he smashed the phone with his boot and returned it to a dirty pocket where it joined other bits of forgotten detritus accumulated over time.

CHAPTER 2

A GIFT THAT KEEPS ON GIVING

Man has suddenly fallen from God and is still in flight.
The Fall is not enough for him; he cannot flee fast enough.

—*Dietrich Bonhoeffer*

ON THE SAME DAY NADIA IOVAN WENT MISSING, FOUR THOU-
sand nine-hundred and seventy miles, multiple cultural worlds, and seven
time zones away, Eric Kissane left his office at WOWL, Inc. for the last
time. He drove his beloved Porsche Carrera around the Capital Beltway to
the Department of Motor Vehicles. It was a blustery Thursday afternoon.
Kissane maneuvered his high-powered sports car at a disappointing speed
through heavy traffic, up the George Washington Memorial Parkway, over
the Potomac River to Tyson's Corner in Virginia. Once-bucolic farmland,
with a lone filling station called Tysons, had given way to high-end shopping malls and towers of glass and steel for beltway bandit corporations
that feed off the Federal Government.

Kissane's task in Tyson's Corner was mundane and his mood was
foul. Pulling into the parking lot of the DMV, he groaned at the sight of a
queue stretching out the front door.

Welcome to Tyson's Corner Department of Motor Vehicles
New procedures have been initiated to make
your visit brief and pleasant.

"Not a chance in hell," Eric muttered, reading a sign posted on the door after inching along for ten minutes just to get inside. He looked at his watch, read the sign again, and hoped at least the brief part true. With a two o'clock production staff meeting, he couldn't afford to spend hours in a lame government office. It would be tight, he thought, but with luck he should make it back to the office in time for his meeting.

"Yes?" a voice at the Information Desk said. Not looking up.

"Driver's license," he replied with equal economy.

Eric was handed the ubiquitous clipboard, given a number pulled from a machine, and told to wait his turn.

He hesitated briefly.

"Excuse me, ma'am, could you give me some idea how long the wait might be?"

The public servant knew better than to meet the public's eye. She shrugged her substantial shoulders and, offering little help, replied:

"Somewheres between one to two 'ours, I'd say."

A chorus of groans went up behind him. "You've got to be kidding," Eric exploded, slamming the clipboard on the counter.

"Oh dear... it can't take that long." A young woman juggling a baby in one arm and paperwork in the other let her lament slip almost apologetically. "I drove all the way to this DMV because it's supposed to be quicker... average wait only 30 minutes it said online. But your manager promised..."

"She must have meant yesterday, honey, because today, as you can see, we are very busy. Next."

Eric reached down and picked up the baby's pacifier thrown for the umpteenth time on the dirty floor. Glad he didn't have a baby to keep quiet while waiting, he offered an encouraging word to the harried young mother, took his ticket, and wandered off to accept his own fate. It would have been satisfying to demand to see the manager and lodge a complaint. But he was fairly certain his "suggestions" would not be at all welcome or do any good. Loath to waste energy on so fruitless a confrontation, Eric sat down with the rest of the tired patrons watching a digital scrolling screen, waiting for their number to come up.

Tightly grasping his escape ticket, B 467, Kissane leaned forward in his seat, watching the process with expectation for several minutes until the truth sank in... he wasn't going anywhere soon.

Eric pulled out his smartphone and caught up on his messages, including an e-mail from Randy Tate on tomorrow's program. Clear and concise as usual. A quick glance gave Kissane all he needed to know. Tomorrow's guest was a young Christian hip-hop artist currently making a big splash and enough controversy to be good for business. It looked to Eric like a typical interview, unlike yesterday morning's disaster of a show with his brother-in-law, Jeff Lorten.

Jeff had been on Eric's talk show to pitch his new book, *Balancing Your Act... Another of Life's Little Instruction Books: How to Avoid Sacrificing Your Family on the Altar of Career in Eight Easy Steps.* The target audience was young, upwardly-mobile, eager-to-be-successful men. Eric had found the whole thing distasteful. Not only was the book yet another in a series of countless rip-offs of the original *Life's Little Instruction Book*, but also a typical example of the Lorten family using its own media to hype its own products and make even more money. Not that Eric minded that exactly, it was the mother's milk of his own success and he could hype with the best of them, it was just that his brother-in-law was so obvious. And, Eric felt, the company had crossed the line when they purchased tens of thousands of copies of Jeff's book (selling them through a third party) to boost sales and achieve best-seller status.

The ebullient Jeff had talked his way breathlessly through all eight points during the hour-long show, managing to mention in nearly every breath a sports or business star, senator or congressmen who had benefited from his personal attention and very own brand of spiritual wisdom. Now, even an ordinary Joe could have the benefit of such wisdom for only $26.95 hardback. Jeff relished his role as counselor to the rich and powerful; Eric was not impressed. After the program the men parted, as usual, too aware of one another's failings to be friends.

Eric finished reading a short bio on his guest for tomorrow's talk show, "bad boy musician turned good" who was now hugely successful. Shouldn't be hard to sell, he thought. It was a popular theme. Kissane checked the progress on the digital board.

Very little, it appeared.

He continued to stare at the digital screen, frustration growing.

Only three out of fifteen cubicles paid for by taxpayer's dollars were actually operating, and they appeared to be manned by overworked and undermotivated people moving in slow motion, seemingly oblivious to the seething crowd held captive by their apathy.

"Probably turned down as greeters by Wal-Mart," Eric muttered to no one in particular. The harried young mother laughed.

Number C980 now being served at window number 9.

At least the computer voice was perky.

Numbers were being called in (seemingly) random fashion. Even the windows, he noticed, were not sequential.

Customer number A200 now being served at window number 12.

Customer B450 now being served at window number 9.

Time was crawling by.

Customer C981 now being served at window number 9.

The bizarre process was driving him nuts. Like a kidnap victim with Stockholm syndrome, Eric began to focus on the woman at window number 9. She was a stout, middle-aged woman going soft around the jowls with a loosening of the flesh above the elbow, but pleasant enough in a plain sort of way. Unlike her colleagues, she was processing customers before they aged noticeably. He tried to catch her eye. Gave her a smile, hoping it would encourage her to work faster.

Overcome with an irrational urge to raise his hand and shout, "pick-me, pick-me", Eric decided he really was losing it and tried to calm down.

1:30 p.m. came and went.

Furious but trapped, Eric called his producer and bailed on the afternoon meeting. "Do the best you can without me, Randy, and brief me later. I'm not giving up and coming back to this hellhole another day and I'm well and truly mired here for now."

He began to pace.

Eric strode back and forth across the length of the room, cell phone in hand. He was amazed that some people were quietly reading books, playing with their kids, acting like it was completely normal to be trapped in a stuffy, inefficient government office. Not him. He had important things to do and the tension was killing him.

With nothing left to do he called his wife in New York on the off chance she might actually answer. Kissane had recently decided to work on his marriage. To his surprise, he had actually found himself missing Rachel a little during her recent extended trips.

"Rachel?"

Long pause.

"You answered?"

"Eric. You called?"

"Um. Yeah... thought I would. How's the conference?"

A trifle longer pause.

"Fine," she said very slowly and interrogatively.

"Good. Good. I was thinking about picking you up at Dulles tonight? What time's your flight getting in?"

"Around eight, I think, but why the sudden... I mean I can take a taxi as usual."

"No, why don't you let me collect you. I'm not busy tonight and... well, I'd like to. We could catch a late dinner or something... I'm stuck here in the DMV at the moment. I missed my afternoon briefing with Randy... I've been here for hours and I swear, Rachel, it's making me crazy. Worst run place I've ever seen... " he realized he was rambling nervously into what might have been dead air on the other end.

His wife often made him nervous.

"The clerks are floating," he rambled on. "Chatting with each other instead of actually working, the number sequencing is clearly calculated to keep people in the dark and prevent rioting. I guess, in fact... it's bizarre. I feel like I'm trapped in a Kafka novel."

"It's the DMV, Eric. Hardly Kafka."

"What do you mean, hardly Kafka? You think I can't make literary illusions because I'm not a scholar?" He hated it when she got on her snotty intellectual high horse.

"No, I mean you shouldn't make them inaccurately," Rachel replied, sounding as supercilious as she felt. "Kafka's world was filled with elegiac madness, not mediocrity... but I've got to run now, Eric. Thanks for the offer but making a connection at the airport is more trouble than catching a cab. I'll just see you at home. After dinner."

Angry. And now humiliated as well as nuts with frustration, Eric pulled up the forbidden phone number on the small screen, his thumb gently rubbing the send button. Itching to push it. Fear and a small dose of guilt were combining to make him jumpy recently, so even though he had not tired of the woman who had been in his life for the last two years, he knew his relationship with her must end.

Eric hadn't called Cricket Hartford in weeks. Unlike other women, he knew she would accept the end as easily as she had the beginning of their long affair.

Eric wanted to hear the rich, Southern lilt of her throaty voice one more time. Just a short conversation while he waited couldn't hurt, he rationalized, and it would surely ease his tension and calm his nerves. Cricket would make him laugh at the absurdity of his predicament and, if he referred to Kafka, *she* wouldn't sneer.

Now entrenched in a power struggle with Ronald Lorten, his brother-in-law, who happened to also be his boss, Eric knew he couldn't afford even the hint of a scandal. Radio had been a stepping-stone to what he really wanted, his own television talk show. Soon, he thought, his face will be as famous as his voice.

Now serving customer number B466 at window number 3.

It was close to 2:00, and his number was finally getting close. Eric stared at his phone as if looking for a sign, gently stroking the screen with his finger.

One last time and then a new start.

One little swipe and modern technology took care of the rest. The soft Southern voice answered on the first ring.

He agreed, like he knew he would, when she invited him to come by as soon as he escaped from the DMV nightmare.

Finally, miraculously, B467 ran digitally across the screen in little green dots, and Kissane was called to window number nine. Feeling generous now that freedom was in his grasp, Eric smiled at the woman he had been watching and was not at all surprised by the grateful response he saw in her eyes.

Jessica Bennett had worked at the DMV for ten years. She had seen it all. The good, the bad, and the ugly. The famous, and infamous, but she had never in her life looked into such pale blue eyes set in Mediterranean Levantine dark skin. The contrast was stunning. Trying not to be obvious, she feasted her eyes on his strong chin and close-cropped black hair. He was wearing tight Levis, black Italian boots, a silky shirt and black cashmere jacket. He had a voice to match the looks. Like honey from the rock, smooth as an FM radio announcer paid to lull you to sleep with a little night music.

"You're doing a fine job, Ms. Bennett," Eric said, looking directly into her eyes. "Can't be easy dealing with this crowd."

"Nice of you to say so... we don't get much of that," she mumbled and watched as the gorgeous man put a check by organ donor. Generous as well as handsome, she thought, adding, "I wish more people would do that."

"Might as well," Eric replied in his mellifluous voice. "In the event... I won't be needing them anyway, right?"

Jessica took her time taking his picture. The camera loved the handsome face.

She knew it was silly, but the memory of his smile, kind remark, and dark good looks and icy blue eyes stayed with her the rest of the afternoon.

Jessica Bennett was surprised to see Eric Kissane again the following morning when she unfolded the *Washington Post*. His picture was on the front page above the fold. Not the DMV mug shot she had taken of him yesterday, of course, but a publicity photo that was set alongside the disturbing image of a smashed red Porsche Carrera on Glebe Road. The driver, well-known talk show host of the right-wing media giant, WOWL,

Inc., never regained consciousness, according to the newspaper report. He was pronounced dead yesterday evening at Inova Hospital in Fairfax. Speed, according to a state trooper on the scene, had been a factor in the crash. The *Style* section of the paper carried a non-flattering story on the dead man's illustrious family by marriage and included a detailed profile of Eric Kissane's brother-in-law, the colorful CEO, Mr. Ronald Lorten. No pictures of the widow, Rachel Lorten-Kissane.

Well, lucky girl. Jessica sighed, imagining the widow's beauty must have matched his own. Being married to such a man even for an afternoon would have been more bliss than she was likely to know in a lifetime.

Ms. Bennett thought about Eric Kissane for days, fancying *she* had been the last recipient of his gorgeous smile.

CHAPTER 3

A Piece of the Pie

I will show you something different from either
Your shadow at morning striding behind you
Or your shadow at evening rising to meet you:
I will show you fear in a handful of Dust.

—*T.S. Eliot*

ENOCH ARNHEIM WOKE FIRST. A RARE OCCURRENCE. LAURA'S new position as spokesperson for the State Department required long hours. She was often last to bed and first to rise, eager to catch up on what had happened during the night around the globe. Maybe, he thought, gazing at the woman he loved in a deep sleep, she had been called out to Foggy Bottom during the night and was catching up.

Laura was a strikingly attractive woman; the aggressive intelligence and drive needed to maneuver in the high-pressure world of politics and world events were softened as she slept, making her even more beautiful to him.

He got up, letting her sleep, and went to shower in the guest bathroom.

Enoch was impressed by Laura's meteoric rise at the State Department. Impressed and trying not to be jealous while he remained stuck in a mid-level management position at the IRS.

He had the coffee brewing when she joined him.

"Sorry," Enoch said with a peck on her warm forehead, her hair still damp from the shower. "Hope I didn't disturb you." It was quiet in the kitchen; thick brick walls muffled the sound of traffic rumbling over the cobblestone street in front of the Georgetown townhouse they shared.

"Anything serious keeping you up last night?" he asked, pouring her coffee and motioning toward the toaster. "Muffin?"

"Please."

He pushed the State Department mug across the immaculate granite counter toward her.

"Nothing new. Except a particularly graphic report on yet another human trafficking ring uncovered in Eastern Europe yesterday. What is it with men?"

"Those men or men in particular?"

She shot him a don't-even-go-there-at-this-hour look.

"Look, it's going to be a long day. If you get home first would you put together a salad for us?" she mentioned on her way out the door. "The makings are all in the fridge."

They both knew he *would* be home first. Unless something big was breaking at the Internal Revenue Service that no one had bothered to tell him about. Enoch needed a scandal of sufficient proportions to get media attention. He needed to win a big case.

"Fat chance of that," Enoch thought half an hour later as he swiped his security card and entered the massive IRS building on Constitution Avenue.

* * * * *

Across the river in Arlington, Cricket Hartford noticed lavender crocus peeking through dirty brown snow as she ran out in pajamas to get the

Washington Post. Convinced her luck was changing, Cricket saw the flowers as further confirmation. A sign. Back inside, she breathed in the dead air of the condominium and imagined it smelled as sweet as honeysuckle and jasmine after a rain. This day had, she decided, in some mysterious way, been foreordained just for her, crocus and all.

The morning sky was clear blue, a color that would lamentably disappear into the steamy dog days of Washington, D.C. summertime. Senators, congressmen, lawyers and lobbyists, everyone important would leave the nation's capital to "nonessential personnel" and take hearth and hound to the beach. Politics, business, and even mistresses, were left behind in August to cope with the heat and compete for parking space with sweaty tourists.

A satisfied smile crossed Cricket's face at the thought that while "nonessential" accurately described her life as well as her job... at the moment... all that was about to change.

The talking heads were their chatty, chirpy selves but Cricket switched them off, bored with her television companions this morning. Her mind was elsewhere.

Mug, plate, and knife went into a stale-smelling dishwasher. Wiping toast crumbs from a once green Formica countertop she noticed the faded picture hanging above the sink. A younger, more optimistic self had put it there twelve years ago. It was an ordinary photograph with a common theme; an antebellum mansion in pastoral Stafford County, where she had grown up on the edge of a small town, within dreaming distance of such estates.

"Where *has* the time gone?" she muttered into the dead air of her apartment.

Cricket was a Valley girl. A Shenandoah Valley girl. At a very early age she realized she had a gift. Boys were attracted to her, good boys, bad boys, almost any boy she set her sights on, and most of those she didn't still wanted her. An ability to attract men without really trying had proven useful and easier than working hard at academic pursuits for which she had far less aptitude.

"Go with what you've got, girl," was about the only advice her mother ever bothered to impart. That, and to keep her nylons in the freezer to make them last. Cricket had followed her mother's advice religiously. She had used her power over men cheerfully, disdaining women who couldn't. Or wouldn't. And when an early relationship took her to Washington, Cricket moved up the government ladder the old fashioned way, one man at a time.

But Cricket was getting tired of the climb. A few months ago, she noticed the last in a long line of men becoming distant, she recognized the signs with something like panic. Cricket knew her flower was fading, and she was still "nonessential". No one's boss, no one's partner, no one's wife, and no one's mother.

She left the kitchen and stepped into the shower, letting the water wash away the years in Washington while imagining summer in the countryside. Cricket wouldn't need a mansion, and she didn't want to return to Stafford County. A cottage in the country near Washington D.C., somewhere along Goose Creek in Middleburg's rich hunt country, would be fine. Along with an antique shop to keep her busy and provide ongoing income.

It was nearly 8:30 when Cricket finished toweling herself off in front of a full-length mirror. She could see some telltale signs of aging skin and more than a hint of gravitational pull on the figure she'd kept tight as a teenager's. But that didn't matter as much now, and she certainly wouldn't miss the endless hours of exercise and near-starvation dieting it took to maintain her finest asset.

The charcoal-gray suit chosen the evening before still looked right in the light of day. Washington business with a touch of sex. The tight skirt was slit high to reveal her long legs in silky black nylons. A white silk blouse buttoned demurely to the top. Cricket's eyes were gray and set far apart above high cheekbones which were covered with still-luminous skin.

Her thick, naturally blond hair was pulled back and off her neck, framing an enticing if not perfectly symmetrical face.

By the time the faux Viennese wall clock hanging in the small space by the door (that her realtor had euphemistically called a "hall") had chimed nine times Cricket was ready to go. The space by the door had barely enough room for a small table and one person; two if tightly intertwined. She picked up her leather Coach briefcase that *he* had given her and checked the manila envelope one more time. There were pictures of them snuggling together on Virginia Beach, by the fireplace in Telluride. And in her apartment. Proof enough and, if Mr. Lorten wanted more, she would happily comply.

Careful with her yearly physical and blood tests, Cricket Hartford knew she had not had been infected with HIV when she had started a three-year-long affair with Eric Kissane. A regularly scheduled blood test a few days after his death revealed he had given her more than expensive gifts. If Eric had known that he had the virus and had not revealed that to her, then he was guilty of a crime. But Cricket was not looking for justice, just a nice house in the country. Eric Kissane couldn't be made to pay for what he had done to her, but his family could. And, she thought, they probably would.

No longer a death sentence, HIV was still a major blow and her anger grew as she read and watched stories about his illustrious family during the days after his death. Pictures showed lines of limos disgorging Christian politicians and celebrities for the funeral at a mega-church outside the Beltway in Virginia. Investigative reporter and wit, Tom Willis, quipped, "If someone had dropped a bomb during the funeral it would have taken out the entire right wing of the Republican Party."

A cab appeared as if by design as Cricket stepped outside her door. Further proof, she thought, as she put her long legs delicately into the back seat of the grubby car, of the friendliness of fate on this... her day.

* * * * *

Ronald Lorten knew that God loved him and had a wonderful plan for his life, including becoming President of the United States. In the meantime, he had to deal with life's little annoyances. Lorten frowned as he looked at the single sheet of paper on a broad expanse of polished oak that was his desk. Martha, his tiresome secretary who didn't even demand to be called his Administrative Assistant, continued to give him a hardcopy of the day's schedule as though she didn't trust electronics.

Martha, the daughter of the famous biblical scholar Dr. Wilbur Culberson, was an unmarried, middle-aged, mousy little person; small in a prepubescent sort of way, mediocre, and careful to a fault. She carried her Bible to church in a handmade quilted cover, and was terrified of her boss.

Ronald had no idea, nor did he care, what Martha did in her off-hours, but he wouldn't have been particularly surprised to learn she still lived at home and cared for her aging parents. He might have been surprised, however, to know she was mostly content to do so.

The Culberson name carried a certain weight in evangelical circles. There were generations of them in Christian academic and artistic circles: college presidents, musicians, professors, and editors. Maybe the gene pool had thinned out in her case, she thought, and she assumed incorrectly that Mr. Lorten had hired her because of her name, despite her limited looks and ability.

Ironically, it was just the opposite. Her boss cared not at all about the famous family name and had chosen Martha because of her dullness. He put up with her ponderous pace gratefully, if not always patiently.

As CEO of WOWL, Inc. Ronald Lorten had learned the hard way that a secretary who attracted him sexually distracted (not to mention tempted) him, so he had hired Sarah before Martha. Sarah had seemed perfect, much too thin and angular for his taste. Smart and efficient. Only smart turned out to be even more difficult to manage. Sarah had proved to be neither naive nor sufficiently intimidated by him. Her increasingly penetrating questions worried him long before he found a good excuse to safely fire her without threat of litigation. Lorten didn't need a secretary who questioned his decisions or made moral judgments about his habits and lifestyle.

So when it came time to hire again, Ronald chose happy-just-being-a-secretary Martha. He often had to stifle his desire to scream at her to move a little faster, to look in a mirror and at a calendar at the same time, and join the real world. She was perfect and he knew it.

Martha knocked hesitantly on Lorten's door, then opened it a crack.

"Your first meeting this morning is a ten o'clock, sir — a Ms. Cricket Hartford... otherwise everything is clear, yes?"

"Yes, Martha. Perfectly clear, thank you. I don't really need you to go over every detail on the schedule with me. I can read."

"Yes, sir. But, sir, I did want to remind you as this Ms. Hartford called yesterday afternoon to confirm..."

"And so you have," he snapped. "And about that appointment... give it fifteen minutes, then ring me. I don't know what this woman wants but I know I don't have time for it, whatever it is."

Lorten had no idea how the woman had managed to get through to him on the private line one evening last week after Martha had left. Despite her many failings, Martha was a good gatekeeper, and the fact that this unknown woman had his private number worried him. But something in her tone of voice had kept him from refusing to see her. It was a strange call and he would be glad to have the short meeting over with.

"Yes, Mr. Lorten," Martha said. She had hoped he would be less stressed after the funeral and accompanying press following the sudden death of his brother-in-law.

She tried again.

"And the mail sir, are you finished with it?"

The mail came to Martha's desk each day after first being sorted in the mailroom. She was getting more confident about what was personal (that went to her boss unopened), what was important (those went on top), and then the myriad of requests, offers, and invitations (that she had to read and synopsize). Martha walked a fine line between bothering her boss with too much mail, and missing something he would acutally want to see. She found sorting the mail just another stressful part of her very stressful job.

Lorten didn't bother to look up or answer her question. He pointed to a stack of letters on the corner of his desk. Martha stepped into the private lair of Ronald Lorten; the sound of her low heels cushioned by a thick Persian carpet. She picked up the mail and noticed the scrawled "no" on the top letter. It was from the rapidly growing organization, International Justice Organization, asking for airtime on WOWL to promote their efforts against the growing sex trade in underage children around the world.

She hesitated, holding the letter in question out for him to see.

"Are you sure about this, sir? It's such an important cause."

Ronald actually counted to ten before answering with what he thought was a very controlled response. "Yes, Martha, I did see it, as my written response clearly indicates. And do please try and remember I don't pay you to offer suggestions. Now, since I have things to accomplish, which are *not* written on this damn piece of paper, please take the mail, answer it as indicated and call me exactly fifteen minutes after that woman enters my office. Can you do that, Martha?"

"Yes, sir," she replied, shocked at the profanity but meekly assuming that grief over the death of his brother-in-law was making him more irritable than usual. It was his first full week back in the office since the funeral. Martha assumed her boss had been helping his sister take care of the myriad amount of details created by a death, especially a death so sudden and violent.

"Only one more thing, sir, Connie asked me to remind you about dinner this evening at Little Thai with the Ohlssons." She closed the door before he could reply.

Ronald remembered. His wife had reminded him at the breakfast table. At least he was looking forward to that; an evening with his best friend would be a welcome break from all family all the time, since Eric's death and funeral. In fact, he had no intention of working late tonight; except for the morning interruption he meant to spend the day working on preliminary plans for the Christians in the Media Action Committee (CITMAC) conference he was hosting in the fall.

Ronald expected to be elected president of CITMAC at that conference, which would be nice in a stepping-stone kind of way, but his real goal could be seen from his window up Pennsylvania Avenue. Lorten had a fine view of the White House. His influence had played a major role in the midterm elections that saw the House and Senate returned to Republican hands and the Party owed him.

Lorten hated how the current residents of the White House were tarnishing the people's house with lies and socialism. He was becoming more and more convinced that God had placed him in a position of power for "such a time as this" — to defeat the left and restore America to Christ. He leaned his big frame back in the soft leather chair, snakeskin cowboy boots on the desk, and gazed down Pennsylvania Avenue with a smile on his face... until he remembered the annoying appointment on his morning schedule.

Lorten had sensed a veiled threat in the charming voice when she called. A subtle something had made him agree to her request for a meeting. His brother, Jeff, usually handled disgruntled donors and he cursed himself now for not passing her off to him.

Resigned, he buzzed Martha and asked for a second cup of coffee. This time in a more charitable voice.

But Lorten couldn't keep the upcoming meeting out of his mind and a righteous anger began to grow in him, and an eagerness to take this woman on if she did turn out to be an angry donor. We really are doing good work, he thought, listening to the strains of a familiar hymn played by a new group as it came softly over his intercom. He was tired of people who wanted him to live in poverty just because the business was a Christian one, and he was tired of trying to explain this fact to moralistic busybodies jealous of his success.

In an effort to throw off his anger Ronald turned his attention to the mail. He enjoyed reading some of the vast number of response letters received every day. It helped him keep his finger on the pulse of his audience. As he read, he realized with some guilt how glad he was that Eric would no longer be a factor in the business. Eric had been making more and more demands. A much larger salary, more airtime, more control of content. And he had even been demanding a television show. Now Ronald no longer had to deal with his popular but erratic brother-in-law. And the station wouldn't suffer any with his departure, he thought, in fact the sympathy factor might actually help ratings.

With that small epiphany Ronald made a note to have tapes of Eric's more popular programs packaged and made available immediately to his grieving fans. In the midst of this satisfying marketing moment, his brother-in-law's richly modulated tones came in over the radio in an advertising spot for a company called *Witness Wear*.

"Avoid the nerd factor," his rich baritone cajoled. "Be cool and committed to Christ at the same time."

"Be rad-ic-a-l-ly cooooollll," Eric's seductive voice entreated as effectively from beyond the grave as in life. The sound of crashing waves in the background and roar of a powerboat engine created the image of a water skiing dude witnessing with his wet t-shirt sucked into ripped muscles.

Lorten made a mental note to have all *Witness Wear* ads redone with another reader. Making money selling his brother-in-law's programs and continuing to hear his voice intruding into the day were two very different things indeed. It wasn't his fault that Eric drove his car into a tree, Ronald thought. His death was tragic but it would, he admitted to himself, make life so much easier.

CHAPTER 4

A GRAVE ENCOUNTER

The folly that man does, or must suffer, if he woos
A proud woman not kindred of his soul.

—W.B. Yeats

WHILE RONALD LORTEN PREPARED TO MEET HIS UNWELCOME 10:00 a.m. appointment, his sister sat alone on the cold ground of a nearby cemetery. A dusting of frost clung to the old headstones. Winter grays would soon give way to sprigs of yellow forsythia and blooming daffodils. But the promised warmth was still weeks away and Rachel Lorten-Kissane shivered as she leaned her back against a grand old oak spared by the developer's axe for two hundred years because of its place among the dead.

Tears were running down her cheeks. Her first tears since news of Eric's death reached her came from a deep well of complicated emotions. A spider was busy spinning its web on the turf covering Eric's grave. Silky strands held onto drops of dew creating a tiny crystal cathedral. The beauty of the web, the quiet of the place, and the cold reality of the grave unleashed many emotions.

Rocking back and forth, legs pulled up against her chest, head on her knees, Rachel let out a series of little sobs. The tears *were* real but confused by release, regret, shock, relief. She had no intention of making regular pilgrimages to her husband's grave. In fact, she didn't intend to come again. While it had been a terrible mistake to marry Eric, one she had regretted very soon after her vows were uttered, he *had been* her husband for eight years. His death was brutal and shocking. Rachel tried and failed to shut out an image of his body mangled in the ruins of the car he loved. Marrying Eric had been the only thing in her whole life that she was absolutely certain had truly and completely pleased her mother. He was handsome, talented, smooth, and he became famous. Everyone had loved him. Except her.

She thought her parents, John and Alice Lorten, had optimistically named her, their only daughter, Rachel, and in what seemed almost like betrayal, God had given them a *Leah* instead. She had spent her teen years in conflict with her mother when she refused to spend time and energy focused on clothes and diets, "overcoming her limitations", as her mother called it.

"You have a responsibility to make the most of what God has given you," had been her mother's mantra. "You must work at loveliness, Rachel," she whispered in pleading, said in frustration, and shouted in anger.

"I'm sure," Rachel whispered into the morning silence, "that my mother will miss you, Eric, and my brother will find a way to make your death profitable for the company." But her voice lacked the sarcastic bite her mother hated so much and instead held a twinge of real grief.

Waves of emotion continued to rise up in Rachel and a pile of soggy pink Kleenex grew beside her.

She had been sitting by the horse fountain in Mozart Platz taking a break between classes at the University of Salzburg when she saw Eric Kissane for the first time. He was standing nearby reading a tourist map. Rachel thought then, and still, that he was the most handsome man she had ever seen. He was everything the lumbering Nordic Lorten men were not. Slightly built with black hair, dark Levantine skin, and beautiful blue eyes. That day by the fountain, far away from her family, Rachel forgot to be wary.

No one even remotely as attractive as Eric Kissane had ever paid attention to her; not, at least, when she was on her own and away from her family. Not for herself and never for long. Growing up the only daughter of a very important man in the world of media power brokers had presented challenges outside her natural coping skills. 'Celebs', as her family called them, were a continual presence in her young life. The Lorten family was important to the political right wing of the evangelical world and to Christian broadcasting artists and authors who needed the same forum and access to the masses as the politicos. Unlike her mother, who thrived as the epicenter of the social order that swirled around them, Rachel had always hated it.

Surprised by Eric's proposal and even more that she accepted, they wed soon after in a charming seventeenth-century Lutheran Church with a few of Rachel's acquaintances from the University of Salzburg witnessing the vows. Eric had seemed as vague about his family as she had been about her own.

When the Lorten clan turned out in force to meet the newlyweds at Dulles International Airport a month later they heaved a giant, collective sigh of relief at the sight of Eric, who for his part smiled at his new family with more warmth than he had his wife at the altar.

Rachel's tears continued to flow as she remembered her beautiful wedding and pathetic marriage. A warming sun melted the dewdrops on the spider's web ruining the illusion. Emotion spent, she calmly ran her finger over the cold granite slab, feeling each freshly carved letter.

Eric Charles Kissane

5 August 1971 – 13 March 2015

She had resisted using her mother's flowery suggestion for an epitaph: "Faithful Husband and Son of the King". Not so much because of its excessive sappiness, which was cause enough, or because she thought

Eric had been unfaithful in the physical sense (she didn't think he had) but because it was fundamentally untrue. Eric's hypocrisy, while indeed lapidary, would be hard to convey on a gravestone. So Rachel kept the earthly slate simple; the facts were few and she left to God without comment the mystery of his mortal soul.

"Mrs. Lorten-Kissane?"

"Yes," she answered, fumbling with the phone as she got back in the car. "I guess I still am."

A momentary embarrassed silence followed and Rachel had the distinct impression the caller wasn't exactly sure how to proceed. But after a prolonged clearing of his throat a man's voice said, "I am calling from the Office of Decedent affairs at Inova Fairfax Hospital and I need you to come in as soon as possible to discuss your husband's courageous gift of life. I *am* so sorry to bother you but we have one more... er... small thing to clear up."

"No," Rachel snapped. "If there are papers to sign please use the fax or send a courier to my attorney. I'm certainly not 'coming in' today or any other day to discuss a private decision my husband made that in no way relates to me."

Rachel felt her tone of voice, while civil, had given a clear and definitive final answer, so she was surprised by the insistence at the other end of the line.

"Unfortunately ma'am," the young man said with more force, "it isn't quite that simple. I know this is a difficult time for you... but we really do need to see *you*, not your lawyer, in our office as soon as possible. It's a confidential matter. One that requires your immediate attention. Would later today be possible?"

"No. It *really* is not possible." Rachel started the black Lexus LS Sport Eric had bought her for Christmas last year and said, "Whatever it is you want to tell me I don't want to know. My husband did a good deed, hopefully some valuable tissue was harvested," she shuddered. "I think that's what you call it — a terrible word; anyway, Eric is dead so this can't concern him and I assure you it does not interest or concern me!" She tossed the phone onto the empty passenger seat but despite her brave words, Rachel's hands were shaking as she turned left on Drainsville Road outside the cemetery gate.

* * * * *

Later that same day, when Tom Willis at the *Washington Post* was nearly ready to leave the office, he took one last call. It was a strange tip from a low-level clerk in the Office of Decedent Affairs, the Organ Donor Unit at Fairfax Hospital.

Willis, the most dreaded of all investigative reporters in D.C., had the head of a Cro-Magnon man with a thick skull, high forehead, broad square face and bushy eyebrows. He also had intelligent eyes and a sarcastic grin that redeemed his otherwise homely face. Mr. Willis might, from a distance, appear dim, or as if his eyes were closed. No one who knew him, however, would so describe the journalist. Married to his work, the only marriage that had worked, Tom Willis was known for taking chances and following leads.

He pondered the implications of the call long after hanging up and in the end decided to file away the information for possible future use.

CHAPTER 5

A Plan in Place

. . . thus, began the shifting of evangelicals to the GOP
and the shifting of the GOP to the right.

—Pat Roberson

It was nearly nearly 7:00 p.m. when Connie arrived at Little Thai Restaurant in downtown McLean. Temperatures had dropped precipitously during the last hour, dispelling all hopes of the early arrival of spring. She shivered at the March wind blowing an ill will outside her snug Mercedes.

Stopped at the traffic light on Chain Bridge and Old Dominion, Connie Lorten tried Ronald's cell again. Still no answer. Mad, and getting madder, Connie wondered again what on earth could be keeping her husband from answering his phone or the many messages she had left throughout the afternoon with Martha. "If he isn't in trouble he soon will be," she muttered to herself, pulling off Old Dominion Road into the parking lot of the restaurant.

Little Thai was known for its fine food. And as a place where the well-known and well-heeled were assured the privacy they craved from the fame they had sought.

McLean, a near-in Washington suburb on the Virginia side of the Potomac River, was home to politicians of all ideological persuasions.

Located in a more fashionable than most strip mall, Little Thai was sur-rounded by old neighborhoods of red brick ramblers from the sixties and increasingly more upscale neighborhoods right up to and overlooking the Potomac River. Little Thai was twenty minutes from Capitol Hill, five min-utes from the CIA, where senators and spooks in suits picked up bagels and coffee at the local Starbucks on their way to work, just like ordinary folks.

The town might look like any other leafy suburb in Middle America; it was, however, anything but. The Federal Government was a vast life source, not only to government workers, but to beltway bandit companies and all who feed from the political trough. The most powerful people in the most powerful country in the world called McLean their hometown and Little Thai was a hometown haunt for many of them.

Connie, however, was not thinking whom she might see while din-ing at Little Thai tonight, but rather why her husband was avoiding her messages and phone calls. His hapless secretary, who seemed even more hapless than usual, had repeatedly muttered vague excuses as to where Ronald was and why he was not answering the phone. Whatever excuse her husband might have for not being in touch, short of kidnapping or heart attack, would not do.

Ronald and Connie were meeting his best friend, Pastor Leif Ohlsson, for dinner. Leif was an old friend with a new trophy wife and Connie had no intention of making small talk with her in Ronald's absence. She nei-ther liked nor disliked Charleen, the new Mrs. Ohlsson, but she felt (and probably had shown) contempt for the man who had been unable to con-tain his sexual appetites for a decent mourning period.

Connie Lorten drove around the crowded parking lot getting more and more furious, looking in vain for her husband's matching silver Mercedes. A few minutes and several gestures later, all notable for their distinct lack of sociability from people trying to park, Connie gave up. She parked, put on her sweetest smile, and headed for their usual corner table.

"Leif... Charleen... how lovely to see you. It seems my husband has disappeared off the face of the earth, which is very thoughtless of him."

The pastor stood, gave her an air kiss on both cheeks. Connie noticed Leif's ever present bodyguard at the next table along with a companion, hired to help him blend into the convivial atmosphere. There had been threats against Ohlsson's life a few years back and while Ronald wouldn't say so directly to his friend, he suspected Leif enjoyed the power of walking around "with protection".

"Not to worry, Connie," Leif assured her with a smile. "These things happen to important people, and we all know how important Ronald is, now don't we?"

The new wife had big hair, bigger breasts, and a worse nervous giggle than she remembered. Oh dear Lord, Connie thought, spare me. But she addressed her with great restraint and in a very civilized voice.

"How nice to see you again, Charleen... what a colorful scarf. Looks so warm. I saw a similar one at Neiman Marcus in the Galleria yesterday, should have bought it but I thought this miserable winter was over."

"Sweet of you to notice," the new wife cooed. "Leif never notices a thing I'm wearing..." She let the sentence trail off into space, an embarrassed grin on her face.

Thinking silence the better part of valor in the face of an obvious retort to the new bride's ditzy remark, Connie moved smoothly to all things safe including the weather.

Leif Ohlsson was senior pastor of Washington Bible Church, a twenty thousand member mega-church with buildings and concrete now covering many acres of a previously woody area just inside the Beltway. It was a measure of his power and confidence that the pastor defied sentiment (from family and congregation) and married a much younger, very beautiful woman, less than a year after the death of his wife. Too young and too soon. That had been the inevitable reaction of many in the congregation, especially the women. Men found it in their hearts to be more forgiving once they saw her. Leif's grown children were furious, but the pastor assumed they would get over it as the congregation would, given enough time.

Patience was not known as one of the pastor's spiritual gifts. Tapping the table and fingering the menu, the man was unable to contain his frustration.

"Let's order!" It was a command uttered with the authority of one used to authority. "Ronald will understand. I've got a meeting with some deacons at 8:30. Who knows what they'd cook up if I'm not there to mind the store."

Apart from the mixed metaphor, Connie thought it a splendid idea; anything to move the miserable evening toward a quicker conclusion. She ordered a favorite house red from the hovering waiter and brought up the latest scandal at the White House. It was a safe and common topic that exhausted the next fifteen minutes until Ronald Lorten, finally, came charging through the door. His usual immaculate suit was decidedly rumpled and his face flushed.

"Sorry, so sorry I'm late."

Ronald greeted Leif with a slap on the back and sat down without recognizing Charleen... or his wife.

"Really... sorry everyone, I got held up. Unavoidable really. Couldn't get away." In the midst of his extended excuses Ronald realized his mistake; he jumped back up and through the small space around the table to brush Charleen's cheek with a kiss. Rather clumsily done and utterly unlike socially smooth Ronald Lorten.

"Hello, dear," Lorten threw out vaguely in the direction of his wife, wiping sweat from his brow with a napkin.

"I presume your secretary is dead and you've lost your cell phone," Connie observed. "As those are the only obvious reasons I can think of that would explain you keeping us waiting and dropping off the radar this afternoon."

But even as she spoke the edge was coming off her anger. Something *was* wrong with Ronald. He wasn't ill, as near as she could tell, but he had a stricken look about him that was decidedly unlike her always-in-command husband.

"Well, actually we didn't wait," Leif pointed out. "We ordered without you. And for you. Hope you're in the mood for red curry with lemon grass, Thai hot."

Soon small dishes of rice, accompanied by a variety of colorfully prepared delicacies made of ingredients not grown in America's great heartland began appearing on the table, absorbing everyone's attention for the next few minutes. A pot of green tea and four tiny cups were added to the crowded table and soon the aroma and pungent taste sensations further mellowed the company. By the time coffee and sticky rice were served, even Ronald was beginning to believe the story he was telling was actually more fact than fiction.

At first he had been pleased when Cricket Hartford had walked into his office, precisely at 10:00. She was a very attractive woman with an aura of sophistication and ease, not the pious, small-minded, disgruntled little donor he had been expecting. She sat down, crossed her exquisite legs (leaving the skirt split open as it dropped) and then, in a most amiable and seductive manner and without a hint of emotion, laid waste to his very life.

Lorten had no idea how long he sat slumped over the desk after her dramatic departure. Martha had followed his instructions to the letter and buzzed him at 10:15. When there was no reply, she timidly knocked on the door, and opened it a crack. She saw the stricken look on his face, heard his barked command not to disturb him again. By anyone for any reason. Martha obediently withdrew and, as always, did exactly as she was told.

Ronald couldn't remember leaving the office or how he came to be walking on the Mall near the Vietnam Memorial. He did remember staring at the black granite wall with the rows and rows of names, thinking at least those poor guys died honorably. And better still, anonymously.

Lorten had wandered on the Mall among the monuments and throngs of tourists imagining the delight of his enemies, when they learned of the muck Cricket Hartford was about to sell to the highest bidder. The scandal, and he knew it would be a scandal born gleefully on the liberal airwaves and in the mainstream papers by all his enemies, would destroy the reputation of WOWL and deny him the power to do good for his country. His life's work was in danger because his sister couldn't keep her husband home. Not that he particularly blamed Eric for *wanting* to see other women, especially one as beautiful as Cricket Hartford. Rachel's sharp tongue and supercilious attitude to everyone in the family, including her husband, was no doubt more than Eric could bear.

Finally, when the sun began to set behind the Lee mansion atop Arlington Cemetery, Ronald realized his thousand-dollar suit was not keeping him warm. A deep-seated survival instinct seeped back into his consciousness as he realized the lateness of the hour. Multiple parking tickets blew away as he sped back across the Roosevelt Bridge and up Route 66 to McLean. He knew Connie would be fuming but the germ of an idea, a possible way out, had started to grow and he couldn't be distracted by her repeated efforts to reach him. Once in the restaurant, talking with his friend, the idea developed quite naturally in the telling.

"And quite frankly," Ronald went on, draining the last of his strong black coffee. "The timing is so amazing, it has to be providential. Yesterday, I got a letter from IJO, an international ministry fighting the human trafficking trade. The importance of the cause captured my attention right away and I realized we should do something to help fight such suffering and injustice. Then today, I saw another report on the *Today* show. It is hard to look at this stuff and not be touched. And moved. Little kids sold as sex slaves." He shook his head.

"Then, after reading that, it just all came together for me and I realized we had to take action. I took a walk on the Mall to think about it, and the longer I walked, the more troubled I became. I am convinced we cannot remain silent in the face of this tragedy. We have the media might, and the network, to raise much-needed cash for intervention, prevention, counseling centers, re-training. You got it. It's a huge problem that requires a big response."

Three faces looked back at him, clearly surprised. Charleen had tears in her eyes.

"I saw the *Today* story this morning as well," Leif replied, surprised at his old friend. "It is shocking what those kids suffer. Some looked to be about ten years old. I wish there was something we could do."

"Well, that's the thing," Ronald pounced. "I think there is. Something we can do, I mean. We are the richest most powerful nation in the world and Americans have very generous hearts. Leif... if we use our combined resources we could really *do something big*. You have used the political power of your congregation to move people to the ballot box and you can mobilize them again."

Surprised by Ronald's out-of-character indignation over anything other than American politics, Leif tried and failed to change the subject to a more comfortable one for his bride. He had hoped this dinner would help establish the old foursome camaraderie enjoyed for years before his wife died.

Missing what Leif thought were fairly obvious cues to change the subject, Ronald pressed on.

"We could at the very least draw more attention to the problem. Raise some funds to build a center somewhere in Eastern Europe to help the victims. What do you think? We've taken on challenges together before."

"I don't know," Lief answered nervously. "This isn't exactly the kind of mission outreach we usually go in for. We have enough trouble influencing our own nation on social matters. I can't see that we would have much clout in Bosnia or Romania or some other basket-case country where this stuff goes on all the time. And I've read that most of the victims return to the street after they are rounded up anyway."

"Well, I'm surprised at you, Leif Ohlsson. I really am," Charleen remarked, as she removed her husband's hand from around her shoulder, stiffening her back. "Seems to me I remember you standing up there in the pulpit and repeating over and over that no one is past saving, or too broken for God to heal."

Oh good grief, Ohlsson thought. All I need is my wife fired up over some hopeless cause, some politically correct liberal notion that will upset the congregation. He emptied the last bottle of wine into his glass, trying to think of a way to move the conversation to a safer topic when a different angle occured to him. Perhaps, this is exactly what I do need to change the perception of the congregation about Charlene. Leif was not unaware of the snide "trophy wife" remarks.

When he spoke it was measured. "I'm sorry, dear. You're right. I just meant it would take a huge amount of investment, experts, and people on the ground that have experience in this kind of thing. You can't just pick these poor kids up and send them home with a few dollars."

Not totally appeased, the new Mrs. Ohlsson kept her eyes on Ronald and asked if he had a plan.

Glad for the unexpected ally, Ronald pushed forward. "Well the first thing we can do and this is where my media influence will come in handy, is to draw attention to the problem. People are really generous and caring if you give them a reason to be. So we expose the problem of human trafficking by giving it a face, making it a cause, something like... and I'm just thinking out loud here... maybe we could call it our 'generation's holocaust'."

"Not quite a holocaust," Leif said at what he thought was an overused and inappropriate comparison.

But with one look at his bride's face, he tried again.

"I'm not saying we should remain silent, I'm not saying we shouldn't explore this. I'm just suggesting it would take lots of time and lots of planning. That's all I'm saying, sweetheart."

"Good. Glad to hear it. But every day we wait more young kids are picked up and used as sex slaves."

Connie was surprised to see Charleen standing up to her new husband. Surprised and impressed. But she was also fairly certain the current news story about a problem existing for years was not the cause of her husband's disappearance this afternoon, nor his sick pallor and rumpled suit.

"Charleen is right. Every day this problem goes on unchecked young boys and girls are abducted. We need to raise awareness and funds, and we need to begin now."

Unable to ask Ronald what had really prompted this sudden moral outrage, Connie smiled, nodded, and listened like the adoring political wife she would need to be if Ronald did make a presidential run.

"We can get several conservative senators and congressmen on board," he went on enthusiastically. "Men who will be facing tight re-election campaigns in November would be only too happy to help... show the compassionate conservative angle... "

Not wanting to be the Grinch, Leif began to add helpful suggestions.

"I suppose it's possible for you to mount a campaign and wrap it up with a big finale right before the election at the CITMAC conference in October."

"We, my friend! Together we can move mountains. I was thinking about something with a retro feel, but using all the latest social media. It would be fast and effective, like an old-fashioned Bible trivia contest... which would have the added benefit of calling attention to biblical literacy and as a vehicle to get the attention of the older generation. The Millennial generation might be tech savvy but the Boomers still have the bucks."

"Crass, but true," Leif agreed. "But how do we engage them in this contest idea?"

"Radio," Connie said laconically.

"Well, there is that," Leif chuckled. "How many radio stations do you own across the country, anyway?"

"Enough," Ronald added. "And on every one of them we are pushing a Christian worldview, as in our Republican party talking points. We'll show those damn Democrats that 'right-wing Republicans' can out-social their social conscience. Getting rid of this President isn't going to be easy, despite our current rhetoric to the contrary, and this plan is good on principle and good politically."

"I don't know a great deal about the issue of human trafficking," Leif said, "But I haven't been living in a cave the last few years. This is, if not a holocaust, certainly a terrible scourge of our time. The Church should do good, not just talk about it."

Charleen smiled at her husband and let him return his arm to her shoulder.

"I'm sure both of you guys, especially my husband, know more about all this than I do," she said. "But it seems to me that maybe, rather than a contest, maybe we should do something more substantial like a conference that brings together theologians to explore and study the existence of evil and the justice of God. That might, well, be more useful in bringing attention to this issue and bringing about real change. But you're the experts."

She looked down at her hands, checked her perfect nails and hoped she had not overstepped.

"That's a good idea, dear," Leif replied, surprised at his wife. "But the thing is Ronald here knows marketing and how to get people's attention better than we do, so let's leave that part to him. And Connie," he went on, "the Lorten mansion in Great Falls would be the perfect venue for a big celebration. Do you think we could use it to throw a big party and announce the winner of the contest? Maybe show a film produced in the country that receives the assistance? That would get maximum attention from the press a month before the election. We could time it to correspond to the CITMAC conference."

Certain her husband had not fundamentally changed since break-fast, Connie was still wondering what on earth had lit this fire.

"I would have to ask Ronald's mother," she replied carefully. "Since it *is* her house. But my mother-in-law loves putting on a party and she would be willing to do almost anything for her precious son and the family business."

No one seemed to notice the irony and with amiable goodbyes the satiated diners left the warmth of Little Thai.

Leif and Ronald continued their conversation in the parking lot, shadowed by Leif's bodyguard. Connie took her own car and drove home with a growing list of questions for her husband, while Leif's puzzled dea-cons waited at the church wondering whether or not to start the meeting without him.

"What a nice man," Charleen said, leaning toward her husband in the closeness of the car. "You know, before tonight I had been just a teensy bit afraid of your best friend but he's really a sweetie. Connie seems a little cold, if you don't mind my saying so, darling. Beautiful of course, for a woman her age, but completely unmoved by the need of those poor girls. Not at all compassionate like Ronald. Now I can see why he's your friend." She rubbed her husband's leg, nails scratching his suit pants on the inside of his thigh, raising the hair on the back of his neck.

Leif Ohlsson was glad for the rosy glow his wife had taken away from their dinner, but he hoped her naiveté did not really extend so far as to imagine Ronald Lorten was in the same league as Mother Theresa.

Ronald was not entirely comfortable with thinking the miraculous solution had come to him directly from God. Entirely. But he was relieved that it had come to him. Hugely relieved, in fact. He simply couldn't deny that, as a solution, his plan not only provided for WOWL to continue its vital work and at the same time do real good for poor victims of sexual violence. He knew Leif would continue to come around, especially with the new wife pushing him. Connie, however, was not fooled. Exactly what to tell her occupied his mind on the rest of the short drive from Little Thai to the grand neighborhood known as Potomac Overlook, where Ronald and Connie lived alone in an obscenely large house they both loved.

Mixing an element of truth, along with pure pragmatism, he explained to his wife before they retired to bed how the company was facing a lawsuit over possible financial malfeasance, which he had learned of this afternoon. And he further explained to his equally pragmatic partner that the humanitarian campaign, which was a good and righteous thing, would divert attention from what might prove to be a messy investigation. A good offense, he concluded, is always better than any defense. And people were easily distracted by shiny objects.

Relieved to hear it, Connie put the whole miserable evening behind her as she stepped into her deep tub, surrounded by candles and soothing light she slipped under the steaming hot water scented with French Lavender & Honey bubble bath.

* * * * *

The WOWL Awareness Campaign was presented to the senior management team at WOWL, Inc. two weeks later. Ronald Lorten invited Leif to join him and the rest of the team, which included his brother Jeff, the Chief Financial Officer; Charlie Rice (manager of the fund development department) and Martha. Martha was going to be key. He introduced her as his personal Administrative Assistant and go-to person on the project. Ronald watched his compliant secretary tear up as he described the suffering and plight of the kids caught in the sex trade. He did not give her credit for encouraging him to take a second look at the letter from IJO. But he knew she wouldn't expect him to.

"Brilliant," Jeff said several times. "Absolutely brilliant, my brother." "Brilliant" was Jeff's new overworked go-to word for emphasis. But he was not alone in his excitement. There was a general air in the boardroom of something important happening. Functions were assigned. People got on board. Doing good was intoxicating. There had been a barrage of negative publicity in the press following the death of Eric Kissane that had focused on the rich celebrities who showed up to his funeral in droves. The life-style of the Lorten family became fodder for the liberal press, led by the *Washington Post* and *CNN*. A general air of excitement during the meeting reflected the feeling that this new project would change the message in the scandal-loving city of Washington, D.C.

"Eat this, you liberal-loving heathens," Charlie Rice wanted to say with a fist pump. Instead, he quietly made a note to task his senior accountant with creating the budget for what had just come to be known as *The Awareness Campaign.*

Jeff would head up marketing and launch the Bible trivia contest, using the Internet, Facebook, and Twitter. All WOWL-owned radio and television stations and bookstores across the nation would take part, advertising and encouraging local events. Leif Ohlsson would get his mega-church congregation on board to help launch the project in the summer.

"How about a Bible Trivia Board Game to go with the campaign?" Martha suggested. To her astonishment everyone agreed. Someone was immediately tasked with checking patent rights and another with coming up with a design.

Everyone was engaged. There was a slight undercurrent of protest from the marketing team when Ronald explained that an outside consultant, Wharton & Wharton Consulting, would take the lead and work directly with him, but no one had the temerity to actually object. Ronald was a hands-on CEO; everyone expected him to make the decisions and drive any project this big. And with so much good will in the room, it would have seemed bad manners to question the decision.

"Okay, people. This is brilliant," Jeff said. "Let's make the city sit up and take notice! We might even get good press in the *Post*!"

General amusement at such an absurd suggestion was heard along the carpeted corridors as people dispersed back to their individual offices. Feeling a part of the team for the first time since she nervously set foot in Mr. Lorten's executive suite, Martha Culberson was happy to be at WOWL.

CHAPTER 6

PATTERNS

Mercy and truth are met together.

—A Psalm of the sons of Korah

RALUCA AND HER FATHER PAUSED AT THE FRONT DOOR OF THE police station. He placed an encouraging hand on her shoulder and squeezed.

"You'll do fine," he said.

The red, yellow, and blue flag of Romania hung limp above the crumbling green plaster façade of the building. It had been three weeks since Nadia disappeared with no news and no clues. Despite Raluca's tears and pleading, the village policeman continued to insist the girl had, like so many other Roma kids, simply run away.

Local law enforcement in Tirnova consisted of one Mircea Stefanescu. He was a piggy man, quarrelsome and slovenly. It had been Raluca's misfortune to burst into the police station after Nadia went missing and to catch the officer napping, head back, mouth open, feet resting on the desk. Not happy to be disturbed over a girl missing for only a few hours (especially a Gypsy!), Stefanescu had brushed off Raluca's concerns. Born to cheat and steal, one less Roma in Tirnova was not necessarily a bad thing in the policeman's estimation and nothing Raluca could say changed his mind.

Until someone else changed it for him.

A week after Nadia Iovan went missing, Officer Stefanescu filed a missing child report in hopes of ending the daily, hysterical visits of her friend. His superiors at the county level, also uninterested in a missing Gypsy girl, bumped the file up to Bucharest in time-honored bureaucratic-cover-your-backside-style where it landed on the desk of "The Hunter", as he was known in the division for Trafficking and Exploited Children. Detective Inspector Radu Kunis was interested in finding girls like Nadia, but he was known as "The Hunter" because of his dogged pursuit of the men who preyed upon them. The case of Nadia Iovan interested him. It was, in fact, what he had been waiting for: a trail not yet grown cold.

"Damned man treating this missing girl case like the crime of the century," Stefanescu grumbled to his wife soon after the Detective Kunis arrived in Tirnova. "The man's taking over my station and using me like a damned lackey."

Mrs. Stefanescu smiled as she bent over the stove, spooning home-made chicken soup into a large bowl for her husband. The satisfied smile was replaced with a look of sympathy when she turned to place the bowl and a large chunk of dark bread on the table.

Detective Inspector Kunis arrived on a Sunday afternoon with the power of his position riding on big SUV wheels, an attractive female assistant by his side, and the absolute authority to take command of the two-room police station and local resources, namely Officer Stefanescu and one rusted-out Dacia.

Stefanescu had spent the last twenty-four hours trudging around the village, bringing in neighbors, the girl's teacher, the owner of the café, and even the senile grandmother for interviews, just as he was told to do. Word of what was happening spread throughout the village via the local 'social media', which was faster than Facebook.

Now it was Raluca's turn. Stefanescu glared at the girl who had caused all this trouble as she and her father entered the room.

"You'll do fine," her father whispered again in her ear again as they sat down on hard wooden chairs softened with handmade cushions. One window was open in the stuffy room; two would create the dreaded 'current', considered by most people in Romania as the source of everything from muscle ailments to the common cold.

It was a grubby little room, but the Inspector from Bucharest filled and changed it with his six-foot-two frame and commanding presence. He was wearing a dark suit, very white shirt, and thin red tie; the scent of aftershave mixed with that of stale smoke in the room.

"Hello, Raluca." The Inspector leaned his big frame in a slight bow to her and took her hand first, then her father's. "My name is Inspector Kunis, this is my colleague, Officer Emilia Pasca, and we are here to help you find your friend. I'm really very sorry for your loss."

Raluca was surprised; the man's kindness unexpected.

He went on:

"I had a best friend when I was your age, so I can imagine, a little, of how hard this must be for you."

Stefanescu snorted as he leaned against the wall behind his own desk, glaring at the backs of the detectives. Especially the lady cop from Bucharest! And, he thought, catering to the hysteria of young girls would hardly cut down on real crime. He rested his arms on the shelf that was his belly and wondered why Bucharest had really sent this high-powered investigative team to his little town.

The rickety wooden desk had been cleared of its usual clutter and now held only the inspector's well-used briefcase (lid open), one small plastic bag, and a pad of paper on the scratched surface. Officer Pasca sat ready to take notes on her laptop.

"We're working on finding your friend," Inspector Kunis went on. "But we need your help."

"Oh dear," she said, fighting back tears when it was clear that the man didn't have news but only more questions. "But I don't know anything else."

The woman officer picked up the plastic bag and handed it to Raluca:

"Do you recognize this?" she asked.

Raluca turned the bag over, pushed the plastic around a little and realized at once it was a smashed cell phone. Seconds later reality dawned.

"Oh god," she gasped. "Oh god, it's hers. It's Nadia's cell phone... she wouldn't go anywhere without it. Not on purpose. What happened, where did you find it... "

Neither detective answered her questions.

"Look again," Ms. Pasca said. "How can you be certain it's your friend's cell phone? They all look pretty much alike to me. How do you know for sure?"

Raluca smiled through her tears and pointed to the Justin Bieber sticker covering the back of the scarred phone. "Nadia *loves* Justin Bieber."

"Well," he chuckled, "most girls your age do, don't they? Did you call Nadia's phone after you discovered her missing?"

Raluca nodded miserably. "I don't have a cell phone, but when I saw her grandmother wandering around their yard calling Nadia's name, I knew something was wrong so I ran home and called her cell phone number. Several times. Then I came here, to the station, to get help but," she looked at Officer Stefanescu, "but he told me to go home and not bother him about a runaway Gypsy brat."

Embarrassed, the local policeman started to protest.

"That's exactly what you said," Raluca went on. "You didn't care — now it's probably too late."

"Where did you find it?" Raluca asked, looking at the plastic bag with her friend's beloved cell phone in it.

Inspector Pasca answered:

"Actually, the local shepherd picked it up early the next morning as he took the animals to pasture just a few kilometers west of town, not far from the road. He wasn't sure what it was at first. Then it rang. I don't think he knew how to answer it. At any rate, the shepherd eventually put it in his pocket and forgot all about it. Until we arrived and started asking questions, that is."

Saying, without saying, that someone should have started asking questions earlier.

Kunis put the bag with the phone in his briefcase and closed the lid. "And on its own it doesn't tell us much, anyway."

Even Raluca knew that wasn't strictly true. The cell phone told them a great deal. It told them which way Nadia was going when she left the village and that she had not left Tirnova of her own free will! She would never have *thrown away* her phone. Someone else did that for her.

"But," the man from Bucharest went on, "you can help. I need you to answer some questions for me. It's important that you think carefully and answer truthfully."

The inspector's own daughter was about Raluca's age; the girl's suffering moved him. He saw an inner strength and a singularity of purpose, despite the puffy eyes and drawn look of grief on her young face.

"Now," the experienced investigator said, and knowing sympathy wouldn't help, forcing himself to use an authoritarian tone. "I need for you to close your eyes and go back to that morning. You have to tell me everything you can remember. Forget your previous statement. Tell me the story of that day like it is the first time you've ever told it. And fill in all the details, even ones you think don't matter. Like what the weather was like that day, what you were wearing, what Nadia was wearing, everything that happened after you entered the street on your way to pick up your friend for school until," he paused, "until you dropped her off that afternoon."

"Waste of time," Stefanescu muttered quietly and then quickly covered his intemperate remark with a cough. The man sitting at his desk was, after all, a senior detective. It was one thing to brush off a little girl, quite another to mess with Bucharest.

"Close my eyes?"

"Trust me. It will help."

She felt shy and silly, but she did as she was told. Trying hard to remember exactly what the day had been like from the moment she opened the gate to let out the geese and started down the street to Nadia's house. The old woman painting the tree. Nadia's weird clothes and their argument. The weather... everything she could remember, including the farmer with the butchered pig and Nadia's overreaction to it. She didn't know how long she talked. The only other sound in the room was the tapping of computer keys, the heavy breathing of Stefanescu, and the creak of the wooden floor as he shifted his weight from leg to leg.

"I should have listened," Raluca moaned when she opened her eyes. "I can see that now. I should have believed Nadia when she said she wanted to get out. She was asking for help, wasn't she? And I didn't listen. I thought it was just her usual complaining about life in Tirnova. And I'm so ashamed, but I was tired of her complaining, so I didn't listen. Maybe she was so unhappy she did run away?"

"And throw away her cell phone?" the Inspector asked in a quiet voice. "I don't think so. And no one saw her getting on the bus, so it leaves the question of how."

"And where is she now?" Raluca asked. It was rhetorical, of course. Clearly no one knew. Not even the important Inspector. "A person can't just disappear into thin air... it doesn't make sense."

It makes perfect sense, Officer Stefanescu thought. The girl is with some of her thieving relatives, begging on the streets somewhere. What he said was, "It's clear Nadia Iovan ran away. About time you admit it and let us all get on with our lives."

But Nadia Iovan had not run away. Of that, Detective Inspector Kunis was very sure. With the number of missing kids increasing and a shocked world press shining a light on the tragedy, his government was finally willing to appropriate needed resources to this often-ignored problem.

"It's a business," he had told his boss, the Government Minister. "And like all successful business, they have a business model, including calculated risk factors and cost analysis. We find those; we find the people selling our children as sex slaves."

Patterns were emerging. Reports of missing kids in one area were followed by similar abductions in different counties. Kunis knew that the so-called "second wave" of abandonment started when Romania joined the EU and desperate people went in search of high-paying jobs in the West, leaving kids like Nadia with relatives unable or unwilling to care for them properly. These kids were a target of the traffickers, vulnerable, but not as 'damaged' as street kids and worth more on the high-end market.

Detective Inspector Kunis did not much like the grubby, prejudiced, narrow-minded man who passed for the law in Tirnova. And he wouldn't put it past Stefanescu to take bribes and look the other way if need be, but somehow Kunis did not think the men who were running the sophisticated international trafficking rings would risk dealing with the likes of him. They knew the natural prejudice against the Roma community. What the poor bastard didn't know, Kunis thought, was that he could have been making money off his prejudices if he were only a slightly smarter policeman.

The inspector wanted to find Raluca's friend before it was too late, but he knew there was a slim-to-none chance they could. Kids were picked up all over the country and taken to holding points near the western border until a "quota" was reached that made the risk of moving them across the border worthwhile. What he did not know was what exactly that number might be, how many kids had already been abducted in the current round-up, and how soon they would be moved. Romania was still excluded, because of corruption, from the EU's Schengen passport-free travel zone. Time, he knew, was the only thing possibly on their side, and it was rapidly running out. After the girl was across the border she could be moved anywhere in Europe. Chances of finding her were reduced to near zero.

The men who took Nadia had counted on the fact and she had no one who cared enough about her to sound an alert, a miscalculation on their part this time. Nadia Iovan had left behind someone who cared very much. And while she might be young, Kunis was impressed with his witness. Her quick action had given them at least the possibility of finding Nadia, and of stopping the men who took her.

He stood up and moved around the table, then half-sat on the edge and leaned close to Raluca.

"Look at me," he said. "What happened is *not* your fault. I want you to know that and remember it always. Even if you had said something to your parents or a teacher the day Nadia went missing, they wouldn't have known what to do or been able to protect her. So don't let a false sense of guilt over what you *should* have done get in the way of what you *can* do now."

This important man confused Raluca. He scared her but she was beginning to trust him. To think he might really care about what happened to Nadia.

"And I know," he went on, "I know you were a great friend. I've talked to lots of people around here and I keep hearing the same thing about how you and your family took care of Nadia, and her grandmother, after her parents left. You stood up for her at school when kids teased her. You didn't abandon your friend when her parents did and that took courage. Courage and kindness."

Raluca knew it wasn't true; she could have done more. She could have stopped Nadia from leaving that day but instead she had refused to go with her to the cafe. She felt embarrassed, not comforted by the kind words.

"Can I go home now?" Raluca heard, and hated, the whine in her voice.

"Not yet." The big man stood up, stretched. And went back to the chair behind the desk. He picked up his notes and glanced through them. Then, in whispered tones, conferred with his colleague before addressing Raluca again.

"What was Nadia like during class that day? Did she participate as usual? Did she seem more distracted? Did she write down her assignments for the next day?"

Trying hard to tell the Inspector everything about that day, he surprised her with a question that wasn't so easy to answer.

"Did you and Nadia like to spend time in chat rooms on the Internet?"

Her father shifted uncomfortably in his seat.

"Chat rooms? I'm not even sure what that is," she said not-altogether-truthfully.

"Oh, Raluca, I think you know what a chat room is. But let's start with a simple question. Did the two of you spend time on the Internet? Watching videos of cute little kittens, perhaps?"

A reluctant nod. And small smile.

"Did you ever talk to strangers online?"

"No." Raluca knew her answer was too quick and not totally believable. "No. But... I mean, no I didn't, but I have watched Nadia do it a few times."

After a long uncomfortable pause, the Inspector went on.

"This is very important, Raluca. I don't think I have to tell you how important it is. Did Nadia ever mention any names or details about someone she met online?"

Oh dear, Raluca thought. Reality dawning.

Thinking back as hard as she could, taking her time before answering. "I don't think so. No, I'm sure she didn't. Not a name."

"Did she tell you which chat room she used?"

"No."

Inspector Kunis believed her. They could probably get something from the computer but he had hoped for, if not a miracle, at least a lead.

Raluca's father was a simple man of another time but he was not unintelligent. He didn't understand computers or chat rooms but he knew something about the hearts of men. Methods may have changed, men hadn't. And it wasn't just Raluca who was beginning to understand the implications of Nadia's online connection. The people of Tirnova knew how to protect their children from the usual dangers, he thought, but have no idea how to protect them from the modern ones. It could have been, he understood only too well, his own little girl snatched away to the worst kind of horror. The thought left him shaking and holding tightly to her hand as they walked home together.

CHAPTER 7

HEWERS OF WOOD & DRAWERS OF WATER

How hopeless it is to tidy away the past, even for others.

—*E.M. Forster*

ENOCH'S PRAYERS WERE ANSWERED. HE PULLED HIS CLASSIC Austin-Healey into a parking spot barely big enough, even for its diminutive size, and heaved a sigh of relief. The lights were all off in his Georgetown townhouse. It was nearly eleven and he didn't want to explain his late-night drinking with the guys to Laura. Frustrated with his boss, who was (in his estimation) a closeted anti-Semite and redneck that also happened to be a near genius, he had joined the guys for happy hour drinks. Enoch had stayed at the pub long after everyone else had gone home. He had more drinks than he should have and in a sloppy frame of mind came to the conclusion that Director Johnson refused to retire in order to thwart Enoch's ambition. Clarity of mind did not return as he walked off the drink before driving home. In no mood to explain, he crept up the creaky old stairs and slipped into bed.

Unlike Laura's position at the State Department, Enoch's job at the IRS was neither powerful nor visible. They had lived together since Enoch finished law school five years ago. Neither was ready to commit to marriage. He suspected her hesitation stemmed from increasing disappointment with his lackluster career. She saw him as wasting his talents, toiling away in anonymous trenches at the IRS. His reasons for waiting were less clear to him. But Laura was making more demands on their time together and that was adding up to growing tension in the relationship. He did not appreciate being her escort to high-powered political functions. And he also didn't appreciate her pressure to use her influence in the administration to help him secure a better job.

Enoch was determined to "make it" in D.C., but he intended to make it on his own. He loved his job; it was like being a cop without a gun, a detective without the bodies. And however hungry he was for his boss's job, he was willing to wait until Johnson either moved on or made a major mistake.

"We have to talk," Laura said, as Enoch rushed through the kitchen on his way out the door. His head pounding from too much drink and too little sleep.

"Okay. What's up?" he asked, looking at his watch. "Can it wait until tonight?"

"No, actually it can't. Please, sit down. This is important."

Enoch put his laptop next to hers on the perfectly clean counter and dropped his tall frame onto the edge of the chair. The kitchen was spotless. We pay a fortune for a cleaning lady and no one lives here long enough to mess anything up, Enoch thought.

She sat down across from him.

"I have wonderful news, Enoch. I hoped to tell you last night but I finally gave up and went to sleep before you got home." She was trying to keep frustration about last night out of her voice... as she wanted to get him to agree to an interview today at the State Department.

"The Office of Personnel called me yesterday," she went on. "Finally, it looks like there is an ideal position that would be perfect for you. It is not as senior as I would like, but definitely a step up from where you are and we would be in the same agency... the same world, so to speak. But we're going to have to act fast. You need to come over today to meet..."

He cringed. Laura was so intent on convincing him that she missed the cues.

"Hold on, Laura," he interrupted. "How many times have we had this conversation? I don't want you to get me a job. And certainly not at State. I like the position I have for the time being. All I need is one good high-profile case and I will get Johnson's job. And your suggestion that I drop everything at the last moment and run over to Foggy Bottom today for an interview implies whatever I might have on my schedule today is utterly unimportant. I think I resent that."

"Oh please, don't be so dramatic. I'm not suggesting anything of the sort. Just that this is a great opportunity and it's important. To both of us. And since when did you start liking your job? You graduated law school at the top of your class and you're telling me you're happy working in a dead-end, low-level IRS position for a man you can't stand? Or are you waiting for a mythical perfect case to drop into your lap or for Johnson to drop dead of a heart attack from his terrible diet? Is that your plan, Arnheim? Is it? Because that doesn't sound like a very good plan to me!"

She was on her feet now. Furious. And frustrated beyond belief. How could he not possibly see what she was offering him?

He stood up, picked up his briefcase, and answered in a deceptively calm voice. "I am late. I know you mean well and we can talk about this tonight."

They both knew how quickly this could escalate. Something neither of them really wanted.

Laura didn't answer and she didn't linger long, either, in their spotless kitchen.

"Stupid male ego," she fumed, turning her car toward Constitution Avenue. Having lobbied hard to get Enoch a hearing, she decided she would make an excuse that would keep the door open; admitting to herself she had handled the morning badly. But, she thought, if only he had come home on time last night, they could have discussed this wonderful opportunity in a civil manner. Always pragmatic, Laura determined to repair the damage this evening. She would pick up a nice bottle of wine and a good steak on the way home, and then they could discuss the issue again. Concentrating on Enoch's unreasonableness, Laura nearly hit a large black SUV that cut her off as she turned right into the underground parking garage.

"Men!" she screamed, shaking her fist at the driver. Laura continued to mutter about more-or-less the entire gender while she was forced to crawl around the block in heavy traffic before finally pulling into her reserved space. She was fifteen minutes late and more flustered than was good for the State Department Press Secretary.

"Damn you, Enoch," she muttered, pounding the elevator button. When the doors opened Laura put Enoch out of her mind and the best diplomatic smile she could muster on her face for the crowd inside.

CHAPTER 8

MARTHA IN THE MIDDLE

The Scriptures uniformly call us not so much to reflect on justice as to do justice.

—Miroslav Volf

MARTHA LEFT THE OFFICE EARLY. SHE WALKED ACROSS CHAIN Bridge Road to the Metro stop at Rosslyn in a fog. The short train ride to Arlington where she lived in the modest brick rambler of her childhood did nothing to clear her head.

"I'll just be a few minutes," she said to her mom as she walked out the back door into their small garden, pleading the need for some air before dinner.

The Culberson yard, like the house, was a humble one. Years ago, Martha's mother had created a goldfish pond. The fertile Virginia soil around the pond, once carefully tended by Mrs. Culberson, was now over-grown with weeds and bushes that needed clipping, the small bench she had placed by the pond to watch the sun flashing off the colorful fish as they cut through the water was all but consumed by the rambling catmint. The fancy fish were long since dead. Dirt and leaves settled on the surface of the water and sank over time. Replenished with rainwater, life grew in the tiny bog at the bottom of the pond. Frogs moved in, laid their eggs in large gelatinous sacs from which tadpoles emerged and then morphed from fishlike creature to frog; the few that survived completed the cycle by hibernating in the mud.

Martha sat on the bench staring moodily into the murky waters, her thoughts back at the office. She was still wondering why her boss, after months of growing compatibility as they worked together on the Awareness Campaign, had exploded at a chance remark she made at the end of the day. Ronald Lorten had gone from camaraderie back to condescension in a split second.

Something was moving in the water. Martha leaned closer, pushing aside dead leaves and green growing fungus, she watched, mesmerized, as a teeming mass of tadpoles grazed like tiny sea cows along the moss-covered stones in the pond.

April, May, and June had passed since Ronald Lorten presented the Awareness Campaign to the WOWL team and asked her to be his "right-hand" on the project. Proud and excited, she had taken on the new responsibilities and the obsequious countenance that had so irritated her boss had (unbeknownst to her) gradually been replaced by a growing confidence. She didn't even resent the fact he had never given her credit for suggesting that the IJO human-trafficking mission was worthy of support from WOWL. She didn't even mind that he had never thanked her for the Bible Trivia Game idea, even though it was selling in all their bookstores across the country and had actually helped raise awareness of the campaign. Until today, with everything ready for the official launch on Monday, tired and happy after another busy week, Martha had been sitting quietly at her desk when Mr. Lorten shouted, "Come into my office, Martha, and take a seat."

He was leaning back in his chair, snakeskin boots on the desk.

"We've done good, don't you think?" he said with a hint of Southern heritage showing. "We've worked as a team and pulled this thing together. You should go home early today and enjoy the weekend. You've earned it. And get ready for Monday; it's sure to be madness."

Sitting there with her boss in the fading light she had felt something close to companionship. Drawn into a false sense of camaraderie by his apparent change of heart toward her, Martha spoke her mind.

"You've been working very hard as well, Mr. Lorten. Don't you think it's time for the consultants to step up now? They should send their people over sometimes. We could use their expertise on site when we go live on Monday. Even Charlie said we are paying them big money without much to show for it."

That was the moment, she thought, still staring in the pond, that he had pushed back from the desk, dropped his boots onto the thick Persian rug and snarled at her with the old disdain in his voice. "Don't worry about details that don't concern you, Martha. Just do your job. I decide if Wharton & Wharton Consulting is worth the money."

"Come in to dinner, dear," Mrs. Culberson called from the kitchen door.

Martha's mother had made her husband's favorite comfort food that evening. Old-fashioned meatloaf with lots of buttery mashed potatoes and hot stewed tomatoes on the side. The brilliant mind of Dr. Wilbur Culberson was, like his body, wearing out. His thin old frame was stooped and his hands shook sometimes, making eating difficult and often resulting in embarrassing spills. Over the years he had invited many students to dine with them and Martha missed the stimulating theological discourse that had marked many evening meals in the Culberson home.

Mrs. Culberson was eager to hear Martha's stories about work at WOWL, especially after long days shut in taking care of her ailing husband.

"So tell me," her mother said, "are you ready for the 'launch' as you call it?"

Martha appeared to be giving more attention to the meatloaf than it deserved and missed her mother's question. She was still wondering about the uncomfortable end to her day with Mr. Lorten.

"Martha? I asked you a question."

"Sorry, Mom, yes, yes, we're ready," Martha said. "In fact, it will be very exciting. We're going live on radio, TV, and the Internet by the end of next week. All the publicity spots are ready and some of them are really clever. I just hope we get a good response. It's such a great cause."

"It all sounds wonderful, dear. Except the Internet is such a danger-ous thing, isn't it? Used for all kinds of wickedness?"

"It's a good thing if you use it for good, Mom, just like the radio or TV, it's just another tool."

"Well, that could be. But this all sounds like a lot more work for you."

Mrs. Culberson knew it was selfish, but she missed her daughter and resented it when she was away too many evenings and weekends.

"More work means more money, too. I will get a nice bonus."

Dr. Culberson looked intensely at his daughter, a quizzical smile on his old face. "What did you do to your hair, dear? It looks different."

"Oh, Dad," Martha laughed. "Are you only noticing now? I changed it over a month ago. At the same time I got contact lenses. Of course, I wore glasses in high school for a year before you noticed."

He chuckled.

"I believe I was busy working on the Old Testament translation of the NIV Bible at the time. Focused on ancient Hebrew verbs, one might be forgiven missing the odd detail."

She patted his hand. "You missed more than a few odd details during my childhood, but none of the important ones. And I'm glad you like my hair. I'm told it makes me look years younger."

"Everyone looks years younger from where I'm sitting," he replied. "So tell us about this campaign and the 'launch'. Whatever that means."

"It means as of Monday, everybody who listens to Christian radio owned by the Lortens, or goes to their bookstores and participating churches, will hear about the campaign to help stop human trafficking. It's a good thing, Dad. Don't look so skeptical. The company knows how to tell a story in a way that touches people's hearts."

"And people's pocketbooks. It might do some good, Martha, but it won't do the Lortens any harm either." Dr. Culberson's shaky hands replaced his cup in the saucer, spilling a little weak decaf coffee on the table.

"Wilbur!" Mrs. Culberson exclaimed. "What on earth do you mean?"

"I mean it won't do the Lortens any harm either," he said in something like the old tone that commanded immediate respect. "And explain please, daughter, why WOWL is now pushing biblical literacy with this campaign? I have never known them to be concerned about it before. Certainly none of their radio or television programs are aimed at improving anyone's knowledge of the Scriptures."

Martha smiled at her grumpy father.

"You just never liked Christian radio."

"No, I just never thought radio could be 'Christian' by definition. It is an odd logic that says having declared oneself a follower of Christ, thereafter one can declare whatever endeavor they engage in as 'Christian'". Seems more like marketing to me. But never mind, maybe I'll enter this little contest."

"Sorry Dad, contest rules. No clergy, no professors, no family members or staff. But back to your point about Christian radio. I don't know what you mean. Of course the radio and television stations of WOWL are Christian."

"They might include some such content or at least rhetoric," he grumbled. "But you can't just call something 'Christian' and then market it as ordained truth."

Long past the time when Dr. Culberson usually grew too tired to talk, he continued with more animation that Martha had seen in months. Like many elderly, her father suffered from what his doctor called "sundown syndrome". His mind got tired by the end of the day, making it harder for him to concentrate and communicate as the day wore on. But not tonight.

"Martha," he pressed, "why do you really think the Lorten family has decided to spend so much time and energy on something not even remotely related to the American political scene? This is not the cultural war that they are usually fighting. Why this and why now? It has been years since they have used their media might to invest in major aid programs. Ronald's father was a good man, but I can't remember him actually focusing on biblical literacy or large aid efforts either. This new concern is out of character. You are sitting right there outside the door of the big man, Martha, so what do you think is behind all this?"

"I'm more than sitting outside the door, Dad," Martha said with more hurt in her voice than intended. "I'm Mr. Lorten's administrative assistant, I'm helping make it happen!"

He ignored, or missed, the hurt in his daughter's voice and carried on with unusual clarity.

"Ronald Lorten, like many others, has blurred the line between faith and politics for a long time and built a tidy empire doing so. He's a businessman, so as a businessman, he has a reason for this charitable action. My question is, why this one and why now? Have you asked yourself that, Martha? Have you thought it might be to divert attention from something, shall we say, less... charitable?"

"Dad! That's ridiculous."

"Yes, more than ridiculous," Mrs. Culberson jumped in. "It's a scandalous suggestion, Wilbur. I won't have you worrying Martha like that. Ronald Lorten is a fellow believer and this is a Christian ministry... you shouldn't even say such things."

"On the contrary, my dear, that is precisely why we should question such things. And I don't like the fact that you are mixed up in this, Martha."

"Mixed up in this? Dad, you make it sound positively criminal. How can you say that about a ministry?"

"First of all, WOWL has not been a ministry for a very long time. It is, however, a very powerful political instrument. A political instrument used to propagate the assumption that a particular political position is morally superior to all others. I worry. That's all, Martha. I worry for the Church. I worry for you."

Dr. Culbertson was becoming more and more agitated, upsetting wife and daughter. His finger shook as he pointed it at Martha.

"The Lortens of this world keep demanding that America should become a Christian nation again, when it never was a Christian nation. The founders rejected the idea of special entitlements or entanglements with religion from the very outset. Besides, the Church is Universal, not national, and its role is to call men and women, not the nation, to Christ."

"Wilbur... " his wife said, patting his hand. "Calm down, dear. You're getting excited."

"Perhaps," he agreed, fire fading from his eyes. "But there is more than a hint of nationalism in the right-wing rhetoric of the so-called Christian right. That's dangerous."

"But Dad," Martha finally interrupted what had turned into a lecture. "Can't you see that's the point of the Awareness Campaign — it isn't political at all."

Dr. Culberson looked at his daughter with longing. He felt a desperate need to protect her, to warn her. But it was no use. He could feel tiredness taking over.

"Remember what G. K. Chesterton said?" He was smiling now. "The Church keeps going to the dogs. And every time it does, the dog dies. This time, the Church is going to the political dogs."

Glad for the lighter tone, Martha laughed. "Well I don't think the church is going to the dogs, and if so it isn't the fault of my boss alone."

"Maybe not alone, but he's doing his fair share. Mark my words. This Awareness Campaign is not all that it seems to be."

"Well, I'm sure I don't know what has gotten into you tonight, Wilbur," Mrs. Culberson fussed, cross with him for upsetting Martha. "But I say if what Martha is helping the company do will help this bring attention to human trafficking and gets people interested in the Bible — well it's a good thing. They are both good things. I've always said you could do great things Martha, and so you are — just ignore your father, dear. He doesn't know what he's saying."

Her father did look worn out, but Martha was fairly certain he knew exactly what he was saying. She stared into her empty coffee cup wishing he hadn't chosen this night to find the mental energy to see clearly what she was trying very hard to ignore.

The Culberson trio sat quietly together for several minutes as light faded from the room. Each troubled, for different reasons, by the conversation. The light was going out in the old scholar's eyes. His head began to nod.

Wife and daughter stood to begin the nightly ritual of helping him to bed.

Later, when Martha went to say goodnight, her father looked at her with still-troubled eyes and tried once more to make her understand.

"It was so sudden and so out of character, Martha. I knew Ronald Lorten's father. He might have been concerned for these young victims, his son I'm not so sure about."

"Oh Dad, don't go on about that... it's okay. I promise I'll tell you if I see anything that seems wrong. I've been involved with all the details. Please trust me and stop worrying."

She closed the door to his room more quickly than usual.

Later, when Martha stood at the kitchen sink, hands in the dishwater, she thought about her own preoccupation recently and wondered about her father's words. Would she have noticed if something was amiss? Or had she been too busy enjoying her new role? Too busy thinking how she would spend her bonus? Or enjoying the newfound camaraderie with colleagues too much?

Martha's cheeks flushed at the memory of rushing to Tyson's Corner Mall when one of the women in accounting mentioned a sale at Talbots. She had acted like a teenager looking for the right clothes to impress her peers.

Two expensive suits later, Martha had stopped into the Red Door Salon and made an appointment for a haircut and ended up with a new look. People had noticed the change and complimented her.

What am I trying to prove, she thought, hands still submerged in the now cold dish water, embarrassed at what she realized people must be thinking, must be saying to each other, about how she had put on airs. She wondered what her father would think if he knew she had been looking at the Christian Cafe online dating site. Not that she believed their marketing slogan (Find God's Match for You Here) in a literal sense, but, she sighed, it would be nice to meet a Christian man.

The very ordered, settled life of Martha had undergone unexpected changes and it was more than her hair, contact lenses, and wardrobe. She liked having more responsibility and the admiration of her colleagues. She didn't want to go back to being mousy Martha.

Ronald Lorten would have been happy to know Martha's first thoughts the next morning were not related to questions raised by her illustrious father but rather on whether or not she could afford the Anne Klein jacket rejected last week as too expensive. Martha brushed the tiniest amount of blush on her checks, kissed her father on the top of his head, and went to work rushing across Chain Bridge with no thought of deep or troubled waters.

* * * * *

As Martha was making her way to the office Monday morning, Nadia Iovan was on her way back to Tirnova.

She went there in her mind every time her body was violated. Nadia knew now, now that it was much too late, that she wasn't the smart girl who got out, but the stupid girl who got caught by wolves. She was a selfish stupid girl who deserved to be devoured by wolves for abandoning her own grandmother. Memory of home was the only place she could go to get away. So she floated above her dirty body and escaped to the things she used to hate but couldn't remember why. The animals in the street, silly traditions like painting trees. Boredom. Oh how Nadia longed for the simple pleasure of boredom. And she talked to her best friend. Sometimes to Adi, Raluca's little brother. And she talked every day to Baba, pleading with Baba to forgive her. Wondering if her grandmother had enough to eat. If Raluca was really going to check on her. But no one heard her words. After her throat closed that day in the forest the only words she had were the ones in her head.

The driver had not waited long before pulling the SUV off the road onto a rutted track in the forest. They forced her from the car and took turns. Then carefully covered the leather seats with a blanket to absorb the blood and covered her with another before driving across the country toward the border and a bribed guard standing by to get his cut. Nadia had screamed and cried when they raped her in the forest. Then her words were all gone. Once out of Romania the men handed her off to other wolves and she never saw them again. It didn't matter how much men beat her, and withheld food and drink and promised if she would talk she could go to the easier places in nice cities with rich men and a softer life. You are young and beautiful, the wolves told her. It doesn't have to be the most danger-ous streets and meanest men. But it didn't matter what terrible things they did or less horrible things they promised if she would start talking again like a *normal* girl because Nadia wasn't normal anymore. Her silence was not a choice. Like everything else she'd lost, her voice was gone for good.

Now, looking back as she floated above her body, Nadia wondered why she had hated home so much. She told herself if she could go back and see Raluca and take care of Baba, she would never ever complain again about life in Tirnova. But she knew she couldn't ever go back. Not in her body. That body couldn't ever be clean. Even if she escaped from the wolves by the door, the ones on the road, the wolves in the trucks, and the ones on the street, she could never go back. People would look at her and see what she had done. They would know. She couldn't wash it off. Nothing would ever wash it off. Nadia remembered going to church with Raluca and her family and hearing about God's love and forgiveness for sin that made one clean again. If only that were true, she thought, knowing nothing could ever wash her stains away.

So Nadia went home in her mind, where summer gardens were always in bloom, the plum trees along the roadway were whitewashed, and friends sat together under a grape arbor waiting for a cool breeze at the end of a long day. She longed for that place in the same way she longed for the daily needle, which took care of all the other longings.

CHAPTER 9

A PERPETUAL PLACE

A speckled cat and a tame hare
Eat at my hearth stone and sleep there.

—W.B. Yeats

LEAVES WERE BEGINNING TO FALL WHEN RACHEL FINALLY moved into the old carriage house that sat in the woods at the outer edge of the Lorten property. She was alone in her new home for the first time as the sun began to set. The architect had proclaimed the reconstruction a masterpiece, then took his leave. The place was finally free of movers and contractors and their materials. Ellie, Rachel's best friend, who had helped carry in the last few things, was out buying Lebanese take-out for their dinner.

Rachel had left the ugly McMansion she had shared with Eric the day after his funeral and lived in a hotel while the crumbling historic structure was being recreated into her image. She had left behind furniture, furnishings, and even a walk-in closet of unopened eight-year-old wedding gifts that had conveyed to the new owner. Rachel brought the cats, a small cellar of fine wine, her large library, and Persian carpets collected in the Caucasus.

Looking for a hearty red wine to go with the spicy lamb that would also be sufficient for the celebration at hand, Rachel rummaged through a row of unopened boxes. She chose an *Octagon* from a Monticello vineyard, then commenced exploring her new home while waiting for Ellie's return. It would be easy to hear her car, any car, approaching down the private lane that wandered through the woods from Old Dominion Road to her house.

Ellie was married to Rachel's least favorite brother, Jeff, who happened to be on his way to Bosnia with her other least favorite brother, Ronald. This, she knew, was semantically impossible — but true, nonetheless.

"Semantics be damned," Rachel shouted to the open beam rafters and was rewarded with a small echo in the nearly empty living room. Lovely, she thought, I shall live here alone and have agreeable conversations with myself.

She opened closets that smelled of sawdust, touched cold granite surfaces and warm wooden ones made from the old Black Walnut tree that had long stood guard by the front door. Killed by a lightning strike years ago, the seasoned hardwood was used by the craftsmen to make kitchen cabinets, doorframes, and built-in ceiling-to-floor library shelves.

Merry and Pippin were curled together, sound asleep on the new sofa. Like Rachel, the cats had been displaced until construction was complete. Free now from the Kitty Kennel in McLean, a rather less luxurious exile than her D.C. hotel suite, the cats had spent the day exploring hedgerows and eating field mice before curling up to catch the last rays of sun on the softest spot in the room.

The persistent roar of cicadas came through open windows. The woods were filled with the bug-eyed insects on a mission to find a mate. When last seen the cicadas had burrowed into the ground, set their alarm for seventeen years, and waited. Like Rachel, they were back. As if directed by an invisible conductor, the fevered pitch of the cicada mating call rose higher and higher until, as if on cue, they all released together before ramping up the amps once again. The noise of it was driving people crazy. And out of their yards. Garden weddings were rescheduled indoors. Outdoor parties cancelled. Even the President of the United States and the Prime Minister of Russia had to move their Rose Garden ceremony inside the White House. Personally, Rachel liked the noisy creatures and figured after seventeen years of waiting underground the cicadas deserved the stage.

"Sing on cicadas. Sing on," she shouted over the deck into the woods, feeling like a monarch of the glen instead of the owner of a few untended acres of woods. Rachel exulted in the moment. She took in the sounds, the earthy smells, and the beauty of towering sycamore trees that lined the creek and stretched their massive white limbs above the yellow, bronze, and saffron hues in what had been until recently a very green wood. It was hers and she was home.

I will still be here, she thought, when snow silences the creatures. And I will stand here listening when spring peepers fill the night with their music and fireflies light up the summer sky. Seventeen years from now, I will still be here in my perpetual place to welcome the cicadas back again.

Built in the late 1700s, the carriage house was remodeled in the Sixties as a four-car garage; then it stood empty for decades crumbling from the weight of the vines seeking to reclaim it. Rachel's parents purchased the property two decades ago with plans to tear it down, but the Lortens could not actually see the carriage house from their mansion and soon everyone but Rachel forgot it even existed.

Money was not an object. After convincing her mother to sell, she worked with an architect experienced in historic restorations. They gutted the inside and added a two-story open stairwell with a copper skeleton that framed and enhanced the wall of glass. Built-in overstuffed benches followed the curve of the windows and made it possible to curl up with a book and read while watching birds soar by at eye level. No curtains would be necessary, the woods provided the privacy.

Fourteen can be a silly season in any girl's life, but Rachel's teenage years were also filled with grief over the loss of her father who died too soon, conflict with her mother, and a never-ending stream of important rich and famous guests wanting the publicity WOWL could grant them. She resented the presence of the greedy strangers in her home and avoided the social swirl by hiking through the woods to the crumbling carriage house, taking with her plenty of snacks to eat, lots of books to read, and candles to read them by. One summer she hauled an old beanbag chair through the brambles. The blue plastic split, leaving a trail of beans like breadcrumbs that a family of field mice followed to the source and enjoyed a bountiful winter. The following spring Rachel found the chair greatly diminished in size and an earthy rodent smell permeating the room.

Rachel smiled at the memory and wondered if the builders had found any bits of blue plastic when they ripped up the flooring. The mice had probably also enjoyed the black and white journals she hid under the floorboards over the years. Her diaries chronicled daily frustrations with her mother and brothers and life in the big house. Hiding them had been satisfying but unnecessary since none of the people in her life had time for, or would have been interested in, reading of her teenage angst.

She walked from the deck back inside and sat down cross-legged on the densely woven Persian. She lifted the edge and ran her hand over the restored wood, found and pressed a small groove that released a plank and revealed a copper box hidden in a shallow recess.

Asking the builder to put a hiding place under the hardwood floor had been as foolish as hiding her diaries there as a girl, but it was a sentimental whim he indulged, accustomed as he was to wealthy clients with eccentricities. Rachel liked her whimsical little box hidden under the newly restored floor despite the fact it would serve no purpose. If only, she whispered, if only I could hide Eric's secret so easily.

Rachel had intended to lock the medical records from Inova Hospital in her desk, but sitting there on the floor a much better, and more satisfying solution came to her. She rushed downstairs at the sound of Ellie's car coming down the lane, quickly retrieved the hospital folder from her briefcase and was pulling the edge of the carpet over the hiding place, with Eric's secret inside, when the phone rang.

"Oh," she jumped. Like she had been caught in an illegal or illicit act.

She let it ring until her mother's southern accent, pitched in a permanent whine when talking to her daughter, further shattered the peace.

"Rachel, darling... please, please... pick up the phone and talk to your mother. I hope you're not moving those heavy boxes by yourself... you get a boy to do that... hallo... hallo... Rachel please pick up the phone dear... well... call me when you're settled."

"Stupid, stupid, stupid," Rachel said tracing the cord to its source and yanking it from the wall.

"Hello, where are you?" Ellie's sane voice preceded the aromatic scents of the Middle East wafting up the open stairwell. "You sound like you could use a cup of tea. And stop panicking — your mother could have intruded by phone as easily if you were in Gstaad."

"Oh thank goodness you're here, I'm starved. And forget tea, I've found the wine."

"Well done," Ellie said setting out the goodies on a crate holding books.

They sat on one of Rachel's favorite carpets, a Turkish prayer rug, and sipped the fruity flavored Virginian wine in plastic cups and devoured the lamb masala, goat cheese, and tzatziki dip with plastic forks.

Jeff had met Ellie when she came home with Rachel for Thanksgiving break during their junior year of college. The marriage looked picture perfect on the outside. Beautiful wife, cute kids, successful husband. Jeff was the charismatic, handsome, Lorten. People liked his big personality that filled a room the moment he walked in. The way he listened so intensely, with compassion and support. Jeff had pursued Ellie with the same enthusiasm he now applied to getting important people to his Bible study groups on Capitol Hill. Jeff needed a beautiful wife and Ellie was, more often than not, the most beautiful woman in the room. But what Jeff didn't need and could not abide was competition. Early in the marriage Ellie learned to be the beautiful accessory. She learned to subsume an intellect that more than matched her husband's. For all his popularity, Jeff Lorten was insecure. He needed his wife to be his moon, reflecting his brilliance, and she had learned the emotional price of doing otherwise.

A breeze blew through the French doors, bringing not only the roar of cicadas but a woodsy smell of dried grass and autumn leaves that mixed with fresh paint, wood stain, lingering sawdust, cardamom, and garlic. It was a moment to savor and Rachel couldn't think of anyone in the world she would rather share it with than Ellie.

They toasted with a little more wine, clicking plastic against plastic. Waterford crystal had never seemed so fine.

"Oh, before I forget, I brought you a housewarming gift. I made it myself," Ellie said, tossing a brightly wrapped parcel.

Rachel unwrapped it to find a pair of pillowcases embroidered with a Yiddish proverb: 'Sleep Fast. We Need the Pillows.'

"Ha, how very droll, Ellie," she laughed. "And I suppose you embroidered them yourself, which is very annoying. I couldn't even sew on a button that came off the other day because I don't own a needle."

"You don't own one because you don't know what to do with one," Ellie added helpfully.

Maybe it was the wine or rich food, or maybe it was just the moment, but Rachel, overcome with emotion, swiveled away from the box table, knelt and kissed the floor like it was the Holy Land.

"Are you praying?" Ellie asked, laughing at the sight. "Because I don't want to disturb you if you are. But you do look pretty silly."

Rachel sat back up.

"Oh, I forgot you were here."

"Clearly! Well that's the thanks I get."

"You know, maybe I *am* praying... at least I am experiencing extraordinary feelings of thanksgiving. I'm not sure if I'm as thankful as I should be to God or just this beautiful moment. I feel thankful to you, that's for sure, for helping me choose the furnishing for this perfect place and for... carrying up the last box. And being my best, maybe only, real friend. I am even feeling thankful to my mother; an unusual emotion... must be the wine, for finally giving in and selling the carriage house to me. I am just so glad to be here without Eric... I know how terrible that sounds. It's not as though I'm glad his life was taken from him — just that mine's been restored to me... if you know what I mean."

Ellie knew. She had felt more than a few guilty thoughts herself that widowhood would be easier than making her own hard marriage work.

They sat in silence, comfortable understanding silence, for several minutes. "Well, at least... at least *you* have two beautiful children."

"Hmm. Good thing that men's only role in procreation involves pleasure and none of the pain. Otherwise I probably wouldn't have."

"True. In fact, otherwise the whole darn human race would have died out long ago."

They giggled like girls. Like the college roommates they once had been.

Rachel drained the last drop of wine.

"Isn't this place perfect, Ellie? No one but you knew how much I hated that house. Eric's McMansion. It was like my marriage... with an expensive brick front and vinyl around the back."

"Umm, I know a little about phony coverings myself... and yes this place is utterly magnificent. I'm glad for you, Rachel... and, and I hope it will be your permanent place... if that is what you want it to be."

Ellie had serious reservations about her friend moving into a place so close to the family. She had lobbied for a house in Old Towne Alexandria or Georgetown where one could get the same old world charm with none of the proximity to her famous and dominating family. She had even encouraged Rachel to make a total break, take a job in Europe, and move far away from Virginia for a few years. But now that it was done she was grateful Rachel would be close by.

"I know what you're thinking, and it does seem odd that I have chosen to stay here, but this never seemed like part of my other world, I have loved this place and dreamed of living here since I was a little girl. It always held a little mystery, a little danger and most of all a little disorder, which was very welcome. I could escape here. Of course, nobody noticed me missing or bothered to look for me, but still it felt like I was escaping. And it was wild. Untouched by landscaper's tools and devoid of cute little trimming and plantings. I pretended this was my home and that I had a different last name. Now it really is mine."

"Yeah, but the last name thing didn't work out so well."

The incongruity of Rachel keeping her name hyphenated with Kissane was left unsaid because they had discussed it so many times. Rachel theorized it was a subliminal decision based on foreknowledge that her new name was going to be just as burdensome as her maiden name, so why bother to replace the old? Ellie insisted that it was a suppressed desire to remain a Lorten despite lifelong protests to the contrary.

"No, it didn't turn out so well. And I admit I could have thrown off the Lorten name, but I didn't and now I am glad because I'm not too crazy about Kissane either and well, let's face it, I'm not likely to replace either one of them so I'm destined to remain a hyphenated woman."

"Or you could drop the Rachel and the Lorten. And the Kissane, and like people in the witness protection program, you could get a new identity. Or maybe you were adopted and you can go find your real parents and use that name."

"Very helpful I'm sure; however, since I look like my dad the adoption thing isn't likely. By the way, what is the family saying about me moving here?"

"You mean other than your mother's endless lament — why would Rachel want to live in that horrible little rundown place?"

"No matter what I do my mother laments."

"Jeff thinks you're crazy. Nothing new there. "

"Jeff is probably right. Just smell that air. Fall smells so good. Like fresh apple cider and vegetables with the dirt still on in farmer market stalls. I have been hanging out smelling the vegetables, and you know what Ellie, next year I'm going to grow a little garden and take up canning."

Ellie rolled her eyes.

"You might actually want to rethink that. Canning doesn't really seem like you."

"No, I'm serious."

"Canning? We are talking about putting vegetables in jars, right? Whatever for?"

"You know you're right, it should be called jarring, but never mind, I'm going to can fruits and vegetables. Because I want to, I think maybe it's a lost art. I'm going to can tomatoes. I am going to can pickles. I am going to can peaches — after that I am going to pick blackberries myself and can those too. Then my boss will probably can me because I will never write anything again but I don't care because my books will be replaced on my shelves with color-coordinated fruits and vegetables. Much more valuable than books. My mother has always been trying to make me 'get over' the book thing as she calls it... so I shall."

Merry, Rachel's oldest and very fat cat, trotted into the room, drawn by the smell of lamb; he dropped his bulky body near the humans, sniffing the meat. Rachel stroked her happy cat and it produced the deep bass purr she loved.

All was quiet for several minutes, except for the purring of the cat and screeching cicadas, until Ellie roused herself and proclaimed her friend a fraud.

"Actually," she said, "I don't think one actually 'cans' blackberries, Rachel, or pickles for that matter. I think you 'pickle' cucumbers and one 'makes jam' with fruit. I grew up in Indiana and I know these things and if you are going to go domestic, which I doubt, and do not recommend, you better at least learn the lingo."

"And," she went on, "I think it's pretty presumptuous of you to assume because you and your snobby world of East Coast elite do not 'can' that it's a lost art. In fact, I should think there are plenty of women canning their little hearts out at this very moment in the place you all so quaintly call Middle America or the provinces."

Rachel groaned.

"How true! How depressingly true. So like me to discover something not lost at all. Ah, well... I shall just continue eating my way through fall then and depend on Trader Joe's in the winter. Eric always said that the only domestic thing about me was that I lived in a house so maybe I should leave canning to Middle America."

"Oh cheer up," Ellie said as her cell phone rang. "I admire your insouciance, if not your skills on the domestic front."

The call was Justin, Ellie's oldest.

"Oh dear... yes, sorry," she said. "I'm still at Auntie Rachel's. Um no... you go ahead and eat without me. There is a Caesar salad with lots of chicken in the fridge. I'll be home soon. And start your homework."

Ellie and Jeff's two children were going through the difficult adolescent years. Justin, the oldest, was openly miserable and would probably be trouble for a time. Sally was moody but would undoubtedly turn out as lovely as her mother. Jeff did not like his sister or her influence on his wife and kids. He had been marginally less angry about Ellie's time with

Rachel since Eric's death, "be nice to the widow," kind of thing. And while Jeff was away in Bosnia, Ellie could enjoy her friend's company without his inevitable withering condemnation afterwards.

Despite the camaraderie of the afternoon, the shared work and meal, Rachel was glad when Ellie finally took her leave an hour later. There was a weight of shared knowledge between them. Having told no one on earth beside her doctor and Ellie that Eric had HIV when he died, Rachel sometimes wished even her best friend didn't know. It made the knowledge more real, somehow, and sometimes it invaded the quiet moments when they were together, taking some of the air out of the room. Rachel could pretend to everyone else that her handsome husband had died and left her a widow. End of story. Ellie knew the truth and sometimes even her unspoken sympathy added to Rachel's burden.

The sun had long since set behind the Blue Ridge Mountains before Rachel got tired of unpacking boxes. She took one more tour around her new house, enjoying each room, then wandered out onto the deck, not wanting the day of new beginnings to end. Sitting in the swing with Merry and Pippin on either side for balance she pondered the moment. Life was going to continue to be complicated, but it would be better here than in any other place in the world. Of that she was certain. There was no imprint of Eric here. None with the exception of what was possibly lurking in her blood and on a piece of paper in the box under the floor. Rachel felt that she was gaining control and today she had officially pushed the "reset" button on her life.

* * * * *

The thin young man behind the desk stood like a soldier at attention when she opened the door of the dingy office near the morgue in the basement of Fairfax Hospital. "Please have a seat, Mrs. Kissane. My name is Andrew Nichols, er... ah... thank you for coming... I mean please have a seat... Mrs. Kissane."

Poor lad had clearly not been long in the job, Rachel had thought charitably, hoping to make the visit brief; she put on a thin smile to ease his mind.

Mr. Nichols, manager of the Donor Unit, who called the day she visited Eric's grave and did not give up over the ensuing weeks, left ever more threatening messages until Rachel finally gave in and found herself in the windowless office with some idea of what must be coming.

Dressed in her usual dark clothes, Rachel self-consciously assumed young Nichols took it as a sign of mourning or simply bad taste. In reality, the woman in front of him was imposing, attractive and dignified, with a strength that quite intimidated the young man.

Perched on the edge of a small wobbly plastic chair, Rachel leaned toward the desk; not with an air of expectation but inner resolve; ignoring the young man's clichés of solace, she told him firmly to come to the point.

"This is not easy and I do apologize, Mrs. Lorten-Kissane, you have had such a shock... let me begin by saying how important it is for more people to do what your husband did... I mean being an organ donor is heroic and I um... have seen lives saved because people like your husband are willing to give the gift of life to another... "

Trying not to frighten the young man, Rachel interrupted and quietly but firmly demanded he save the platitudes and tell her immediately the reason she had been summoned, although something like the truth had begun to dawn long before the dreaded words stumbled out.

"The problem is, Mrs. Lorten-Kissane," he mumbled. "We cannot use them... "

"Look, we discussed this on the phone. I didn't make a trip here to hear you repeat that my husband's donated organs are diseased and you can't use them... it seems moot now for you to tell *me* he was sick. It can't possibly matter now, surely. I am telling you either get to the real point or you can tell it all to my lawyer. I do have a lawyer, Mr. Nichols, and I have to tell you I am feeling very harassed by this hospital."

He got to the point.

"Your husband's tissue tested positive for the immunodeficiency virus, Type 1 (anti – HIV 1). Our laboratory, which is appropriately certified, did extensive autopsy tests on all the, um... physical evidence to determine if there was evidence of other sexually transmitted disease, or IV drug use such as needle tracks and um... "

Unable to meet Rachel's steady gaze, the young man had kept his eyes on the report and went on reading. "We are required by law to notify you, the spouse or partner, of the deceased person so you can be tested... "

His voice trailed off.

"Stop," Rachel leapt to her feet and shouted. "Do stop now."

So there had been a point to the "required consultation" after all. Eric, whom she was quite sure was not remotely homosexual and would never have damaged his body with drugs, had clearly been promiscuous. Any remaining illusions about her husband and their marriage disappeared into the dank air of the hospital basement.

Rachel forced herself to sit and continue in a steady voice. "Mr. Nichols, you are only doing your job. I'm sorry I shouted, but let me make myself very clear: if I hear of any leaks from this office, I can, and will sue. I will hold you personally responsible if anything even remotely like a hint of my husband's medical condition finds its way into the press. Do not, under any circumstances, contact me again. You have fulfilled your duty to the letter of law. I have been duly notified. The public is protected. My lawyer will be in touch just to be sure we are clear on the privacy issue. My husband was something of a public figure and I expect this hospital to ensure this private information does not find its way outside the confines of this office."

She didn't remember taking the report with her when she stumbled out of the office, down the corridor, past the morgue and out into the bright sunlight. She didn't remember much of the drive home, but the report was there in the car seat next to her when Rachel got there, proving it had not all been just a bad dream. In the days and weeks that followed she read through the Health and Human Resources data and other scientific papers she could find online about HIV. She told Ellie and her doctor what she had learned. She got a blood test and was told the good news that the virus was not yet evident in her bloodstream. The bad news was, it could be dormant and undetectable for months. Eric had slept around, and what he had done would remain with her. The question was whether or not that fact could remain hidden in the little box under the beautiful hardwood floor.

* * * * *

Moonlight filtered through the treetops and lit the meadow — Rachel could see up to the edge of the woods where darkness pulled in the last of the evening light.

Pippin, the smaller of her cats, was a hunter. Her belly full of mouse, Pippin growled when the swing moved, disturbing her sleep. Rachel held the swing still with her foot, wishing she could so easily stop the facts of Eric's past from invading her present. Scandal could erupt at any moment if one of the women decided to come forward and tell her story to the tabloids. She told herself that with each passing day that was less likely. But she also knew if her family ever found out what Eric had done they would blame her. Blame her for her inadequacies as a wife. Blame her for causing Eric to stray.

"Oh dear God please, please, please do not ever let my family find out," she whispered over and over, less prayer than mantra.

Hope and fear were mixed with exhaustion when Rachel finally let her feet move and set the swing in motion. The cats jumped off in disgust and went to find a fixed location in which to spend the night. Rachel went inside to sleep for the first time on her new bed with crisp, out-of-the-box sheets covered by a fluffy new eiderdown comforter.

CHAPTER 10

CHOSEN

I heard the old, old men say,

Everything alters,

And one by one we drop away.

—*W.B. Yeats*

THE WAITRESS WAS NOT OLD BUT LIFE WAS WRIT LARGE UPON her plain face. Deep, jagged wrinkles, not finely etched lines of normal aging, cut into thin cheeks and creased a heavy brow. Stocky legs held up a shapeless torso shrouded in an ill-fitting white uniform. Dr. Culberson was not in the habit of being rude, especially to those for whom life has been unkind. He was also, however, not in the habit of ignoring plain facts.

"Miss," he motioned the waitress to their table and pointed at his plate. "This is utterly inedible."

She stared at the old man through tired eyes.

"So? Ya want me to take it back? Or what?"

Its replacement, another plate of congealed gravy straight from a tin covering meat of questionable origin, ringed by large hard peas, was much like the first.

"I'm sorry, Dad," Martha said, smiling at her father, who, despite his frustration with a disappointing meal, had just experienced a triumphant evening. "We should have just gone straight home and enjoyed hot but-tered toast with jam by the fire."

He nodded, still staring at the plate of food, struggling to hold onto even his anger as his mind grew more and more tired.

When the invitation first arrived Dr. Culberson said he was not well enough to attend. He was aware of fading mental capacity and wanted to avoid a sentimental, maudlin event fraught with the potential for embarrassment. But, in the end, Martha convinced her father to go. She had accompanied him to the National Capital Church early in that eve-ning where friends, students, and fellow theologians had gathered to give tribute to his many contributions to the Church in America over the last fifty years.

Culberson's intellectual force had helped create the 'evangelical' movement out of what had been a legalistic, ingrown worldview of the fun-damentalist Fifties. And while Dr. Culberson personally harbored doubts about where the movement was currently heading, he had been honored and humbled by the standing-room-only crowd and tributes from his col-leagues that evening. The old man privately hoped his scholarly work, including an eight-volume systematic theology, would endure, while other efforts like the magazine he helped launch would, like grass, wither and fade away. What had been conceived as a scholarly journal intended for rigorous review of current cultural, political, and social issues, had sunk to just another marketing-driven, inspirational rag in his view. But the evening had been a success. Alert and feeling stronger than usual, buoyed by adrenalin, Dr. Culberson had managed to meet and greet many old friends during the reception; his sharp wit and wisdom was evident in a brief thank you speech.

Laid up by a cold, Mrs. Culberson was home in bed, so Martha agreed when her father suggested stopping for a bite to eat at the new diner on Route 50, the one that advertised... "Food from the Fifties".

"I didn't think they meant it literally," he grumped.

"Oh, Dad," Martha laughed, patting his hand. "Just think about tonight instead of the bad food. 'Greatest theologian of our age,' Dr. Anderson called you, and so you are. Greatest father, too. I was so proud to be there with you."

Dr. Culberson finally looked up from the miserable plate of food at his daughter, his head shaking slightly. "Thank you, dear. I just wish your mother could have been there with us. She has put up with a great deal of silence from me over the years. Supposedly thinking deep thoughts was probably an excuse for not thinking enough about the two of you."

"Never mind all that now. We all make mistakes and I just hope I can look back on my life one day and see even one accomplishment that really matters... you have so many."

It had been hard, at times, growing up an average person in the shadow of such a great man. Martha had held a series of uninteresting office jobs since college and then, when needed, moved back home to help take care of her aging parents and work at WOWL. Now, with the Awareness Campaign, Martha was hopeful her life was beginning to really count for something. At this very moment, her boss, Jeff Lorten, and Pastor Leif Ohlsson, were on their way together to Sarajevo. The money raised would help so many victims of human trafficking and hopefully help catch the criminals who preyed upon them. Martha's cheeks blushed with pleasure at the realization she had helped make that happen. She hoped the company would continue its focus on such important issues in the future. Maybe someday, she thought, I can go and visit the Justice Center that would eventually be built with the WOWL funds raised through the campaign. She wanted her life to count for more than just typing letters for Mr. Lorten and putting up with his bad moods.

Lost in her own thoughts, Martha didn't notice the deep frown on her father's face as he struggled to find a way to thank her. He knew that without his faithful and generous daughter he would soon be in a "care" facility, a cruel euphemism for institutionalization.

But Dr. Culberson had never been able to say the simple things in life very well.

Martha took the pained expression on her father's face for continued frustration over the meal.

"Maybe we should just go home and have that tea and toast," she suggested. "This has been a big night and I don't want you to get overtired."

"It's not me who has to go to work tomorrow. You've been working such long hours. I worry about you, dear."

"Oh Dad, I like my work now. The Awareness Campaign has been very exciting. A winner of the Bible Trivia contest has been chosen, a Mr. Phil Grant from Minnesota. I will be showing him around when he comes, as a guest of the station and to attend the CITMAC conference. Things are going to get crazy busy when Mr. Lorten gets back from Bosnia, so I'm taking the rest of the week off while he's away. Do a little shopping and help Mom around the house."

Dr. Culberson grumbled something under his breath about her boss and WOWL, Inc. He didn't trust the Lorten family and thought his daughter much too naïve to recognize the rapacious nature of the media empire.

Martha ignored her father's muttered remarks, she had heard them before, and went on valiantly trying to chew and swallow a tough piece of meat.

Dr. Culberson suddenly gave his plate a shove, dropped the knife and fork on the table and stood up. "That's it! We're going home."

His well-worn tweed coat hung on a greatly diminished frame but he wrapped his wool scarf around his neck with a flourish, tossed his ubiquitous hat at a rakish angle on his head, and tapped his walking stick for Martha to join him.

Surprised by her father's decision to leave without paying the bill (despite her protest) she nevertheless took his arm and steadied him toward the door.

The waitress rushed to block their exit.

"I'm sorry, sir. But you haven't paid for your food."

"I'm sorry too, miss. But you haven't served me any."

Sensing a disaster, the manager quickly intervened and offered free meal coupons and a polite "try us again sometime" as they went out the door. It was bucketing down rain as the old scholar and his daughter walked together to the car.

"Throw those coupons away, dear," her father said as he sank back into the seat, shivering from damp and exhaustion. "My memory really *is* fading; food wasn't as good in the Fifties as I remembered."

"Nothing wrong with your memory, Dad," Martha said starting the car and turning up the heat for him.

But there was much wrong with his memory and the great mind that had just been celebrated by peers and young scholars alike was no longer a force in the Church, or in the family. Martha realized this and she missed him already.

* * * * *

"Hello," Darcy Grant called to her husband; standing on an open beam above her, hardhat on his head, hammer in his hand.

"You won," she said, waving a white envelope embossed with the corporate seal of WOWL, Inc. in Washington, D.C.

"Won what?" he called down over the sound of jackhammers in the street. "The lottery?"

"No Phil, we don't play the lottery. Come down here so I can tell you."

Phil waved at his lovely wife and started making his way down through the gutted old house.

"You can't work in those clothes, lady," Elder Harris said, coming into the room and giving Darcy a hug. Ed was pastor of the local church and their very good friend. He took her arm and helped her navigate across what was left of the floor in the shell of a once nice row house in a poor Minneapolis neighborhood.

"No kidding. Actually, I didn't come to work. I'm on my way home from school and have a surprise for Phil... I couldn't wait to tell him."

A grin spread over his broad, friendly face. "You're not... ?"

She laughed. "No, nothing so wonderful, Ed. I haven't been to the doctor. I've been to the post office."

Ed had been their friend since college, when he was one of the few black faces at Taylor College in Indiana. Ed and Shirley had five great little kids now and she tried hard not envy them each new pregnancy.

"So what's important enough to bring you down alone?" Ed asked, wishing he hadn't been stupid enough to jump to the wrong conclusion. His friends had wanted a baby as long as he had known them, but now with Darcy in her early forties, it wasn't likely to happen for them and he cursed himself for bringing it up.

Plaster was dropping on their heads as Elder Harris led her outside to wait for Phil. A bright blue and white sign that read "Rock Creek Presbyterian Church — Habitat for Humanity" was hanging over the door.

Litter was blowing across the street in a stiff wind while grown men stood idle against buildings. An aura of despair was in the air and struck Darcy again, as it did each time she came to the inner city.

She held out the fancy envelope for Elder Harris to see.

"Remember the Bible contest thing Phil entered? Well, he won," she said proudly. "My husband, the Bible trivia whiz kid is on his way to Washington, D.C. to schmooze with the big boys at WOWL and some political conference."

Ed laughed out loud.

Phil was not so amused.

Early the next morning, as light warmed the rich oak table Phil had crafted to fit their recently remodeled kitchen and breakfast nook, the two sat discussing the unexpected news. They preferred to call their occasional but intense disagreements "discussions".

"I think you should go alone, dear," Darcy said to her husband as she filled their cups for the second time with black coffee. They had been over this ad nauseam the night before and she had failed so far to convince him. "You'll manage fine without me."

"Of course I'll manage," he replied, testily. "That's not the point. I want you to go because I won't enjoy it without you."

Sparkling clean windows framed the backyard. Phil could see down to their dock on a tiny lake. He wished his lovely wife wasn't so infernally practical. Disappearing summer would soon become a bitter Minnesota winter. He was finally tired of the cold. Fall was lovely but as a precursor it no longer held any charm for him. Soon gray days would take over, followed by white ones, and spring would only be a distant hope.

"Just go. You need a break and it will be fun."

Phil didn't answer but kept staring at the slick brochure in his hands. He knew it had nothing to do with fatigue. He really hated to admit to himself that he didn't enjoy anything as much without her, but it was true. It particularly annoyed him because it made him feel like he was turning into his dad. What he had once perceived as weakness in his father's dependency on his mother now seemed like love to him, but he hated the comparison all the same.

Tall and angular, with fine bones and short black hair starting to be peppered with gray, Darcy Grant was a handsome woman who exuded confidence and capability. Their marriage was a real partnership and he had never ever seriously looked at another woman after they fell in love in college.

The contest had been part of a publicity campaign to raise funds for refugees in Bosnia and at the same time encouraging biblical literacy. The Grants had both been encouraged that their favorite radio station was engaging in two worthy causes and, on a whim, Phil entered.

He enjoyed the challenge and, after winning at the local station level, progressed to the regional. Then, and without really meaning to do so, the national contest. He liked the idea of using the new technology for good instead of evil; using the Internet had allowed the station to avoid the expense of travel and fostered continuing interaction between the contestants via the newest medium of communication. Phil still talked to some of the folks he had met online during the contest. It was one more example of the innovative and creative approach he had come to expect from the broadcasting giant WOWL. But he had not expected to win and now that he had, was acutely embarrassed. He could still see the amusement in Ed's face when Darcy showed up yesterday with the announcement.

"Well, maybe I won't go either," he said, still looking through the packet of information about the trip. "It was silly to enter."

"Phil Grant, don't be ridiculous. You've enjoyed WOWL programs for years and it will be fun to meet the people who make them happen. Look," she said pointing to a picture of the Washington Monument, "this is great stuff. Not only will you get to see Washington, but also visit the corporate offices of the station and meet lots of 'Christian personalities' at a gala reception in the Lorten's Great Falls home. Go on Phil... go for it. Show those 'Christian personalities' that accountants can have fun too."

"Doesn't that phrase strike you as a little odd?"

"Do you like 'Christian celebrities' any better?"

He growled a response.

Darcy stood up, taking the cups with her, laughing at him affectionately as she began clearing up.

"Lighten up, dear. We are in danger of becoming old fuddy-duddies, disapproving of everything. Emotionally cold Swedes. That kind of thing. Go and have a good time." Wiping up the already clean counter, Darcy held the wet dishcloth still for a moment and said, "It's so sad about Eric Kissane's death. Now, I would have liked meeting *him*."

"Oh so you would have gone to meet Mr. Talk Show Host with the gorgeous voice — but not to be with me, huh?"

She ignored her cross husband, knowing his good humor would return soon enough.

The brochure had pictures of Washington monuments, the Capitol, and cherry trees turning fall colors around the Tidal Basin. Visiting the nation's capital was part of the prize. Phil had always wanted to visit D.C., the Smithsonian museums and art galleries — but not alone. He found Darcy's practical nature, not for the first time, extremely annoying.

She finished up at the sink and joined her husband who was still glowering at the material. She poured them more coffee. It was a morning ritual. They liked to get up early, have time to read the Bible, then pray together before sharing the morning paper with a second cup of coffee. Theirs was an easy trust, a peaceful friendship, based on years of shared joys and values. Each of them were capable in their own fields, still neither were completely satisfied with pursuits apart from one other.

Phil was surprised and not very pleased by his wife's reluctance to join him.

"So it's the money, huh?" he asked somewhat rhetorically. They both knew they could afford for her to go, but they had agreed long ago to spend money based on stewardship, not a cash balance.

"That, and the fact I probably can't get anyone to stand in for me at school," she added. "But we did spend a lot of money on the kitchen and our trip to Europe. And Ed is counting on us to help with the next Habitat house."

"I know all that," he snapped. "And it seems a little cheap, don't you think, for the station not to pay for the winner's spouse to go along?"

"No, I think it's good management," she answered in her implacable way. "It's a Christian radio station after all. I'm sure they have better things to do with their money than throw it around on contestants. Like the current campaign to fight human trafficking."

Phil and Darcy were careful with their money; being good stewards was important to both of them.

Darcy looked at her husband and wavered inwardly in her decision not to join him and decided to reconsider if he was still insistent tomorrow.

Six months ago Phil's accounting firm, Grant & Associates, Ltd., had been hired by the District Attorney of Minneapolis to investigate a pyramid business scheme that was beginning to unravel. He had helped it unravel only to find it led very close to home, right in the Grant's own neighborhood. She had never seen him so miserable as when their fellow congregates had accused him of standing on the side of the world against the church. When in reality it had nothing to do with the church, but everything to do with several members of the congregation who had joined in a questionable financial get-rich-quick scheme and ended up on the wrong side of the law.

Several families in the church had started selling the 'natural beauty' skin products called Fine-Skin a few years ago. They, in turn, had recruited several families in the church who, in turn, recruited still more and so the 'Christian business' grew. How spending large amounts of money, and encouraging others to spend large amounts of money, on skin and beauty products was in any way Christian, remained a mystery to Darcy. She resisted all invitations to attend the Fine-Skin parties to discover her best 'season', quite happy (thank you very much) to go through life never knowing whether she was a spring or a summer.

Some people in the congregation had made big money fast, moved into larger houses and bought better cars. Condescending, it seemed to her, when the Grants refused to join this new way to wealth. The church grew too, from the increased giving. Phil and Darcy understood the anger directed against him for his role in exposing the unethical practices of the scheme. Only the pastor's unfailing support had made the whole episode tolerable.

The antique clock on the kitchen wall began its slow, ponderous chimes, announcing it was seven o'clock. Before it chimed its last, Darcy was out of the kitchen and getting ready for work. Phil sat there alone for a few more minutes before deciding to accept the invitation and visit D.C. as the grand prizewinner and special guest of WOWL. And not just to see the sights. He was restless. He hated conflict and the whole Fine-Skin case had brought a heap on his weary head. Then with the realization this morning that he was getting as set in his ways as his dad, it had all come together like an elusive reconciling of figures on a financial page. It balanced. He would go to Washington and enjoy the city and meet the people at a great Christian ministry. Maybe they needed a new financial controller.

The Grants had moved into their present house fifteen years ago, shortly after they were married, when Phil was a newly certified CPA, long before he became senior partner in his own successful firm, before Darcy became director of the academically acclaimed Rivendell Christian Grammar School. Despite the fact the Grants could have leveraged this house up to a much more expensive one, they chose not to play that particular American game. They both longed for children to fill a bigger house but when that didn't happen they shared what they had with others. Besides, they had a great yard with plenty of space for their flowers and vegetables. They liked their neighbors. And on quiet evenings they could hear frogs on the lake, and watch the ducks and other waterfowl that made it their temporary home during migration.

Darcy's father had teased them about their 'lake', suggesting it was more of a large puddle. And this morning, that was pretty much how it looked to Phil as well. A messy brown puddle.

The phone rang, interrupting Phil's morose ruminating.

A friendly voice from WOWL was calling to inquire about his trip to D.C. "Congratulations, Phil. Can I call you Phil? We are so excited to meet you. It's no small thing to have beat out thousands of contestants all over the U.S., in fact," the voice paused to take a breathe. "I can't wait to meet the man who knew the name of Absalom's traitorous advisor, Ahithophel. Amazing. Quite amazing."

Phil groaned inwardly as the chirpy voice went on praising him for his amazing knowledge. But he didn't back out. Phil Grant was on his way to Washington D.C.

CHAPTER 11

FOUND

. . . In vain you rise early and stay up late, toiling for
Food to eat — but he gives his loved ones sleep.

— A Psalm of Solomon

WHEN INSPECTOR RADU KUNIS RETURNED TO TIRNOVA THE AIR
was filled with a tangy aroma of zacusca, the traditional preserve made
from eggplant, red peppers, onion and wide variety of herbs. Smoke from
outdoor fires, over which the zacusca cooked in vast copper kettles for
twelve long hours, signaled the change of seasons.

Little had changed since Nadia's disappearance in the spring. The
shepherd took the animals out in the morning and brought them back in
the evening. Crops were planted and harvested. New babies were baptized. Old people, including Nadia's Baba, were buried in the cemetery on
the high hill outside of town. Most of the people in Tirnova had forgotten
about the Roma girl who had vanished without a trace.

Raluca had *not* forgotten. She had not given up hope. She helped
her parents with the garden and animals; she studied and read and waited
for word from Inspector Detective Kunis. At his suggestion she and her
brother Adrian created a Facebook page for Nadia and were surprised by
the response. The story connected with people around the world. Whether
it was nostalgia for simple village life or the mystery of her disappearance,

for reasons as varied as the people who wrote messages back on Facebook, her story resonated.

The hundred-year-old mud walls of Nadia's house were crumbling now, the satellite dish losing its grip on a collapsing roofline. Raluca had rescued a few things she thought her friend might want again someday, and kept them in a box under her bed.

Grape arbors were heavy with ripe fruit, and nuts could be heard dropping to the ground, when the man from Bucharest arrived. He appreciated the sad irony of being the bearer of bad news in the midst of such fecundity.

Kunis decided to meet Raluca in her home this time to avoid the sneering presence of Officer Stefanescu, whose racism and appetite for gossip would quickly spread the plight of Nadia in all its most lurid details throughout the village.

Raluca's mother only had a few hours' notice to make the living room, which doubled as Adrian's bedroom, look presentable for their illustrious guest. She placed cut roses in the blue crystal vase, and set out coffee cups and a plate of sweets, covered with napkins to discourage flies that were not discouraged. The air in the room was stuffy and would have benefited from a cross breeze, but she couldn't risk "the current".

The Inspector bumped his head on the lintel as he entered the tidy room. The family followed him in and took the less comfortable chairs. Unable to endure the hospitality formalities, Raluca blurted out the burning question. "Have you found her?"

The Inspector put down the cup of coffee he had just received, cleared his throat, and took a moment before answering in a grave voice knowing the sorrow his news would bring.

"I think so. I think I've found her but I'm not absolutely certain. It's complicated."

He picked up the cup again and took a sip, relishing the sweet, strong brew as he began to carefully make his way through the tale, leaving out the harshest details. The good news was a network of criminals perpetrating the abductions had been found in Bosnia and some of the leaders arrested. The mafia-like tentacles of the human trafficking ring stretched across Eastern Europe. The bad news was that over a hundred kids who had been forced to work the streets in the sex trade were found in a stinking basement in Sarajevo, brutalized and traumatized. The kids had been moved into a shelter where they were safe for the moment but in only marginally better living conditions than what they had known at the hands of their captors. One of the girls in that shelter was most likely — but as yet formally unidentified as — Nadia Iovan.

After months of waiting, of wondering, Raluca had trouble taking in what the Detective was telling her. She was unable to comprehend what brutalized and traumatized meant, never mind "sex trade". What she did understand was that Nadia might still be alive.

"You *think* Nadia is one of those kids? What does that mean, you think? Either it is or isn't her. Right?"

Kunis understood the frustration.

"It just isn't that simple," he said, wiping crumbs from his mouth. He folded his napkin, laid it on the table and smoothed it with his finger. Then he leaned his big frame toward Raluca, hands clasped between his knees, wishing so much that he could lessen the pain of it.

"Listen, I know this is hard but you have to understand the condition these kids are in. They are suffering from traumatic stress disorders, they are malnourished and many appear drug-addicted as well. It is still chaotic."

He was watching the impact of his words on the bright young face, thinking how extraordinarily self-contained and mature she was for a village girl. The dedication Raluca had shown to her friend over the past months had confirmed his first impression of her and continued to impress him.

"Nadia wouldn't do drugs," Raluca stated with finality.

"Maybe not willingly."

There was no way to make this easy. Detective Kunis picked up his cell phone and swiped several times until he came to the picture of the girl he thought was Nadia.

It was very quiet in the room as Raluca stared at the grainy image. She was sitting on the daybed couch between her mother and father, they were holding onto her for support. Finally, she gave a simple nod, affirming what the Inspector expected.

"It is Nadia," she whispered.

Adrian looked at it next, the blood draining from his face.

"Are you sure, Raluca? Maybe it's not." He handed the phone back to the Inspector, shaking his head. "Why didn't you just ask her name?"

"I asked," he said. "But she couldn't answer. Actually, no one in the shelter has heard her speak. They're not even sure she's Romanian. This girl," he said, turning off the phone, "is mute. We think she was targeted through the Internet — one of the chat rooms she used, so whoever took her knew her name, but she could have been moved many times since then. As you can imagine, records are not kept. I'm so sorry. For all of you."

The trail had led Inspector Detective Kunis where he had always known it would. He sighed.

"When can we bring her home?" Raluca asked, avoiding the reality that Nadia didn't have a family or home to come back to.

"You can't!" His answer was quick. And firm. "Not now and not for a long time. You have to understand, she needs professional help."

"So... is she getting this professional help now? In this shelter place?"

He thought about what he had seen. It was a long way from helping anyone. He knew many kids would simply end up back on the street. But the tough cop who was able to track down and take on human traffickers, corrupt police, and city officials was unable to speak the whole truth into such vulnerability.

"No," he said, with regret. "She isn't. But I am on my way back to Sarajevo now and I promise to see what I can do."

Having delivered his message and confirmed the identity of one more victim, Inspector Detective Kunis stood to go. Ducking lower this time, he cleared the door on his way out without mishap.

"I don't want you to get your hopes up, but some Americans are arriving tomorrow and they are bringing money to build a facility to help kids like Nadia."

Raluca's face lit up. "That's great."

"It is, but don't get your hopes up," he said. "These things take time." He didn't need to add the obvious. Nadia didn't have time. She needed help now.

Mr. Moldovan picked a luscious bunch of grapes hanging over the courtyard gate as they walked the Inspector to his car.

"These are for your journey, Sir. I want to thank you for all you've done for my daughter. And Nadia."

The big man leaned down and gave Raluca a tender hug. "I'm so sorry I couldn't have brought you better news. Just remember where there's life there's hope. And your friend is alive."

"And she needs me," Raluca said. "I have to go see her. There isn't anyone else. She doesn't have anyone else."

The policeman hesitated, thinking of what she would see.

"I don't think that's a good idea," he said. "Not yet. And I can't take you with me, anyway. I'm not allowed to have civilians in my car. But I promise to go visit her. And see what I can find out about getting help from the Americans. I'll tell her you'll be coming someday."

Raluca knew when she was being put off.

"I thought you said not to get my hopes up about the American help, which is months, if not years, away. You know they won't do anything special for just one girl. She can't even ask for help and she won't trust you. How can she, when to her you're just another stranger? And a man. Please take me to her. I've saved enough from my egg money to buy a train ticket to Sarajevo."

There was a long pause. Raluca's parents expected the Inspector to tell their daughter no so they wouldn't have to.

"Okay," he said, moved by her determination. "If you can get to Sarajevo, I will take you to her."

Later that afternoon Raluca walked up the hill to sit by Baba's grave. The last of the leaves were blowing off a stand of stunted trees marking the edge of the cemetery. She sat on the warm ground thinking about tomorrow, when she would travel with her father on the train to Sarajevo.

"Baba," Raluca whispered, her words scattering like the leaves, "Nadia is alive and I'm going to see her soon. And I'll bring her back one day. I promise."

CHAPTER 12

ONE GOOD DEED

. . . we played the flute for you and you did not dance:
sang a dirge, and you did not mourn.

—St. Matthew

THE SMELL OF FRESH BREWED COFFEE DREW RONALD LORTEN to the galley when he rose from his comfortable bed high above the Atlantic. It was seventy degrees below zero at thirty-five thousand feet but toasty warm inside his Gulfstream GIV jet. His brother Jeff, who hated to fly, was still asleep with a little help from Ambien.

Pastor Leif Ohlsson had brought Ned, his ever-present bodyguard, on the trip to Bosnia and they were already enjoying their first cup of coffee when Ronald joined them in the galley. The steward handed Lorten a mug emblazoned with the WOWL logo.

"Morning. Morning everyone," Ronald boomed, leaning down and looking out the small window but failing to see any signs of light on the horizon. "Hmmm. Smells good in here. When's breakfast?"

"When you are ready for it, sir," the steward replied.

Lorten glanced at his Rolex. It was 5:00 a.m. Sarajevo time.

"We'll give my brother half an hour. Then we eat. It's going to be a long day in Bosnia-Herzegovina." He stretched out "Herzegovina," rolling each letter slowly off his tongue with his slight Southern drawl.

The WOWL documentary film crew and publicity team had been in Europe filming for a week and would meet them at the airport to capture their arrival in Bosnia and follow them throughout the weekend. Ronald Lorten was more than ready for the day to begin. It would be a vindication for him. A justification of the decision he made to save the company from Cricket Hartford's threats. The Awareness Campaign had been more successful than he had dared to hope, accomplishing what he needed from it and a great deal more. Lorten was looking forward to the groundbreaking ceremony of The Justice Center for Exploited Children in the center of the old city of Sarajevo, built in the crater of a bombed out building. The Center would house offices of investigators, legal experts, and a state-of-the-art aftercare facility with counseling and therapy for the victims. He would put in the first shovel and present the four-million-dollar symbolic big check to the executive director of International Justice Organization (IJO), who would build and operate the programs. The occasion would be celebrated in colorful Balkan style with bands playing, flags flying, and beautiful children dressed in traditional costumes.

While Ronald Lorten couldn't share it with any living soul, he had a growing sense that God had blessed the plan he had conceived in such desperation, bringing beauty out of the ashes. The fact that he had received a letter from IJO requesting support for their efforts to stop human trafficking the same day Cricket presented her blackmail demands had to be more than coincidence. More like providence. He had managed to protect the important Christian voice of WOWL, his possible presidential bid, and raise millions for victims of unspeakable violence.

Ronald Lorten felt very good about himself as he gazed into the darkness again and saw the first light of the rising sun. Not only did he feel good, he felt safe. It would be, he thought, a pleasure to share this triumph with Cricket Hartford. He wanted to tell her that good had come from her evil intentions. And, irrational as it was, he actually just wanted to see her again.

He wouldn't contact the woman, of course. Lorten was many things, but suicidal was not one of them.

Unable to sit still and wait for breakfast, Ronald took his mug and paced back and forth through the plane, chatting with the pilots and stretching his legs. He hadn't felt this happy since he helped the Republicans win control of the House and Senate in the midterm elections.

People were fed up with politics-as-usual coming from the current administration and Ronald was proud of his role in fomenting the unrest in the electorate with endless telling and retelling of the salacious details of each new scandal emanating from 1600 Pennsylvania Ave. In fact, he thought, it was looking increasingly possible that the Republicans might just defeat this President next November. Ronald knew his name was increasingly mentioned to head the national ticket and there was plenty of time for him to throw his hat into the ring. It would be a shiny white Republican hat.

Lorten often sat in his office looking up Pennsylvania Avenue to the beautiful mansion he could see from his window. To have a real Christian and true conservative in the Oval Office would help restore Christian values to the nation. "God has chosen you for such a time as this," his friends kept telling him. And Lorten, who hadn't officially decided to run, knew that adding compassionate to his conservative image couldn't hurt. He had Cricket Hartford to thank for that and the irony was not lost on him. Republicans were often condemned for being the party of rich white people, for rich white people, and by rich white people. Which wasn't true, he thought, thinking of the millions of conservative Christians across American who had given of their hard-earned money to help kids they don't even know in Eastern Europe. And he would be happy to make that known during his campaign.

Lorten took one of the comfortable swivel chairs by the table now being laid for breakfast. He opened his laptop and pulled up the day's detailed schedule. Martha had continued to do a good job with the details. And a good job of not asking questions after he squashed her early inquiry about Wharton & Wharton Consulting.

The schedule looked good. He was eager for the groundbreaking and official ceremonies in the morning, and lunch planned for them with the Mayor of Sarajevo, the U. S. Ambassador, and other city and national officials. Lorten could do without the local color, including dancing girls in traditional garb, but he was looking forward to meeting the law enforcement team from Romania who had tracked down and exposed the ring of human traffickers working across Eastern Europe.

Ronald was less happy about some of the other things on the agenda. They were scheduled to visit a shelter in the afternoon where they would meet some of the recently rescued victims. And the last thing on the schedule was a walk on the streets where the kids had been forced to work. Ronald liked to tease Leif for not going anywhere, including out to lunch, without his bodyguard, but this time he was glad Ned would be with them. He wasn't looking forward to actually meeting the kids in the shelter or the mean streets where they had been forced to work, but Lorten knew he needed to be seen getting into the trenches where the war against traffickers was being fought.

"How great is this, Leif?" he said. "We are about to land in Sarajevo, my old friend. Imagine how exciting it would have been to do this during the war. Dodging snipers at the airfield."

"Imagine all you want. I prefer peace and safety, as I would very much like to return to my lovely bride with all my limbs," Leif huffed.

"Wimp," Ronald chuckled. "Still, you must admit it would have made for an exciting film. "The headlines! 'Lorten brothers and megachurch pastor shot at while delivering aid.' Has a nice ring to it!"

"Oh, I think our press will be just fine without the snipers. Fox News has a correspondent on the ground and journalists from the networks and CNN have been notified — some might even probably swallow their liberal bias and show up as well."

"You mean from the people who've claimed the Awareness Campaign was just a publicity stunt?" Ronald said. "Not likely."

Leif had had a few questions too along the way, from that first night when Ronald brought it up while they were dining with their wives at the Little Thai Restaurant. It was so out of character for his friend, and the whole idea seemed to come upon him so suddenly. He had thought it curious at the time, but over the months since Ronald had worked hard on the details, putting his heart and soul into the project. Leif had done his part, too, involving the congregation. Charleen's participation had helped smooth some of the troubled waters over his recent marriage. People saw her in a new and more positive light. And now the old friends were about to reap the reward of a shared project. Leif was looking forward to the day as well, and had already decided on the text for next Sunday's sermon, Micah 6:8: "This is what God requires of you, that you act with justice, love mercy, and walk humbly with your God."

When the fluffy omelets with hot sausage and fruit on the side arrived, the men tucked in. Demi-glass bowls of butter, marmalade, and honey offered a choice of spread, for crispy hard rolls. Fresh-squeezed grapefruit juice and more hot coffee followed.

"You boys sure know how to travel," Ned said as Jeff finally joined them halfway through the meal.

"And for that we are truly thankful," Jeff replied, as he bowed his head in prayer before partaking.

Well sated, the men pushed back and buckled up.

An overnight train from Bucharest was pulling into the main train station in Sarajevo as the WOWL Gulfstream jet began its descent.

* * * * *

Stiff from leaning against her father's shoulder during the night, Raluca put on the new fleece jacket she loved. She twisted and stretched, and jumped up and down to get the kinks out while her father gathered up the rubbish from their cramped carriage. He tossed empty water bottles, leftover breadcrusts (from sandwiches brought from home) into the small bin under the window. The rolling motion and clacking sound of the train had finally put Raluca to sleep, despite her excitement and nervous anticipation, but her father never closed his eyes. He was too afraid to sleep. Too afraid of what his daughter would have to face in the coming hours and what it might do to her to finally see Nadia again. Not her friend, but a traumatized victim of unspeakable violence.

Raluca spotted the tall Inspector first. He was waving at them over the crowds as they entered the cavernous train terminal.

"Follow me," he said after warm greetings. "I'll buy you some breakfast. Bosnian style."

The small café was filled with cigarette smoke and the smell of frying meat and onions. Kunis ordered cevapcici and eggs with a local cheese-filled sweet bread and strong tea for everyone.

It smelled delicious, but her stomach felt like it was still rolling down the track, so Raluca pushed the plate of spicy food to her father, nibbled the bread and sipped sweet tea while listening to the Inspector.

"I couldn't get you a seat in the official ceremony or at official lunch, of course. I have to attend," Kunis explained. "But I will meet you outside this address at about 2:00. I might be late but I'll be there — do not go in without me."

"And please remember, Raluca," he went on. "You won't have much time with Nadia today — I had to pull strings to just get you in. An official delegation of special guests, including the Americans, will also be visiting the shelter this afternoon. I promised the director we would be out before they are scheduled to arrive. They don't want anything getting in the way of what will be a tightly choreographed visit."

Raluca had no idea what that meant or any desire to meet any Americans. All she could think about was that after all these months she was actually going to see her friend again in a few hours' time. The fact that Nadia couldn't talk anymore hadn't sunk in, and anyway she was sure Nadia would talk to her.

Threading their way into the busy street the Inspector gently cupped his big hand over Raluca's elbow and looked at her hopeful face.

"Are you ready for this?" he asked. "I mean really ready? It's not going to be easy and you must promise me you won't say anything to Nadia about going home. Or ask her any questions. You will have to be patient and not expect too much this first visit. And try not to cry too much. You don't want to frighten her. Okay?"

"Okay," she nodded. "I've brought some cake. She loves my mom's walnut cake, it was her favorite, and I thought it might, well, remind her of home."

"Good girl," he said. "That's perfect. Now remember, you have to do exactly what I say. When I say to leave her, we go. No drama. No argument."

It took a few minutes for their eyes to adjust to the dim light of the shelter. Raluca followed her father and the Detective down a flight of stairs into a large room that was filled with too many bodies and too little air. The stink of urine and cheap antiseptic made her already-churning stomach lurch. Afraid of throwing up, she took a sip of water from a bottle in her backpack and took out the carefully wrapped walnut cake for Nadia. Dozens of kids were milling around a big room with what looked to be staff carrying trays of cookies and bottles of soda to a long table set up for the upcoming reception for the Americans. The three of them made their way through the main room and down several dark hallways.

Raluca saw her first. A huddled mass, curled up in a fetal position on a bare mattress. She was wearing a tank top that hung on her bony shoulders and her stick-like legs stuck out of very short shorts.

Everything the Inspector had told Raluca about how to treat Nadia went out of her head and she rushed to the bed, collapsed by her friend, holding her and sobbing. "Oh Naddie, oh dear, what have they done to you? Oh my God, what have they done to you?" Raluca's body shook in agony as she held her friend, then taking off her jacket, covered Nadia's naked limbs with its warmth and softness. Tears streamed down her checks and spilled onto the filthy matted hair of her dear friend.

Time stood still as the men watched, helpless, both aware that despite all the instructions they had given Raluca this was, in fact, the only adequate response to such injustice.

* * * * *

Ronald Lorten's day had been perfect, the sun shining down upon him like a blessing. Exuberant crowds overflowed into the street at the groundbreaking ceremony. The Mayor was effusive in his gratitude. A huge cheer rose up when he pushed his snakeskin boot into the dirt, breaking ground for the Justice Center for Exploited Children. Even the media seemed impressed and moderately friendly.

"Now to the hard part," Ronald said, as their driver stopped the dark green Range Rover in front of the shelter. The neighborhood was a long way from the mayor's palace and colorful city center where the other events had taken place.

"Okay, let's get this over with. We're running early but I'm not hanging around this area waiting — it's not like these kids are looking at the clock or have something else to do."

"This *is* important," Leif said, offended by Lorten's tone. "We can at least show *these kids* as you call them, that we care. They are, after all, the victims we came to help."

"Don't preach to me," Ronald snapped. "I know who we came to help. I just don't see how it's going to help anyone to stare at their suffering. What we can do is provide funds for the people who are equipped to help them and that, my friend, is exactly what we have done. So don't get on your moral high horse with me. Remember this whole thing was my idea in the first place."

"Sounds to me like you do need a little preaching to," Leif replied, unintimidated by Lorten. "If Jesus washed feet I think we can at least eat and drink with these kids. And since we have a translator I, for one, want to meet some of them and hear their stories."

Jeff was less happy than Ronald about going into the shelter. Nearly phobic about germs and neurotically fastidious, the idea of actually eating and drinking with prostitutes made him queasy. "As a psychologist, I happen to agree with my brother," Jeff said. "Our presence might just further traumatize the victims."

"Well, we're here and we're going in, so let's just do it," Ronald said. He motioned to the arriving film crew to follow him.

It wasn't that Raluca had refused to leave Nadia's bedside — the Lorten group simply arrived earlier than planned.

"Damn," Kunis muttered when he heard the noise of the arriving dignitaries.

"Wait here," he told Raluca's father. "Just keep her here and away from the Americans, I'll come back to get you both when they've gone."

He made his way back to the main room and paused at the doorway to watch the official party of VIP guests. A camera crew was capturing Ronald Lorten interviewing staff and some of the victims.

It didn't take long for a formal thank you from the director of the center and Mr. Lorten's touching reply in kind. Then the group began moving toward the door but something caught Ronald Lorten's attention and he turned back into the room. It was Raluca, running through the crowd to reach the Americans. Before Kunis could stop her she grabbed the sleeve of Ronald Lorten and began pleading with him, tears running down her face.

A bodyguard moved quickly to rescue him from the distraught girl and the Inspector gently took ahold of her shoulder to move her away.

"I'm so sorry, sir," he said. "This poor girl has just been reunited with her friend who has been missing for months. She was one of the girls recently rescued from the street and is in terrible condition. It's been a shock, please forgive us, you have done so much... "

Lorten held up his hand, motioning everyone to back off. "It's okay, calm down and give me a little space. I want to hear what this girl has to say."

Douglas Boyle had made many short films for WOWL and he knew "the shot" when he saw it. Motioning his team to follow, he trained a camera and an open microphone on Lorten and the distraught girl and moved in as close as possible without getting in the way of the moment. He followed as they walked across the room and down a corridor into another one.

Nadia was still huddled on the cot, eyes staring into the distance, as they approached. She pulled the fleece over her legs and shuddered as the group neared, shutters clicking.

Ronald Lorten turned to see his camera crew doing their job; it was the job he paid them to do, but something snapped and he became irrationally enraged at their intrusion.

"Get out of here," he shouted, waving them off. "All of you. Get out! This is private."

"Private," Douglas scoffed as he retreated with his crew. "I've never seen a Lorten shrink from the camera before." But he went, they all went and left Ronald Lorten alone with the Romanians. He sat beside Nadia on the dirty bed and listened as Raluca told the story, Inspector Kunis translating every word.

While Jeff and Leif waited in the car, fuming over the delay, Ronald Lorten listened to the story; from Nadia's abandonment by her parents, to the day she went missing from Tirnova.

Raluca's words managed to get past his usual defenses, his schemes, and his ambitions and his pride. Layer after layer was stripped away to what had once been a heart of flesh. Ronald Lorten wept.

"Here," he said, handing all the bills he had in his wallet to the Inspector. "Take this, it's all I have on me. Get Nadia moved out of this miserable place and into a hospital or clinic where she can get the help she needs now until the Justice Center is built. I will wire you more as needed."

Raluca didn't understand everything but she knew a miracle was taking place.

"I'm sorry, sir," Kunis apologized. "I couldn't possibly take your money. We have presumed upon your time and generosity already. It wouldn't be right to ask you to help one girl after all you have done to help so many. It's too much."

Used to getting his way, Ronald Lorten brushed off the protests.

"Will a thousand dollars be enough to move her out of here and into a clinic?"

"Yes, that is more than enough but... "

"Good, that's settled. Except that this is a private transaction. Will you promise to make sure she is moved and promise to keep my part in this just between us?"

Raluca wanted to thank this larger-than-life man, who had stopped and listened, and now was actually going to help Nadia. She wanted desperately to thank him, but all she had was the still unopened walnut cake her mother had made for Nadia. "Here," she said. "It's Nadia's favorite cake, she would want you to have it."

Looking embarrassed and mumbling thank you, Lorten took the crumpled package.

"Someday Nadia will be able to thank you herself," Raluca added.

"I don't deserve your thanks. And I don't deserve hers. Just keep taking such good care of your friend."

And then he was gone, taking all his American power and money and a slightly-smashed walnut cake with him.

"What took you?" Jeff snapped when his brother finally joined them in the SUV. "We've been cooling our heels... God only knows what you were doing."

"Exactly," his brother replied. "And I intend to keep it that way."

BOOK TWO

CHAPTER 13

MATH

And what does the Lord require of you but to do justice,

to love mercy, and to walk humbly with your God?

—*The Prophet Micah*

PHIL GRANT WAS STILL UNCERTAIN ABOUT THE WISDOM OF HIS trip as he boarded Northwest flight #903 to Washington D.C. Cyrus and Mary Osterhus rode along when Darcy took him to the airport. The pastor and his wife were good friends but Phil thought there had been altogether too much hilarity at his expense in the car. Like lawyers, he assumed, who must endure lawyer jokes, he did not find accountant jokes particularly funny.

"Be sure and check the books while you're there," Mary kidded him.

"I hope Ronald Lorten knows you are a whiz at more than Bible trivia," Cyrus added.

"That and the fact that you've brought down empires with your number two pencil," Darcy giggled.

"Oh, how very droll," Phil had responded, trying not to sound as peeved as he felt.

The plane turned and banked over downtown Minneapolis on its way east as his wife and friends sat down to a big piece of pie at the Betty Crocker Pie Shoppe.

A smiling steward offered Phil *Time* magazine. It lay in his lap unopened. He had things on his mind other than current events. Like the fact he was about to make a fool of himself as the token "real person" from outside the Beltway. The nerd from Rosewood, Minnesota trying to play with the big boys in D.C. It would be like high school graduation award ceremony all over again, he thought miserably. He could still remember how everyone cheered wildly for the athletes, whistling and stomping, followed by polite clapping as he took the platform to pick up numerous academic awards. Being a nerd before Bill Gates made nerds cool had not been easy.

The air was rough as the plane climbed, each jolt an exclamation point to the idiocy of his decision, for he now saw it for what it was: an opportunity to be embarrassed on a national level.

"Oh no," he groaned as the plane took a particularly jarring plunge.

"Hate to fly do you, sonny?" the elderly lady sitting next to him inquired kindly.

Embarrassed and not inclined to explain his fear had nothing to do with flying, Phil picked up the magazine and pretended to read.

* * * * *

A few hours later, Cricket Hartford heard the plane carrying Phil Grant to Washington D.C. fly over as she led her visitor inside "Wit's End Antiques". People in the small village of Middleburg paid for the privilege of living in peace and quiet so near the nation's capital, and they resented the noise of occasional aircraft flying low on approach to Dulles.

"Sorry about the noise," Cricket said, showing perfectly white teeth behind a smile that made Willie a little weak at the knees. "Planes should not be allowed to disturb our peace and quiet, right Mr. Richards?"

Willie Richards was a local contractor, not one of the landed gentry; just a hard-working guy trying to make a living. He was only too happy to do business with Middleburg's newest transplant from D.C.; he needed work and she was easy on the eyes. A competitor had underbid Willie in the spring for the major remodeling job on the old house Ms. Hartford had purchased at the edge of the village. It was now a high-end art and antique business with a finely appointed living space for her on the second floor. But now she wanted more light and better views of the horse farms and rolling hills outside her windows and he would be happy to make that happen. For the right price.

"So what's the bottom line?" Cricket inquired as Willie continued to fiddle with his calculations.

They were sitting on the small deck at the back of the shop that faced the fields. The door was open to a kitchenette where she made her afternoon tea. There was a small television on the counter turned to Channel Nine News; Andrea Rowen was interviewing Mr. Ronald Lorten, the new president of CITMAC. He was explaining his vision for leading the organization going forward, utilizing the power and potential of Christian broadcasters to get out the vote in state, local, and national elections. Ms. Rowen inquired about his intentions for the "other presidency" and when he planned to announce his candidacy.

Cricket turned up the sound to hear her old friend Ronald Lorten skillfully avoid the question.

Willie Richards noticed her interest.

"Friend of yours, ma'am?"

Ms. Hartford was a classy looking woman and he figured she knew lots of important men up in Washington. He had no idea how well.

"No, I don't think you would say we're friends... exactly," she replied. "I did meet him once though." She turned her attention back to the subject at hand. "So do you have a final number for me?"

"If we do it right, meaning bigger windows and skylights, it will add considerable expense."

Cricket stood. She smiled confidently.

"Do it right, Mr. Richards. I'll take care of the finances."

"Yes, ma'am," Willie said, adding a slightly higher profit margin.

Cricket made herself another cup of tea after the contractor left and thought about things. Seeing Ronald Lorten again made her think. Again. Sure, she had her beautiful house and she loved living in Middleburg, but the antiviral drugs were expensive. The shop was making a small profit but there would be growing medical costs as long as she lived. The Lortens got off easy, she realized, still angry that they were unscathed while she suffered an uncertain future of ill health and eventual poverty. Cricket really hated to visit Ronald Lorten again, but as a businessman he would understand. Expenses had been higher than expected, and as the new president of CITMAC, he would undoubtedly like to continue getting good press — especially if he made a run for the White House. And for the price of finishing her house he could do just that.

* * * * *

Martha was going over the final edits on an advertising pamphlet for WOWL's spring event: "Innovations in Marketing Your Faith Conference" before setting off to the airport to pick up Mr. Phil Grant.

It was hard to focus on a conference not coming up for months when there was so much to do for the one starting today. These last few weeks had been a blur of activity as the big event approached. Ronald Lorten was becoming more distant and critical as the pressure increased. Maybe it was time to move on after all.

"Oh well," Martha sighed, first things first. The flyer was due back in graphics this afternoon. She read through it again, making sure she had incorporated all the changes Ronald had scribbled over the text.

MARKETING YOUR FAITH

ANOTHER IN A SERIES of WOWL
LEADERSHIP CONFERENCES

Make NEW CONTACTS AT A POWER NETWORKING RECEPTION at Noon ON OPENING DAY! With special guest GREGORY STILLCOT, author of *Hyper-marketing: A Five-Step Strategy to Effectively Marketing Your Faith-based Ministry.*

Sing Along with the Award-winning *Hereafters* at a live, private concert on FRIDAY NIGHT followed by a RECEPTION with "President and CEO of WOWL, Mr. Ronald Lorten and other dignitaries, CEOs, authors, television, and radio personalities.

You will return home armed with the knowledge, the know-how, and the knack for **Marketing Your Faith.**

* Rooms at the Hyatt Regency in Washington DC must be booked at least one month in advance for a discounted price of $350 per night.

Feeling a little sick from the hype, Martha went to the garage where her old Camry was parked. She did not usually drive to work, preferring to take the Metro, but Jeff Lorten had asked her to be the official representative of the company welcoming the contest winner and she couldn't very well ask him to join her on the Metro. Martha had made a small paddle sign with the name Phil Grant in bold letters so she could join the scrum of limo drivers at the exit gate. She tossed the sign onto the car seat, thinking it probably wouldn't be that hard to pick out Mr. Bible Trivia Guy in an airport filled with high-powered D.C. types. Oh dear, she thought, ashamed of herself. I'm beginning to think like a Lorten.

CHAPTER 14

THE GALA

The creatures outside looked from pig to man, and from man to pig, and from pig to man again; but already it was impossible to tell which was which.

—George Orwell

Aﬀᴛᴇʀ ᴛᴡᴇɴᴛʏ-ꜰᴏᴜʀ ʜᴏᴜʀꜱ ɪɴ Wᴀꜱʜɪɴɢᴛᴏɴ, ᴘʜɪʟ ᴡᴀꜱ ꜰᴇᴇʟ-ing full. To be wined and dined was taking on a whole new meaning. And against his wife's best advice he ate a late and hearty lunch before the evening gala, which promised to offer more rich food.

"'Heavy hors d'oeuvres' doesn't mean weenies in a blanket of badly baked white dough like it does here in Minneapolis," Darcy reminded him. "Go to the event hungry, taste everything, and come home to tell me about it, dear."

He should have listened, but with time to kill and calories to burn, Phil meandered down Constitution Avenue wondering at the miles of marble that had been quarried from the hills of the new republic and planted on what had been mosquito-infested swamp at the time. The government had grown too big, of that Phil was sure, but the size and grandeur of the stately structures lining the National Mall filled him with a pride in his government that he had not expected.

America might be less than its most rabid patriots assume but more than its enemies understand, the modest man from the Midwest decided, walking along the grand boulevards that belonged to him as much as anyone.

Yesterday, he had walked around the cavernous conference hall filled with booths advertising media outlets from around the country. Christian broadcasting was big business and WOWL was the 800-pound gorilla in the room. The WOWL booth included a short video on the Awareness Campaign, which he would see tonight. Social issues were front and center on most of the booths, and they covered the range of concerns from Constitution issues, abortion, homosexuality, prayer in school, and stem cell research. Voting records on all representatives were provided with "conservative" ratings. Phil always voted Republican and wondered how a good Christian could do otherwise.

Not a walker by nature, his feet were killing him after wandering around the conference center, so when Phil saw a copse of trees near the base of the Washington Monument he decided to let his lunch digest more slowly. Spreading his jacket on the damp grass, he leaned back against the trunk of a small cherry tree and sighed with something close to contentment. Except that he missed Darcy.

Phil wanted to reach out and touch his wife's hand and hear her description of the people passing. Merely a blur of humanity to him, Darcy would see individuals and find each one endlessly fascinating. Missing his wife, but still angry with her at the same time, he wondered how he would get through tonight's social occasion alone. He was dreading the enforced coziness of the upcoming drive with Martha Culberson to the Lorten home in Great Falls, but most of all being introduced as the contest winner in front of that glittering crowd of Christian celebrities.

Phil watched as harried-looking tourists with whining kids trudged by his spot near the monument, ticking off yet another item on their sightseeing list. A frazzled schoolteacher with a sport whistle herded a mob of grade-school kids into a long yellow Fairfax County school bus idling by the curb. A steady stream of young, fit, government workers jogged down the grassy Mall. A homeless man, dressed in layers of clothing and surrounded by his life possessions lay sleeping on a nearby steam grate undisturbed by traffic, sirens, and screaming school kids.

A family of Japanese tourists joined Phil under the shade of the trees. Looking tired, the young mother sank gratefully down on a blanket spread by her husband and laid her sleeping baby beside her. Unlike their parents, two small boys bounced around full of energy, completely uninterested in resting on a blanket. They jumped up and down, pulling on their father and pointing at the kiosk at the base of the monument. Like all the others, it sold miniature Washington Monuments, tourist trinkets, soda, popcorn, candy, and hot dogs. Their father appeared to be trying to interest them in the real thing instead of the kiosk but in the end he gave in. Having won the day, the little lads skipped happily beside their father toward the queue, straight black hair bouncing up and down like tops on mops.

A few remaining leaves on the small trees provided shade for mother and baby. A tired contentment written on her pretty face, she too leaned her back against a tree and rested. Noticing Phil's attention and acknowledging it for what it was, she smiled back at Phil without a hint of the usual paranoia attached to the smiles of strangers. She welcomed his attention, knowing it was benign. And perhaps she felt his longing and sympathized. That tender, unspoken communication filled him with a wave of sadness so strong, a longing for the children they had never been able to conceive so deep, that he turned his eyes away. The agony threatened to pull him under into the debilitating grief which visited him at the oddest moments. It came unbidden. Like now. Phil envied the strangers their children and wondered for the millionth time what it would feel like to watch Darcy cradle a baby in her arms, hold a tiny hand in his own, listen to a tiny voice, and know the simple joy of buying a piece of kitsch or sugary cup of cold soda on a warm fall day in return for the smile of child.

He knew coveting was a sin but it was one he committed on a regular basis when he saw young families.

Phil stretched his long frame out on the grass and closed his eyes, willing himself to think of other things. His urge to explore a possible career change in D.C., the same urge that had propelled him to accept this trip, had cooled. He knew changing places wasn't an answer to his current restlessness, the pain of childlessness, or his discomfort with people in the community he had offended. He would endure the evening festivities, still certain that "nerd" was written on his forehead like the mark of the beast, then go home where he belonged.

Phil's official tour had been everything WOWL promised. He had been given a private tour of the Capitol by Jeff Lorten and had even met some of the senators and congressman that attended his Bible Study. Martha had toured him through the building that housed corporate offices, studios, and multiple recording booths, all state of the art. They sat in on a little live Cathy Pardue talk show, as she tried to fill the big shoes left by Eric Kissane. Then they listened to the marriage counseling team taking live calls and giving advice to people discussing the sordid details of their private lives over very public airwaves. The tour concluded with a cappuccino in the plush conference room.

Stiff and sore from sitting on the ground, Phil stretched out on the grass and closed his eyes. Wind was whipping the fifty flags around the base of the monument and the comforting sound of it put him to sleep. He slept until a large Labrador (leaping for a Frisbee) landed on his still undigested lunch. Waving away the apologies of the dog's owner, Phil stood up and looked around. The little family was gone. All that remained was a flattened patch of grass where their blanket had been spread; that, and his envy.

Uniformly pruned dogwood trees lined the lengthy gravel drive that led off Georgetown Pike to the Lorten home. Phil wished he could see the trees in their spring splendor with shimmering white blossoms under the towering oaks that dwarfed them and gave the drive its grandeur. Light was fading fast as Martha drove her modest car behind a line of decidedly not-so-modest ones up to the columned doorway where valets waited.

Darcy's warning reminded him. "Don't be surprised if they have a mansion, Phil, and don't be judgmental. The Lortens probably have old money and an inherited estate. I mean... if it's big enough to host the gala... so don't go jumping to conclusions and get on a moral high horse."

Darcy was right about the size, but he had no intention of judging anyone. He just wanted to get through the evening without too much embarrassment and go home to her.

"There will be lots of famous people here tonight, Phil. You will meet politicians, musicians, and authors; it'll be fun," Martha said as they inched along.

"I'd just as soon not meet the celebrities, if you don't mind," Phil told Martha, almost pleading.

"But Mr. Grant, you *are* one of the celebrities tonight."

"No, really. I don't want attention." But he knew how disingenuous that sounded given the fact he had showed up as the recognized winner of the contest tonight.

Martha's laugh was not unkind. "Nonsense, it will be fun."

Fun like a root canal, he thought.

The receiving line stretched through a foyer that looked as big as his house.

"So this is the famous Mr. Phil Grant from Minnesota," Ronald Lorten greeted him with a firm handshake after Martha's introduction. "Welcome and congratulations. Mr. Grant won our Bible Trivia contest, Mother," Ronald said, passing Phil down the line to a fashionably dressed woman on his right.

She took his hand. "It's lovely to have you, Mr. Grant. And congratulations on winning our little contest! I hear you were better than people from all over the United States! I am so impressed that anyone could know so much about the Bible."

Jeff Lorten took over from his mother in welcoming Phil. He pumped his hand like a politician while playing to the crowd around them.

"Answer this question, Phil Grant, and you shall pass. What Old Testament judge ran his sword into the belly of a king sooooo fat the sword disappeared up to the hilt in it?

Acutely embarrassed and wanting only to move on, Phil mumbled, "Ehud," without thinking of the inevitable consequence of his correct answer.

"Yes," Jeff clapped. "Ten points for Mr. Bible Trivia guy. And the name of that very fat king? Sorry, overweight king — 'fat' is no longer politically correct and Lortens are always politically correct, right!" The crowd around them laughed.

"Eglon," Phil muttered in order to escape.

There was more applause and a few gasps of admiration for such breadth of biblical knowledge.

"What'd I tell you... is he amazing or what..." Jeff patted Phil on the back before passing him along the receiving line to his wife.

"I'm sorry about my husband," Ellie Lorten explained in a small voice. "He means well... and we *are* glad to have you here, Mr. Grant. I'm sorry your wife was unable to join you, but I'm sure Martha is taking good care of you this evening."

"Very nice lady," Phil mumbled to Martha as they finally moved away from the Lorten line and melted into the glittering crowd of people. He wondered to himself how men like Jeff Lorten managed to get women like that.

Waiters in white jackets carried trays of sparkling drinks in fluted glasses through the milling guests. Bite-size canapés of crab cakes and flaky pastries filled with savory meats and exotic cheeses were available from roving waiters and on the heavily-laden buffet. A table dedicated to desserts was decorated with a towering cone of cream puffs swathed in burnt spun sugar. Afraid to ruin the edifice, Phil settled for a strawberry dipped in dark chocolate and rued his large lunch.

Flower arrangements the size of small trees stood about the room.

"George Washington stayed here a few times," Martha said, continuing her role as tour guide. "He was a guest while surveying the Potomac River. Washington laid out plans for the canals around the falls that are now called Great Falls. It's a lovely park. The Lortens have remodeled and built on, of course, but the estate is very historic and they feel it is important to preserve it for the community, including a humble carriage house at the edge of the estate where the first president once stabled his horses. I think Rachel Lorten-Kissane, the widow of Eric, has just moved in there."

"I don't think I've met Eric's widow, is she here tonight?"

"No, I haven't even met her. She doesn't participate in the family business."

Phil was not really interested in meeting any more Lortens. He wanted to know what such an estate was worth but was too polite to ask. "So are we very close to the Potomac River?" he asked instead.

"Oh yes, you can see it from the Lorten property, just a short walk from the house to the bluff overlooking the river," Martha explained.

"My wife would have loved all this, especially the history. Darcy is a really good teacher."

Martha smiled and said she was certain Mrs. Grant was a very fine teacher.

Much to his surprise, Phil had enjoyed his conversation with Martha during the drive to Great Falls. He had been impressed to learn that her father was the famous Dr. Wilbur Culberson.

"So who actually lives here?" Phil asked as they balanced their overflowing plates of food while sitting near a fountain in the garden.

"Alice Lorten. The matriarch."

"Gosh, just one woman in this big house?"

"And a small staff," Martha explained. "Alice and her husband John bought it when the company began to grow."

Wishing he hadn't asked, Phil adopted what he hoped was a casual tone. "So it hasn't been in the Lorten family for generations?"

Martha was spared further uncomfortable questions by the appearance of Jeff Lorten, who bounded up at that moment.

"Come with me, Mr. Grant. It's time to introduce you to some important people in the Christian world."

Mercifully, the meet, greet, and eat part of the evening appeared to be coming to an end as Jeff and Phil arrived back in the Great Hall.

Strains of "Amazing Grace" filled the room, not over a sound system as he first thought, but performed live by a famous artist.

Drawn by the song and the singer, people gathered from the gardens; Ronald Lorten stood to the side behind a Plexiglas lectern set on a small riser.

"Isn't she something?" Lorten said after sustained applause.

Then with his most commanding presence, Ronald began to speak.

"How wonderful to have all of you in our home tonight to celebrate the culmination of a great CITMAC convention and the Awareness Campaign. I'm so glad y'all took time to come all the way out here to our little house in Great Falls and I trust you've had enough to eat and drink."

Scattered laughter and more applause followed.

"I am honored to take on the leadership of our conference of broad-casters," he said. "And I pledge to you to use my position, along with all the might of WOWL, to help call this nation back to Christ. To work to get Christians elected. To fight for the unborn... against a creeping secular-ism and socialism. We must not be silent and we must not grow weary as we wage this war to push back the forces of evil that seek control of our nation. There are those who would turn this once-Christian nation into a pagan, post-Christian culture but I promise to be a voice crying in the wilderness. I promise to be the one standing on the wall on your behalf. I promise to defeat that agenda. It is time to take our country back from the secular humanists, the elitist big government, and the liberal press that would silence us."

Lorten delivered his address with the skill of a natural born politi-cian and with the response of the crowd drowning out his words, Ronald paused with precision to let it happen before going on.

"Do you see a vast right-wing conspiracy gathering here? Or do you see a humble army of God's people dedicated to the defense of our liberty, commitment to our Constitution, and fighting ready to return this country to the Christian principles on which this great nation — the greatest ever given by God —was founded?"

Like a good politician, Lorten let the response of the crowd make his point before going on. The room was electric.

"We are here tonight because we share a common goal and that goal is to bring America back to its roots. We are no longer a fifth column oper-ating in enemy territory, we are no longer the silent majority... and do not," again he held up his hand for quiet before concluding, "do not be tempted to listen to the slander that will be spread around to defeat us. Instead, remember that our battle cry here tonight is... enough is enough. Enough is enough!" Ronald led his guests in the chant.

Despite himself, Phil found he was joining in the refrain meant to echo all the way down the Potomac to the White House.

"Before we conclude this grand evening," Lorten went on, "I have a short video I would like to share with all of you. As you know, WOWL, along with the Washington Bible Church and my good friend Pastor Leif Ohlsson..." He clapped his arm around Leif's shoulder as he stepped forward. "Together we have raised funds and awareness for one of the worst evils of our time, the sexual exploitation of children around the world. And tonight we have the privilege of showing you a film that reveals the help provided by the Awareness Campaign. But before we see that I want you to meet..."

"Oh, no," Phil mumbled as Martha took his arm and led him to the small podium where Lorten's big hand pulled him up.

"I want you to meet one of the ordinary Americans who had a part in our little project. Mr. Phil Grant, winner of our Biblical Literacy Contest. Phil represents the kind of people across this great land who care about God's Word and who care about helping people in need. Please welcome now Mr. Phil Grant of Rosewood, Minnesota."

Phil could feel himself being led up two steps of the small raised dais. It was happening again, he was back in high school, the nerd trooping up to the podium to receive one more academic award in front of bored classmates who wanted to get on to the cheerleading and football trophies. Not for the first time in his life, Phil wished he had been born with bigger biceps and a smaller brain. Right now he wished he hadn't been born at all.

Lorten grabbed Phil's hand, clapping his arm around his shoulder. "Over a million people from churches and communities all across America took part in the contest through radio, TV, and social media. All of that helped spur interest in God's Word and biblical literacy. My friend here, Leif Ohlsson, got his congregation behind this campaign and it spread across the country. By the way, you want to get out of the way when his congregation gets moving."

The popular pastor received the warm welcome and leaned into the pulpit to add his remarks. "Remember when the *Washington Post* called evangelicals... called us... poor, uneducated, and easy to lead? Well, the *Post* should just drop into our church some Sunday morning and see if my congregation is poor or uneducated. And I can assure you they are *not* easy to lead."

Phil had never been at a rock concert but he thought it must be like this. Charged, out of control, and very cool. Lost in the moment Phil forgot his own humiliation and happily realized the brief introduction was over.

It was a long time before Phil went to sleep that night; he had trouble digesting the rich food and coalescing images of opulence and soaring rhetoric into some kind of coherent meaning. Phil wished he didn't care that he would always be remembered, if anyone remembered him at all, as the geek who knew Ehud ran his sword through the fat belly of Eglon.

He had found it hard to describe the evening to Darcy, especially the image Lorten had so powerfully conjured up of that group of men and women as leaders in the army of God, leading foot soldiers like him into battle against a pagan culture.

"So what's wrong with that?" Darcy asked. "It's true and a metaphor that's been used before."

Darcy was accustomed to her husband's slow thought process and she snuggled under her blankets in their bed at home, waiting patiently while Phil stared silently at a stain on the carpet in an impersonal hotel, holding his head in one hand, and the phone in the other. "Does the Battle of the Bulge mean anything to you?"

"Oh Phil," she laughed. "It's not something I think about every day... whatever do you mean, dear?"

"Well this feels like that, like this big bold brassy move by fiery generals who have moved way out beyond their supply line."

"Maybe, but the Battle of the Bulge succeeded. The generals gambled and won. The cultural war is real, Phil. Some of the people you met may seem too flashy for our taste, but they do have influence. People follow them and that's not a bad thing. Sometimes it takes... fiery, colorful generals. Let's face it; no one would follow us in the culture wars."

Dissatisfied with her argument but too tired to defend his still-disjointed thoughts, Phil closed his eyes and didn't speak.

"Oh, Phil... I'm afraid you've eaten too much rich food. Come home and we'll talk."

Phil knew it was going to be hard to explain it to Darcy, but he had been fighting a growing sense of unease since his first glimpse of the corporate headquarters of WOWL, Inc. It had grown as he wandered throughout the cavernous Washington Convention Center filled with booths of successful marketers of today's evangelical world. He had heard nicely packaged but insipid speeches and clever marketing rhetoric that claimed success by numbers and technique. Not one word about the caring for the poor. Justice. Or mercy. Then in the Lorten mansion, while eating the best food he had ever tasted in his life, and mingling with the rich and powerful of the evangelical world, he realized he had become part of it. Clapping, cheering, empowered. Sucked into the moment! Never given to drink, Phil didn't recognize his symptoms as those similar to a hangover. He had a pounding headache, bad taste in his mouth, and a weight in the pit of his stomach. It kept him from sleeping and gave him time to think.

A friendly United Airlines representative, awake at 1:30 a.m., said it would cost Mr. Grant three-hundred and fifty dollars to extend his stay in D.C. until Monday. With dread in his heart over the path he was about to take, Phil gave her his credit card number and rebooked his flight home to Minnesota for late Monday afternoon.

CHAPTER 15

CRICKET RETURNS

A worried man with a worried mind
No one in front of me and nothing behind.

—Bob Dylan

THE WALL CLOCK CHIMED ONCE FOR THE HALF HOUR AS MARTHA stowed a new designer purse beside her desk on Monday morning. With the CITMAC conference and Great Falls party now behind her, Martha was looking forward to a quiet morning of catching up on a backlog of work.

Housekeeping always arrived before Martha, made the coffee and put fresh cut flowers in the executive suite. She bent to smell the flowers, poured a cup of her favorite Royal Cup blend, and settled in for a quiet day.

Charlie Rice had requested final figures from the Wharton & Wharton Consulting account. Her first task of the day would be to prepare those and get that out of the way. Still a sensitive subject, Martha was careful not to ask any questions about their role in helping Ronald with the campaign. He gave her the data; she sorted it and passed it along to the Finance Office. End of story.

"Morning, Martha," Ronald said, breezing through the door. "Things should be a little quieter around here this week and I'm sure you are ready for it."

"Yes, sir. It will be nice. Congratulations on the lovely party, by the way, and the good press on your CITMAC speech and election. You must be proud."

"More like relieved," he said honestly, then added, "We all worked hard and now we can relax a little. In fact, I'm playing golf with the guys this morning."

Good, she thought, the day looking better and better.

"Call Charlie and Jeff and remind them to meet me in the parking lot in fifteen will you?" Ronald called over his shoulder as he disappeared into his office.

It would be the usual golf foursome: Rice, the two Lortens, and Ohlsson. Reverend Ohlsson saw golfing with congregants as an important part of his ministry, "good way to spend time with his flock" — especially the richer sheep.

Half an hour later, her boss out of the way, Martha was focused on the computer screen and so missed the soft sound of the heavy glass door opening. She did, however, hear it swoosh closed, and looked up with a start to see the smiling face of Phil Grant.

"Oh my goodness," Martha gasped. "What happened? Did you miss your plane? Did I make a mistake on the tickets? Mercy me... what have I done? You said you'd take a taxi to the airport... I should have... "

"No. No. No, nothing like that," he said holding up his hand to interrupt the flow of apologies. "Everything is fine... may I sit down?"

Phil Grant was a nice man. She had enjoyed getting to know him and showing him around during his stay as a special guest of the station. But something seemed ever so slightly different about the man this morning. His shoulders had a less self-effacing hunch.

"My tickets were perfectly in order. You did everything just right. It was me; rather, it was I who decided to stay another day. I attended a service at the National Cathedral Sunday morning and visited the arboretum in the afternoon. I have a flight out this afternoon. But actually, I do have a small favor to ask of you."

It wasn't really a favor as much as a demand. And one she was not at liberty to refuse.

An hour later, Mr. Grant of Minneapolis left her office carrying copies of WOWL's 990 tax record for the past three years. They covered the one nonprofit station in D.C., the old original radio station kept for charitable purposes. IRS regulations required the 990 tax form be made available upon request to any donor. Mr. Grant was clearly a donor and had a right to ask, but she sincerely wished he hadn't. The thought of explaining this surprise request to Ronald, and to Charlie Rice, made Martha's heart race. In fact, she felt a little faint.

Possible implications of the request were not entirely lost on Martha. Her lovely day now in shambles, she determined to put it out of her mind and at least accomplish some work.

But Phil Grant kept coming back, invading her thoughts and ruining her productivity. Martha found herself staring at the screensaver, her mind like the interweaving tubes writhing and twisting, running through the same endless loop of mental gyrations. Mr. Grant had a right to ask for the tax records of the company, and maybe it was just professional curiosity. Still, he had been in such a hurry to return to his wife. The extended stay must have been expensive and he had not seemed to her the kind of man to waste money. Try as she might she couldn't come up with a non-disturbing reason that Phil Grant had spent his time and money in order to pick up hard copies of WOWL, Inc.'s tax records.

In retrospect, the contest winner's penetrating questions during the party at the Lorten estate seemed ominous. Her answers had been straightforward, hopefully. Ronald would never forgive her (and he would most certainly fire her) if something she said prompted their guest to explore the finances of the company.

Unable to concentrate, Martha decided on an early lunch. Mr. Lorten allowed her the use of his private deck when he was away and she usually enjoyed the perk of sitting high above Pennsylvania Avenue with a view to the White House. But today Martha had looked forward to chatting with her friends in the dining common and giving them insider Lorten gossip about who wore what and who was with whom at the big event. But today, sat alone in the exclusive perch, oblivious to the view or the taste of her sandwich.

Martha, flushed from the sun's rays, returned to her desk hoping her boss would remain on the golf course all afternoon so she could avoid telling him about the unexpected visitor.

Long before Martha made her escape for the day she looked up to see another unexpected visitor to the Executive Suite. A well-dressed woman, vaguely familiar and *very* beautiful, had slipped quietly into the office. Making a mental note to tell the receptionist at the main entrance to do a better job of keeping-the-gate, Martha's manners were nonetheless in place when she politely suggested the woman was in the wrong office.

"I don't think so. I'm here to see Ronald Lorten."

"Sorry, miss, but he doesn't have any appointments for today. And I assure you," Martha said, taking the appointment book out of the top middle drawer where she had just placed it, "Mr. Lorten is not expecting you. However, I'll be more than happy to schedule something for a later date."

Pen held hopefully over the book, Martha suggested, "Maybe something in December? Mr. Lorten really has a very full schedule until then. Would that be good?"

Unfazed by Martha's evident fluster, the woman calmly took a seat. "Thank you, but today will be fine."

"But Mr. Lorten isn't even in today," Martha protested. "So there is really no point in waiting. I assure you he does not see people without scheduled appointments."

"Too busy golfing, is he?"

"How do you..." Martha stopped. The confidence and presumption of the woman was breathtaking.

"I saw Ronald in the parking lot," she explained, smiling. "He was unloading golf bags. So I expect he will be here any minute."

Seriously flustered now, Martha tried again.

"Well, you still can't see him."

"Oh, not to worry, I'm sure Ronald will give me a few minutes."

"Why don't you give me your name... I'll pencil you in and then you can call to confirm. Because Mr. Lorten really is tied up all afternoon." That lie bothered Martha, but now her desperation was growing to get rid of the woman before Mr. Lorten returned.

"*There is no mistake*, Ms. Culberson. I am here to see Ronald and I'm quite confident he will see me. Let's just have a wait and see."

"Well, that just isn't possible. I make all the appointments and while we all make mistakes... uh, I'm pretty sure I uh... didn't... I'll double check the computer but everything in the computer is here in this book."

"Please don't trouble yourself. It's not in your book, nor on your computer, and I assure you I don't mind waiting for Ronald."

"Oh dear," Martha said mostly to herself, shocked by the seductively dressed woman and her casual use of Lorten's first name.

She seemed calm on the outside, but Cricket's nerves were actually not much better than the flustered secretary's.

Cricket, who had worked for difficult and demanding men, had great sympathy for Ms. Culberson. Putting up with important men was not something Cricket had to do anymore, thanks to Ronald Lorten. She must remember to thank him.

Martha caught sight of her boss through the glass door, breezing down the hall toward his office with the smug look of a man who had just beat his friends at golf. She sighed inwardly, thinking wistfully of what the day might have been.

The sight of Cricket Hartford sitting demurely on his dark chocolate leather couch, one silk-stocking-covered leg folded neatly over the other, stopped Lorten in his tracks. He stood unmoving for several seconds, his sunny glow draining away. Martha saw his fear and watched in horror as her boss motioned, without a word, for the woman to follow him into the private suite.

"Hold my calls, Martha. No one interrupts me, including you, for any reason."

The heavy door closed.

All thoughts of Phil Grant fled from Martha's head at this new, even more troubling, development. And then, as if an unseen director was orchestrating events to ruin her life, Charlie Rice barged in with a thick file he had to "show the boss at once."

Martha jumped up, protecting the door with her body.

"Gee, you don't have to be dramatic, Martha. Ronald told me to come on up."

"Well, something came up and he's not available now. Why don't you come back, Charlie... I'll call you when Mr. Lorten is free."

Charlie Rice was a very observant man and an astute reader of facts and faces. He looked at the obviously troubled and usually malleable Martha blocking his way and tried again.

"This really can't wait, Martha. Some donor came in while I was gone and requested three years' worth of 990 forms. I need to discuss it with him straightaway. By the way, you sent down for the request. Who ordered these?"

"Oh dear," she said, still standing her ground in front of the door.

"Oh dear who, Martha?"

"Phil Grant, sir," she mumbled, half under her breath.

Charlie Rice looked like a man sobering up before he wanted to.

"PHIL GRANT? The ingrate! What could Phil "the-whiz kid Grant" want with the corporate tax returns? I thought he was long gone. Why didn't you ask me before just handing them over?"

Since the first part of the question was clearly rhetorical, Martha went right to part b.

"Because you were not here, sir."

"Well, that's gratitude for you. We bring the guy out here, treat him like a king and then he thanks us by... by requesting copies of... what was it again, three years, the maximum number we're required to provide... that's a helluva way to thank us, don't you think?"

Before she could stop him Charlie was charging toward the door.

She was up in a shot, blocking it.

"I'm serious, Charlie, Mr. Lorten is with someone and he said he was not, under any circumstances, to be disturbed. Sorry, but that means you, too."

Rice was shocked that Martha could move that fast and even more surprised she was standing up to him. This new Martha was maybe not so good after all. She had lost weight, changed her hair, got contacts and was wearing new clothes. And now she was standing up to him. Charlie briefly entertained the idea that maybe the Awareness Campaign had benefited more than the victims, then he dismissed the thought as ludicrous. Martha was not clever enough to pull such a thing off. Well, he could ask questions later. But he wasn't just anybody and Ronald could not have meant him when he told her no interruptions.

Rice reached behind Martha and opened the door. He saw his friend leaning forward, elbows on the desk, head in his hands, staring with a look of horror at a woman in the high-winged back chair, her delicate profile to Charlie.

Not stupid, he backed out, shutting the door as quickly as he had opened it. But the scene stayed with him. That and the fact Mr. Phil Grant of Rosewood, Minnesota wanted to look at their books. CFOs hate uncertainty and the whole afternoon was turning into a black hole of it.

Bound by Mr. Lorten's command to guard the door, Martha knew she would have to stay until the mystery woman left, then — genuinely sick from nervous tension —she would go home early.

In the meantime, too nervous to work, she tried to remember when the woman had been there before.

She flipped back through the appointment book month by month without finding any unexplainable appointments until she came to March. There on the 15th of March was a Ms. Cricket Hartford, 10:00 a.m. Now it was coming back to her; that day had turned out to be a disaster as well. Mr. Lorten had disappeared after the appointment, upsetting his wife, who hadn't been able to reach him. But, try as she might, Martha couldn't remember anything odd about the following days. Soon after that they had all been caught up in working on the campaign.

Inside his office, Ronald Lorten was not taking Cricket's new demands well.

"What in the *hell* do you think you're doing coming here again?"

Cricket waited through the expected rant.

"How dare you come back... how dare you... I kept my part of our deal and it didn't include phase two. You have put us both at risk coming here again and if you think for one minute that I'm going to give you more money, you are sadly mistaken."

Cricket Hartford looked as lovely, and as healthy, as she had seven months ago. Ronald watched her calmly cross her long, exquisite legs, not even bothering to tug the short skirt down to a more reasonable location on her thighs.

"Oh, do stop being so dramatic, Ronald. You should be glad I showed up. A highly paid consultant on a big project should certainly spend some time in the office, and with the CEO. You can always say I came for a small celebration together over the successful conclusion of the project. Otherwise, it might look like you have created a *fictitious* expense account. And I thought it was time to get to know some of the other players in the company; like maybe your brother, Jeff. He went golfing with you this morning, didn't he? I would like to meet him someday... not as tall as you, I noticed. But I know a Lorten when I see one, as I did just now, taking his golf clubs from your Mercedes to his. Your sister, however, looks more like you. Probably more than she would like, poor thing. Oh don't worry — I haven't met Rachel — but there were pictures of her in the *Post* when her husband was so tragically killed. I recognized your pastor friend as well. I have an idea about his church, but more on that in a minute. Who was the other man who made up the golfing foursome this morning... the one who just poked his head in the door... let me guess... your moneyman? CFOs have a certain look; I've always found it attractive, personally."

"I bet you do. How many CFOs have you had?"

Cricket had a very enticing laugh. Soft, without a hint of cackle. With the initial nervousness of facing him over, she was enjoying the encounter. "It's fun to chat, but let's get down to business."

Cricket had managed many men like Ronald Lorten in her life; he neither interested, nor intimidated her. This was business and she knew she had the upper hand. He'd lost control when he let her in the door.

Unable to remain seated, and unable to bellow like he would have liked, Lorten paced silently back and forth across the thick carpet.

"I like your boots, by the way," she offered. "I have always liked men who wear cowboy boots. They're ostrich, aren't they?"

Lorten didn't correct her and kept pacing, trying to keep his eyes off the woman so he could think.

Having risked everything to avoid the scandal this woman had threatened to unleash on her first visit, Ronald thought his nightmare had been over. He felt an equal measure of anger and self-pity. Anger at his sister for getting him into this mess. And self-pity because he had managed to do good while avoiding a scandal that would have hurt her too. It didn't seem right that he was once again the one at risk.

"Sit down, Ronald. Listen."

He sat. Elbows on the desk, he leaned toward her. "Cowboys. CFOs. I get the impression you like most men."

"Not most," she laughed. "For instance, I don't like you much. I think you are arrogant. Probably delusional and definitely self-righteous. I saw you on television Saturday night, by the way, TBN did a little piece about the gala and I listened to part of your acceptance speech at that CITMAC Convention. Quite impressive, actually."

Cricket was perfectly aware of the effect she was having on poor Ronald Lorten. He looked so miserable but also a little lecherous at the same time.

"I didn't know you were such a big wheel. Really, I had no idea on that first day when I came to see you. I'm impressed. And your house, oh my god, what a house you've got out there in Great Falls."

"It's not my house. It's my mother's house," he said, miserably. "But do get to the point. I assume you didn't come to thank me." He was just a tiny bit hopeful that maybe this visit wasn't another blackmail attempt.

"But if your aim is to ask for more money, I assure you I can't create any more 'fictitious accounts' as you so delicately and accurately described it."

"Oh, I think you can, Mr. Lorten. I even know how. Remember, that's what I'm paid for — I'm your consultant. And, for what it's worth, it will be the last time. I miscalculated my expenses, that's all. It's not personal, and I'm not greedy. Just practical... and unlike probably hordes of others I don't have a vendetta against your family or your organization. In fact, I personally loathe the current administration and I wish you the best of luck trying to defeat them in the next election."

Cricket uncrossed her legs, sat up straight, and tugged on her skirt, tapping her manicured nails on the desk. He took note of the change in her body language and she took note of the resignation creeping across his face.

"Okay, let's drop the dramatics. We are, after all, both pragmatic people and the fact is I need another $100,000. That's peanuts to you and don't try to deny it. You could either give it to me from your personal funds, or, and I think this might be best, use your church this time instead of the company. It will be safer."

He sucked in his breath. Shocked at her chutzpah. "My church? You're joking. This might come as a surprise to you but I don't control the budget at our church."

"No, of course you don't. I know that. I'm not a pagan, you know. I've been going to church lately, to a lovely little stone church in Upperville, Virginia built with Paul Mellon money. Now that family makes yours look like small potatoes... but I digress. Last week at church someone gave the Deacon's Fund report and it made me think of a safe way to do a little business. I know you're good friends, even golfing buddies, with your pastor, Leif Ohlsson. I'm sure he'd be happy to help."

Ronald saw no point in denying where he went to church or with whom he golfed, so he waited. She clearly knew that and a whole lot more.

"A Deacon's Fund typically has very little outside oversight. I checked. The IRS does not go after churches. They could, but they just simply do not. It isn't worth the political capital it would cost them. They are set up to help the needy and as they distribute funds already received by a 'nonprofit', there are no additional tax-deduction issues for the IRS to care about. It's an accepted way for churches to help the needy, in this case, you. You are very much in need of a way to pay me," she smiled at her little joke. "And any payment that large from your personal account might raise questions with your accountant or your wife, so you have to admit the church idea is a good one. So you make a donation to the church in the amount of $100,000, designated for the Deacon's Fund. Then you and your pastor friend pass it through to an AIDS foundation, namely me, and the beauty is that your contribution will be tax-deductible."

He couldn't believe his ears. He couldn't believe her bloody nerve. He couldn't believe he had no choice but to do exactly as she suggested.

"What a fascinating proposal, Ms. Hartford. I'm so glad church has been helpful for you recently. Let me see if I have this right. You're sitting in the pew singing 'The Old Rugged Cross' while figuring out how to rip me off yet again. You are not only a criminal, and make no mistake this is a criminal proposition, you are also terribly naïve. I can't pull off such a crazy scheme, and even if I could, I wouldn't expose my church... like you forced me to expose my family and company. I think you should just go. Just get out of my office. And by the way," he said, half under his breath, "how do I know you're telling the truth about your exposure to HIV? You still look healthy to me."

She took that as a compliment. "Thank you. However, that's not the point and you knew that in the beginning. The pictures I have of Eric with me are scandal enough. My accusations are provable with a simple blood test. But now, the scandal about Eric that you so wisely paid to suppress pales in comparison with the cover-up; isn't that just always the case in Washington? If you want to take our little dispute into the open, go ahead. I made you that offer before, when we were discussing the fact that your brother-in-law had not been abiding by all of the Commandments. You wisely came to the conclusion that a public airing of my problems would benefit neither of us; less so now that you have this new position as president of the Christian Broadcasters Association or whatever it is. And, I think it is safe to assume, serious presidential aspirations."

He glared, recognizing defeat but not quite ready to give in.

"My guess is you don't care enough about your sister to do this to protect her. Although, you might want to find a way to warn her that she has also been exposed to HIV. And, by the way, while it might be very hard to prove that Eric Kissane infected *me*, not the other way around, but is that really an issue you want to explore in a public forum? Although the press would find it fascinating. You have already committed a couple of felonies; fraud, money laundering, and God knows what else. Those are the relevant facts. What are you more worried about — God or the IRS?"

His shoulders slumped. Ronald Lorten was beaten.

"Well, whatever," she went on, figuring he probably wasn't interested in the fine philosophical points. "I can only help you with the earthly powers, I'm afraid. This is not hypothetical. You stole money from donors and you cannot possibly, especially in this high political season with so much at stake, allow the measly little amount of money I am requesting today destroy everything you have worked for and achieved. If you are squeamish about the church, do it out of your own personal petty cash. You wouldn't miss it."

"No, but unfortunately my wife would," he mumbled. "She watches our personal books."

"Well, I'm sure Mrs. Lorten would agree to a tax-deductible donation to the poor given through the Deacon's Fund. And, well, feel good about it."

Slumped, unable to even look at her, Ronald swiveled his throne-like chair so he was facing the street. The sun was shining on the White House. Removing a man like the current president was more important than anything he could think of; important to the country, important to the world.

When he turned back Cricket knew she had won.

"How do I know you won't be back?"

She took her time, savoring the victory.

"You don't. I could give you my word, but that wouldn't mean much, I suppose? However, given your options it doesn't matter if you believe me or not. And by the way, Mr. Lorten, I want you to know I feel comfortable doing business with you. I think you would do many things to retain your power, maybe even rationalize breaking the law for the good of your company. Or for your God. That was clever — by the way, how you used helping the victims of such terrible violence to hide the first payment. I felt good about it actually, being fairly certain you would not have started that campaign to help those kids without me."

She had meant to make him angry. And it worked.

Her taunt made him crazy. Lorten rose out of his seat and moved toward Cricket. She was unfazed by his physical threat. "Calm down, Ronald. We both know you won't actually hurt me. From what I've read blackmail can be dangerous, I don't have any other personal experience, but I'm pretty sure violence is against your religion. Comforting thought, that."

She left him then with clear instructions and a promise. Do this and you will never see me again.

He had no idea if Cricket Hartford stopped to talk with Martha on her way out. He sat at his desk, wondering how it was possible that she had managed to be seductive while at the same time driving a dagger into his heart. For the second time. He simply couldn't go through this again and yet he knew she was right; he had no choice. If she leaked the story of the first blackmail and cover-up, it would mean not only personal but political ruin. This time it could mean prison.

Tears sprang to his eyes. How could this have happened? He had managed to protect his sister and do God's work of mercy at the same time. The face of Raluca Iovan and her friend Nadia came back to him. The rest of the campaign might have had mixed motives but the end had been justified for so many girls like Nadia. "Oh God," he prayed. "Why are you letting this evil woman destroy your servant? And hand a victory to your enemies? Why, Lord? How long is this going to go on?"

Ronald couldn't remember ever liking his sister very much. She was always so different. Such an ugly duckling. Arrogant and snotty to her mother who, it seemed to him, had always tried to help her daughter improve herself.

"Damn. Damn. Damn," he mumbled in desperation. If only Rachel had satisfied her own husband none of this would be happening. Her snobby intellectualism had probably driven him away and into the arms of Cricket Hartford. Ronald had watched Rachel treat her husband with the same condescending manner she treated the rest of the family, which didn't, of course, excuse him. Eric should have been able to control his appetite for outside sex. Ronald had never fallen into that trap despite plenty of opportunity.

Pacing again. "Think," he told himself. "Think."

He could understand Cricket's position. A member of the Lorten family had harmed her. And the amount she was asking was modest. Before he left his office he was beginning to think... as outrageous as it was, that the Deacon's Fund idea just might work. He would do the right thing by Cricket — protect his miserable sister (again) and maybe keep the threat at bay once more.

* * * * *

Unlike her brother, Rachel was having a lovely day. She was enjoying a lively conversation (instead of reading another dry policy manual in her Institute of Russian Studies office) with an interesting man who had wandered into her office quite unexpectedly.

"My name is Enoch Arnheim," he said with a slightly lopsided smile. "And I'm from the IRS." The man moved a pile of papers and took the only other chair in her cluttered office.

"But, I'm not here about your taxes!"

Rachel liked the smile and couldn't help noticing how good the man looked in his perfectly tailored suit. She pushed back a strand of unruly hair from her face and tried not to think how rumpled she must look by comparison. Mr. Arnheim went on to explain how a friend at the State Department suggested he seek her advice about his upcoming trip to Russia. He had promised to take his elderly parents back to the village they had escaped before the war. What were the risks to such a trip, he wanted to know.

An hour later, when he invited her to continue their conversation over a cup of coffee, she said yes.

It did not occur to Rachel then, but once before she had agreed to join a handsome, interesting, man for a cup of coffee by the horse fountain in Salzburg and it had changed her life.

CHAPTER 16

THE FEDS

It is not a matter of wisdom
Or virtue
So how can you condemn
The unreason of others.

—*Czeslaw Milosz*

ENOCH ARNHEIM HEADED BACK TO HIS OFFICE ON FOOT AS MOST Washingtonians were driving west along the busy boulevards of D.C., pouring across the bridges over the Potomac into Maryland and Virginia for the evening commute back to the 'burbs'.

Looking at his watch, Enoch picked up the pace and swore under his breath. He had stacks of work to do and Johnson was on his back to close more cases. He had enjoyed talking with the Russian scholar. He had found her insight on modern Russia fascinating, if not exactly what he had hoped to discover (namely a good reason not to take his parents to their long lost village). But now he would have to work late.

It was a short walk across P Street back to his office in the massive marble structure that housed the most despised of all governmental offices: the IRS. Enoch's tall, lean frame looked impressive and at home on the Washington street where a Brooks Brothers suit or some more modest imitation was de rigueur and where the mark of success was often measured by the stiffness of one's starched collar.

In rare introspective moments, Enoch figured his obsessive (but not quite compulsive) attention to health, fitness, and wardrobe was simply a reaction to his father's utter neglect for his.

Hurrying along Pennsylvania Avenue next to the crush of cars driven by irritable and impatient commuters, Enoch thought about the interesting afternoon that had made him so late. Aware Laura had probably been trying to reach him, he tried her private number before taking off his coat at his desk. She didn't hide her irritation.

"Where have you been? I've been trying to call for an hour... I need you to meet me at the Old Ebbitt Grill in an hour," she demanded. Her voice sounded stressed.

Fighting his natural response, he calmly reminded Laura where he'd been; they had discussed it in detail last night, including the fact it would require him to work late tonight.

"But I thought you gave up the whole idea of helping your parents take this ill-fated trip to discover long-dead relatives."

"No, Laura you told me I *should* give it up. Slight difference."

"Don't be testy, I've had a hard day. And I thought I talked you out of wasting your time in that probably Republican-funded think tank... with some Russian scholar grown fat sitting on his bottom lamenting the end of the Cold War and its politically lucrative market for virulent anti-communists... no, tell them I'm not ready to make a statement... oh Enoch, sorry, I got distracted. Where were we?"

"Sitting on our heavy Russian bottoms thinking subversive Republican thoughts."

"Very funny. Enoch, listen. I hope you didn't let someone cloud your thinking... you don't have time to waste on your parents' crazy schemes. You do let them take advantage of you, you know."

She could spin the flimsiest State Department release into major breaking news, and keep condescension out of her voice when discussing nations that the U.S. clearly despised with diplomatic skill that earned a salary twice as good as his. But let his family in their lives and she took on the tone of a shrew.

"You wasted the afternoon," Laura went on. "And you knew I would need you tonight. To keep the potentially lecherous Irishman at bay." Tension had grown in their relationship since Enoch had turned down what she knew was the perfect position for him in the administration. But both were trying and Enoch did not want to add fuel to the growing fire. He kept his own voice, if not his words, neutral.

"Sorry about tonight, but I'm sure you can manage. And I rather resent the implication that my time was ill spent trying to help my par-ents... they *are* my parents, for god's sake — and I didn't say I wasted the afternoon. I said I spent it."

"Oh please, Enoch. What did they ever give you but, as you said, the 'cloud of their dreadful past'".

"Their faith, for one thing," he snapped.

"Which you've rejected. Give it up, dear boy. Guilt doesn't become you. Just tell your folks... nicely, of course... that it isn't a good idea for them, especially at their age, to take this trip into the past. And that *you*... make this part crystal clear... that *you* don't have time to go running around some godforsaken place in Russia, looking for long-dead relatives."

There was a long pause while Enoch pondered the wisdom of this conversation, at this time, in this place.

"Enoch? Are you still there? Don't get difficult about this, please... you know we talked about spending a week in the South of France next spring and you can't take off time for both trips... think about it..." She had lowered her voice; softened its edge. "Europe is so nice in May and we need some time away from the pressure. Just *be* together... oh, sorry again, can you hold, I have to take this... "

Enoch laid the phone down and started going through the notes on his desk while Laura took another call. The South of France with Laura did sound infinitely better than schlepping around Russian Moldova looking for the past with his parents. And a week together out of Washington might do wonders for what he knew was a fraying relationship. But his parents didn't ask him for much and, since they were uncomfortable with his living arrangement with Laura, they rarely visited him. He found less and less time to go to Brooklyn to see them.

A few months ago, encouraged by their friends, Benyamin and Ida decided to return to Europe. They had left as children from a displaced persons camp where they met. They wanted to find and reestablish contact with any, even distant, relatives. Enoch had promised to find out what he could about such a trip, but had kept putting it off, hoping they would forget. Until one day his mother called and said they were booking tickets, so... was he coming already or not?

In an effort to find a way to dissuade them, Laura had put him in touch with Fred Wohlers on the Russian Desk at State. Mr. Wohlers, whom Enoch knew slightly from a function he attended with Laura, had enlightened him to some of the harsher realities of travel in that part of the world. Unable to give him much more than the usual State Department regurgitation, Fred suggested Enoch check out the Institute of Russian Studies (IORS) for a better perspective.

So Enoch had taken the advice and made an appointment with a senior fellow at the Institute of Russian Studies (IORS), hoping to convince his parents that their plan was a futile and possibly dangerous thing for them to do, given the frail state of their health and instability of the region. He had gone to his appointment today expecting to ask a few questions, framed to get the response he wanted, so he could convince his parents not to go.

Enoch hadn't expected Rachel Lorten-Kissane. For some reason he was surprised the Russian expert turned out to be a woman. When he was ushered into her office, his first thought was that he recognized her "type" from women in his doctoral program, mind-over-body types. But once he got over his preconceived expectations about Dr. Lorten-Kissane, he found her a brilliant scholar and a very interesting woman. The lady Ph.D. had been wearing a cotton sweater over a casual dress with low heels; altogether too casual for his taste, in every way unlike Laura's power suits, which were professional and sexy at the same time.

But he did find that Ms. Lorten-Kissane had an air of self-confidence, without the need to impress, which was a refreshing change from the typical D.C. ego. She had a lovely smile with straight white teeth, beautiful skin untouched by makeup and gray-green eyes with striking black curly hair. He thought her a handsome woman. And as near as he could tell, Dr. Lorten-Kissane had been impervious to his first impression charms.

"Hello, Enoch, you still there... "

He picked up the phone.

"Still here."

"Well, since you spent so much time with this expert, he must have given you dozens of reasons why your parents shouldn't go off on this madcap trip?"

"Actually, the he was a she, and she made Moldova sound interesting... in fact, a little like the South of France."

"I'm kidding, I'm kidding," he went on into a deadly silence. "Let's talk tonight, I have lots to do. I'm sorry about the Old Ebbitt tonight but you will do fine alone. Eat garlic, they'll stay away."

He hung up and sat thinking for a moment about the woman he loved and the one he had just met. Laura moved with lightning speed all day. The powerful must be peripatetic, in order not only to accomplish their important tasks, but also to intimidate. Retaining power can be more arduous than acquiring it, it seemed to him. Scholars, on the other hand, don't have to move so much. Thinkers think and they can do so while sitting. Which takes less motion. And connectedness. Ms. Lorten-Kissane had a phone on her desk, but he could imagine her working all day without ever getting a call. Laura couldn't go five minutes.

The afternoon had proved to be a welcome interlude. As Ms. Lorten-Kissane talked, he had found himself interested in a world he had spent his whole life trying hard to ignore. Enoch wore his Jewishness close to his vest, took no part in children of survivors groups, and especially hated it when Gentiles cried over Jewish pain. But when Rachel Lorten-Kissane described her own visits to Eastern Europe and the old, sad Jewish communities that remain dotted over still-desolate countries, he felt no defensiveness at her muted but genuine emotion.

Maybe, he reasoned, switching on his computer, he had found the day enjoyable only because it was a break from the all-consuming political game around which Laura's life now revolved. It dominated their time together, their conversations, and both their schedules. She had become increasingly absorbed with the internecine struggles at State. Every day brought a new crisis at Foggy Bottom, and Laura sometimes acted like the future of the republic rested on her shoulders. Enoch wanted to remind her that the money and prestige in the job were as tenuous as the President's popularity and would probably end with the next election. The State Department and the state of the world would go on pretty much as before.

Enoch had come away from his appointment with nothing to stop or even discourage his parents, which had been more or less the original purpose of his visit. But he was more convinced than ever that it would be a mistake for them to go alone and he really didn't have the time to go with them. Or the inclination. Enoch's mother would use the trip as a prolonged occasion to chide him to marry a nice Jewish girl. The only passion his parents had in life was for him to carry on the family line.

Frustrated that the day (while pleasant) had not resolved his problem, he set about to work, making up for lost time.

Most of the offices on the fifth floor were empty now. A few hours of quiet and he could catch up. A file of new information on the Moody case was on his desk. It was a straightforward and routine. One Ralph Moody started a charitable organization and became its chief beneficiary, filed as a standard 501(c) 3 scam. It followed the pattern, find a tearjerker cause, use clever fund raising, send enough money to starving children to satisfy the donors with a happy ending picture, and pocket the rest as salary. Americans are generous by nature, he believed, especially when that generosity is tax-deductible. Enoch despised people who preyed on others' emotions for their own profit, and bringing a scum-ball like Ralph Moody to justice was why he liked his job so much (and why he wanted to remain at the department). According to Laura, his job filled a certain need in him to crusade, and he thought she was probably right on some level. But he enjoyed the mental challenge and "the hunt"; finding the thread of deceit or fraud, unravelling it, and then bringing the weight of the Federal Government to bear upon white-collar criminals was satisfying.

He put aside the Moody file and started through his in-tray. A letter from Rosewood, Minnesota caught his interest. It was well crafted by a professional accountant, not the usual hysterical donor, recently enlightened to the facts of life. Mr. Phil Grant had a professional eye. There was no emotion — just the facts. After years in the department, reading thousands of such letters, Enoch knew the genuine article when he saw it. The man had a good grasp of the financial issues in question and his letter appeared to have an absence of malice. There was almost a tone of regret in the firm, clear prose. The writer knew his way around a 990.

Enoch laid the letter down. Thought about it for a few moments. Picked it up and read it again.

It wasn't the alleged misconduct that got his attention; he saw that every day in small fish like Ralph Moody. Enoch could successfully investigate people like that for years and never get promoted,. But Phil Grant of Rosewood, Minnesota was suggesting that the IRS should take a look at one of the most important Conservative media giants in America. Everyone in Washington, D.C. and half of America knew the name of the organization being accused by Phil Grant of serious wrongdoing. And the case had landed on *his* desk. Enoch could not contain his excitement. He couldn't wait to tell Laura. This was the break he had been looking for, and if Mr. Grant was right, it could make his career.

Too tense to sit, Enoch jumped to his feet and strode out to make a copy of the letter. For some reason he felt the need to file the original while it was in his hands. Calming down, he sat down to make some notes.

The facts were these: Mr. Grant had visited WOWL in October as their guest and winner of a contest. But he saw more than his hosts expected him to see and before he left Washington, Mr. Grant requested and received copies of the 990 tax records for the not-for-profit station of the giant WOWL, Inc.

Enoch felt a tightening in his chest, his fists clenching and unclenching. He often got a "feeling" about cases. And though his plodding, unimaginative boss liked to mock him about his hunches, this time he knew he was right. This case was real. And it could be huge. The Lorten family's media might extended throughout the country and he knew the administration was seriously worried about their political clout. These were the kind of people Enoch instinctively disliked and distrusted, purveyors of overt religious propaganda, and scions of power in the conservative wing of the Republican Party.

If the facts supported the concern of the writer, only then would this be his big break. And he must not get too excited, caution would be required. This opponent would bring very deep pockets and major political heft.

Enoch walked down the hall and poured himself a cup of stale coffee from the communal pot and nuked it for one minute. Watching the seconds count down on the microwave an uncomfortable thought dawned. How and why did Johnson give him something so potentially important? His boss had a greedy and discerning eye and he knew as well as Enoch the stakes of such a case. Hence, the scrawled note attached to the letter: "Take a close look at this one and talk to me Monday."

For whatever reason, Enoch had a case worthy of celebrating. Hoping to make amends for standing Laura up for dinner, he stopped on the way home to pick up flowers as a peace offering. His parent's trip and the enjoyable interlude with Dr. Lorten-Kissane were forgotten. He maneuvered his vintage car into the last available parking spot on their small Georgetown street shortly before 9:00 p.m.

If things progressed quickly on this investigation he would be far too busy to take his parents on a trip next spring, which would make Laura happy. And if it could be wrapped up in time, they could celebrate with that trip to France before the end of the year.

Already contemplating his first move the next morning, Enoch wondered idly as he charged up the brick steps of their Georgetown brownstone... what if Dr. Rachel Lorten-Kissane was in any way related to *the* Lorten family of WOWL, Inc? But quickly dispelled the thought as ridiculous before he even opened his front door.

CHAPTER 17

PTL

The church must be reminded that it is not the master or the
servant of the state, but rather the conscience of the state.

—*Martin Luther King Jr.*

Pleasantly plump, and easy on the eyes, Betty Logan tended to boxy suits in primary colors. With short, tight skirts that reduced her stride to mincing little steps, she created a signature sound that announced her presence around the fifth floor of the Internal Revenue Service building. Betty's overly neat boss was not easy to work for but he was fair. And she liked his crooked, little boy smile.

Engrossed in his reading, Enoch missed the give-away sound of Betty's approaching steps. Folder in one hand, other planted firmly on her hip, Ms. Logan stood in Enoch's doorway looking over the top of her glasses, waiting for her boss to motion her in for their scheduled briefing.

Betty had worked in the department for years, an able administrative assistant who was mostly content to remain behind when a series of bosses moved up the ladder. She knew, in her case, it was not so much a glass ceiling as it was her own limited training and ambition that kept her at the same level year after year. Betty liked to go home at the end of the day, have a beer, take her dog for a walk, watch the TV, and no amount of the women's lib guilt would move her to agitate for the job currently held by her handsome, much younger boss.

"Helloooo," Betty said, dropping her glasses, which were held by a pink spiral cord, onto her chest. She wore her going-gray hair in a tidy bun at the back of her head. A line of bright red lipstick stood out against light colored skin. She was a picture of organized, don't-mess-with-me efficiency.

"Okay, Betty, I do see you. Come on in and take a seat."

Her chair was positioned near the desk slightly to the side of Enoch so they could view papers together. She took it.

He leaned back, looking eager as a schoolboy.

"So tell me all about the illustrious Lorten family, Betty. Give me the dirt. And begin with the widow of Eric Kissane, the guy with the golden voice on the radio talk show."

Enoch now knew that the interesting woman he had met on the same day Johnson had given him the WOWL case file was indeed part of the family he hoped not only to investigate but to bring to justice. As unbelievable as the coincidence seemed to him, and despite the fact that the lady didn't fit any of his stereotypical expectations of a right-wing Conservative Christian, he was fascinated by the coincidence and wanted to learn more about her.

Glasses back on her nose, Betty opened the file.

"Sorry to disappoint you, sir, but there isn't much on the widow. She seems to avoid the press. And her family. The lady is some kind of scholar at a think tank. Not too unusual for D.C."

Enoch's voice sounded overeager, even to him.

"Maybe, but it's odd for this family. Did you happen to note which think tank?"

"Hmmm," Betty looked through the pages of notes. "No, it didn't seem important. But there is this." She pulled out a clipping from the *Washington Post*.

Enoch took it. It was a story about the funeral of Eric Kissane with a small picture of his wife entering the church in a group of family members.

"Which one is the widow? The beautiful one?" he asked.

"Nope. The pretty one is the sister-in-law, wife of Jeff Lorten. Now, Jeff is going to be of interest, but I'll come to him in a minute."

The picture was not good; it was grainy and taken from a distance. The widow's face was partially covered but it confirmed what he already knew.

Having trouble concentrating on Betty's description of the corporate structure of WOWL, Inc., he kept looking at the picture and trying to reconcile the thoughtful and interesting woman with the family of right-wing fanatics.

"Unlike his sister, CEO Ronald Lorten is always in the press," Betty was saying.

Enoch returned his concentration to her narrative about the Lorten family.

"It will take some time to fully research him, but the key facts are easily known and without dispute. Ronald Lorten runs the place. He is the CEO and Chairman of the Board at WOWL. The company, as you know, hefts a ton of conservative weight with their media empire. They are heavily invested in partisan politics, some would say right-wing politics; the family helped change the balance of power in the mid-term elections and is hated by the White House. Hate not being too strong a word here. They are seen as a threat by the administration in the next presidential race. Ronald Lorten also just got elected president of Christians in the Media Action Committee (CITMAC), so he wields a very big political stick. Younger brother Jeff works in the company but appears to spend most of his time as a guru of sorts to Congressmen and Senators, especially the disgraced ones. He holds Bible studies on the Hill and has written a book. It doesn't sound like my kind of reading, but the gist is... how to manage your career without falling off a 'tightrope' into all kinds of scandalous affairs, sexual and otherwise. It's about living your life at the pinnacle of power... and still being nice to your kids... that kind of thing."

Enoch wasn't that interested in Jeff Lorten or his book, at least not yet. He was, however, very interested in the CEO and fascinated by the sister.

"Is this all you found on the widow? I seem to remember the *Post* made a big deal about the funeral of her husband."

Betty looked up from her file, beginning to wonder about his interest in what appeared (at least to her) the least important player in the Lorten lineup.

"No," she responded without inflection. "That's about it. I mean you can find her credentials and degrees, which are pretty impressive, a list of articles she's written, but very little actual copy on her as a private person. She leads a very quiet life for a member of such a public family. What you are going to see is what I've already given you," she laid the file on his desk with just a slight look over the top of the glasses for emphasis.

She paused, and then let her curiosity get the best of her.

"Why do you think Rachel Lorten is important? The woman isn't an active participant in the business. She is a recent widow and it hardly seems fair to drag her into this... her brother, the CEO, is the target. Right?"

Enoch smiled but didn't respond.

"Close the door on your way out, will you, Betty? I need some quiet. No calls, please."

Happy to oblige, Betty took her mincing little steps back to her desk, glasses bouncing on her chest as she walked. This case was looking very interesting to her, too. It might be a big break for her boss. Taking on the

Lorten media giant would be a political, as well as legal, battle but Ms. Logan had seen many of the mighty fall during her years in Washington and figured WOWL was as susceptible as other overgrown, overconfident power brokers. The mighty do fall, and often make a very satisfying splash when they land.

Enoch Arnheim was an enigma to Betty. And to the other women in the office. Driven but not difficult, polite but never talkative, he gave very little away. And that's how she described him to her friends who always wanted to know what it was like to work for the handsome "other half" of State Department spokeswoman, Laura Stellar. He seldom mentioned her and there were no glamor shots of Ms. Stellar on the agent's desk.

Once the door was closed Enoch immediately began the long methodical read through the file. No matter how unimportant something might look at the outset of a case he had learned to ignore nothing. He'd sort the wheat from the chaff later.

It was getting dark outside before Agent Arnheim returned every-thing to the file in the order Betty had arranged it. Stretching his aching muscles, he strode around the room, his head nearly hitting the hanging light each time he passed. Pacing and thinking. Smiling and pacing.

His assistant was right, Ronald Lorten ran the company and would be the main target. His brother Jeff would be complicit. Both took sala-ries that would easily qualify as inurement and as Mr. Grant of Rosewood, Minnesota, had so correctly assessed — this, along with all kinds of ben-efits that were not obviously illegal but certainly questionable added up to enriching themselves at the expense of donors and shareholders. But inurement was a weak case; on its own, the general public still believed in the freedom to get rich and enjoy it. Rather than resent wealth in oth-ers, most Americans were inclined to idolize them and hope to join the ranks someday.

Enoch knew he would have to have an airtight case. The IRS could not be seen to be unfairly targeting conservatives again. Not after the Cincinnati office 'tea-party' scandal. He didn't want House Oversight Committee Darrell Issa coming after him for unfairly going after conservatives.

He looked at the letter from Phil Grant again. Then he read all of Betty's research one more time.

Ronald, Jeff, and Rachel Lorten had inherited the majority amount of stock in what was still a modest but growing company upon the death of their founder father over a decade ago. Despite that fact, Rachel currently held no position in the company and didn't take a salary from the family firm. She was still a voting member of the board of directors and a majority shareholder. Until his death in March, Rachel had been married to the most popular (and consequently, one of the most powerful media) personalities in the firm. His radio talk show had been reaching millions of listeners everyday all across America. Enoch wondered how Rachel Lorten-Kissane could be as removed from the family business as it first appeared, or if perhaps she wanted it to appear that way. He needed to talk to her again and felt reasonably sure she would comply. If he could come up with a plausible reason.

Enoch's random chance meeting with Rachel Lorten now seemed downright propitious. Since he didn't believe in fate or a divine being who guides all things, the extraordinary nature of the meeting couldn't be providence, but it sure felt like more than a happy coincidence . . if not luck itself.

"Betty," he called her desk. "Would you please order some pizza to be delivered about seven? Enough for three. Johnson is joining me and he eats more than two normal people."

A few minutes later, focused again on the case, Enoch's cell phone rang. It was Laura.

"How's your day been?" she asked.

"Good. Good. Busy. How about you?"

He listened to Laura's account of her day at the State Department too distracted to focus on world affairs.

"How's the new case developing?" she asked, trying to keep excitement out of her voice. He could hear it and he understood it. The little he had told Laura about the possible Lorten investigation had changed her attitude from 'get out of that dead end job'. She knew at once what it could mean to the administration. He had reminded her that one word to anyone at the White House and it would get leaked. The leak would be easily traced from him to her and that would not only end his chance to investigate the Lorten family but probably the case itself. Secrecy at this point was absolutely critical.

He was surprised she had mentioned it over the phone and cursed himself for telling her anything at this early stage. When he didn't answer she changed the subject. "By the way," she said apologetically. "I'm sorry but I'll be late again, I have to join the Romanian Ambassador for dinner. Let's make up for it with some time together this weekend, okay?"

Enoch was happy for some extra time to work. And glad Laura hadn't made him feel guilty about not joining her and the diplomats for dinner.

"Sounds good. Say hello to the Ambassador for me. I'll think about you enjoying your rack of lamb while I eat greasy pizza with Johnson."

She laughed. "Poor Enoch. Toiling away in the trenches for the American people."

"Love you, too," Enoch replied.

Increasingly difficult of late, Enoch's boss was becoming more and more isolated as the old administration faithful moved out and new young Democrats moved into the IRS. Commissioner was a political appointment; Johnson's replacement would be decided with much political maneuvering and require a lucky break for anyone wanting the coveted job.

Commissioner Henry Johnson was a slob. Brilliant, but a slob nonetheless. He had been in his office so long it even smelled like him. The IRS building was officially smoke-free, like all government agencies, but that didn't stop men like Johnson. Stale smoke hung in the air despite an air purifier stuck under his desk. But it was the clutter that drove Enoch crazy. Files were strewn all over the desk with more on the floor and books were piled precariously on shelves and chairs. The old man, as Enoch thought of him, despite the fact he was still well on the safe side of sixty, had a mind like a steel trap, otherwise the disorder would have defeated him long ago.

Enoch felt certain that Johnson was an old school anti-Semite, even though his superior had always been careful not to give overt evidence of such bias. His barbs about working with a New York Jew were tossed off as jokes. Laura thought Johnson's bias, if it did actually exist, was more likely cultural than racial. Enoch was a Yankee. And a liberal.

Johnson came from a southern good-ole-boy network, went to church with his pious wife on Easter and Christmas, and was counting on that to qualify him as Christian just in case the doctrines of the faith (to which he had been born and raised, but basically ignored) turned out to be true.

As much as Enoch disliked working with Johnson, he did not question his basic honesty. He had never known his boss to cheat, sweep anything under the rug, or stack the deck unfairly in an investigation. He was not above the occasional bias, but who wasn't? Every agent was biased, and the bias was suspicion.

"There's enough dirt out there without making any up," Johnson had told Enoch when he hired him. "Stick to the facts."

The usual mess greeted Enoch as he arrived half an hour later with the pizza. A possibly true story was often told that one day, when a newbie arrived from house cleaning to clean Johnson's office, she saw the mess and assumed a break-in. Johnson was not amused when the police arrived to investigate.

Enoch pushed the piles on the desk to one side and put the pizza down, along with his notes that included Betty's research and press clippings about the Lorten family

"So whaddaya got?" Johnson asked. "Besides pizza."

"Too soon to know for sure," he replied. "So far we have a letter from an irate donor, a guy who had given substantial amounts of money over the years to various appeals by WOWL, Inc. — the Christian broadcasting..."

"I know who they are," Johnson snapped.

"Okay. So the donor won a contest, some Bible trivia thing connected to a campaign to raise funds to help prevent human trafficking in Europe. He gets invited to visit the corporate offices of WOWL, the CITMAC conference, and to attend some gala out in Great Falls as his prize. You know, schmooze with the celebrities, that kind of thing. Problem is the contest winner happened to be a very smart accountant and it seems he saw more than the Lortens intended. Bad luck for them. Before leaving, he asks for copies of the 990s on the one station that's still run as a not-for-profit radio station."

"Yeah? So what? We talking fraud, tax evasion? What?"

"Like I said, it's too soon to say for sure. They obviously had highly paid legal counsel along the way and may be operating on the right side of the thin edge of the law. The whistle blower, this Phil Grant, does not appear to be your usual malcontent; his concerns certainly warrant a closer look. My initial research shows that the Lortens started out as a little non-profit outfit. The timeline then runs something like this: they raised the initial capital to buy the first radio station from small-time donors and it grew like crazy. When the oldest son, Ronald Lorten, took over at the death of his co-founder father, he took the company from a charitable ministry to a very successful, for-profit business over the next decade. And it worked a treat. They expanded across the U.S., leveraging funds, donations, and profits into massive growth. They bought up radio and television stations, bookstores, and got in early maximizing use of the Internet and new social media. They continued with limited eleemosynary projects (the founder had a genuine desire to do charitable works) through the original WOWL radio and television station that retained its 501 status. The accountant has a good eye, I'll give him that, he came up with the same questions I would have asked."

"Yeah. But you're one biased son of a bitch, Arnheim. Am I right?"

"If you mean," Enoch said in measured tones, "biased because the Lortens are Christians and I'm Jewish... that would disqualify me from a great many cases this department receives."

Johnson leaned his chair back and looked at his agent, calculating how far to go with his taunts. He knew Enoch wanted this so bad he could taste it. And he knew why. He chuckled.

"I'm just yanking your chain a little, Enoch. Lighten up. But keep in mind these are fundamentalist Christians who spend their time trying to e-vangelize people," Johnson said, drawing out his syllables. "Hell, they probably even want to e-van-jew-lize you. I wouldn't blame you for wanting to get them."

Enoch barely kept his cool.

"You know, sir, I am going to ignore how extremely prejudiced and politically incorrect that was so we can get back to the point," he replied.

Johnson laughed at having successfully needled Enoch, in reality though, he did have concerns about the agent's ability to be objective on this case. The reason he let it fall into Enoch's hands was because it could turn out to be too hot to handle, and not bring the glory he knew his subordinate was seeking, but the wrath of a very powerful voting block of the U.S. public.

Unbeknownst to Enoch, the Commissioner had held the letter from Phil Grant for a few days pondering what he wanted to do with it before passing it on to his talented but ambitious subordinate. Johnson realized its potential and its hazards. There were still a lot of evangelicals in this city (and in the country) who believed that the government, as a matter of principle, was out to get them. He had floated a few questions about the Lorten family past his wife, Edith, who had a great many friends in that community. Her response was, much as he expected, fiercely defensive. But in the end Johnson concluded that this case couldn't and shouldn't be buried, but that he didn't want or need the heat personally. In his career *or* his marriage. The Lortens were not "trailer park trash" like Jim and Tammy Faye Bakker or Jimmy Swaggart had been. The sophisticated Lorten family had many friends in high places. And despite its merit, the case was highly technical, which the government might win in court, but was very likely to lose in public opinion. After giving it a great deal of thought, Johnson decided his wife's response was probably a pretty good barometer of the support the Lorten family could count on in a pitched battle with the government.

After consuming too many pieces of lukewarm, soggy pizza Enoch tossed the box wondering why he kept ordering the stuff.

"Someday I want to succeed you as Commissioner, but then I think they may give me this office and I figure it wouldn't be worth it."

His boss snorted. "Forget the usual pleasantries and get on with it, Arnheim. Tell me more about the whistle blower accountant in Minnesota. Have you talked to him yet?"

"Actually, I have. And Phil Grant is not your usual disgruntled guy with an axe to grind. He sounds smart, with a firm grasp of the issues, and I sensed he might be genuinely sad to find out the truth behind an organization he's supported for years. Seems his wife listened to Eric Kissane's talk show every day, as did most of their friends. Grant has a little righteous indignation thrown in and I think he feels personally wronged from years of giving to what he thought was a good cause. Probably hard to sort out all his feelings and everybody hates to find out the people you looked up to are charlatans instead of saints. Still, he is not a raving madman, but a very careful accountant and maybe even a good citizen."

"Okay, so where is this taking us? Can the good citizen help us make a case?"

"I think so. We can probably prove inurement without much trouble. All the top executives live like kings, especially Ronald Lorten, the CEO, and his brother Jeff. Ronald pulls in several million a year, Jeff not far behind. Maybe tax or mail fraud, as well. Looks like some dodgy fundraising methods but frankly it's all pretty boring unless we can make the case with the public of excesses in compensation. People don't especially like rich people living off the donations of ordinary people."

"In other words, even the people of Wyoming might be offended?"

"Are there any people in Wyoming?"

Johnson laughed. He finished off a can of Diet Coke and looked at the paper Enoch had prepared with the central facts laid out concisely and cogently. Enoch waited for him to skim it.

"Sex always helps. Conservative family values and all that. Turn up a sex scandal and even the Christian public opinion will shift faster than you can say... "

"Sorry, sir. Nothing obvious has turned up yet, but it's early days still."

Enoch looked at his watch. It was getting late and he had more reading he wanted to do on the case tonight. "I need to be getting out of here."

"Sit down Arnheim... we're not through."

"I want to know how they got this big and this rich. Any sign of real fraud or riches gained from questionable foreign investment? Like, say, partnering with an African dictator in blood diamonds? In other words, do we have any damn thing other than good old-fashioned milking-the-donor cow?"

Enoch laughed. "I don't see anything quite as dramatic as diamond mines, sir. At least not yet. Seems its just the all-familiar methods used by many of these radio stations and para-church organizations. They start small using straight donations and then they raise money by selling tax-free bonds for legitimate religious programming or other kinds of ministry. The profit from sale of same is used to finance expansion that gets privatized for personal wealth. Like most small Christian stations, WOWL started out as a mom-and-pop, modestly sized non-profit, 501(c)3. They raised money (through tax-deductible contributions) for new towers and transmitters, and when they received more in donations than required to purchase the designated equipment they used the 'extra' to buy up other radio and cable television stations. Then, a few years ago, the company sold all but the original Washington station, WOWL Inc., back to themselves as 'for-profit' businesses at below market prices and they subsequently made a fortune. Retaining the one as a not-for-profit to raise funds for charity, like the recent, and very successful, Awareness Campaign. Most donors think the whole media empire is still a non-profit, charitable organization, when in reality that little non-profit station is just the tip of the Lorten iceberg. Seems like they tried this the other way around with a few of the smaller stations in the hinterlands when they started losing money. Set up another non-profit corporation, sell the non-profitable station for an excessive amount to the parent corporation (keeping the profit in the family) then raise funds to pay for it through donation appeals on air. Back in the 70s the message that raked in the dough was a virulent version of anti-communism plus Christianity, a profitable mixture. They raised a ton of money for smuggling Bibles into Eastern Europe. And now it's the 'cultural wars' that keep people giving. Fightening against abortion, for gun rights, to defeat the homosexual lobby, expose the liberal media for its mendacity. Lorten is a master at firing up the base."

Johnson was not surprised at the facts. He didn't admit it, but he was impressed with the speed his subordinate had accumulated them. He was careful in his response.

"It's still not illegal in this country to spend time and money defending and propagating different points of view. You are keeping in mind that we are barely out of the penalty box for 'flagging conservative" groups applying for tax-exempt status'. I don't exactly want another such scandal on my watch so you better be damned sure you are right before you breathe a word of this outside this office."

"Obviously, sir. I will be careful and I understand the risk. These kinds of schemes are more-often-than-not unethical as hell, but marginally legal. But this one is bigger! Huge. Not just the assets, which stretch across the country, but the political power they wield using radio, television, Internet, and all forms of social media."

"Bigger isn't illegal, Agent. It's just more tantalizing to you. So get your financial people working on the accounting details. I would be very surprised, given their legal counsel, Dudley, Smythe, & somebody, if this will be easy. And remember: unlike some of the people we go after, the Lortens have considerable resources to fight back and lots of people who will believe the Federal Government is out to get them (again). They will scream bloody political and religious persecution and liberal bias. Hell, they'll blame the White House and all kinds of other shit. Americans do have a rather strong affinity for the right to free speech. Try not to forget that, Arnheim."

"Again, I am aware of the risks, sir. But I think the facts will support the case. Any helpful suggestions other than to watch out for backlash?"

"You might want to look into misuse of restricted income. In fact, this recent supposedly charitable thing with human trafficking might be a good place to start. And see where all those funds actually went, despite the news coverage of them arriving in Sarajevo to dedicate a new facility or some damn thing to help those kids. Look at how much they raised. How much actually got to Bosnia. All that. You know that tele-evangelist Bakker didn't go to jail because his dog had an air-conditioned doghouse. It was the sex and fraud that brought him down. We could use a good scandal to go with these numbers, if you catch my drift. Don't make it up if it isn't out there, but don't miss it either, Agent. You might loathe my messy office, but I know you want the title, so don't bloody well miss it."

"I don't intend to, sir."

Enoch decided not to tell his boss yet that he had accidentally met one of the principals in the case. He would like to explore Rachel Lorten-Kissane as a source before telling his boss about her.

But, like he could read Enoch's thoughts, his boss asked.

"Do you know anyone on the inside? Anyone who might talk out of school?"

"Give me a break. I've had this for what, a few days? And it's not like I know lots of people in the right-wing Christian community."

"Just see who you can find who knows the family. Find someone who is willing to discuss the family. Off the record is fine. Check out your sources in the press. This family gets lots of coverage. Get out of the office and start looking. The rest of this case is not going to come in the mailbox from Minnesota."

The men worked for half an hour more before Enoch finally escaped from the smoke and mess into the beautiful fall night. Laura was not home when he arrived. Enoch got a cold beer from the refrigerator and switched on the eleven o'clock news. Bored by the time the anchorman, Gordon Peterson, got through the first five minutes of murder and rape in the District stories, Enoch went into the kitchen, dropped his tall, thin frame onto the uncomfortable retro fifties kitchen chairs Laura had picked out, propped his elbows on the pale pink granite table, and consumed a pint of Ben & Jerry's coffee ice cream.

Enoch wondered what was keeping Laura. Business dinners didn't usually take so long. The growing rift between them and his lack of interest in her pulling him up by her bootstraps might get even more complicated with the potential of his big break that could, ironically, help her too. The demise of the Lorten power base could mean a win for the Democrats, and if the current administration stayed in power, Laura would too. He pondered the strange turn of events while staring into the empty carton. The Lorten case could be big enough to advance his career. But despite his initial excitement, he knew Johnson was right, winning wouldn't be easy. And the climate for the IRS could not be worse. Conservatives had just proved there was bias in the agency and would be happy to pounce if he got this wrong. He wanted attention, but not the kind you get in front of an angry Oversight Committee.

Johnson said, "Look for scandal that will add legs to the story, and help us sell this in the press." No one in Washington had a nose for scandal like his friend over at the *Post*. And Tom Willis would still be up, the man never slept. Enoch would be careful not to leak, but a small fishing expedition couldn't hurt. Anyway, Enoch liked talking to the old newspaperman. His mind was one large filing cabinet.

He rang. The reporter answered.

They threw around jolly insults, laughed about some of the current stories in the press, and generally shot the bull together for some time before Enoch came to the point.

"Any scuttlebutt floating around about the Lorten family recently?"

There was a noticeable pause on the other end.

"Why do you ask?"

"Now, Tom, you know I can't say. Actually, it's personal," he lied. "I met the widow of Eric Kissane, the talk show guy killed in his fast car in March. She works over at Institute for Russian Studies and I'm checking out some things for my parents before they travel in that part of the world. And I found her interesting... highly intelligent and not at all what one would expect of a right-wing-fringe-possibly-fanatic fundamentalist Christian."

Tom's laugh was more of a snort.

"I'm not sure they're that bad but, as you say, an interesting bunch."

"So heard anything about them lately? Or her specifically?"

"Probably the same things you read... stuff always floats around people that controversial and powerful. But I can't say I've heard anything recently that's worth your time."

Both men had lived in D.C. long enough to know the "Potomac two-step" and each did it quite well.

Keeping his voice even, Willis moved piles of papers on his desk, desperately looking for a note from several months back. Someone, sounding scared but excited, had called him from Inova Fairfax Hospital (Organ Donor Unit) with a highly inflammatory tip. He couldn't remember the exact date but he remembered the tip.

Enoch ended the call with a false-cheerful last try.

"Well, if you think of anything, let me know, okay?"

"Hold on. I'm a little confused," Willis said. "Usually the leaks come from you to me. Seems to me like you're looking for information to flow the other way."

"A really clever river can run in both directions, you know."

"Well, all I can say is I'm glad you didn't go into science, my boy. Take care and say hello to the other half of D.C.'s 'most beautiful power couple'."

Enoch hated that Style Section gossip moniker, but coming from Tom Willis it was a friendly jab.

"Stuff it! You should be so lucky!"

Several minutes later, the newspaperman found the note he had scribbled back in March. It was about Eric Kissane. A married man, who is a pillar in the Christian community, shouldn't have HIV. Especially if one was also married into the most powerful Christian media conglomerate in the U.S. Now why is the ambitious Enoch, the bulldog IRS agent, all of a sudden interested in the Lorten family? He had seen pictures of the widow and he figured with a girlfriend like Laura Stellar, Enoch's interest in widow Lorten -Kissanen was not as personal as Enoch had hinted.

The reporter noted the time and details of his conversation with Agent Arnheim and made a proper file headed: WOWL – Kissane/Lorten family. Next time this came up (and now he knew it *would* come up) he wouldn't have trouble finding this very interesting piece of information. Timing was everything in his business. Timing and instinct. Tom was good at managing one and born with plenty of the other. He pulled out one of his favorite Cubans, sucked smoke into his already polluted lungs, and thought about things, with a satisfied smile on his wrinkled face.

Enoch set his alarm for 6:00 a.m. in order to get in an hour at the gym to work off the pint of ice cream and pizza, and then he went to sleep thinking about how to get Rachel Lorten- Kissane to see him again. This time they would not discuss his family, but hers.

* * * * *

Martha Culberson's day had begun with the usual boring task of scrubbing Ronald's calendar for the month. Her boss had a way of agreeing to appointments to please people, then giving Martha the task of notifying them of cancellation.

The second mail delivery of the day came at 4:00 p.m. Martha carefully sorted the always-heavy amount of mail, threw away the junk, opened the non-personal letters that she would answer, and took the rest unopened to the desk of Mr. Lorten. Her heart stopped when she saw the letter from Phil Grant.

Ronald knew Martha did a good job of discerning personal from non-personal mail and seldom made mistakes. Today had been no exception. A letter from Mr. Phil Grant, Minneapolis postmark, in a company envelope, return address Grant & Braucht, P.C., went directly onto Ronald's desk unopened.

It didn't take long for the explosion.

"Call Leif," he barked at her. "And Jeff. Tell them to meet me here at 5:00, and tell them it's urgent. And then take the rest of the day off. I won't be needing you."

While Martha called Jeff Lorten and pastor Leif Ohlsson, Ronald re-read the letter. It was short and to the point.

Dear Mr. Lorten,

As a Christian brother I believe it is only right I inform you of a letter I have sent to the IRS in which I described my concerns relating to the information observed from my visit to WOWL and 990 tax returns supplied to me by your office. It is with a very heavy heart that I have taken this action but I cannot, in good conscience, ignore what I now know.

It is my intention, by informing you of my actions, to give you time to consider your position and take steps to restore your financial policies to a strong legal and ethical position and so possibly ease the impact if an investigation ensues.

It is abundantly clear from scriptures that we all must obey the laws of the land, must render unto Caesar what is Caesar's, and be above reproach for the sake of the Gospel. It seems clear to me that you have taken the tithes and offerings of God's people under false pretenses and used these resources to enrich yourself, your family, and your company. I pray that you will be able to see beyond what will be understand-able anger directed at me and act quickly to make changes that restore the company to ethical, transparent, and charita-ble policies that are consistent with the image communicated to donors and sponsors. If you admit where you have made errors I am sure you can forestall a major investigation by the government and restore the witness of WOWL.

I have every desire to see the station make things right for the good of our shared faith.

Sincerely,

Phil Grant

CHAPTER 18

A MEETING OF THE MINDS

*They acquire the habit of always considering themselves as standing alone,
and they are apt to imagine that their whole destiny is in their own hands.*

—*Alexis de Tocqueville*

OHLSSON WAS ON HIS FEET, SHOUTING. SPITTING HIS WORDS inches from Ronald's face. Waving upstretched arms as if in worship instead of fury. Around and around the room he unleashed his tirade at a volume used to reach the back row of the stadium-like "sanctuary" of his church.

"You are one crazy, mixed-up, sorry son-of-a-bitch. Excuse my language. And utterly out of your mind. You had no right to put my church at risk by drawing us into the Awareness Campaign to save your own miserable hide. I should have known you would never go out of your way to help anyone unless it was politically or monetarily motivated. Spouting all that crap about caring for the victims of human trafficking, because it was crap, not real concern! I should have known. You had no right to suck me into this. No right. Now, as you so delicately put it, since I am already 'involved'... let me see if I got this right... now you are suggesting I should put the church at further risk, this time by actually laundering money through the Deacon's Fund."

Spent and defeated, Leif collapsed into the wing-backed chair next to Jeff Lorten, who had been stunned into silence by his brother's revelation of the blackmail.

"I can't believe you've done this to us," Leif mumbled. "I just simply can't believe this is happening."

Lorten waited. He wanted very much to at least defend one lone act. To say, *I did care, at least about the suffering of one young girl.* He had been in contact with Inspector Detective Kunis in Romania only once since meeting Nadia Iovan in Sarajevo. The man assured him that she was doing as well as could be expected. He had found a good facility for her in southern Austria and, he assured Lorten, she would be moved to the new Justice Center when it opened next year. The girl had yet to speak, but the staff was hopeful. Ronald knew he couldn't and wouldn't tell Leif or anyone else about helping her. Making it part of his self-justification would turn even that one possibly good thing to dust.

The men were alone in the Executive Suite. Martha had gone home for the day before they arrived. So Leif could rant all he wanted and no one would hear. He expected Jeff's reaction to be less volatile and less voluble. But no less angry.

Jeff, always a little afraid of his bigger, older, tougher brother looked stricken. He was shaking his hands like a pianist limbering his fingers, then running them through his hair. Unable to speak.

"I knew it," the pastor went on, a hint of self-pity in his crushed tone. "I knew something was wrong from that first night you arrived late at the restaurant pretending you had been overcome with the suffering of sexually exploited victims and a deep desire to rescue them. I knew it."

Ronald waited a moment before speaking.

"Interesting point, don't you think? Probably what any investigation would conclude as well. You knew and yet you went along."

"Bastard!" Leif shouted, jumping to his feet again. He moved aggressively around the desk like he was going to hit his old friend. "You unmitigated bastard."

Jeff, too, was on his feet, trying to calm the situation. Comfortable only with emotional violence, the kind he used against his wife, he put his hand on the pastor's shoulder and tried his best counselor voice.

"Leif. Calm down. Listen, this won't help. Let's at least hear Ronald out. I can't believe he has put us all at such risk without a plan... you must have a plan, brother, please tell me you have a plan. Because if word of this gets out it would do more than sink WOWL, it would ruin me as well. I will be finished on Capitol Hill."

Assuming the worst of the reaction was over, Ronald began in a measured voice. Leif was a practical man and would listen to reason; Jeff would do as he was told.

Choosing his words carefully, Ronald began maybe the most important speech of his career. Both Leif and Jeff were seated again looking at him with something like pleading.

"First of all, you should both remember I didn't get us into this mess! My beloved sister is to blame. It was her husband who cheated on her, and the victim of that relationship wanted restitution for the terminal illness he gave her. A somewhat understandable response on the part of the abused party, I think. Second, I had no idea it would put your church in any jeopardy, Leif. You have to believe me. I could have managed the campaign through WOWL alone but you were there that night. After the shock of the blackmail request, I started talking and you were interested. Don't pretend you didn't like the idea for your own reasons. It was your wife who encouraged you to participate. So, please drop the victimhood thing. It doesn't become you. And, yes, Jeff, I have a plan. We can still contain this thing and no one will be ruined, or even hurt. But I need your help."

There was a silence that, if not friendly, was at least silent. With no further protests, Ronald went on.

"First of all, we keep in mind that there are two separate issues to consider. One is the donor complaint letter, the other is the Hartford blackmail. It's their *convergence* that is the problem."

"Take the Phil Grant letter to the IRS... on its own it's probably not very damaging. Jeff, this is where you come in. You will be involved in meetings with Charlie Rice and the lawyers. None of them must ever know anything about the blackmail. We have to have a solid wall between the two issues. I can't afford you not knowing what was going on and asking stupid questions. And we can't risk the IRS doing an in-depth investigation right now because they might, and I want to stress here, *might* find the fictitious account I set up to pay Cricket Hartford. So we want to move the donor complaint issue out of the way as soon as possible. And, as it turns out, we raised so much money during the campaign that the consulting fee I used won't even be noticed. Except for the fact the consultant didn't do any work. I'm not sure how much my simple secretary Martha notices. I used her basically as a cutout for the nonexistent consulting firm. But she did meet the woman. First back in March, and then again yesterday; I don't think she made the connection but it is a possibility."

Leif groaned, head back staring at the ceiling. Jeff continued to run his hands through his hair.

Ronald continued to make his case.

"But the real issue now is not to make a bad situation worse by a second payment through the company. I simply cannot risk it. That is why it must go through the Deacon's Fund, Leif. I wouldn't do it if I had a choice. There is no need to panic but there is, however, a need to act. Quickly and carefully. Nothing said in this room gets beyond this room, for starters. Jeff, don't get tempted to tell your wife, who would, no doubt, tell our sister."

"You think I would actually do that?"

Ronald held up his hand signaling an end to further protest by Jeff on that point.

"Let's keep in mind we are not just protecting our company or your church, Leif, or your career, Jeff, but our nation. The IRS would love nothing more than to come after us and deal a blow to the administration's main foe. As the recent scandal has proved. Agents in the IRS have been known to target conservatives. We might be able to use that. The stakes don't get any higher. We can't afford Cricket Hartford leaking even a hint of scandal now and to prevent that I have to make this one last payment. The Deacon's Fund is a safe way to do it. I put up the money, Leif. Not a cent of church funds will be used or misused. And there is no way the Feds will check out the Deacon's Fund. They never have. Never will. Furthermore, it isn't a good time politically to go after a mega-church like yours, so stop being such a little girl and listen."

"The insult added to injury doesn't help," Leif shot back.

"First of all, this idea is not risk-free as you very well know, but let's say I am stupid enough to step out even further on this limb with you and agree to use the Deacon's Fund. What's to say this Cricket Hartford woman won't be back?"

"Because I say so!" Lorten snapped. "You're going to just have to trust me on this one. I say she won't be back for more and I have my reasons." In reality he had nothing but a gut instinct and his belief that Cricket Hartford was really not a bad person, just a desperate one caught in a bad spot.

Leif rolled his eyes at the idea of trusting Lorten's instincts, but managed not to state the obvious.

"But what if people find out?" Jeff moaned. He was having trouble following Ronald's argument since all he could see was his own ruin. "A scandal will be the end of my ministry on the Hill. I'm supposed to be the one helping others 'walk the tightrope of power without falling off'... this thing will kill me if it gets out."

"Do stop whining, Jeff. You have the least at stake. You can just become one of the boys in your group. Most of the men you work with have made morally questionable decisions and they will be even more comfortable with you if they find out you have too. Confession loves company. Think of all the divorced marriage counselors. People seem to like talking to people who share their weaknesses. You would be fine. Eventually. But the company, and our political power, that is another story. And Leif, I hate to remind you of this, but try to remember where the majority of funds came from to build your little empire over there at Washington Bible Church. So, all three of us jolly well better make sure no one ever reads the name Cricket Hartford in the *Washington Post,* unless it is in the Obits."

"I think she's bluffing," Jeff added somewhat feebly. "She can't tell anyone. She's the criminal here and blackmail is still a crime. She should go to jail! So let's call her bluff."

"She wouldn't be the only one to go to jail, little brother. And she doesn't have to expose herself in order to implicate us. That is the Sword of Damocles she's holding over our heads. All she has to do is leak enough information to the press, anonymously, so it catches the eye of the Feds who, we happen to know, are already thinking about investigating us, thanks to that ingrate Phil Grant. The IRS will be looking for any hint of scandal, salivating over the *hope* of a scandal, sex being the very best kind, to get the public's attention, to add to what would otherwise be a boring case of accounting details. The lady doesn't even have to put herself at risk to get their attention. And don't forget she knows the ways of Washington and has more than a few friends in high places. Men who would probably be happy to do a little favor for one in return."

Defeated, furious and afraid, Jeff and Leif fell silent.

"Okay," Ronald said, taking their silence as acquiescence. "Here's what we do. No paper trail. No computer trail. No cell phone messages. No pillow talk." He looked at Leif. "Nothing. We only discuss this in person. Leif, I will give you a check but you have to keep it anonymous. No one on the Deacon Board can know the source of the donation. The Clerk will see the check but good ole Lewis can be trusted to do your bidding. So, my check for $100,000 will be made out to the Deacon's Fund and Cricket has set up a bank account in the name of the fictitious AIDS Charity with a P.O. box address somewhere out in the country where she lives. Leif, you will make the request to the Board the very next time they meet. You *know* the Deacons won't say no to you. They never do. But you should make sure there are no minutes of the meeting. Mistakes happen. Files get deleted.

"So Cricket Hartford stays quiet. I get the lawyers to handle the Phil Grant accusations. Maybe I'll find a reason to let Martha go sometime soon, which I have to say would be a relief anyway. Her earnest, doormat personality is making me mean. Come on, guys, trust me. We can't sit around and wait for this to blow up in our faces."

One of the many problems with his friend's plan, Leif thought, was that 'good ole Lewis' Robinson, clerk of the Deacon's Board for many years, was a meticulous and principled man. Making the minutes disappear wouldn't be easy. Possible but not easy. Lewis wrote up the files after each meeting and e-mailed them to the Records Office. Down the road a month or so, he could ask to see a year's worth of minutes and then send the attachment back to Records with that one missing. Removing the hard copy from the file would be even easier. And Ronald was correct; no one had ever investigated the Deacon's Fund, either the amount or the purpose. The auditors were accustomed to large donations being processed through the committee and had never questioned any of the payments. Still, his head was throbbing as he tossed back an Excedrin without water before surrendering. His rich baritone voice, the magnificent organ of communication that moved tens of thousands of people every Sunday morning, was barely a whisper when he agreed.

"I'll set it up for tomorrow's meeting. Might as well get it over with because if I think about this too long I might just blow the whistle on you myself."

CHAPTER 19

BERTA'S BETTER BAGELS

Before I built a wall I'd ask to know
What I was walling in or walling out,
And to whom I was like to give offence.
Something there is that doesn't love a wall.

—*Robert Frost*

NAKED LADIES STOOD IN A ROW NEXT TO THE WROUGHT IRON fence of Berta's Better Bagels Shoppe, their desolate single stalks now stripped of once ample pink blossoms.

"Why did they ever choose a name like that?" Rachel asked as she knocked over one of the spindly stems with her car door.

"Because men love them, I guess," Ellie laughed.

"The flower?"

"No, dummy."

It was mid-morning when the friends arrived at the Bagel Shoppe. Ellie had sounded upset when she called and asked Rachel to meet her for coffee.

The privately owned shop was squeezed between much larger, modernized office buildings on increasingly expensive land. People had been grabbing a cup of coffee and one of Berta's Better Bagels on their way to the Arlington Metro stop for years. Not much had changed inside since the proprietor had decided to bring New York bagels to Northern Virginia over a decade ago.

Still warm for late fall, the front door was propped open. Inside, the familiar yeasty smell, mingled with slightly burnt crust, greeted them. Untouched by clever marketing ideas, the shop, like Berta's freckled face, had settled into a comfortable slow decline into middle age. A yellowed *Washington Post* eatery review from 1990 was still taped to an old fashioned cash register assuring readers they would enjoy the "charm and absolutely delicious homemade bagels baked daily by Berta herself". And most everyone did.

Berta had been kneading, rolling, kettling, and baking the real thing for the neighborhood since long before upscale chain bakeries started providing uniformity and a plethora of choice from spicy jalapeno to sweet raisins. A loyal following remained with Berta's Better Bagels because of her Jewish grandmother's recipe, the authentic taste, and her own hard work (combined with genuine interest in her customers). Berta never wanted for customers and customers never wanted for the familiar comforting taste.

Oak bins with glass doors held the handmade, irregular-shaped plain, poppy seed, or onion bagels. Three small Formica tables provided a limited eat-in sitting room but most people grabbed their bagels on the run.

The coffee was weak, but philosophical patrons reasoned accurately that one cannot have everything in this life and forgave the failing.

A growing immigrant population from Africa and Asia had changed the dynamics of the neighborhood and Berta, the friendly baker, loved the diversity. She was happy to let the world come to her. Everyone received the same friendly welcome in the comfortable old shop.

Berta was behind the counter when Rachel and Ellie arrived, her thick ginger hair stacked in an unruly bird's nest atop her head. Handcrafted silver elephants dangled from her ears and graced her long neck.

Rachel had been visiting the shop since she was in junior high, before the family moved from Arlington to Great Falls. A great deal of teenage angst had passed from Rachel's heart to Berta's broad shoulders; she got fresh baked bread and a secular confessional. But the friendship never transcended the confines of the bakery. As a teen, Rachel thought she was alone in receiving the special brand of compassion served with her bagels, but truth was that many struggling and lonely souls found kindness (as well as comforting carbs) in the little shop.

"Good morning," Berta greeted them. "Sharing one again or splurging on a whole bagel each today?"

They took the usual. One plain bagel shared between friends.

"I'm glad I don't have to count on you two for my profits," the proprietor laughed, slicing the still-warm bagel and filling a tiny glass pot of cream cheese for each plate.

"Did you remember to bring me pictures of your new house?" Berta asked Rachel while pouring the pale brown liquid into big china mugs.

Suitably impressed after studying each picture of the restored carriage house, Berta pronounced it a masterpiece and congratulated Rachel on a brilliant design.

Glad to rest her tired feet, Berta sat chatting unaware that Rachel and Ellie really wanted to be alone.

"How's Lewis?" Rachel inquired, trying to be friendly but hoping for a short answer.

"He's tired. That's how my poor Lewis is. I keep telling him to resign from the Deacon's Board — those meetings go on until all hours. But does he listen to me? He has been clerk for ten years! Sometimes the meetings run so late he's so tired when he gets home, he doesn't know if he is

Arthur or Martha. It's too much for him, especially when the meetings get contentious."

Rachel and Ellie laughed at her funny, old-fashioned expressions.

"What's to disagree about?" Ellie asked. "Aren't they just there to help distribute money to people in need?"

"You have no idea," Berta sighed again, finally getting up to serve a late-arriving commuter.

"So what's up?" Rachel asked quietly now that they were alone. "You sounded so upset on the phone. Is it Jeff? The kids? What's up?"

Ellie shook her head.

"No, no nothing like that. I'm sorry to worry you, and take you out of the office. But I really needed to talk to you. Now."

"It's okay. I'm always glad for a chance to get out of the office. So tell me what's wrong."

"Last night," Ellie lowered her voice to a whisper. "I overheard Jeff talking on the phone. And what I heard really scared me. I couldn't sleep and as soon as the kids left for school, and Jeff the office. I called you."

"What? What did you hear?"

"Jeff was talking to Ronald. And he was furious. More than furious. Scared. And it was something about the company. Do you know what's going on?"

Rachel laughed. "You're kidding, right? You know my brothers wouldn't tell me anything and with Eric gone I, thankfully, know even less about the family business. But who cares, whatever it is, if it's about the company, we don't have to worry about it. Except, I have to say I have been surprised and pleased to see them actually do something good recently. The Justice Center in Sarajevo will be a great thing for all those victims of sexual violence. I almost feel proud to be a Lorten lately... so don't burst my bubble. Let it go... they'll work it out."

"Please listen to me, this is serious. I think Jeff and the company might be in legal trouble. I would have to worry about that... rather a lot actually. Can you imagine what a scandal would do to our kids at this age? Especially Justin! They don't need the trauma."

"What kind of trouble?" Rachel was not nearly as unconcerned as she tried to sound. "What exactly did you hear?"

Keeping her voice low, Ellie continued, "I went to bed before Jeff, not unusual, but I couldn't sleep and decided on a snack so I went downstairs and heard him talking on the phone. Something in his voice made me stop. I hesitated outside the door, not meaning to lurk there listening like a kid through the keyhole, but when I heard his tone of voice, well, I couldn't *not* listen. He was saying something about a meeting, and that he had thought about it more and just couldn't take the chance of putting his career or the family at such risk. And the strange part is he mentioned your name a couple of times."

"Are you sure he mentioned me?" Rachel tried not to gasp. "How? What did he say?"

"Something about not caring about what it did to you. Which makes no sense unless, unless there is some connection to Eric and that is why I am so upset. Why I had to tell you now, Rachel."

Rachel couldn't speak. But she could think, and nothing comforting was coming to mind.

Ellie went on.

"I tell you, whatever it is, Rachel, my husband sounded more upset, more scared than I can remember... he didn't come to bed all night and he was gone when I got up this morning. Blackmail is all I can think of. What if someone from Eric's messy past is blackmailing the company? What other kind of legal trouble could it be? Oh my God, my God... the press will love this. I'm mostly sorry for what it will do to you, but I'm also worried about Justin and Sally. They're at the age where being embarrassed is worse than being dead."

Rachel could actually think of several ways the company might be in trouble other than blackmail. Please Lord, she prayed, let it be something more mundane like an irate donor. It had happened often enough before and the lawyers would know what to do.

"Was that all?" she asked trying to sound unafraid. "What else do you remember?"

"Not much. I thought about just walking in and confronting him, forcing him to tell me what was going on. Then I remembered how well that kind of thing works with Jeff and changed my mind."

"Okay," Rachel said, trying desperately to find a reasonable explanation other than the worst one. "First of all, it's not necessarily anything to do with Eric. So let's not jump to worst-case conclusions. It has been nearly nine months and no one has come forward yet to have their fifteen minutes of fame by claiming an affair with him and I think they would have by now. I mean, why wait so long? That just doesn't make sense. At the time of his death or shortly thereafter, that would have been their moment to exploit it if they meant to do so. And besides, the revelation of his affairs would cause a scandal and hurt the station, but it wouldn't put my dear brothers in legal jeopardy, so I don't think it could be that... "

"It would if they gave in to blackmail," Ellie stated the obvious.

"Okay. That's true but it is also highly unlikely that Ronald would go weak at the knees at a threat and give into blackmail. Certainly not to protect me, and why would he be telling Jeff about it now? So let's focus on what you actually heard and possible explanations."

Their divided bagel was growing cold. Rachel went on.

"Ellie, I've known for a long time that Ronald skates on the thin edge of what is legal in business practices. He justifies it with 'we are doing important work for God and the current laws are punitive. The IRS is out to get conservatives'. That kind of thing. 'Liberals control the media and without the voice of WOWL the other side won't be heard'... etc., etc., etc. Sometimes donors get upset about the lifestyle of company executives, especially Ronald. But it has never risen to the level of actual charges. Part of the company is now for-profit and under different Federal guidelines. And I know Ronald has a phalanx of expensive lawyers whose job it is to ensure the company stays legal, if not absolutely ethical. Maybe this time a disgruntled donor has made a serious charge. Or something was just mismanaged and someone found out. I imagine Ronald was asking Jeff to lie, and Jeff was refusing to do so because as everybody in Washington knows the cover-up is always worse than the crime. Just think Nixon, Reagan, Clinton, to name a few. I mean, Jeff counsels people like that all the time. I can imagine Ronald asking Jeff to fall on his sword for the company and Jeff not exactly being willing to do so."

Ellie did not look convinced.

"And your name came up why?"

That, of course, was the point she was trying very hard not to think about.

"Not sure. But I am the fourth largest shareholder after Ronald, Jeff, and mother... maybe it was a fight about whether or not to bring me into the discussion."

"Not likely, Rachel."

"Okay, maybe not likely. But possible. Unethical, I would believe about Ronald. Criminal, I don't think so. He isn't that dumb. Another possibility is that the administration is pushing the IRS to rattle the cage for political reasons."

"Didn't you tell me a handsome IRS agent came to you see you about getting information for his parents' trip? Maybe that is a little too random? Have you seen him again?"

"See him again for what? And I didn't remember calling him handsome."

"You did. And don't change the subject. I hear this heated conversation right after an IRS agent 'just happens' to come see you. Don't you find that strange?"

"No, I think the man wants to prepare his parents for a safe trip into an unknown part of Russia. Not like they are going to the opera in Moscow. But back to what you overheard... what to do is nothing. Just hope it goes away."

"Well, that's a great strategy."

"Do you have a better one? I, personally, am not inclined to call either one of my brothers and ask them if they have been blackmailed recently. Especially not about my late husband."

Ellie grinned. "It would be funny if it wasn't so scary."

They nibbled their bagel and tried to drink the bad coffee, both caught up in those scary thoughts.

Ellie knew that if a highly publicized family scandal exploded it might just set Justin, already angry at life, over the edge and in full flight from his faith. And despite her assurances to Ellie, Rachel knew the problem very well could be related to Eric's sordid past.

If Eric had been as promiscuous as the medical evidence seemed to support, there had to be several (probably very unprincipled) women out there willing to extort money from the Lorten family to keep it quiet.

"So," Ellie finally said again, "What are we going to do?"

"Well, we can't go back and change the past so we will just have to go forward, one day at a time."

Rachel knew her answer was annoyingly cliché but she didn't have anything better.

"Sorry, but a cliché now just isn't very helpful. And it's no time to be philosophical. I want to do something to protect my family. To protect you. There must be something we can do. Maybe I should talk to Jeff?

"Oh, good heavens, no! Don't do that. While every marriage counselor in the world would disagree with me, I think communication in marriage, especially in yours, is highly overrated. And now isn't a good time to start. He's your husband, but I strongly advise you not to confront Jeff about what you heard. This may go away on its own and the less you know about it the better. Just continue taking care of your kids and the millions of things you seem to get done for other people every day... and taking me out for Lebanese food occasionally... and don't say anything. Don't ask anything. And stop listening through keyholes... remember that very important lesson drilled into us as children. In fact, as Hegel said, at least I think it was Hegel who said, 'we do not need more instruction in life, just reminders.' Well, anyway, let me remind you to stop listening to Jeff's private conversations. Better not to know some things. And this might be one of them. We can at least take comfort in the fact that the law firm of Dudley, Smythe & Dudley are paid to be very, very good at what they do."

"Maybe," Ellie said sounding not all that convinced. "And we need to pray."

Pray for what? Rachel wondered. That God would prevent justice if justice needed to be done? If WOWL had broken the law, or heaven forbid, had been blackmailed and used ministry funds to pay off the blackmailer — should she pray the crime goes undiscovered? My first prayer, she thought, is simple and selfish: protect my privacy. And my second prayer is for Ellie and the kids. The first, she knew, was not only selfish but morally questionable. She had chosen a particular path and it was hardly God's fault if logical consequences had followed. In order to spare her privacy, a crime might need to go unpunished. Please God, she prayed silently, please sort that out. But she had to suspend logic to believe God could, or would.

"Of course I will pray," Rachel assured her. "I pray for you and the kids every day. And for your husband, my brother whom I don't like very much, I pray that God will spare him from what he probably deserves. If not for whatever this is, then for how he treats you."

Rachel sat in the quiet of the bagel shop for some time after Ellie left. Her thoughts were not nearly as uplifting as the light breeze blowing through the still-open door or Berta's warm smile.

CHAPTER 20

DINNER PARTY

Ain't it just like the night to play tricks when you're tryin' to be so quiet?
We sit here stranded, though we're all doin' our best to deny it
And Louise holds a handful of rain, temptin' you to defy it.

—*Bob Dylan*

ELLIE WATCHED THE BLUE SHEET FLOAT GENTLY DOWN UPON Justin's bed like a parachute coming to rest. She gave another sharp snap and it lifted again, gathering air before settling now perfectly centered on all four corners — so unlike her life. Ellie was thinking how nice it would be to just have her friends for dinner tonight without Jeff, when she looked up and saw his brooding presence in the doorway.

"Really, Ellie," he said with contempt. "I thought we paid Manuela to do that sort of thing."

Justin's room was chaos, reflecting his current state of mind. But she saw no evidence of real anger or self-destruction. And she looked for such signs. Life was not easy for anyone in the Lorten household, especially Justin. Means did not equate with satisfaction, or things with joy. They had way too much in the way of means but were, in her estimation, woefully lacking in simple family joys. Their lifestyle made her uncomfortable, but she had to admit it also made her very comfortable.

It did seem ridiculous to Ellie that their children each had a lavish suite of rooms instead of a simple bedroom. The actual bed was situated in a spacious area that included a couch and comfortable chairs; adjoining room included a personal bath, walk-in closet, and study. When she asked, what had happened to just sitting at the kitchen table to do your homework, it had not gone over well with Jeff or the architect.

Jeff and Ellie's house was red brick Georgian on five very expensive acres. It was modeled after the stately homes in Williamsburg, classic but with every modern comfort. They lived very, very well. She wasn't exactly sure what inurement meant, but she knew it had something to do with their lavish lifestyle paid for from the family business that had once been a true Christian ministry. It felt wrong to her too but Jeff thought she should be glad for all the things their money could buy and took any questions about it as criticism.

Manuela's husband Domingo tended the grounds. Their immigration status was not clear but Ellie liked the Honduran couple and knew how much they needed the better-than-average wages that she managed to pay them despite Jeff's views on the subject. The couple enjoyed their own living quarters in the bottom level of the house with a private entrance from the back garden. Domingo kept the roses pruned, created and tended flower gardens, and trimmed the trees and boxwoods to perfection. Not a weed could be seen in the lawn. He cut flowers from the garden daily which they enjoyed for nine months out of the year. Long stemmed bouquets of peonies were now scattered throughout: on mantels, coffee tables, even in the empty guest rooms and on the island in the kitchen.

Unlike the children's large and underused bedroom suites, the spacious gourmet kitchen, overlooking the English garden, was well used. There was a high volume of entertaining required of the very connected Jeff Lorten, and Ellie encouraged the kids to have their friends over on a regular basis. She liked to cook for the family but Manuela was the real master of the culinary domain, brilliant at making ordinary healthy meals for the family or gourmet feasts for important guests. The cook looked less than happy as Ellie joined her in the kitchen. Manuela was frowning as she spread simple butter chocolate frosting on a flat yellow cake. The dessert did not meet her high standards and compliance with the strange dinner menu had put Manuela in a rare bad mood.

Ellie's (and Rachel's) college friends, Bob and Susie Redmond from Indiana, were in D.C. for the Nurserymen Association meetings and were invited to dinner. Ellie and Rachel had met Bob and Susie on their first day of college in the dining common. It was the first of many meals shared together during the next four years. Geography had created distance, but not estrangement, in their friendship, and Ellie was looking forward to hosting *real* friends for a change instead of Jeff's high-powered colleagues or clients.

"Oh, yummy," Ellie said, dipping her finger into the chocolate frosting.

"I could have come up with something better than this tasteless yellow cake, ma'am. Like my Jimmy Cake. You all love a good Jimmy Cake. It isn't too late... "

Ellie grinned and patted the much shorter woman on her shoulder.

"Don't worry, Manu. No one will blame you. It's a college thing and tonight is all about walking down memory lane with old friends."

"So that explains macaroni and cheese made with *Velveeta* cheese?"

Ellie nodded, fighting a desire to laugh. Manuela had visibly shuddered at the very idea of using processed cheese in her cooking.

"Well," she snorted. "I cannot see Mr. Lorten being very happy with macaroni and cheese made with *Velveeta*!"

"Well then, let him eat cake."

The classical allusion was lost on Manuela, who went on frowning as she tried to make sense of a dinner party with such a terrible menu.

Ellie left her cook with the food preparation and went to check out the dining room. Everything looked perfect. The bold blue of her Royal Dalton China contrasted nicely with the snow-white tablecloth. While the menu might be college fare, the setting and wine would be fine. The table-cloth was from Bosnia. A gift, she presumed, pressed on Jeff at the airport, last minute, since he had tossed it in his case and out onto the bed when he unpacked. Jeff did not talk much about the trip to Sarajevo except to say he was glad to be out of that "dreadful place". Ellie liked the delicate handcrafted work and wondered about the woman who made it, why she felt the need to thank one of the Americans. Maybe it was someone whose daughter had been abducted. The fine cotton cloth was stitched around the edge with crocheted cutout rose patterns set diagonally from a petal shaped center. A bouquet of tall sunflowers brightened and lightened the mood. Ellie wanted everything perfect, but not formal.

It was after eight when Jeff joined his wife, his sister, and their guests in the library where pre-dinner drinks were being enjoyed along with bite-sized savory meats and soft cheeses on crackers. Strips of bacon wrapped around almond-filled figs, skewed with toothpicks, were an exotic addition Manuela had added to show her culinary might before the terrible meal to come.

"Jeff, Bob. Bob, Jeff. And," Ellie said, turning to Susie. "Susie, this is my husband, Jeff. I think you all met at graduation but there were rather a lot of people there and... "

"Nice to meet you, Bob. Susie. Hello, Rachel." Jeff's firm grip and friendly smile disarmed the somewhat nervous couple. They were not accustomed to dining with powerful media moguls.

"So what do you do out there in Indiana, Bob?" Jeff asked, managing to make Indiana sound a little like a foreign country.

"I manage a nursery."

Desperate to keep a rising panic out of his voice, Jeff wondered how he would endure an evening with a man who took care of children.

"Really? Isn't that... rather, I mean, wow that must be awful... ah rewarding," he stuttered.

"A plant nursery, dear." Ellie said, coming to his rescue. "Bob started a very successful chain called Green Acres Nurseries. Bob and Susie are here for the American Nurserymen and Landscape Association meetings."

Plant business, Jeff decided, might be marginally less boring than managing children.

"Well done," he said with gusto. "America needs small businessmen like you. Without so much government regulation you could probably be doing even more business. Am I right, or am I right?"

Dinner was not spectacular but Manuela's addition of arugula salad with lemon garlic vinaigrette was a welcome relief, especially when washed down with a fine Malbec. "You know some of us no longer have the metabolism for college food, Ellie," Rachel said, piling her plate with the salad.

Bob begged to differ and happily ate two big helpings of the creamy pasta.

"You look wonderful, Rachel," Bob said. "You are wearing the years well, despite this last hard one."

"Hear, hear," her brother said, raising his glass. "To Rachel. She has been a very brave widow. And we all miss Eric," he added dishonestly.

"What are you going to do now that you're on your own?" Bob continued. "Go back for yet another degree? We think of you as the perpetual student, Rachel. Smarter than all of us combined."

Jeff choked on a piece of arugula but mustered a smile worthy of a loving brother.

"Rachel's newest interest is architecture," Ellie explained. "She just designed her new home in the family's old carriage house and it is magnificent."

"I didn't actually design it, Ellie. I had an architect but I envisaged it and it came out rather well. I'd love to show you guys if you have time tomorrow morning."

"Let's all meet there for breakfast. Not that Rachel can cook but I will pick up bagels from Berta's Shoppe on the way if you could manage the cream cheese."

"Very funny, you don't need to bring anything. I'm rather domestic at the moment. And since we all skipped breakfast during college I won't have to recreate some bad 'memory' food."

"Hey, I like dining common cake," Susie replied, finishing up a second piece.

A sliver of moon hung in the starless sky as Jeff and Ellie waved goodbye to their guests at the door, their smiles fading as it closed.

"Finally," Jeff said. "I thought they would never leave. And was it absolutely necessary to serve that dreadful food? Lord, that was awful, Ellie."

"Oh... it wasn't so bad," she said, trying to avoid a battle. "We enjoyed it." Ellie had expected an outburst; she knew she would pay for having been herself at dinner and not playing the adoring wife.

"Well, I don't know if your guests enjoyed it. And you never stopped talking. It was embarrassing how you and Rachel totally dominated the conversation. In fact, you might have had one glass of wine too many."

She *had* participated more than usual in the conversation, voicing her own opinions instead of confirming whatever position Jeff postulated. He had never been able to abide even the suggestion of independent thought from her in front of other people. How anyone so gifted could be so insecure never ceased to amaze Ellie.

They moved side by side but not together toward the kitchen, carrying dessert plates and coffee cups from the dining room.

Coke cans and potato chip crumbs were scattered on the marble counter top.

"Damn kids," Jeff growled when he saw the mess. "Go get them down here right now. They're old enough to clean up after themselves."

"They probably would if we didn't have a maid who regularly did that for them," Ellie suggested. "Jeff, please don't take your bad mood out on the kids. Shout at me if you must but not them this time."

He slammed a stack of plates on the counter.

"What does that mean? This time? What is that supposed to mean? I'm not in a bad mood and I don't 'take things out on the kids'. I am a mature parent capable of deciding when my children need discipline. In fact, I'm a bloody expert in the field and I think I deserve at least some respect and support from my wife."

It hadn't been a bad evening. She was sure only Rachel noticed Jeff's tension and frustration with the conversation. His gifts were small talk and charm and both had been on ample display to the guests during dinner.

"I'm not in a bad mood," he said again. "Why would I be in a bad mood anyway? Other than having been forced to listen to banal college memories and consume bad food while pretending to like both!"

Ellie put her perfectly manicured hands on the sparkling marble countertop; leaning forward she looked at her husband in earnest, wanting to find a way to live in peace with this man. Silence and subservience had not worked over the years and it scared her how much she was beginning to envy Rachel's singleness.

"That's rhetorical, right?" she said. "I mean, Jeff, you can't really pretend this anger you have against me whenever I show the slightest individuality in a social setting is not real. You take it out on me and the kids get caught in the backdraft of your anger. I'm tired of it."

None of the many people who looked to Jeff Lorten for spiritual and emotional support would have recognized the man staring at his wife, anger and contempt distorting the amiable features he was known for.

"You are an ungrateful, irrational, and disrespectful wife, Ellie. After all I've done for you, this is the way you thank me." He waved his hand around the room. "I provide this beautiful home, with everything you could possibly want, but do you thank me? Or appreciate it? Or even pretend to be a submissive wife? God forbid. And now after putting up with your pathetic friends and my miserable sister all evening, on top of a terrible day at work, you accuse me of being in a bad mood. I am not some kind of an emotional cripple that explodes for no reason. God Ellie people pay me to help *them* manage emotion and they are grateful. You can't even show minimal respect for me as your husband. Never mind recognize that I am an authority in the field of how to discipline children."

"I think you know this has nothing to do with a few crumbs on the kitchen counter or my choice of menu," Ellie said in a quiet, defeated voice

"You never worry about my needs, Ellie. It's always Rachel this or poor Rachel that. Or the kids this or the kids that. You never have anything left for me. I'm struggling with a boatload of terrible problems, maybe even dangerous ones at the company, and I could use a little support."

The kitchen was suddenly very still.

"Dangerous problems at the company? What kind of danger- ous problems?"

As much as Ellie hated the state of her marriage, she dreaded real upheaval.

There was so much between husband and wife that divided and hurt; yet, they had two beautiful children far away upstairs in a house so big people didn't have to really live together most of the time, but who did need their parents to hold it all together for them.

"What terrible problems, Jeff?" She blurted out, forgetting Rachel's advice. "I heard you talking to Ronald the other day on the phone and it scared me. Please tell me what's going on."

He looked at her then, really looked at his wife whose beauty still amazed him but no longer moved him emotionally. He hesitated, some part of him wanting to confide in her. She held his gaze, willing him to speak. It might be too far back to real love, but vows, children, and time bound them.

The moment of wanting to share with his wife passed.

"Don't worry about it. We've had problems before and it's nothing Ronald and I can't handle. But whatever you do — for God's sake — don't mention this to Rachel. She's already on her moral high horse so keep her out of it."

"And," he added as a parting shot over his shoulder, "Next time, don't eavesdrop when I'm talking on the phone. I'll tell you what you need to know and when you need to know it."

CHAPTER 21

SECOND MEETING

I have sinned, my Father, and I am afraid of my sin.

—Fyodor Dostoevsky

ENOCH SAT LOOKING AT HIS TELEPHONE, ABSENTMINDEDLY TAP-
ping his pen, while trying to figure out how to get Ms. Lorten-Kissane to
see him again.

Morning sunlight highlighted a few specks of dust on his otherwise
immaculate desk.

He ran through the options in his head again before dialing.

A friendly, *"Hey, enjoyed our last meeting — let's do it again."* An
option, but one with potentially uncomfortable social side effects.

Or maybe, *"I have more questions about my parent's trip"?*

Weak.

*"Turns out I'm investigating the Lorten family business and
thought you might give me some inside info on your illustrious and possibly criminal brothers."*

Probably not.

Rachel did not strike Enoch as either naïve, uncontrollably romantic, or the least bit stupid. But he did think she had enjoyed their meeting

as much as he had and in the end Enoch simply invited her to join him for a cup of coffee and she simply said yes.

Rachel arrived first and took a table by the window. Enoch's long strides looked eager to her as he strode up the street. But then, she reminded herself, she had no idea how Enoch usually walked.

She was only mildly surprised by his call. Rachel assumed the man wanted to chat more about the dangers of traveling to remote spots in Russia. It was nice to meet an attractive, interesting man and she looked forward to seeing Enoch Arnheim again. Whatever he wanted, she was glad he'd called.

"It's chilly out there, isn't it?" he said, rubbing his hands to together after shaking hers.

Rachel sensed a problem right away. Maybe it was her finely tuned Lorten antennae for sensing people with agendas. Maybe it was his smile. Not lopsided like last time. Something was different. Her heart sank a little.

Signature coffee mugs at Café Ole resembled small bowls without handles. Rachel cupped her hands around the warm ceramic, slowly sipping the hot strong liquid and growing nervous. Enoch took his time, then ordered South African Rooibos tea. It was the fad tea of the month in Washington, D.C.

Social pleasantries exhausted, Rachel put down her cup, leaned back, shoulders straight as though bracing for a blow.

"So, maybe you should tell me why you called. Really."

"What do you mean?" he mumbled, startled by the question. Recovering quickly and desperate to keep the meeting on a friendly basis. He lied.

"Does there have to be a reason? I enjoyed our talk the other day and thought it would be nice to do it again."

Rachel's voice had held no hint of wariness over the phone. He simply couldn't imagine what had changed since he ordered tea. But where her eyes had been warm and lively when he sat down, now they were wary. Enoch looked at the woman across from him and found her more attractive than he remembered. Laura would probably call her overweight and unsophisticated. He found her interesting.

He liked her masses of dark unruly curls.

And her intelligent grey eyes.

There was something very non-Washington D.C. about her. Brooklyn, maybe?

She waited. He hedged.

Eventually he told her something of the truth.

"Look, I did actually think of a few more questions about my parents' trip, but that is not why I asked to see you again. And as much as I enjoyed our last meeting, I would not have presumed upon your time in order to continue our discussion of the current 'Wind in the Willows' production at the Folger Theatre or whether or not the Vermeer exhibition at the National Gallery is worth the long wait."

Rachel stiffened a notch more.

Enoch noticed and wondered again what he was missing. Nothing personal had arisen during their last meeting... she had not mentioned being a widow... he hadn't mentioned his living arrangement. Near as he could remember there had been no flirting on either side. It had been a friendly, professional meeting. Strange, maybe I read the scholar right and misread the woman, he thought.

"So why did you call?" she insisted.

Enoch pulled a camel colored cashmere scarf from his neck, a gift from Laura on their one-year anniversary, and laid it carefully in his lap while trying to find a way to thread what was becoming a very tiny needle.

"Well, it's about *your* family this time, actually, not mine."

Rachel went from wary to angry in a split second.

"I don't talk to reporters. Even one as clever as you. Using a story about your parents seeking their family lost in the Holocaust is pretty low even for the *Post*, so I'm assuming you're from the tabloids."

She fumbled with her coat, trying to get it on and stand up at the same time, wondering how she could have been so stupid. Or emotionally vulnerable.

"Reporter!" Enoch was really rather relieved. "I'm hardly a reporter. What made you think that?"

Rachel didn't go but she didn't take off her coat either.

"Not a reporter? Okay, so who are you? And why did you come to see me with that travel story? And... you have about two minutes."

"It wasn't a story. Everything I told you was true. My parents are planning the trip and I don't think they should go. I wanted some good reasons to talk them out of going, or at least prepare them. I work at the IRS, which I think I mentioned when we met."

He waited.

She nodded.

"I knew absolutely nothing about you when I came to your office — except you had been recommended by a friend from the State Department. Period. Full stop. You could've been an orphan for all I knew about your family. I wasn't hiding anything then and I have no intention of doing so now... "

"Seems like you have discovered I'm not an orphan in the meantime. How did that come about? And why would you want to talk to me about my family unless you're looking for a story? And, by the way, your two minutes are about up, Agent Arnheim."

"I know we shouldn't believe in them, but it *was* a coincidence."

Now Rachel Lorten-Kissane was getting interesting on a whole new level. Why on earth should she be so sensitive about her family that she jumps to conclusions about tabloid newspapers? The Lortens are famous, but hardly rockstars.

"So, here is what happened, I needed professional advice. We met, I enjoyed our talk and learned what I needed to know for travel in Russia. End of story. I went back to my office to work and — this is the coincidence — there was a letter involving WOWL, Inc. I knew about the Lorten media empire, of course, who doesn't? But I had no personal interest and didn't even stop to wonder if you were from *that* Lorten family until I saw that letter and made the connection. Believe me, Rachel, please. Our meeting was random. End of story."

"But it wasn't end of story, was it? Because here we are and you want to talk about the Lortens."

Rachel believed him. Up to a point. Still here she was with an IRS agent who had just announced he wanted to talk about her family. A reporter might have been less dangerous.

"Go on," she said, needing to know why Agent Arnheim had really called her.

"Reading through the brief, shareholders reports, etc., I came across your name. I couldn't believe it... I was stunned at the coincidence. But since it isn't a very common name, I assumed you were in fact a member of the Lorten family."

Surely, she thought, my brothers can't know about an IRS investigation if the agent in charge only received the initial inquiry last week. The conversation Ellie overheard suggested they might, which meant the man was lying.

"So IRS agents believe in coincidences?" she asked, trying to go back to a lighter tone, needing now to know more.

"Usually, no, we don't," he grinned, sensing she was relaxing. "But coincidences do occur."

"Ah. By the very virtue of the word."

"Exactly."

They might, she thought, but a busy man would hardly take his time to meet her again in order to chat about the philosophical possibilities of randomness and chance meetings.

She loosened her coat.

"Okay, let's assume coincidence for the moment, Agent Arnheim... I guess I should call you Agent Arnheim, since this is clearly an official IRS meeting. I have to say I am not thrilled you used a fairly dishonest pretext for getting me to come out for coffee with you... and you must know from your initial research that I am not part of the family business. So what could you hope to gain by talking to me, I can't imagine."

It was starting to rain outside, dreary D.C. drizzle.

Enoch knew he had botched the meeting but he was determined not to give up such a fortuitous opportunity. He really wanted to ask her why she hadn't asked the most obvious question: Why the IRS would be investigating the family businesses.

"Could we start over? I'm sorry I didn't tell you over the phone... but frankly I didn't expect such a, shall I say, visceral reaction. Just the mere mention of your family led to ah, a rather unexpected response. It's not like I used our previous conversation as a means of getting to know you because of the case...far from it. And I have been very up front with you now... I did enjoy talking with you before and no harm in doing it again. And you must admit the coincidence of meeting you and the same day receiving the case... well, at the very least it seemed like something I wanted to tell you."

Rubbish, she thought.

"Oh... I see! You just wanted to take time out of your busy day to share this amazing coincidence with me. In an ironic sense — so we could wonder together over coffee at the random nature of life. Somehow," she leaned across the little table and stared into his eyes. "Somehow, I don't think so. And let's be honest, you knew if you mentioned wanting to talk to me about my family I would never have agreed to come. Which is why you didn't mention it. So don't feign surprise at my negative reaction upon learning that instead of a friendly chat about my given field of knowledge and your need for said knowledge or God forbid that we just enjoyed each other's company enough for another get-together. Instead you were in pursuit of information about my family because you are investigating them. Which really can't be good, can it? And I'll be honest with you... I noticed you were not wearing a wedding ring, so I assumed, ever the naïve fool, that you might have just wanted to get together again. Silly of me, I know... "

"Oh God, no. Not silly... but... " he stumbled.

"Please," she held up her hand. "Let me finish. This is embarrassing enough without you saying something that isn't true. Okay, when you called I just said yes without thinking it through, glad enough to meet an interesting man. I assume your research revealed I am a widow."

He looked uncomfortable.

"Ah. It did. Well, did that make me more vulnerable in your eyes, Agent?"

Enoch thought vulnerable was the last thing that came to mind with Rachel Lorten-Kissane.

"Surely," she went on, "you couldn't have thought me enough of a schoolgirl that you could seduce me by friendliness based on one brief conversation into giving you inside information about my family that might be harmful to them? It's a very curious approach for the government, don't you think, Agent?"

He rather agreed with her and couldn't believe he had tried such an amateurish approach. Only the fact that Johnson wasn't here to see his humiliation kept Enoch from crawling under the table literally;

metaphorically, he was already there. As an experienced agent, he had set out to make an ally and clearly succeeded in doing exactly the opposite.

Finishing off the now-cool dregs in the bottom of the big cup, Enoch tried the contrite approach.

"Would you mind awfully not calling me 'Agent'? Enoch will do."

Rachel wanted very much to call the man Enoch. To think of him as friend, not an agent of the Federal Government.

"I should have remembered my mother's advice about me and men... " Rachel muttered under her breath.

"I'm sure I don't know what that means, but I'm desperately trying to dig my way out here... could I try again, to explain?"

Still wanting to know more about what the government was investigating, Rachel took off her coat and asked a passing waiter for a refill.

"First of all, let me explain something personal... "

"You don't need to."

"I know, but let me. I have bungled this so far so let's get everything on the table. I'm in a committed relationship and sort of assumed you knew about it because it makes the press occasionally. I guess I get so used to people knowing that my partner is Press Secretary at State and assumed you read the gossip columns. Laura and I are... ah... um... together, but not married. She has a high-profile job and it sometimes rubs off on me. I hate it, actually... not the together part but the press part, the 'power couple' line the press employs occasionally. Silly, but there it is. It was stupid of me to think someone like you would read trivia like that. But just because I'm in a committed relationship doesn't mean I can't enjoy the company of interesting women."

"I thought we had already established this little get-together was not because I am an interesting woman, but because I am a woman whose last name happens to be Lorten. This has happened to me before in life as it turns out. Not something I'm particularly fond of."

Despite her sarcasm Rachel was humiliated for thinking, even sub-liminally, that this man might have been interested in her. Of course, she had seen the current State Department Press Secretary on CNN. A remarkably beautiful and brilliant professional; the kind of person Enoch Arnheim would be with. Rachel wanted to flee and go home and hide out with her cats. But there was something more important than her badly bruised ego at stake.

"Forget it... I'm not saying I thought your call was a date... just, oh dear, now that we are both embarrassed could you just get to the point so we can both go back to work?"

"Honestly, I didn't exactly have a point. I just thought it was an amazing coincidence and I did find you very interesting... not at all a ste-reotypical evangelical/fundamentalist. "

"Evangelicals and fundamentalists are not the same thing," she interrupted. "But do go on."

"Okay, see, you made my point. I didn't even know there was a dif-ference between evangelicals and fundamentalists. So anyway, I thought, okay, didn't give it enough thought, but my idea was that you might be open to talking with me and giving me some general background about the community. Like you just did. I didn't expect you to reveal confidential, personal, or company information. I was genuinely curious about you and how you fit into what seems like such a different family. I intruded and I'm sorry."

The waitress came again. Rachel asked for water. Her mouth was dry. Keep your friends close and your enemies closer, she thought. She wanted to believe him, but the timing didn't work. There was no way, not if Ronald and Jeff knew about the investigation before the agent in charge.

"And," he continued, "I didn't want to face you for the first time again in some kind of a deposition situation. I am really sorry, Rachel, I didn't set out to deceive you," he added, not altogether truthfully. He wondered if he could get away with patting her hand in a friendly conciliatory gesture, but thought better of it.

"Well, not to put too fine a point upon it... but you did mean to do exactly that. You suggested by your friendly call that this was just that... a friendly cup of coffee when, in fact, you are doing your job."

He started to protest.

"No, no," she stopped. "I do wonder what you hoped to achieve though."

"A meal maybe? I'm starved. Could we eat?"

It broke the tension. And at that moment Enoch looked miserable and not at all dangerous. She noticed that the cute lopsided smile that made him even more attractive had returned.

Rachel laughed. Too much caffeine and too little food were making her giddy.

"Why not? No harm in eating. I do it all the time."

He ordered the house signature white pizza with gorgonzola cheese and black olives, medium size, thin crust for both of them and a half carafe of Chianti, then changed the subject to safe topics while they waited.

Enoch was surprised again at how much he enjoyed talking to this total stranger.

The pleasant interlude ended when the waiter removed the plates.

Rachel returned to the point.

"Okay, let's start by you telling me about the Federal Government's interest in WOWL."

"Fair enough." He gave a very brief outline, leaving out more than he put in.

"You must know the IRS has looked at the company before, but this time a very astute donor, a contest winner of some sort, it seems, was invited to be a special guest of the company. Turns out the man owns his own accounting/auditing firm and knows his way around non-profit law. He saw more than your brothers intended, I think. It is very early days but I would say the government might have a case, certainly for inurement."

Enoch watched carefully for her reaction, but failed to read any.

"If that means what I think it means," Rachel said. "It will require a pretty high standard of proof. You will have to show egregiously high compensation on the part of the executives, namely my brothers, as opposed to only grubby greed. The question will be, what is reasonable compensation in relationship to the size and nature of a corporation like WOWL, which you must know is rather substantial."

He waited, surprised by her voluble response.

"Of course," she went on, "if a corporation exists for purely eleemosynary purposes, it might make inurement easier to prove. WOWL was once a not-for-profit, charitable, company, but as you probably already know it is now an amalgam of for-profit and not-for-profit companies. The disgruntled donor might not have known that but the lawyers, including you, mostly certainly will have to concede that important legal point. The mainstream media, referred to by my family as the mafia-media, will help you out with stories of excess on the part of my colorful family, of course. They will exaggerate what they know and guess at what they don't. People who don't like WOWL will be thrilled and the faithful supporters across the U.S., people who have donated hard-earned money, may also take exception when you lay out the salaries, the cars, the houses, the plane... you do know about the plane... "

"I know about the plane," he lied.

"I'm sure you do. No heated dog houses, however; my brothers both hate animals."

He couldn't believe the flow, now started, seemed to be unabating.

"And," she went on, "the current administration hates the influence that WOWL exerts over millions of voters. They see it as the head of — what's the term? — a 'vast right-wing conspiracy'. So you will be quite the darling of the Left if you slay their enemy. But despite some disappointment at what might reasonably be called excess on the part of my brother's lifestyle, the rest of the country will, in the end, I think consider my brother's lifestyle as a weakness to be forgiven and redirect their anger against the outsider. Namely, you. And assume you are being pushed by the Administration for their own purposes. Are you, by the way, being pushed by the Administration? Your relationship with someone so visible might be misconstrued as, well, as part of the 'left-wing plot'."

Before he could answer, she finished her lengthy monologue.

"And, as you know, the public does tend to have a short attention span, so unless you have much more than the mansion in Great Falls, a private plane, and couple of Mercedes, you might want to reconsider. So, my point is this: Despite some juicy lifestyle stories, you are going to have trouble winning this case in the most important court in D.C.: the court of public opinion."

Enoch remembered Johnson saying something similar. And he knew it was true. Fine legal, technical, or accounting infractions might exact stiff fines but the powerful family could still come out a victor if seen as the victim of a politically motivated probe. Enoch's gut told him, however, that there was much more to this case than even the astute Phil Grant had discovered. And the answer to that might lie in the fact that Rachel Lorten-Kissane, by his measure a highly capable, measured, and seemingly ethical woman would keep such a distance from her family and become instantly defensive at the mere mention of them.

Enoch was stung by her suggestion that his relationship with Laura might present a conflict of interest. Another point Johnson had made. But she had said a great deal more than he expected and maybe more than she intended, so he kept his voice neutral.

"You seem extremely negative about your own family businesses. What happened to cause such a rift?"

Rachel laughed. "So you want my whole life story for the price of one pizza? Look, it's complicated, like all families, only mine just happened to be more famous. Like Tolstoy said, all unhappy families are unhappy in the same way. So we have a communication empire. It started out small, just a little radio station, WOWL, here in D.C. My father was a man with a mission... to use the medium of radio to reach and encourage the faithful. The programs included lots of preaching and good music, including sacred and classical. It was back before the dreadful 'emotive' talk show format that exploits private lives of vulernable people for ratings. Anyway, my Dad believed, as many people did then, and most still do, that the new technologies of the twentieth century could be used to evangelize the world. Preachers could reach thousands and even millions at a time. I personally disagree with the premise that that is how faith spreads... or that Christ intended the Kingdom of Heaven to come to Earth over the airwaves — although that would be a lot easier than actually meeting, touching, and caring for people. But I'm sure you're not interested in my views of apologetics and evangelism, so I won't bore you."

"No, really, go on."

"Well... even without much effort it seems WOWL grew in those early days of radio and then TV. It was the beginning of television evangelists and preachers. And people liked it. Maybe it is because one would rather accept what a 'famous' preacher says than the local pastor in the little wooden pulpit. So, famous people took the place of trusted pastors, family, and friends because they could publish and sell books, or start big organizations. People like, or at least trust, people who are successful. The man who has baptized, taught, married, and will bury you is ignored in favor of the unknown famous and successful celebrity pastor or talk show person. We live in a celebrity culture and 'Christian celebrities' have the same proportional impact in the church as celebrities do in the secular world. The mega-church, mega-media approach is outsourcing

Christianity to something utterly impersonal. A contradiction in terms, if you ask me, not that anyone does."

"They should," he said. "Sounds good to me."

"No, they probably shouldn't. But here is the point which really is my long answer to your question about what happened between me and my family... I have a fundamental, philosophical, and even theological difference with the family business. I do not believe that a media-generated, marketing-driven Christian culture translates into living out the Gospel, caring for the poor, visiting the sick, adopting the orphan, welcoming the stranger in our midst. WOWL is very nationalistic and political. Frankly, I think that is a serious problem. So I don't love the business. Not so strange my family isn't thrilled with me. I'm sure you've come across it before. Does your family ever embarrass you, Mr. Agent?"

She did not expect or wait for an answer. "Well, mine does. But it could be worse, we could have built a biblical theme park out in the Virginia countryside. Actually, we tried that too, but mercifully it failed."

Rachel leaned back and lowered her voice.

"But I'm boring you... sorry."

"Bored, I'm not. A bit surprised and very interested. I must admit I tend to think of most Republicans as white, Christian, anti-abortion, right-wing, and fairly radical. Nothing at all, in fact, like you. Except for the white part. Seems impossible you come from the same family. You're not adopted, by any chance?"

Now it was her turn to smile.

"My mother often wonders — or wishes —the same thing. Although she is in position to know I am Lorten born and bred. As the Southerners say. I was born a Lorten. My dad died too soon; I was just thirteen. Not a good age under the best of circumstances, and during those years immediately after his death, under my brother's leadership, the business exploded.

Christian celebrities became a fixture in our family and I became an out-sider... since Junior High. Just ask my mother... "

"Wait a minute," Enoch interrupted. "You must have been a very prescient thirteen-year-old if you were opposed to the family business from such an early age."

"Read it however you want. You asked and I'm telling you. Mostly, I just avoided things by spending time alone. In books. Then I graduated from high school a year early, went to college, and then off to Europe to get a graduate degree. As far away as possible."

"Then why on earth did you marry one of those 'celebrities' you dis-liked so much, especially one who worked for your family? Rather sucked you back in, didn't it?"

She stiffened. He had touched a nerve. And she was suddenly aware he already knew a great deal about her.

"I'm sorry, by the way, about your loss," he added quickly. "And I didn't mean to intrude into the personal... but it seems so odd given what you just said about your feelings about the family business and your desire to escape it... to have married back in, as it were."

Rachel looked down, gathering her composure, hoping he would read any quiver in her voice as a sign of grief not to be intruded upon rather than a dangerous topic she wanted to avoid at all costs.

"People get married for all kinds of reasons, Mr. Arnheim. Or not, as the case may be."

"Touché," he replied.

"But back to my reaction to the family business," she went on, eager to redirect. "I don't think I was particularly prescient as a child, probably more like, difficult. I was the ugly duckling... brainy and introspective... I hated all the parties and the people feeding off of our family because I didn't fit in. If I had been the pretty and popular type... I might have loved the attention of all the famous people who were coming and going. Media is the mother's milk of celebrities — Christian or any other kind. Writers, musicians, politicians... they all need a platform, and my family supplied it over the airwaves to millions of people across America. My mother and brothers loved it... and I hated it. It's simple as that. I don't consider myself better than they are... in fact; it's probably pride and arrogance as much as insecurity that caused me to keep a distance. Then and now. I was smart enough to know that when the 'celebs', as we called them, were nice to me it wasn't to me as much as to my family. My mother thrived on it. I resented it."

"Well, then forgive me, but doesn't that make it even more surprising that you married Eric Kissane?"

"Not that it's really relevant, Agent Arnheim, the fact is my husband joined the family business *after* we were married. And as he is deceased I'm assuming he is not a target of this investigation, so let's get back to the subject at hand. My brother's lifestyle might be loathsome, unethical even, but since as far as I know he never takes a step without his lawyer's approval, the government might want to reconsider before you leak a trial balloon to the press to gauge which way wind is blowing. Remember the Lorten brand name does have considerable public support. That, and the fact that my brother is a tad litigious as well. But more importantly... he has the power to make his case the people's cause. The old idea of a 'moral majority' might be problematic from your perspective, and mine too, in that the term suggests a cornering of the market on 'morality', but the majority part isn't a myth. Is awakening that base and mobilizing them for the next election really what this government wants? You might want to ask Laura that question, since her job depends on the administration staying in power. I wonder if a fight with the Lorten Empire is what you all really want."

Rachel regretted the personal jab as soon as it was out of her mouth. He chose to ignore it.

"Maybe not, but what I want is hardly the point, as you must know. My job is to follow the facts. And what the administration wants is, despite your insinuation, completely irrelevant. Our investigations are not politically motivated despite what the pundits say. And you sound a little like you are warning me off?"

Rachel laughed. It was a deep laugh full of real mirth. It was quite the nicest laugh he had ever heard.

"What's so funny?"

"Sorry… " she tried to stop laughing. "You wouldn't understand… all of a sudden I pictured my family… Ronald, Jeff, mother, needing to thank me… me of all people… for protecting them… or warning the government off, as you put it. They would be so conflicted by the need to thank me."

She got her laughter under control and continued.

"No, seriously, I was just giving you friendly advice. You asked me here to get some inside information about the people at WOWL. Well, I'm giving it to you… for the price of one good pizza. And that was one good pizza. I'm sure the disgruntled donor who alerted you to what he saw at WOWL was indeed offended at the lifestyle of my rich and famous family whom he had assumed lived liked humble Christians, and I'm sure the poor guy has a point. I just don't know if it is a point that can be made in the court of law. Good lawyers make good fences, as Robert Frost said."

"That isn't exactly what Robert Frost said. But point taken."

Enoch thought that figuring out where the conversation was going was like driving the Austin on Georgetown Pike. Charging up hills and around corners. And almost as much fun.

"Close enough and even more to the point," she went on, "recent history does seem to show there is occasional bias in who the IRS targets, and if Ronald's legal fences are strong enough you might not be able to breach them. Desire aside."

"Desire? What do you mean 'desire'? You keep suggesting this is somehow personal. Please tell me you are not suggesting some kind of anti-Christian bias. We don't pick cases based on 'desire' as you put it, anyway. I rather resent the implication that I'm investigating a Christian group with a desire to bring them down because I'm Jewish. I am surprised and offended."

It was one thing for his ignorant lout of a boss to suggest that, but he found himself truly angry that this woman, whose friendship he might want under different circumstances, would think so.

Realizing she had touched a nerve, she pressed the point further.

"Oh please, don't be overly sensitive. I wasn't even thinking religious bias, although now that you bring it up it is an interesting point. I was suggesting a liberal political bias. Still your reaction is telling, don't you think? Issues of faith are highly emotional and you won't be able to 'just stick to the facts ma'am' when the press begins its gleeful coverage of this juicy story. I hope you realize that."

Rachel declined dessert, unwilling to waste calories when she couldn't enjoy consuming them. For now, sadly, she had to see Enoch Arnheim as a real threat to the peace she had so recently achieved.

"Liberals are not always hostile, Dr. Lorten-Kissane. The liberal press, as you call it, is not always adversarial. Even the liberal press has given WOWL credit for helping victims of sexual violence and exploitation recently. So then you must be proud of that, too. Right?"

Rachel had wondered about the current out-of-character relief campaign, but was only too happy to assure the IRS agent that her family indeed has done a great deal of good over the years, including the current example.

Enoch fell in beside her as they exited the restaurant. Outside her office, he shook her hand.

"Well," his smile was genuine, the pressure of his handshake firm. "That was an interesting lunch. You are a most interesting woman... if a little scary at times. I enjoyed meeting you — both times. I just wish it could have been... well, you know... I hope the next time we meet it won't be under difficult circumstances."

She had no idea how to reply since she assumed there wouldn't be a next time. Rachel withdrew her hand and with a little nod turned to enter her building.

Enoch went down the street toward his office in the mammoth gray IRS building without looking back.

Rachel managed to smile at the concierge and rushed into the bathroom on the first floor, unwilling to face her colleagues. She was badly shaken. She stood looking in the mirror without seeing anything except the fear in her eyes. Disappointment that Enoch Arnheim had not wanted to have lunch with her because he found her attractive was now buried deep beneath the much greater concern. She found herself wishing, maybe for the first time in her life, that she was beautiful, with the ability to beguile with a sensuality that came natural to other women. And I would use it now, she thought. I would use it to steer Agent Enoch Arnheim away from an investigation that had the potential to ruin her life. If he searched, he would find and expose her husband's promiscuity and the hypocrisy of their marriage for all of Washington, D.C. to see, and worst of all, her family to gloat over. Somewhere out there in the city there were women who knew firsthand that Eric Kissane was not the person he pretended to be on air — and one or more of them was bound to crawl out from under a rock and tell her story when the IRS investigation was made public. Rachel had found she could live with the threat of illness as a result of exposure to HIV, but not the threat of public humiliation. Her beautiful carriage house would no longer protect her and provide the peace she was enjoying for the first time since her disastrous marriage to Eric. Agent Arnheim had to stop before he found the scandal that would make his case.

She splashed water on her face, brushed her hair, and walked back into the lobby and told Mr. Sorensen at the concierge desk to call her office and let them know she wouldn't be in for the rest of the afternoon.

"Yes, ma'am. Are you okay?"

"Fine. Fine. Just let them know, please. I'm in a bit of a hurry."

Mr. Sorenson didn't think Dr. Lorten-Kissane looked in a hurry. He thought she looked sick. But he had been a concierge for a long time and he knew better than to pry.

Rachel drove home down the twisting turnpike, and by some internal and unconscious compass, turned into her dirt road and finally came to a stop in front of the house without remembering how she got there. Both cats greeted her as Rachel walked into her now-endangered sanctuary.

"I wish, I wish, I wish," Rachel muttered over and over to herself as she rocked in the porch swing wrapped up against the cold, tears running down her cheeks. The words of the nursery rhyme she learned from her father kept coming back, 'If wishes were horses, beggars could ride. If ifs and ands were pots and pans, there'd be no work for tinkers'.

Wishing wouldn't help.

Ronald must have learned of the investigation and told Jeff; that was what Ellie had overheard. So Agent Arnheim had lied to her about when he got the case.

Rachel understood full well that if she was going to protect her cherished privacy and remain in the place she had created, she would need to find out what Enoch Arnheim knew, when he knew it, and whether or not it had to do with Eric's past.

CHAPTER 22

NIKITA
SERGEYEVICH KHRUSHCHEV

He never did but what he wanted to do.

—*Karen Blixin*

"ARNHEIM HERE," ENOCH BARKED, PICKING UP ON HIS PRIVATE line.

"Lorten-Kissane here," Rachel barked back. It had taken her two weeks to get nerve enough to call Enoch on the private number he had given her that first day. In case she thought of more information to help his parents with their trip. If he even has parents, she thought, her hands sweating as she held the phone.

"Well, well... Lorten-Kissane indeed," his voice warmed. "Good to hear from you, Lorten-Kissane. By the way, that isn't nearly so effective with a double-barreled name is it?"

She exhaled a small nervous laugh. "Not so much. And you're going to think me quite crazy for what I am about to suggest, but it's a lovely day and I wondered if you'd like to take a walk and have a late afternoon cup of tea on the rocks overlooking the Great Falls. Virginia side, that is."

Enoch had not expected to see Rachel again. Not until it was across an oval table during a deposition. He looked at his watch and thought the opportunity too good to be missed.

"I would, ah, I'd love tea outside on a chilly November day. Do it all the time."

"It isn't chilly, it's sixty-five warm degrees."

"Well, as it turns out I was going to be in your neighborhood anyway and I'd love a cup of tea with you. How about I pick you up around 2:00?"

"That would be lovely. How in the neighborhood are you going to be?"

"As the crow flies, I'd say six minutes, but then the crow flies slower than my Austin. I'm having lunch at the Irish Pub."

"What a nice coincidence. I would certainly call that in the neighborhood."

"I thought we didn't believe in coincidence?" he said and added quickly. "I'm kidding. It would be nice to see you again and I take it this is strictly personal. As in, we don't talk about my family or yours?"

"Not all that personal. Let's call it me making up for being so rude last time."

Enoch retrieved his car from the parking garage under the IRS building and headed out of the city across Roosevelt Bridge. He found himself humming as he sailed down the nearly empty Georgetown Pike with the top down. The road was wide open and he took the curves, drops, and narrow tight corners at the speed for which his car was designed. Falling leaves blowing past him landed in a trail of dancing colors on the black tarmac.

Smiling at the prospect of seeing Rachel Lorten-Kissane again and wondering what had really prompted the mysterious invitation, assuming guilt had nothing to do with it, he pulled into the Irish Pub to make his story about eating in the pub true, albeit retrospectively. Pub grub and a good brew before tea on the rocks with Rachel! A most interesting turn of events for an otherwise dreary day in the office with Johnson breathing down his neck for a progress report on the WOWL case.

Rachel, meanwhile, was not smiling. She was worrying about what she had set in motion as she brewed Earl Grey tea and packed scones and strawberries into a never-before-used tea chest given to her as a house warming gift by a colleague from the office. The tidy wicker basket had everything for a 'proper tea,' including a linen tablecloth, thermos for the hot water, two china cups and plates, and a Scottish plaid blanket. Dressed in Levis, hiking boots, a warm cotton sweater and windbreaker, she pulled her masses of black curls into a ponytail and tucked it through a baseball cap, then walked outside to wait, not at all sure she could pull this off. Sitting on the step staring at the packed tea chest she wondered if she should call Ellie and ask if she thought duplicitousness was one of her spiritual gifts. Rachel realized the tea chest was a mistake. It was silly and pretentious and surely shouted premeditation. She dumped everything in a Trader Joe's brown bag, threw the blanket over her arm, and got back outside just as Enoch drove up in his sports car.

"Is this a real car?" she asked, finding her way none too gracefully into the low seat.

"You have no idea," he replied, storing the bag and blanket in the tiny boot and shutting her door.

"Is that a real carriage house?"

Enoch was impressed with the finely restored structure tucked away on the very private lane.

"Of course it's a real carriage house. I keep all my carriages in it."

The small distance between driver and passenger made conversation easy, even with the top down, as they drove the short distance from the carriage house lane to Great Falls Park. Rachel was amazed how comfortable she felt with him; they had only met twice and the second time with disastrous results. And her family would never forgive her if they knew Rachel was spending time with an IRS agent charged with investigating the family business. Explaining her motives would be met with incredulity and her actions seen as treasonous, but she didn't expect to see any family members at the park. And Enoch seemed friendly enough, so she put her head back and enjoyed the ride.

They walked the short distance up the old canal path, through the woods, to a rocky ledge overlooking the pounding white water below.

The tea was hot, the scones and strawberries deliciously lathered with Devon cream, and the view splendid. Far below, water poured over the falls, dangerous and inviting.

Warmed by the sun and hot liquid, Enoch stretched out on the Scottish reds and watched the high thin clouds drift past with the occasional jet coming in for a landing at Reagan National Airport.

Despite the idyllic setting and outward affability, neither Enoch nor Rachel felt truly at ease. Rachel was wondering how to subtly turn the discussion to the IRS case. And Enoch knew he should be using this heaven-sent opportunity to get more information from a Lorten family member.

'Back to work Arnheim,' he told himself, taking his eyes off three turkey vultures riding the thermals in hypnotic circles overhead.

"Dr. Lorten-Kissane," he said. "Why don't you relax and check out these clouds?" He patted a spot on the blanket next to him.

Tea, biscuits, and me, she thought, wishing life was so simple.

Enoch. She liked his name. His barely discernable Brooklyn accent, engaging smile, and long-legged elegance. His clothes, unlike her own, were perfectly pressed, making her feel even more rumpled than usual. She would love to lie down next to him and gaze at the sky, watch the birds, and listen to the roar of the water below.

Instead she kept her distance, sitting stiffly on the edge of the blanket, making a pyramid with bits of red rock chips.

Enoch turned on his side, propped his hand under his head and looked at the enigmatic woman beside him. She was so unlike Laura, yet he found himself attracted to her despite how stupid and dangerous that could be. He asked the safest question he could think of:

"So what's the town of Great Falls famous for? Apart from water rushing over rocks?"

"Rich people. Miles of McMansions and a few genuine ones. And some famous people live here. Redskin football players and Linda Carter. She lives here too. I don't recognize most of them but we have our share of important people in Great Falls."

"Wonder Woman lives in Great Falls? Cool."

Rachel laughed.

"She does, but she doesn't wear her costume to Safeway. Even Wonder Woman ages, you know. And, well, then there is the CIA safe house. Kids try to find it in the woods near the village shops... hoping someone might actually be torturing people in the neighborhood, somewhere other than school, that is. Oh, and Khrushchev slept here once."

"He did not!" Enoch snorted, sitting up. "The safe house, okay that I can believe, since you are only a few miles down the road from Langley and the CIA. But Khrushchev sleeping in Great Falls sounds a little like a suburban legend to me."

"No, really. It was in 1956. We learned about it in grade school. Ike was in the White House. Khrushchev and Nixon were having the famous 'kitchen debates' around the country, then Khrushchev stops in Washington on his way back to Russia. They show him the Russian Embassy and official residence which he refuses to stay in because it is in Washington — or something. But he demands to stay 'with the people' on a farm. So the State Department scrambles to find a farm close to D.C., one that satisfies security demands, and they come up with a dairy farm in Great Falls. It was then pretty much a sleepy backwater, so even we played our little role in history."

"I don't believe you. You have to show me this farm. If it still exits that is."

"Oh, it still exists. You might have seen it straight up Georgetown Pike from the Irish Pub, where strangely enough you had lunch today. It is a big, white, run down Victorian farmhouse on the way to Chez Francois, the five-star French restaurant, our other claim to fame. Do you often come out from D.C. to eat at the Pub, by the way?"

He ignored that small jab about his 'excuse' to be in the neighborhood (fooling Rachel was not going to be easy, he thought) and eventually the conversation moved on from old Russian dictators to fine French cuisine. Enoch had been watching Rachel build a tiny edifice of stones while they talked, until his curiosity finally got the better of him.

"How Jewish of you. That little thing you're creating looks like a monument of some kind. Like the ones God told the Israelites to make after escaping some enemy or another? So what are you memorializing today? There is nothing dangerous here, as long as we stay back from the edge."

"What edge is that, counselor?" she asked, continuing to pile her tiny rocks one upon another.

"The big scary one with the river below," he answered carefully. "But you haven't answered my question. What's the memorial for?"

"It's a cenotaph, actually. You do know what a cenotaph is, don't you?"

"A grave marker without the body. And thanks, that explains everything. I mean most people I picnic with build them. Ms. Lorten-Kissane, you are a very mysterious lady. Is there any particular reason you are sitting here on this beautiful day drinking tea with me thinking about the dead instead of the living?"

Because, she thought, the dead is why we are here today, Agent Arnheim.

Rachel had visited Eric's grave only once, a few days after the funeral, and she had no plans to go again. Playing with the rocks had calmed her nerves and kept her hands busy. She did not mean to make a monument or a cenotaph and it was a foolish thing to say. Probably a Freudian slip as well. Trying to be clever when she should have been wise.

"I'm kidding," she said, knocking over the rocks. "More tea?"

"No, I was just wondering about your husband. You never talk about his accident, but it must have been so terrible for you."

"Decidedly worse for him."

Background noise, the water below and planes above, faded away and suddenly it was very quiet on the ledge above the falls. Enoch didn't really know what he was fishing for when he mentioned her husband, but her strange, cold response told him he was at least casting in interesting waters. He waited for her to go on.

"But I thought we agreed not to talk about my family today. Strictly personal, remember!"

"That *was* a personal question, Rachel. Too personal, perhaps, but hardly anything to do with the IRS versus WOWL. I'm sorry, but, well, you sit here on this lovely day and make a 'grave marker'. Kinda odd, don't you think?"

Rachel kept her eyes down, afraid of what he would see if she looked into his.

Enoch got on his knees, picked up a stick and scratched a line in the dirt around them, outside the blanket.

"Let's agree that our conversation today is in the *box* and nothing to do with my job. Okay? My question was personal. I don't know how it could be construed as part of the investigation, anyway. Is it?"

Rachel smiled.

"No, of course not. Except Eric worked for the station, it was his life, and so I think of him in that context and assumed you were too. My mistake. And I was kidding about the silly pile of rocks. I fiddle sometimes. My mother would say I'm not very good in social situations. And my mother would be right."

She rubbed out the line in the dust with her finger. "We don't need dramatics."

Maybe not, he thought, but something dramatic had happened. Enoch's sixth sense kicked in with a rush of adrenaline, that investigative instinct, which Johnson denied, and Laura teased him about. The one that made him very good at his job and now it was on high alert.

Enoch had accepted Rachel's surprising and odd invitation as an IRS Agent on the biggest case of his career, but somewhere along the way the day had become more about Enoch the man. He had been enjoying the place. The view. The conversation. The woman.

"Okay, no dramatics," he said evenly. "But please tell me why my question caused such a reaction if your husband's death really has no bearing on anything that might come up in my investigation. What's wrong with a friendly question? And it *was* just friendly."

"Really?"

"Yes. Really! Was your marriage an unhappy one, Rachel?"

She began putting cups and leftovers back in the bag. He tugged at her sleeve.

"It's off the record, Rachel, really. What is it that makes you crumble inside emotionally when your husband is mentioned? Okay, so it's well-controlled crumbling, but you change and I can see it whenever anything close to your marriage is even mentioned. And we sit here on a sunny day enjoying the view and each other and all the while you're building a... a cenotaph? How weird is that?"

A need to talk, a desire to believe him. The breeze. She wasn't sure why, but she let him take her hand and pull her back down on the blanket. Not close, but not miles away either. She leaned her head back and looked at the sky. Like most kids, Rachel had imagined clouds to be something more than dense patches of fog in the sky. She thought of them as a means of escape. Puffy chariots. Charging horses. Airplanes. She felt an irrational desire to escape now. Into Enoch's kind voice.

"My marriage, for what it's worth, here inside this box, is that it never was one. Eric married me in a beautiful ancient church in the Austrian Alps. It was an exquisite setting. He had a good eye, I'll give him that. But it was not for me. It was a calculated move to advance his career. Marrying into the Lorten family media-empire was a very good move professionally. We met accidentally, but he knew immediately who I was. He saw an opportunity and took it. He was talented, but it would have taken him years to advance his career. I was a shortcut. Eric became very popular as host of his own radio show and he was moving on up to television when he died. So, it was a marriage of convenience, which seems a little tacky to me, but hey, hardly the first one in history."

Despite a twinge of guilt with how he had manipulated her to talk, he pressed on. "And you? What was your motive?" he asked.

"Oh, my motive was not any better. Or any more original. His beauty seduced me. And for a time I thought Eric didn't know about my family and really wanted me, and I know it sounds cliché but, he wanted me *for* me. For my mind or personality or something equally sappy. I grew up with famous people, famous in our evangelical Christian world, who were always hanging around our family, and by extension around me, and *not* because we are such lovely people to be around," she laughed. "And I forgot that salient point for a moment there by the fountain in Salzburg."

"I'm not sure I understand that, but let's assume for sake of this conversation it's true. How did he know you were a Lorten when he met you in the middle of Austria?"

"That's a good question. And I never knew exactly, but he had made it his business to know about our family. It isn't that hard. Running into me there was an accident; I think, but who knows? I never did and it no longer interests me. Anyway, my often-vaunted intelligence failed me, but worse, much worse was that my spiritual compass was disconnected. Marriage is sacred and I suborned all thought of God and entered into it for the most pagan of reasons. Love not being one of them. The man was very handsome and I was flattered. The thought of showing up and proving my mother wrong seemed reason enough at the time and maybe it was the only truly fulfilling moment of my marriage, getting off the plane and seeing her face with Eric beside me."

"Proving your mother wrong in what way?" he mumbled, unable to think of a better question when she finished that extraordinary revelation.

"Oh dear, now that is way too complicated to explain. But back to your question. Was my marriage terrible? No, not so much. Eric wasn't mean or given to violent rages. He wanted everyone to like him, including me. He did well. He got rich and famous just like he wanted. His raw talent — which mostly consisted of a voice like the gods — moderate intelligence, no conscience, passion, and good looks, might have propelled him to success in time but he cut several steps by marrying me. Eric got exactly what he wanted out of our marriage and he only had to be nice to me in return. We got along, mostly living separate lives. He would never have done anything to jeopardize his relationship with the family by leaving me, so we would probably have gone on into our dotage, except, of course, for the accident. I think he was perfectly happy to live a life of almost unimaginable banality. He wanted people to recognize him. And they did. He wanted people to like him, and for the most part, that worked out okay too. He wanted wealth, not for its power, but for the stuff he could buy with it. How original," she laughed, thinking how different Eric was from her brother Ronald, who had all the stuff he wanted but never enough power.

"I didn't love him either," she carried on talking, now that the flood-gates were open. "Frankly, there wasn't much, besides his drop-dead good looks, to love. I don't think I ever had a discussion with my husband about any issue, any idea, except in the context of how it related to him. Even his faith. Maybe *especially* his faith. He entered our marriage with eyes wide open and that was the difference. My motives might have been as shallow as his, but at least initially I convinced myself otherwise. We stayed in Europe for a few weeks after the wedding, but when I saw him greet my family at the airport I knew he had lied to me. He looked at them with more joy than he had at me as I walked down the aisle to meet him at the altar in the lovely old church."

Enoch was stunned.

"I'm so sorry, Rachel," he mumbled.

"Don't be. It was my choice."

"No, I'm sorry I asked. You're right, it isn't my business. God, Rachel. I'm really sorry. But, and maybe I shouldn't ask, but if you didn't love him and your marriage was such a desert why not be glad... in a way... that he is gone? I mean, not glad he was killed, of course, but you know what I mean. You can start over, Rachel. And you are wrong about a man like Eric not looking at you. I mean, I don't know about him, but I... "

She reached over and placed a chilly hand over his mouth. "Don't embarrass us both."

At that moment a group of noisy school children came over the rise. The tired voice of their teacher called to them to get back from the precipice.

"Back from the precipice indeed," Rachel said, coming to her senses. She really wanted to tell Enoch what her husband had done to her. She wanted him to finish his dangling sentence. He might hold her and that would feel good. But she knew that wouldn't do. It would shatter the neatly drawn lines. It would change their fragile friendship, bring down her family, and probably make his career. She might even carry the smoking gun he was looking for in the bloodstream of her body, and if he knew that he would never see her even as a friend again, but as a weapon in the government's case. Exhibit A: Motive for blackmail. Scandal. The media would love it; the masses would take it as further proof of Christians as hypocrites.

Rachel straightened up. Inside and out.

"How about you, Mr. IRS Agent? Is your relationship a happy one? I can imagine it must be... what is it the press calls you... a 'power couple'?"

"Very," he said. The mood and moment were gone. Enoch helped Rachel pack the basket and followed her down the trail.

—————

CHAPTER 23

ETHICS AND PUBLIC POLICY

. . . in vain do men serve God, if they only offer
to him trivial and bare ceremonies.

—*John Calvin*

A COLD WIND WAS BLOWING DOWN PENNSYLVANIA AVENUE AS Enoch and Rachel made their way up the street after a lecture at the Ethics and Public Policy Center. Dust and small bits of debris swirled in the air, a howling wind, and honking drivers frustrated by bumper-to-bumper traffic made walking and talking impossible.

"Let's get some coffee at the Willard,'" Enoch suggested, pointing to the old historic hotel across the street.

There had been a few dinners, and the occasional visit to an art gallery, with Enoch, and it felt increasingly like a normal friendship to Rachel who, however, knew better. He rarely talked about the case but she convinced herself the time spent with him was necessary, learning everything she could. Not that he revealed much, and his motives were still a mystery to her, but she would have been happy to know he was frustrated with progress on the case. Bogged down in difficult-to-prove, dry financial details, and despite long hours with Betty's capable assistance, nothing like a scandal was to be found on Eric Kissane or any of the major players.

Not particularly interested in hearing scholars debate some eso-teric theological positions about faith and culture, Enoch had said yes to Rachel's invitation to join her at the lecture more to avoid the escalating cold war in his house. Laura wanted to know more about the investigation than he was willing to tell her, afraid of leaks that could not only get him in trouble with his boss but backfire and ruin the case. She was taking his refusal to tell her details as a lack of trust.

Enoch and Rachel settled in a paneled booth near an open fireplace and took the waiter up on his suggestion of hot mulled wine as a perfect antidote to the blustery day. A few minutes later, warmed by the fire and hot wine, Rachel sighed with contentment.

"Nice to have an after-ski drink without any of the cold and exercise before it."

He chuckled. "I take it you don't ski. By the way, I did enjoy the lec-ture, more than I expected actually."

Enoch pulled a brochure from the lecture out of his pocket and laid it on the table pointing to a quote on the cover by noted theologian Dr. Wilbur Culberson. It read: *"The church has neither a divine mandate nor the authority to articulate particular programs of politico-economic action. When we attempt to pronounce our fallible ideas in the political realm with presumptive piety, they encourage public doubt about the church's possession of an authoritative word of God in the theological and moral realms."*

"So, do you think Christians should not engage in politics?" he asked.

"No, I think they should. I just don't think that pulpits should be used to assign a divine mandate to a *particular* political party or position — left or right. Of course we should try and bring Judeo-Christian princi-ples to bear on the public square; we should be active in the fight against injustice, protecting the weak, the marginalized, the vulnerable."

"Like the unborn?"

"Yes, but hardly limited to that."

"Meaning?"

"Meaning, first of all, the church in America has been silent at some rather critical moments. Like the big obvious one — namely, a fight for civil rights in this country came from the liberal left, not the conservative right. But there are so many other examples less well known, and more recent. Like the aggressive eugenics program that took place in the middle of the Bible Belt up to twenty years or so ago. There were thousands of forced sterilizations and not one peep from evangelicals. Young black males go to jail at a higher rate for similar offenses than young white males. Why isn't that our cause? And we need to have a serious debate about gun control and the death penalty in the context of our belief that every life is sacred. Our moral outrage seems to be limited to abortion. I think that is a problem."

Rachel continued, on a roll now.

"There seems to be a self-indulgent, self-satisfied nature to a set of political positions and rhetoric that have somehow become 'the evangelical litmus test' issues. One does not actually have to love mercy or act justly as long as one votes Republican. A position strongly held and actively pushed by my own family."

Enoch listened to Rachel and thought about his and Laura's liberal worldview. They also held fairly narrow absolute positions with the same moral certainty.

"It's too bad the press doesn't do a better job of giving voice to the kind of thoughtful discussion by evangelicals that we heard today. I have to admit, until I met you, I bought the stereotype."

"Well, if we as Christians did a better job of loving our neighbor as Christ commanded instead of demanding our neighbors think exactly like us and vote with us, we might actually resemble the stereotype a little less."

Rachel sipped the last of her hot-spiced wine. "My theory is that evangelicals emerged from our 'pietistic ghettos' of fundamentalism in the Fifties in a very bad mood."

"Okay. Now you've totally lost me."

Rachel smiled at him.

"I'm kidding. Sort of. I'm sure there are many reasons for the current strain of nationalism in evangelicals. On one hand, it might be a fear of becoming marginalized again — which is a legitimate fear. Having no impact on culture. Or — and I'm afraid this is probably closer to the real reason — we don't want to do the hard work of actually living out our faith. Basically, we want what the Jews during the time of Christ wanted, to throw off the power of Rome by the might of a militant 'messiah.' Or, in our case, a Christian president and elected officials. Actually, in some ways the real message of Jesus isn't any more welcome to his followers today than he was in the first century."

"I hear rumors your brother might be happy to fulfill the role of 'Christian president'."

"Now Enoch, I absolutely refuse to ruin this delicious crème Brule with a discussion about my family. Especially that family member."

He smiled at her as she finished the rich dessert.

"Oh my, that was delicious," she said, wiping her mouth with the fine linen napkin. "There must have been a thousand calories in that. And worth every single one."

"Only if you like that kind of thing," he said.

There was a long and comfortable silence before Rachel went back to the point of the lecture.

"I interviewed Dr. Culbertson a few times and I remember an observation he once made about the danger of political activism that assumes not just moral positions but moral superiority over political opponents. He suggested that the current brand of political activism came along about the same time as the mega-church movement. Which for the uninformed, namely you, Agent Arnheim, is a philosophy of ministry that uses modern marketing, music, celebrity, and media to grow big churches. And they have succeeded in growing really big mega-churches, but at the expense of small communities of faith. These enormous churches are led by charismatic leaders who tend to eschew rigorous doctrine in their preaching and lean toward the more easily achieved emotional response. Using personal charisma, and their powerful bully pulpits, pastors can rally congregations to fight what they see as the moral decay in the country... not with the arduous biblically prescribed means, but through political action."

"Creating a base for the groups like the first Moral Majority and other similar activist groups, I assume."

"Well, it's a theory."

"It feels like some pastors use their large, highly charged emotional gatherings to manipulate."

"Or maybe," Rachel went on, "we are just guilty of intellectual myopia. Reason should not leave off where faith thrives. But if we are not careful, it does."

Their quiet was shattered by a group of noisy dentists in town for a convention who took up a nearby table and ruined the ambiance.

"Oh well," Enoch said, "nice while it lasted. And thanks, by the way, for inviting me today. It was an interesting lecture and discussion. I think I am more and more aware of why you have distanced yourself from the family business. WOWL propagates a political and ecclesiastical movement you fundamentally disagree with... still," he went on thoughtfully, "that's not a crime, I guess."

Immediately regretting his choice of words, Enoch changed the subject. But the issue had raised its ugly head and the drinking dentists had altered the mood and ended their quiet interlude.

Enoch held the heavy door to the street open for Rachel, who bumped into a large man charging through the opening.

"Ronald, what a surprise."

"Rachel? What are you doing here?"

It was an awkward moment. Enoch remained holding the door as the siblings extricated themselves from the unwelcome encounter.

Ronald Lorten didn't notice Enoch. Enoch, however, was fascinated for his first face to face with the CEO of WOWL.

"Well," Rachel explained, "that was my not-very-polite brother, Ronald. Sorry I didn't get a chance to introduce you. He seemed to be in a hurry."

Rachel kept her voice light but she was shaken at having run into Ronald while with Enoch. Comforted only by the fact her brother seldom noticed anything about her and would not have taken note that the man holding the door for his sister also took her arm as they started up the street together.

CHAPTER 24

BRING OUT THE DEAD

. . . It's just a flesh wound...

—The Black Knight

SCALLOP AND SHRIMP LINGUINE SETTLED LIKE A DEAD MASS IN Ronald Lorten's stomach. He pushed the remaining pasta to one side, picking over a few limp spinach leaves, then ordered a Pepcid with his coffee. Running into Rachel as he entered the restaurant hadn't helped his digestion. He wondered, without giving it much thought, about the well-dressed man leaving the restaurant with her. He didn't look like one of her usual slovenly academic colleagues.

Ronaldo, headwaiter at the Willard Hotel, knew Mr. Ronald Lorten and was happy to comply with any request, even the unorthodox ones. Tips were his bread and butter and the big man in cowboy boots tipped generously, especially when dining with others. The waiter slipped Lorten a package of little pink pills with his coffee and decided for the millionth time that Washington power was not worth the price. His customers could keep their high-powered lives. He didn't have their money, but he went home each day without pain in his stomach or fear in his eyes. Getting on top was clearly not the end but only the beginning of the struggle for people with power and money. Ronaldo smiled as the big wheels lowered their voices when he approached. They need not have bothered. Leaking tidbits from private conversations was a surefire way to get fired from the Willard Hotel.

The other men at the table looked as though their food hadn't settled well either. Edward Dudley, senior partner at Dudley, Smythe & Dudley, had been Ronald's lawyer since he took over WOWL, Inc. He inherited the association from his father before him. The second-generation relationship of media mogul and powerful law firm had proved mutually beneficial. And at times contentious.

While Edward Dudley didn't count Lorten as a personal friend (exactly) others might conclude their longtime relationship constituted a potential conflict of interest, so he had invited John Tuber, fellow partner in the firm, to join him for the working lunch and a young hire, Matthew Classen, who would be putting in the hours of research assistance as the case developed. WOWL had been "looked at" by the IRS before and Edward was not yet certain if this time would prove to be different. Instinct told him it was both bigger and more dangerous. To err on the side of caution was a way of life for D.C. lawyers and Dudley was nothing if not a big time D.C. lawyer.

One year out of Georgetown Law School, and giving all his waking hours to be at one of the city's more prestigious law firms, Matt was a typical hire for Dudley, Smythe & Dudley. He was top-of-his-class smart. Personable, aggressive, and hungry for success. Surprised to be included with two senior partners and such a high-powered client, Matt watched the edgy exchange during lunch between the powerful men with interest and excitement.

"Okay," the portly lawyer said, pushing away his empty coffee cup and tugging on his too-tight vest. "Caesar, having accomplished lunch, went out and conquered Gaul."

No one laughed. He didn't expect them to; it was a signal, not a joke.

Ronald took the sign, swallowed his Pepcid, cleared his throat, and began.

"So, you read the letter from Phil Grant. We've swatted this kind of fly before and I expect you to handle the legal side of things; I'll take care of the press when they get wind of it, which in this town, they are sure to do sooner rather than later. Just watch for a column by Tom Willis. 'IRS Investigates Religious Right Media Giant, WOWL.' I could write the damn headline it's so predictable."

Edward Dudley's response was slow and measured, not convinced by Ronald's bluster.

"It's not quite that simple, Ronald. In my opinion this might be different. To use your colorful phrase, it is going to be more than 'swatting a fly'. So, let's start by assuming the worst. Always the best place to start. Then hope to be pleasantly surprised when the worst doesn't turn out to be so bad after all."

Matt was waiting with sharpened pencil and yellow legal pad. Finally, they were getting down to it. His boss went on.

"Let's recap what we know. One Philip Grant, from Minnesota, comes to visit your corporate office as a reward for their nationwide contest. He then attends your fancy party out in Great Falls and is unfavorably impressed by your wealth and lifestyle. Checks out your public tax records for the non-profit and sends a well-argued letter to the IRS suggesting several kinds of financial malfeasance. We assume they have been wasting no time since receiving his letter. Mr. Grant's complaint was sure to get a serious look by the IRS. We know they have assigned a senior agent, one Enoch Arnheim, to investigate. Nothing official yet but his office is leaving footprints. Guess you shouldn't have invited a smart accountant to be your special guest, eh Ronald?"

"It's not funny, Eddie. Who knew mild-mannered Mr. Phil Bloody Grant would stab us in the back?"

Mr. Dudley leaned forward and rested his arms with some difficulty on the table. His arms and legs might be too short and his stomach too big, but there was nothing wrong with the man's mind. His eyes drilled holes into his client, looking for, but not expecting, the whole truth.

"Phil Grant," the lawyer went on, ignoring Ronald's response, "isn't your average run-of-the-mill disgruntled donor. I've checked out his firm. He's very successful. His complaint begins by suggesting inurement. Not easy to prove but very useful in building a case of public opinion. So what do you know about this Phil Grant? Anything you can tell us might be useful."

"I can tell you he is a narrow-minded, annoying, and ungrateful little shit," Ronald snapped. "We host the guy, let him attend our big party, and this is the thanks we get. Maybe he is one of those people who think that because our business is Christian we should live like poor people. Silly envious twit."

"At least he sent a copy of his letter to you — not the *Washington Post*."

"Small favor. And who says he didn't send a copy to the *Post?* They could be writing the story as we speak, or waiting for that snotty IRS agent assigned to the case to give them the dirt. Whoever this Arnheim is, he probably thinks going after a high-profile case like ours will make his career."

Ronald paused while the waiter returned to refill coffee cups and then continued his rant.

"So if my so-called 'lifestyle' is all the Feds have, let them bring it on... we are not in the communications business for nothing and the liberal press hounding Christians plays very well in Peoria. And people are sick of the First Lady, who never misses an opportunity to rail against their right-wing enemies, of whom we are chief, it seems. Hell, the administration is probably *behind* the investigation. It wouldn't be the first time the White House used the tax men to do their dirty work."

Edward Dudley was wishing they had had this conversation in the well-paneled, soundproofed law offices up Pennsylvania Avenue.

"Lower your voice and save your outrage for the press, Ronald. We are talking about what we know, not what you intend to spin. So let's focus on the facts, shall we?"

Lorten was in no mood to heed Edward's advice, lower his voice, or adjust his attitude. He felt betrayed that his longtime legal counsel had brought along another partner in the firm. He could understand the kid being present, briefed, and ready to do the dogsbody work, but the reason for John Tuber's presence was not lost on him. And he didn't like it.

He took another Pepcid.

"Do calm down, Ronald," Edward tried again. "First of all, while you might think it would be fun to take on the government in the press when this breaks, I'm telling you to resist such temptation. But we'll deal with that when the time comes. For now, we know they will try and prove excessive compensation, which could be damaging from a public relations standpoint but not much more. But if they charge tax fraud we're talking a whole other level. Could even kick the entire thing up to the CID."

Red blotches were spreading on Ronald's face, his neck swelling over his collar. With great effort he lowered his voice and hopefully his blood pressure.

"They don't have tax fraud," he said. "Because there hasn't been any tax fraud — and you as my very able counsel should know that as well as I do."

John Tuber was making notes, which had the effect of further irritating Lorten. This wasn't a deposition.

"You," Ronald pointed at young Classen. "You find out everything about this Agent Arnheim they've assigned to the case. Do any of you guys know anything about him?"

Happy for a chance to speak, the young lawyer jumped to reply.

"Are you kidding? That doesn't take research... just read the Style section in the *Post*. He's the boyfriend of the hot press secretary over at the State Department. Her name is Laura Stellar."

"Thank you, Matt," his boss said. "But I think Mr. Lorten is looking for something a little more substantial than his living arrangement. Make a note to check him out."

"Yes, sir," the chastened young man went back to making notes, but couldn't help adding one more comment.

"Actually, Mr. Lorten, I think you met him at the door as you came in. He was with your sister."

Like dropping a rock in a pond, ripples of amazement spread like waves across the table. Finally Ronald found his voice.

"Don't be absurd, boy. That's impossible on so many levels we don't even have time. And don't even think about repeating that. To anyone!"

Matt assured him he must have been mistaken and tried hard not to see his career at Dudley, Smythe, & Dudley slipping away. He wasn't used to volatile and voluble clients in snakeskin boots. Determined not to further infuriate the client, he closed his mouth and lowered his eyes, intent on the yellow legal pad.

Edward Dudley was getting more and more nervous watching Ronald Lorten. Either Lorten was truly incensed by the government's overreach or, and this is what worried him, his old friend was hiding something from him.

Adjusting his substantial weight against the table again, the lawyer pressed his hands together, fingers bouncing off each other. He fixed Ronald with the equivalent of a Paddington legal stare.

"Okay, Ronald, forget about who the investigator is, it doesn't matter. Focus on what does matter. I think we can assume the government has not yet taken the case to the CID because making an IRS case is easier and doesn't cost the taxpayer as much, however... and I want you to listen to me now... however, let's not assume that does not mean that they either cannot or will not do so in the future."

Ronald was listening and thinking, fast. He tapped his teaspoon gently on the table and signaled the waiter for more water. The thought that Rachel might know and be seeing the IRS investigator had shaken him.

"Okay, you're right, Edward. Of course. Nothing assumed. And I'm not worried. Mad as hell, but not worried because I know how good you are at your job. Haven't your legal eagles been watching my every step for the last decade — ever since we went from an unknown, pretty miserable little Christian radio station... to... well, to what we are today. You have been taking care of me all along the way. Watched the sales, the buybacks, the expansion. All of it. All your accountants were on board so, what the heck, it doesn't look like the government has much except a political axe to grind by telling the world I am an overpaid executive. And *that* I know how to fight. Hit me and I will hit back ten times harder."

He sat back, drained his glass of water, and hoped his expression was the essence of ease when he felt anything but.

Leif was furious with him for putting his precious congregation at risk. Jeff was panicking. His useless sister continued to go about life totally unaware. Or worse, was actually talking to the IRS behind his back. Despite all the real and tangible good he had done with the Awareness Campaign, here he was suffering a grilling by *his* own lawyers with his political future at risk.

John Tuber and Edward Dudley received the message just given — that they had a stake in the outcome along with WOWL. In fact, they had been expecting Lorten to remind them of that. In their joint and studied opinion, Ronald Lorten was probably in more trouble than he knew, and hopefully not more than they knew. Either way, his ship could sail very close to their own and both men shared his need, if not his taste, for an antacid.

"Legal is not the only thing that matters here, my old friend, as you very well know," Edward went on, some of the sting out of his voice. "As someone in communications, you should know that better than most. I think some past transactions, while perfectly legal — and we will cheerfully stake the reputation of the firm on that — might... well... take some explaining to your donors, your constituents. However, let's deal with that later. Right now I want to know, I have to know, right here, right now... no messing about with me... what else IRS Agent Enoch Arnheim might know or find out, that you have not yet disclosed to us. I can only do my job if I have all the facts... and I do mean *all* the facts."

Ronald knew this question had to be asked. But he was not pleased his supposedly old friend found it necessary to bring a witness with him, to hear both question and answer. Two of the three men looking at him were not fooled by his expression of hurt.

John Tuber broke the uncomfortable silence.

"Mr. Lorten, I don't have to tell you how important it is for you to answer that question. Fully and honestly! I want to hear your answer — in front of God and everybody at this table — what else, if anything, is there for the IRS to find?"

"You tell me. Your accountants go over our books, sign off on audits, and monitor all new deals, so you tell me. Should I be worried? Hell, Eddie, how long have we known each other? I absolutely wouldn't lie to you, but I'm not the lawyer here."

It was an awkward moment. Neither of the fine gentlemen from Dudley, Smythe, & Dudley wanted to alienate the firm's most lucrative client. The question having been asked and answered at least gave cover to Edward with his partners, so he deescalated the tension.

"Okay, for the moment let's move on. The central question in the end is not how you live, but whether or not you, or other family members, have enlarged your personal wealth at the expense of taxpayers and your faithful donors. Mr. Phil Grant seems to think you have, and he has convinced the IRS to take a very close look. So far it seems they might just agree with him. My advice is we take this very seriously... that's all I'm saying."

"Take it seriously... you think I'd be paying your exalted fees if it wasn't serious? What do I have to do to convince you I'm serious? Put on sackcloth and ashes?"

"Well the first thing you do is shut up when I tell you to shut up. Keep politics out of this. And follow my advice or I can't be responsible for the outcome. You want to try this in the press, you better go get new legal counsel."

Before Ronald had time to respond his lawyer continued.

"And secondly, we make the first move. I don't like to play catch-up. We provide answers before they even have time to think up the questions. We respond before deadlines. We answer all phone calls and e-mails in a timely, and careful, fashion. I want all the surprises to be on our side. You give me everything I want, when I want it, and don't hold back on me, Ronald. Do what I say and I'll take care of the Feds."

Matt's juices were flowing at this exciting exchange. This is why he had joined the firm. They had big clients with national reach, and he wanted to be part of that. He was part of it and he couldn't believe his good luck.

Lorten leaned back until his chair tipped precariously toward the windows facing Pennsylvania Avenue. Passing tourists looked in, probably wondering at the important Washington types lucky enough to be dining in the Willard Hotel. Ronald Lorten did not feel lucky. He felt like killing his brother-in-law... except that he was already dead. Without the blackmail hiding under the surface, this IRS investigation would be standard stuff, easily handled by his capable legal counsel. There was no way in the world he could tell Dudley, Smythe, & Dudley about Cricket Hartford, her HIV, and the two blackmail payments.

"Okay," Ronald said. "That's more like it. I want you to go after the IRS, not the other way around. But what you don't understand up there in your legal tower is this... the IRS doesn't want answers or quick responses or polite phone calls. They want a pound of conservative flesh. My conservative Christian flesh, to be precise. I'm sorry, Eddie, but this is personal and it is political. We can't win if we aren't playing the same game. I'll wait until it leaks but then I'm fighting back. You fight them your way and I'll fight them mine. In case you hadn't noticed we are coming up on the presidential election cycle. Now that the House and Senate are back in Republican control, the White House is the next prize and I damned well intend to be in the race. There is more at stake than my little company. A cultural battle is being fought for the very heart and soul of this nation and I'm not going to stand by, dumb as Balaam's ass, because my lawyer is running scared."

Edward Dudley was not fooled. But he was impressed.

"Lovely speech, Ronald. Practicing for the press is fine and, at the right time, I'm sure you will convince lots of voters and donors that you are the victim here. Maybe even that they should elect you President of this great nation. But do remember not to give me that crap. You will follow my counsel or I can't save you. And do lower your voice."

"I'm bloody well not going to lower my voice! I'm right and you know it. The Federal Government is getting the cart ready and I can hear the cry now... 'bring out the dead.' They want me on the cart... but I'll be damned if I'm getting on the cart... I'm not dead yet."

There was just the slightest pause before Matt, forgetting himself, feigned a perfect English accent and proceeded with a favorite Monty Python quote.

"Oh stop being such a baby and get on the cart."

A terrible silence fell over the group of men.

With his law career at Dudley, Smythe & Dudley now well and truly passing before his eyes, Matt tried to salvage the moment. In an even stronger British accent he carried on:

"Oh stop being such a baby and get on the cart... it's classic... Python, you know, 'Monty Python and the Holy Grail'... remember... the plague cart is going round picking up dead bodies and the John Cleese's character says... " His voice trailed off miserably.

No one laughed. But Lorten was glad for the interruption and used the moment to signal the waiter for the check.

"Thank you, Matthew," John Tuber said as they put on their coats. "I'm sure your college buddies found that kind of thing amusing. Probably not so wise to try it on with clients."

As they moved toward the door, Edward took his client by the sleeve and pulled him to the side.

"You might actually want to ask Rachel about her friendship with Enoch Arnheim, by the way. You might not like it but young Classen was right, I saw them too."

Ronald mumbled something about Rachel not having anything to do with the business and being free to drink coffee with the devil himself. But had he not turned quickly away, the lawyer would have seen devastation written all over Lorten's sagging features. He knew that handsome young IRS Agent wouldn't be having coffee with his sister for the fun of it.

The lawyers walked in silence to their office on the corner of Pennsylvania and 18th Street. The older men were aware that the Lorten Empire might be in real trouble and their firm along with it. The meeting had not gone well. Edward knew the man well enough to know that either Lorten was feeling cornered and wanting to fight back, or supremely confident due to an abundance of innocence. Somehow he didn't think it was the latter.

Edward Dudley pulled the collar of his coat over his ears against the cold wind. He was feeling the effects of too much rich food and caffeine and too little trust between old colleagues.

John Tuber, who had said little during the meal, said even less on the walk back. But when they were alone and behind closed doors, he made his position crystal clear.

"I don't buy Ronald Lorten's self-righteous I-am-the-victim-here routine. Make sure you don't either, Edward. And try not to forget where, at the end of the day, your interest lies. Not with your old buddy, who just might be headed for a very bad end. That campaign against human trafficking didn't buy them enough goodwill in this town to withstand a serious scandal... which reminds me, ask young Matt to go through the details to see if there were any restricted-income violations in that campaign. How much went to build the Justice Center in Sarajevo. How much into the family coffers? And tell the young lad he had better grow up fast, or he'll be doing his growing up at some other firm."

CHAPTER 25

THE PUMPKIN PATCH

Turn back, O man, forswear thy foolish ways.
Old now is earth, and none may count her days.

—*Clifford Bax*

HALLOWEEN HAVING COME AND GONE, PUMPKINS WERE IN short supply at the pumpkin patch on Reston Avenue. Once mountains of sunny orange had been reduced to littered leftovers on well- trampled grass.

In a time when ranging free is no longer an option for children or chickens, something buried in the agrarian past of the American psyche comes to life in the fall, triggering a need to connect with nature. Enterprising citizens, happy to meet this need, marketed harvest nostalgia along with pumpkins and pasteurized apple juice. Lines of minivans arrived like lemmings and disgorged children from government-approved safety seats into a carefully controlled "natural" experience.

Plastic spiders still hung in drooping webs when Rachel arrived to get pumpkins for Justin and Sally. A faded sign reminded children to stay off the pumpkin pile and offered a plastic playground free of splinters and allergic reactions as an alternative to actual hay. A sterilized, pasteurized, and plasticized harvest.

Rachel had promised her niece and nephew pumpkins for Halloween and, operating on the theory that late was better than never, she had found two small, only moderately rotten, gourds and drove to Jeff and Ellie's stately mansion down a private lane off Colvin Mill Run to drop them off.

"Anybody home?" Rachel called, juggling the pumpkins as she opened the front door.

"Hello, hello!"

A welcome shouted from deep in the house invited her to come on in.

"Auntie Rachel," Justin said, giving his favorite aunt a big hug as she entered the kitchen. The lanky teenager was enjoying a snack of chips and salsa. "I'm so glad you're here. But you're like, way early for Halloween next year or about a month late."

"Oh please! Details, details, details," she said, giving him a peck on the cheek. "Take your pumpkin. Give one to Sally. Go. Learn to make a pumpkin pie for Thanksgiving."

Justin laughed.

"Yeah, like you know how. Uncle Eric used to say, 'the only domestic thing about my wife is she lives in a house'."

Rachel smiled at her adorable nephew and set about making tea in the gourmet kitchen.

"He might have said that," she replied, "to which I would have replied... why have a dog and do your own barking?"

"Okay, you lost me on that one."

"It means, you silly boy, why be domestic when I had a husband to do it for me? He liked to cook, design and decorate the house. And was much better at it, so I graciously let him. By the way, where's your mother?"

"She's coming. So who decorated your current beautiful house?"

"Well, now that is different. I designed it. I didn't just decorate it. And to further impress you, I want you to know I'm going to stop at

Safeway on the way home, buy a pie crust and make an apple pie with fruit from my very own tree. How domestic is that?"

"Any fool can put fruit into a pie shell," Ellie said, coming into the room. "The skill is in making the crust, not picking it up at Safeway."

"Don't listen to her, Aunt Rachel," Justin said, taking his leave of the kitchen. "But don't get too domestic, I like you just the way you are."

A dense fog was closing in, settling over the trees in the backyard, as Ellie and Rachel took their tea to a counter island in the cozy kitchen that smelled of fresh baked ginger cookies, which Rachel tried, and failed, to resist.

"So what's up with you? Other than your rather lame excuse of dropping by to bring the kids pumpkins," Ellie remarked.

"Okay, it was a little lame but I did want to see you and it was an excuse to stop at the rather pathetic looking farmer's market," Rachel lowered her voice in case one of the kids came back into the kitchen. "You won't believe the folly I've just committed."

"Not true, I believe you capable of all kinds of folly. But do tell."

"Okay. Yesterday, Enoch and I went to a lecture at the Ethics and Public Policy Center, then stopped in for a bite to eat at the Willard."

Ellie raised her eyebrows in surprise but Rachel ignored her reaction and went on.

"And who should we meet on our way out the door but my dear brother. Not your husband. The other one. It was a little ah... awkward... as the kids say. I didn't introduce Enoch, obviously, and I'm not sure Ronald noticed him. But if Ronald realized I was with the IRS agent in charge of investigating the company, I think he would... well, I can't even imagine what he would do. Probably die of an aneurysm. And, by the way, he was there to have dinner with his lawyers. I saw half the firm of Dudley, Smythe & Dudley at a table, waiting for him."

"Oh dear, Rachel. Did the Dudley brothers see you with Enoch?"

"Well, only one Dudley brother was there, but one is enough and I think he might have. You know Enoch gets his face in the Post occasionally with Laura-the-beautiful. And mother has been frantically trying to reach me... leaving increasingly desperate messages on my answering machine about something Ronald told her. I don't know, maybe the lawyers wouldn't recognize Enoch."

Ellie was no longer smiling.

"Of course they would. Even I have seen his picture with Laura. It's quintessential Washington gossip: beautiful, powerful woman and her..."

Rachel winced.

"I didn't mean it like that. I'm just saying people in D.C. might recognize him."

"I doubt if Mr. Dudley or Mr. Smythe read the Style Section. Especially since Mr. Smythe has been dead for twenty years."

"It isn't funny, Rachel."

"I know. I know. My brothers and my mother already think I was an unsuitable wife but this would make me... an unsuitable widow. And they are probably right on both counts. But they're not right about me being a traitor because of that friendship. If anything it's the opposite."

Ellie looked and felt exhausted. Jeff had been harder to live with recently. As usual he was taking his pressure out on her and the kids. She had taken Rachel's advice and had not asked any questions, but ever since his argument with Ronald that she overheard, her husband's black moods were increasing. Without Eric's talk show as a launching pad for his new book, sales were lagging, which didn't help either. She sighed.

"You know Rachel, maybe you shouldn't be seeing this guy. It might backfire."

Rachel trusted Ellie but didn't want to hear this advice.

"It could," she agreed. "But I think it's worth the risk. I'm still convinced it's better to have some control over where his investigation is going than to stand by wondering when and where it will explode. And I'm encouraged that Enoch seems to be focusing on financial issues that might bring fines but no real scandal. If it doesn't go any further than that, Ronald could agree to take a plea, pay the fines, and spin the deal as harassment by the government. Which has been known to happen. And if it looks like a heavy-handed, targeted attack on a conservative, that could even help his political ambitions."

Ellie thought for a minute before asking the question on her mind.

"And the other reason you're still seeing Enoch? What about the emotional risk of that?"

"Does there have to be another reason?" she asked, then answered, her own question. "We *do* seem to enjoy each other's company. Which is a little strange, right?"

Ellie didn't think it strange at all.

"You cannot be so blind, Rachel, as to think men really see you as your mother thinks men see you."

"Whatever that means."

"You know exactly what it means and we've had this conversation... how many times since college?"

"You tell me, I'm not good in math."

"It means you *are* attractive to men, dummy."

"I don't think Eric thought so."

"Eric was a twit. And he used you... "

"I used him too... "

Ellie remembered the last family Christmas party. He seemed different, more attentive to Rachel.

"Did something change," she asked, "in your relationship with Eric toward the end? Like he was working on the marriage?"

"Ha. Such work would have been too hard for him."

Her flippant remark was not completely honest.

Eric had seemed different in the months leading up to his death, a fact Rachel had tried hard to ignore. Like the day he died. He had called and offered to pick her up from the airport and take her out for dinner. Embarrassed about her condescending response to his frustration at the DMV, she had decided on the way home to try and be kinder and take him up on the dinner offer. But Eric was dead before she landed and kinder words were never said.

"Well," Ellie went on, "even if he *had* changed toward the end, Eric decided to marry you because you were part of the Lorten family, which means he used you deliberately... you just stopped thinking for a while when you met him — affected, as we all were, by how handsome and charming he could be. But that is a very different thing from premeditation. You know you don't give men much of a chance, Rachel — you are so formidable. I don't want to sound like your mother, but you could be a little more vulnerable sometimes."

"Okay, okay, let's drop this ridiculous conversation. It's embarrassing. And Enoch Arnheim must have his own motives having to do with the case. Whatever the reason, obviously not romantic, since he is in love and living with beautiful Laura. But whatever the reason, he is happy to share some time with me occasionally."

"Of course he is. I'm reminded of that great line by Jane Austen... can't remember which book... men are biased by a certain kind of beauty so they end up married to very silly women. A terrible fate, but no man would suffer that with you."

"Oh, I think some men want silly women. Look at my brother, your husband. Your beauty he loves, but your brains intimidate him and, let's face it, threaten his terribly inflated ego. I actually think Jeff would prefer a silly, dumb blonde always smiling at him from stage-right like a politician's wife on Valium."

Ellie laughed at the very familiar Washington image of pert, perfectly dressed politician's wife, smiling vapidly at her man. The perfect accessory for the powerful man. Ellie's laugh wasn't a happy one. Jeff did want a "Stepford" wife. And he had a way of making life difficult when she refused to play that role.

Sally joined them just then and the conversation turned to safer topics while the three girls finished off the ginger cookies.

CHAPTER 26

TEA FOR TWO

Better than any argument is to rise at dawn and
pick dew-wet red berries in a cup.

—*Wendell Berry*

THE RED LIGHT WAS BLINKING ON THE ANSWERING MACHINE when Rachel returned from her evening run the next day. She decided to ignore what was bound to be more hysterical messages from her mother. As usual, Pippin had followed Rachel on her jog along the lane up to the place she took off into the woods for a half-mile trail run. The scrappy little cat hid in the hedgerow, waiting until Rachel looped back to the same place on the road, then sprang at her ankles in mock attack, rolled over in the dirt to be petted, then trotted along into the house for a spot of milk for his bother.

All joy sucked out of the evening routine by the insistence of her mother's phone calls, Rachel forgot to give Pippin his treat, collapsed into the swing on the deck, and dialed her mother's number. Without too much trouble she gave in to a face to face at the Lorten home Saturday afternoon.

Alice Lorten wandered from room to room, unable to find peace while waiting for her daughter to arrive. She was determined to make Rachel listen to reason and had prepared and practiced what to say to her.

Afternoon tea was laid out in the drawing room.

Cucumber sandwiches without crusts and raisin nut tarts had been artfully arranged on a silver tray with the tea ready when Rachel arrived. Mrs. Lorten poured and they sipped the comforting liquid, ignored the food, and made the smallest talk possible while trying to find a way to ease into the reason for the visit.

"Darling," Mrs. Lorten said, putting down her china cup and forgetting her carefully prepared lines, blurted out her true feelings. "You simply have to stop dating that horrible Jewish investigator! Ronald told me you were with him at the Willard Hotel Restaurant. No, no, you listen," she said when Rachel tried to protest the outlandish accusation. "Let me finish. I can see why you might be attracted to this man... you must be desperately lonely without your wonderful Eric... no one will compare to him, of course, and I know you are lonely but, Rachel, you have to ask yourself why he would be seeing you."

Something in Rachel's demeanor gave her mother pause.

In a slightly less strident voice she went on: "I don't want to hurt you, Rachel, but the man is known to be living with the State Department spokeswoman, Laura what's her name... and she is... "

"Beautiful," Rachel interrupted. "Yes, mother, I know he has a partner, and who she is, and what she looks like."

"Well then, then you must know why he's dating you. How can you possibly do this to your family? He's the enemy. You're dating the enemy."

That was not what Alice Lorten had intended to say. She usually failed to say what she intended to say to her only daughter. Rachel had been a difficult child. Now she was proving to be an even more difficult adult.

Trying not to care so much, Rachel looked away from her mother and around the room. Tea had been prepared as though the Queen of England was coming for a chat. She can prepare the house — but not her heart — for me, Rachel thought miserably.

Alice Lorten was perfectly coifed, manicured, and waxed. There was strength in keeping up appearances and Mrs. Lorten was a master of appearances. But today, even with expensive makeup and the experienced hand that had applied it, Alice Lorten's face showed shadows of age and stress. Her eyes were swollen. Tears and anger had taken a toll since Ronald told his mother the family was facing an IRS investigation and that Rachel had been seen with the investigator. He didn't want to confront Rachel yet, but he knew and used the fact his mother would.

Mrs. Lorten's hands were in her lap restlessly straightening out imaginary wrinkles in a perfectly pressed linen skirt.

"Well, say something, Rachel. Don't just sit there staring at me. Tell me why you are dating a man who is out to destroy our family."

Rachel took a deep breath and tried to sound rational, devoid of emotion.

"First of all, mother, I'm not *dating* Enoch Arnheim. I have seen him on several occasions. I met him through my work; we enjoy each other and get together occasionally. As friends. Not dating, okay? Please do not use that silly word which does not apply in any case. Actually, he came to see me about a proposed trip his parents wanted to take in Eastern Europe and he wanted my professional opinion about the safety of travel in the region. They are Holocaust survivors and want to return and see if they can find... "

Mrs. Lorten threw up her arms in frustration and shrieked.

"Oh I don't care about his horrible parents and their travel; I don't care and I don't want to hear it. I'm talking about us, Rachel. I'm talking about our family. Even if you did meet this man before you knew he was investigating the company, surely once you found out you wouldn't have gone on seeing him. Ronald says you are responsible for this mess, although he wouldn't explain how. And I must admit, I don't see how you dating this man could make you responsible for the investigation, but I do see his point about your complete lack of loyalty."

Rachel laughed. "Ronald said that? He said I'm responsible? Well, that is a novel perspective. I don't think having a few lunches with the investigator is probably what he was referring to."

Mrs. Lorten's not-very-bright face struggled with this new idea.

"What do you mean? What else could it be? You have always acted like you are too good to be a part of our ministry. Like we are all beneath you. Even Eric cared more about the family than you do. Still," she paused, looking heavenward, "I must admit I don't see how you could possibly be responsible for an IRS investigation. Arnheim sounds Jewish. Is he Jewish, Rachel? Oh dear, dear, I thought everything would finally be okay between us when you married Eric. But it isn't okay. Is it?"

Mrs. Lorten was crying now and all the pretty work on her face was washing away.

"Mom, please," Rachel said, scooting forward on the chair so she could touch her mother's hands.

"Please, listen to me Mom, for once. Just listen. As much as we misunderstand each other I have never wanted to hurt you — admittedly I have done so sometimes, but it wasn't intentional. At least I hope not. Certainly not by sabotaging the company. Maybe Ronald was exaggerating out of frustration. And, don't you think it's long past the time we could honestly refer to WOWL as a ministry? Still, I'm sure Ronald was upset, he probably said things he shouldn't have or you simply misunderstood him. Please try not to worry. Ronald will take care of whatever is going on, remember that he has very good lawyers. And try not to worry about me. As I said, Enoch is just a friend. I'm not foolish enough to think it could be otherwise."

Rachel could remember with clarity so many other moments in the room, trying to talk to her mother. She didn't remember any that actually succeeded. This time needed to be different. Her mother was bewildered, her world in danger of falling apart, and Rachel desperately needed to avoid adding guilt over hurting her mother to other regrets at the moment.

"Mom, you were with Dad when you started the first radio station, the very first little radio station. It provided good preaching, interesting forums to discuss important issues of the faith, wonderful hymns. It was something good. Don't you sometimes feel that WOWL, that we, have lost our way since then?"

Mrs. Lorten brushed her daughter's hands away.

"That is simply not the point. Don't change the subject."

"In fact, Mom, it is precisely the point. Don't you want, more than anyone else really, that things should be put right, for your sake, and for Dad's memory? If the company has done something illegal or even unethical, don't you think it should be addressed? Wouldn't Dad have wanted that?"

Aware she had utterly failed to convince her stubborn daughter and unable to look directly into her eyes, Alice Lorten stood and went to the window and gazed out across the acres of garden, wringing her hands, rings knocking against rings. Gathering her thoughts and drying her tears, she tried once again.

"Of course Ronald wouldn't let anything illegal happen. Jeff wouldn't either. How can you say such terrible things? You are just jealous of your brothers; you always have been. They're successful and you're not, but I don't know why you can't see the good they do and be glad for that instead of always tearing them down." Her usually soft, seductive southern accent had all but disappeared. At that moment Alice Lorten sounded every inch a Yankee.

"I think it would be better if you just go now, and... maybe you should stay away for awhile until you are ready to apologize. I can't believe you could even suggest the boys have done something wrong. This government agent is a liberal, probably pagan, person who wants to destroy our Christian witness and you are helping him. It breaks my heart as your mother."

Aware that no amount of reason would penetrate years of estrangement, and having little appetite for more pain, Rachel stood up and moved toward the door.

"I am sorry," she said to her mother's back. "I am really so sorry... families shouldn't hurt each other this much. Especially not families who profess to have Christian charity as their spiritual birthright. And while you won't believe it, the truth is I want Agent Arnheim to fail more than any of you. Much, much more than any of you do. However, he is good at what he does and if WOWL has anything to hide I imagine he will find it. Find it all."

Mrs. Lorten turned just as Rachel left the room and shouted after her.

"What do you mean, Rachel, what do you mean?"

She watched her daughter walk across the lawns toward the woods. Like everything else about Rachel, Alice Lorten couldn't understand why she wanted to live alone in the terrible old carriage house. Even with remodeling it seemed odd for a young woman to live alone in the woods.

Ronald had asked her to call after and fill him in on her talk with Rachel, but she needed a glass of sherry to steady her nerves before talking to her son. He wouldn't be pleased. Sipping the soothing liquid, Mrs. Lorten wondered again if Rachel really was her own flesh and blood. Babies are sometimes switched at birth, she had told her husband often enough. To which he had always replied: "Yes, but not ours. She looks just like me."

Cold and damp when she got home, Rachel made a strong cup of coffee with freshly ground beans and took it with her laptop to the library. All hope of enjoying her weekend now gone, she decided to at least accomplish some work. An unproductive hour later, unable to concentrate on a review she was writing, Rachel decided it was time to act. Loath to actually talk to her brother, she sent Ronald an e-mail demanding, not requesting, that they meet first thing Monday morning.

Rachel arrived at the WOWL corporate headquarters at 9:00 a.m. precisely. She parked her car in the spot marked "Jeffery Lorten" since she didn't have a reserved place.

Ronald's administrative assistant, Martha Culberson, was friendly, if a little perplexed at the unusual visit of Ronald's sister.

"Good morning Mrs. Kissane, please go on in. Your brother is expecting you."

Lorten remained sitting behind his massive desk. She sat down without invitation and came right to the point.

"Mother might have told you we had a little talk," she began.

Eager for a fight, he pounced.

"Mother was hysterical after you left. You have been a shit to her for more years than I care to think about. However, I'm assuming you didn't come to talk to me about your appalling relationship with our mother. So say what you've come to say. I have work to do and I can't say I'm exactly thrilled to see you."

"How honest of you," Rachel replied with a thin smile. "You're right. I'm not here to talk about Mom, but I am here, as odd as it may seem, to help you. Admittedly, it will help me too. But you are, above all dear brother, a pragmatist and it is to your pragmatism that I am going to appeal. You can lose a little or you can lose a lot. It's up to you."

Ronald listened while she talked, his face growing red and blotchy, neck swelling over his collar as it did when his blood pressure went up.

"Let me see," he said when she finished, his voice dripping with sarcasm. "Let me see if I've got this straight. You're telling me that your husband had HIV when he died, and you are concerned that some woman — or God forbid, some man out there might crawl out from under a rock and sell their story if the IRS investigation into our finances becomes public? So you are suggesting, and this is very novel, that I plead guilty to all kinds of financial malfeasance in order to protect you from Eric's sordid past coming to light. Is that it? Did I get it right?"

"More or less," she replied, thinking it curious he was not more surprised. "Except, you missed the part about how it will protect you too. If you think the IRS won't find this kind of scandal and leak it to help make their case, then you are not as clever as I thought. And if you don't believe me, ask Edward Dudley if he would prefer to defend WOWL, Inc. against charges of financial malfeasance or defend WOWL against financial malfeasance with a sex scandal as background music. In fact, you can blame the lawyers, blame the accountants, blame the liberals, or an overzealous administration out to get a conservative like you and, voila, you get lots of sympathy, make a deal, pay the fine. Life goes on. You might be a little weakened, but not destroyed. But let the IRS dig around long enough and find the scandal, and the harm to the company, not just me personally, will be catastrophic. If I were you, I would want to know and factor this into my calculations. That's all I'm saying. That's why I'm telling you."

He couldn't believe her nerve. But she was right about the danger, so he proceeded with an abundance of restraint.

"How magnanimous of you."

What he wanted to do was tell her all about the beautiful Cricket Hartford and how he sympathized with Eric if not approved of his behavior. He wanted to tell Rachel about the blackmail. But she might just share it with her friend at the IRS and as much as he hated her for saying it, Rachel's point was well taken. She mistook his hesitation for agreement.

"Think about it, Ronald. If Eric had HIV, that means he had been very promiscuous. Do you really want to risk giving one of those women an opportunity to tell their story on CNN? Or worse, the tabloids? We both know there are people out there who would pay for that kind of dirt on our family. But if you enter a plea, give Arnheim enough to satisfy Phil Grant and the IRS, the Administration can crow a little, you survive to fight, and maybe even run for office... another day."

Then she made a tactical misstep (her first) in the conversation.

"The good news is I think I can buy us a little time with Enoch…"

"Stop!" He shouted. Unable to bear the irony of the moment, beyond fury, he held up his hand to end the insulting suggestion that his sister could actually help him through her connection to the investigator.

"Just stop right there. Are you actually suggesting Agent Arnheim cares enough about you to accept some kind of quid pro quo? I hope you're not so naïve, dear sister, as to think you have anything to give that man that would keep him from his appointed task. Namely destroying us. That is, quite frankly, laughable."

Rachel had watched her brother's face contort in rage and morph to sneer. And while she had expected anger, this was something more and it worried her. He had not even questioned that Eric had HIV when he smashed his car so spectacularly into a tree on Georgetown Pike. Or ask how she knew.

She wondered about that. When his rant ran out of steam, she prodded a little more to see if she could find out.

"How very quaint of you, Ronald, to suggest I might be selling… what is it called? Favors? No. No. No. As you so correctly point out, that is not likely for multiple and obvious reasons."

"Sorry," he replied, slumping down in his chair. He too was considering the dangerous waters they were in and knew that further antagonizing his sister wouldn't help. "I didn't mean that, exactly," he mumbled.

"Of course you did. But never mind. The point is, what will you do now? Whether you like it or not, it is to our mutual benefit to contain the IRS investigation to as narrow a scope as possible. Don't fight it, pay the fines, and it will go away before major scandal erupts. I know you wouldn't give into the IRS in order to protect me from the emotional fallout of having all of Washington tittering about my unfaithful husband. I wouldn't ask you to. But you must see… it isn't just about me. A scandal like this could do terrible harm, maybe irreparable harm, especially if seen in the light of the IRS probe. Phil Grant came out of nowhere. He's not my fault. It's not my fault you've allowed this once wonderful ministry to turn into a rapacious and very politicized business, rationalizing your multimillion-plus salary and millions more in benefits and perks, not to mention those for Jeff and other top executives like Charlie Rice. It is *wrong* that good people all over America give their tithes and offerings to what they assume is a ministry when it mostly makes you rich and famous. So now the business has to answer for its questionable ethical, if not illegal, practices. I admit Eric's behavior has added a potentially much more dangerous element, and that's why I came here to tell you, to warn you. And while I didn't expect thanks I also didn't expect, even from you, such invective. So, as the kids say... chill out. Think about it, and get back to me when you've calmed down."

A moment of silence descended over the room as the siblings, who had never understood or liked each other, struggled with the realization that they might have to collaborate in order to prevent mutual destruction.

"Time is rather of the essence here, Ronald," she said in parting. "It might be good to make up your mind sooner rather than later."

CHAPTER 27

THANKSGIVING DINNER

Once your reputation's done. You can live a life of fun.

—*Wilhelm Busch*

THANKSGIVING CAME, UNBIDDEN AND UNWELCOME, BY EVERY-one in the Lorten family. But tradition demanded the clan's annual gathering at the appointed time and place. Ronald and Connie always hosted Thanksgiving, and Christmas was held at the family estate in Great Falls. Any actual feelings of thankfulness were in short supply this year as the family gathered. Rachel chose to arrive late and slip into her place at the heavily laden and beautifully decorated dining table between Aunt Gladys and Justin. Connie greeted her last guest with a southern frostiness that bordered on hostility.

Norman Rockwell could not have painted a more all-American scene. Candlelight softened the décor if not the mood in the room. The rounded softness of blue hydrangea arrangements on the mantlepiece contrasted with tall grasses sprouting from elongated copper pots on the hearth framing either side of the roaring fireplace. The holiday aroma of roasting meat mingled with the spicy scent of cinnamon, cloves, and sugar.

"Hello, Auntie Gladys," Rachel said, giving her elderly aunt a peck on the cheek and breathing in the strong smells of fine face powder and expensive perfume. Once-chiseled cheekbones had settled into a comfortable fleshiness, but the elegant old lady's smile was as sweet and genuine as ever. Unaware of current family tensions, Aunt Gladys chattered away to Rachel about the weather, parking problems at the Tyson's Corner Mall, and the difficulty of getting good seats this season at the Kennedy Center.

Justin, who usually masked his teenage angst in juvenile and sometimes inappropriate humor, was in a fine fettle, teasing his sister Sally across the table. Then, when he could get in a word between Aunt Gladys's shopping concerns, he asked Rachel how she got away with coming late to dinner.

Justin was fifteen. A dangerous, difficult age in the best of times, and this was most decidedly not the best of times for his family. Jeff and Ellie's oldest child was angry at the eruptions on his face, his father's moods, and life in general. Rachel knew how he felt and she figured he would get over most of it, with time. At least he could see the little ironies in life and exploit them with wit. Justin had a winning smile that hid all manner of pain seething right below the surface.

"So I hear your grades could be better at the moment, young man," Rachel said to him. "Is that true?"

"Is that a philosophical question, Aunt Rachel? Because if so I really couldn't say. Your question is, well, ambivalent at best. And raises other more interesting questions... like what are grades anyway... and better than what? See. It's complicated, but on the other hand," he said, while tucking into a big bite of turkey, "I could say that my grades are probably a true reflection of my esteem for the academic institution my parents are paying through the nose for."

Rachel laughed. His father, who heard most of the exchange from across the wide expanse of table, did not laugh. He glared at his son.

"Hmmm, okay, let me rephrase," Rachel said. "What are you going to do after someone in authority at that overpriced educational institution tosses you out on your ear to consider the meaning of life from a less lofty environment?"

"They wouldn't dare do that to a Lorten," he said cheerfully, scarfing down mounds of mashed potatoes, baked crispy brown under a layer of Gruyere cheese, and more meat than a third-world inhabitant would see in a year.

She munched on her salad and crispy bread.

"You dieting or what, Aunt Rachel?"

"Or what."

Like all teenage boys, Justin's appetite was enormous, but he had been blessed with his mother's height and thin frame and bore no resemblance to the large bones and broad shoulders of the Lorten clan. He would never have to starve to stay thin.

"So, are you going to tell me about your grades?"

"Well, I could quote a little-known philosopher, Wilhelm Busch, you might have introduced me to him, who once suggested, 'Once your reputation's done/You can live a life of fun.' With my academic career in ruins at age fifteen, I guess I might as well begin a life of fun."

"Oh rubbish, Justin, I'm sure I didn't introduce you to any such philosopher. And I'm also sure you will pull out your grades before it's too late. Because despite your best efforts to disguise it, you are a very intelligent boy. And just who do you think would pay for your 'life of fun'?"

Justin kept shoveling. Rachel went on in a lowered voice.

"Because, somehow, I can't see my brother funding your little plan."

Full and past, Justin finally put down knife and fork, and rubbed his stomach.

"You know, Aunt Rachel, you can be very boring sometimes. But let's talk about you. You look," he paused for a moment looking intently at her in the candlelight. "You look different recently... like glowing, or something."

"Glowing? Really, Justin now you *are* starting to worry me."

Alice Lorten chose that moment to assert her matriarchal role and tapped ever so lightly, silver spoon against crystal goblet. Unlike her sister-in-law Gladys, Rachel's mother had readily availed herself of the best plastic surgeons in the country. And her face still held much of the soft glamour bred into Southern beauties. Young John Lorten had loved Alice for her body, not her mind. And even Rachel had to admit he probably got his money's worth.

"I want to thank Connie for this lovely, lovely dinner," Alice Lorten said. "Everything was simply marvelous."

"Here, here." There was more clinking of the glasses. Under her breath, Rachel muttered to Justin.

"Ridgewell's did do a marvelous job. Simply marvelous."

Ridgewell Catering serviced the finest Washington D.C. occasions. They always catered the Lorten family dinner and Rachel had noticed their trademark purple van parked near the servants' entrance when she arrived. The Ridgewell staff was busy in the kitchen, serving the food. Everyone at the table knew Connie hadn't cooked a bean.

Ellie was watching her son and her best friend, glad of their friendship. Justin looked up to Rachel and Ellie thought she would help ease him through the worst of adolescence.

After toasts to Connie's cooking and hospitality, two servers arrived with dessert.

"And for you, madam?" she inquired of Rachel, tilting a silver tray laden with fine pastries. "A lemon tart, mince pie, raspberry cheesecake, or traditional pumpkin?"

Rachel went with the lemon tart. Conversation, as sometimes happens on such occasions, fell silent and into the lull all heard Justin's choice.

"And you, young man, would you like a tart?"

"Yes, ma'am," Justin answered with gusto. "And I'll take one of those little lemon things too."

Ronald glared. He did not find his nephew funny. Ever. And especially not his crude, juvenile attempts at humor at the dinner table. Ronald and Connie had made a conscious decision not to have children; family dinners always confirmed the wisdom of that decision.

The conversation buzz resumed. Politics and dessert were digested together. Finally, when the meal came to a blessed end, Ronald raised his glass and made the usual speech.

"Let's not forget on this Thanksgiving Day that God has been very good to us. We have much to be thankful for and we should always stop and be grateful, not just on this official day of remembrance, but every day of the year."

"Here, here!" Jeff replied, answering with raised glass. "God has been very good to us."

"We've been pretty good to ourselves, too," Justin observed.

Oh, dear, Rachel thought. That's exactly the kind of thing I would have said at his age. People were not amused then. And they were not amused now.

Fed up with his son and with Rachel who always seemed to encourage his bad behavior, Jeff snapped, "Shut up, Justin. That's enough."

"I'm glad you came, Aunt Rachel," Justin said, walking Rachel to her car. "I can't stand these family things without you."

"I know they are bit of a trial, aren't they? But you must admit the food is good!"

He patted a very full stomach. "That it is. So are you going to tell me what's up with you? When I ask Mom she just goes all quiet-like on me. But I know you... there's a... maybe a sparkle in your eyes. So are you in love or something?"

He held the car door open and leaned in to catch her reply.

"None of your business, dear boy. None of your business."

Still leaning into the car he added, "Name this tune," then proceeded to sing to her his best impression of an old rock classic: "Love is just a lie... made to make you blue."

It was a game they played and she answered in a second.

"Roy Orbison, 1960... and I'm not in love." But she smiled at him and thought him not so self-absorbed as his parents might think.

It could have been worse, Rachel thought, driving home. She had managed to avoid a confrontation with her mother and brothers. She had enjoyed Aunt Gladys and being with Sally, Ellie, and Justin. Rachel made a mental note to reassure Ellie, who worried too much about her son. But her thoughts moved quickly from the obligatory family meal, now ended, to the drink she was looking forward to sharing with Enoch.

The Brogue still smelled of smoke despite the current ban. It was a friendly, down-home pub. The place was filled with wall-to-wall people when Rachel arrived and it took a moment for her eyes to adjust to the dark room. There was a lively game of darts on the back wall. Enoch waved to her from the bar, already enjoying his first Guinness. She ordered a diet coke and they took their drinks to one of the high-backed wooden booths that offered a modicum of quiet.

They shared stories of Thanksgiving dinner. Eating too much, with too many relatives. But nothing about her brothers and nothing about Laura.

The food was standard pub grub, comforting and extremely unhealthy. She ordered Bubble & Squeak and he a cheeseburger topped with Stilton and house fries. Conversation ranged comfortably through some inside-the-Beltway political stories.

"Enoch," she ventured over an espresso. "You seem a little down tonight. Is everything okay with your parents?"

"My parents are fine," he answered. "But Laura and I have separated. She moved out last week."

"Oh, I'm sorry," she mumbled, unsure what else to say.

"It's mutual," he went on. "But we are both sad."

"Oh dear, I am sorry, I don't know what to say."

Enoch had never talked about his relationship with Laura. And she had never asked. The occasional small note about them had surfaced in the *Post* Style Section, and that's all she knew about his very private life.

"Nothing, there is nothing to say. And while it is good to be with a friend, and I've come to think of you as a friend, but... that isn't the reason I asked to see you tonight. I have something I have to tell you, something I didn't want to do over the phone."

He paused and she panicked.

"The thing is, the government is ready to bring the case against WOWL. Officially, and that process begins with a formal notification to all of the shareholders. That is going to take place soon and instead of being overjoyed by the prospect of a public fight with your brother, I'm conflicted. I have been hoping for a confrontation with your brother. It will create a media storm, and probably boost my career. Especially if we win."

He held her eyes with a steady gaze.

"But I find myself hoping the case will be settled quickly. And quietly. I hate to think what this is going to do to you. You are so private and as a Lorten that privacy will end. At least for a time."

Rachel didn't know how to respond and managed only to thank him for the heads up, hoping he couldn't read the panic in her voice.

"I suppose you can't say any more?"

He shook his head. "Only that if Ronald is smart he'll settle and not fight this."

She hoped so too.

"Well, thank you for telling me," she said keeping her voice light. "And thanks for the carbs, too."

Enoch's goodbye hug in the parking lot was more tender, and perhaps a little longer, than usual which only made her feel worse.

Unable to fall asleep, Rachel thought about Enoch and Laura. She wondered why they had separated. Trying not to assume what she would like to assume, Rachel forced herself to think about other things, like the more important revelation of the evening. She wondered if she should call Ronald and pass along the news and warn him (again) not to fight the IRS charges. But he wouldn't welcome her call or tell her his plans.

Finally drifting off to sleep, after the help of a Tylenol PM, a high-pitched scream pierced the night and she was instantly awake. Uncertain. The alarm clock by her bed read three. Hoping it had been a dream, Rachel snuggled again under her new eiderdown but before she could sleep the strangled scream came again.

Now fully awake she recognized the cries were animal, probably a fox. But the distress was real and it left her feeling uneasy. There would be no more sleep tonight so Rachel got up and went to the kitchen to make a large mug of hot chocolate, before settling on her reading bench in the library to think about the day soon to dawn.

With pad and pen she organized her thoughts. The many possible scenarios, actions, and reactions of all the players, and the beginnings of her own contingency plan.

BOOK THREE

CHAPTER 28

SNOWED IN

When mirth for music longs,
This is my song of songs.

—*Laudes Domini*

SNOW WAS BEGINNING TO FALL AS THE SHAREHOLDERS OF WOWL, Inc. arrived at the Lorten family estate. Small wet flakes drifted silently to the ground, melting as they settled. Ronald Lorten had asked his mother to prepare the formal living room for what promised to be a most uncomfortable meeting. He chose this less formal setting over the corporate office for the sake of his mother and Aunt Gladys. It also provided a home court advantage over the investigator.

An overweight marmalade cat sprawled, un-feline like, on the Belgian linen sofa. Marseilles chairs in hues of warm yellow were dotted strategically around the room with wingbacks against the walls.

A carved teak table from the Orient divided the room; a lone vase of white roses on the highly polished surface.

The marmalade cat slept contentedly between Rachel and Ellie, unaware of time or tensions in the room, her belly fat spread comfortably over the rich cloth. Connie and Alice Lorten looked neither comfortable nor happy. Aunt Gladys reclined slightly in the Toulouse chaise, nervously crossing and uncrossing her legs, nylon stocking rubbing against nylon stocking. To the more nervous in the group, the sound was as irritating as fingernails on a chalkboard. A silver tea service with china cups was ready to be poured. The tray sat on a low table near the bay window overlooking the formal garden. Snow was adding a frosting to the sculptured fountain.

My mother would serve tea at an execution, Rachel thought, uncharitably. Few of those present had accepted her offer as they arrived.

Lawyers from Dudley, Smythe & Dudley were seated against the wall, briefcases ready like loaded guns. Jeff arrived late, tossed the cat, nudged his wife down the sofa so he didn't have to sit next to his sister, and greeted no one. Ronald, who had arrived first, strode around the room looking at his watch.

Agent Enoch Arnheim was late. Ronald took the delay for what it was, a control maneuver. A game Lorten played often enough to recognize it well. The government was about to officially announce — and lay out its case — for the investigation.

"Agent Arnheim, sir," the maid said, ushering the perfectly tailored, fit agent into hostile territory. It was exactly a quarter past three.

Rachel avoided eye contact. Enoch nodded a greeting to the group in general, opened his briefcase, and began laying out papers on the polished wood.

Aunt Gladys got up and offered the agent a cup of tea.

"Oh do stop it and sit down, Gladys," Alice snapped. "He is not our guest."

Edward Dudley stood and whispered something in Ronald's ear.

Ronald took a seat.

Enoch let tension mount a few moments longer as he arranged his notes and looked at the faces in the room, resting briefly on each one, except Rachel. He recognized the widows Alice and Gladys, the lawyers, a brittle beauty with a nasty scowl he took to be Ronald's wife, and Rachel's friend Ellie, who smiled as she caught his eye. Only two non-hostiles in the room. Soft snores from the overweight cat and a ticking wall clock were the only sounds in the room as they waited for Agent Arnheim to begin. That and Aunt Gladys crossing and uncrossing her legs.

Enoch cleared his throat and started the short, official notice. The government had a strong case, and while Enoch felt there was probably more to be discovered, Johnson was pushing him to make his move, accusing Enoch of dragging his feet. After today's meeting Enoch would "let" news of the case leak to the press. Fallout could go either way, he thought. The religious right might mobilize to Lorten's defense and accuse the IRS of targeting the administration's enemy. Or, hopefully, flush someone with unsavory information — disgruntled workers, an additional irate donor, or something more scandalous — out of the woodwork.

The agent began to read the legal language in lawyerly tones. The IRS was investigating WOWL, Inc. on several counts of inurement, illegal use of tax-exempt ministry dollars, and tax fraud.

It went on for two pages of therefores and wherefores.

Ronald, Jeff, and Rachel were relieved at what wasn't included; the lawyers thought it could have been much worse, and everyone else was stunned to hear the serious nature of the case against the family businesses.

"Bastard," Ronald said into the silence when Enoch finished the last page.

Like glass shattering, it fractured the tension in the room.

"Oh, Ronald," Mrs. Lorten gasped, hand over her mouth like she was the one who had uttered the curse. "Don't talk like that, dear. Lortens don't talk like that — oh dear God... whatever will people think?"

"Probably more to the point, ma'am," Enoch said, "is what the government thinks! But I suggest you listen to your mother, Mr. Lorten, and formulate a more professional response to the charges." He looked around the room again trying to judge the reaction of the expensive legal counsel who would be a formidable challenge in the months ahead. He caught

Rachel's eye and smiled at her before showing himself out of the room and out of the Lorten mansion.

The sky was glowering and the wind picking up. Snow was sticking to the road, covering the grass and dusting the tips of evergreen branches. According to the excited newscasters, a real blizzard was bearing down on the Washington, D.C. metro area. Television news ran announcements at the bottom of the screen listing early school closings and liberal leave for government agencies to give people time to get out of town ahead of the blizzard. A real nor'easter was being promised, the kind of storm that blows in heavy, wet snow off the coast and closes down the city. Enoch didn't buy the hype but he was glad to be on the way before it got worse. His Austin was fun in the sun but not what you want on snow and ice.

"How'd it go?" Betty asked when Enoch called from his car for messages.

"Much as I expected. Let's say I don't think the Lorten family is going to enjoy being snowed in with their thoughts this weekend."

She chuckled. "Well, Johnson is already gone and I'm thinking the newscasters might be right on this one so I'm leaving soon unless you need me, sir."

"Good idea. Leave now and be careful."

He dialed Laura next.

"Why don't you come over and enjoy the snow storm with me this evening?"

Not sure what to make of Enoch's invitation, Laura hesitated.

"Thanks, Enoch, but I'm not sure, I have some work to do."

"It will be worth your while, really. I have something to tell you about the Lorten case. Still background, but I think you will be interested and I promised to tell you before it gets in the public domain. Which might happen soon."

An hour later, covered in snow, Laura knocked on what had once been her own front door.

Enoch invited her to join him by the fireplace.

"Popcorn and brandy? Really, Enoch," she laughed, taking some of both and getting comfortable in a big chair by the fire.

She listened while he talked. Warmed by the brandy and the news.

"This *is* big, Enoch. Even Johnson can't deny you a promotion now. I've read about the widow. Is she your source?"

He knew Laura well enough to know she wouldn't be jealous, but it sounded like it as she went on.

"Are you seeing her for business only or for pleasure?"

Enjoying the idea she might actually be jealous, he didn't grace her question with an answer.

"Because," she went on, "I have seen pictures of Dr. Lorten-Kissane and she definitely does not look like your type."

"What is my type?" he retorted, no longer amused.

Me, she thought, frustrated that she had let her feelings show.

"Intelligent and beautiful. In that order, I would say. But I can't imagine a narrow-minded evangelical like that being attractive to you, on an intellectual level, despite her doctoral degree. And well, like I said, I've seen pictures and she doesn't look your type. A little too scholarly and frumpy for you."

The cozy drink by the fire had not turned out so well. And defending Rachel would only make matters worse.

"Look, Laura, I've had a long day. I promised to give you this and I might be able to give you heads up again down the road with something the administration would very much appreciate knowing before the press."

Her goodbye kiss on his cheek at the door was warm and her thanks effusive.

"Good night," he said. "Be careful in the snow — and Laura, it might be wise not to believe all the stereotype propaganda this administration puts out over there at Foggy Bottom. Not everyone on the other side is simple. Or narrow-minded."

CHAPTER 29

CONFRONTATION

Day by day my mind's afflicted and darkened eyes grow
sounder under the healing salve of sorrow.

—St. Augustine

RONALD WAS PERCHED ON THE EDGE OF A BROAD MAHOGANY desk in his father's old upstairs study, swinging a fancy cowboy boot aggressively back and forth, the other leg planted firmly on the edge of a worn Persian carpet as he waited for his sister. Jeff slouched in a chocolate brown leather chair, nervously twisting and untwisting the cap on a plastic water bottle. Both were experiencing murderous thoughts about their sibling.

"Close the door," Ronald barked as Rachel entered the room moments later.

The tense family meeting with the IRS investigator was over. The widows, Gladys and Alice, were still sitting in the drawing room comforting each other. Alice loved her sister-in-law, but wished she would take her simple hysteria and go away before a snowstorm stranded her there for the weekend. Alice very much wanted to find her sons and grill them on what had just happened, but Gladys was clinging to her like a limpet and talking about the old times when everything was good and IRS agents didn't invade their home making terrible accusations. The agent, lawyers, and other family members had all left, hoping to avoid what television weather people were gleefully calling the 'big one' approaching the Washington, D.C. metro area.

Never comfortable in one another's company, the siblings assessed each other for several uncomfortable minutes of silence in the room that had once been their father's study. Ronald's sharp, "join me in the study," had been more a command than suggestion. He hadn't planned this meeting but the thought of his sister walking out of the house without a care, while he continued to shoulder the burden of the crisis, could no longer be endured. Fed up with her supercilious attitude in general and traitorous friendship with the investigator, he was through letting her off the hook.

"So, are you happy now?" he barked.

It sounded like a childhood taunt, even to him.

"You've put your whole family and everything our father worked for at risk, and then you sit there in our house gazing at the man who's going to destroy us with your schoolgirl crush written all over your face. It's pathetic, Rachel. You're pathetic."

"Ronald," Jeff interjected with a note of caution but was ignored by his brother.

"I didn't believe it could be true, that you would be dating this man," Ronald went on. "But I saw him look at you with something like... "

"Like what?" Rachel asked, interested in spite of herself now.

"How the hell do I know... like he knows you, that's for damned sure!"

Rachel didn't want this conversation but, knowing it couldn't be avoided, she decided to antagonize her brothers as little as possible. Not something she had ever been very successful at — but there had never before been so much at stake.

"Look, Ronald, I know you're upset. That was pretty awful, all of us gathered there like suspects in a crime novel. But it wasn't *his* fault. The government is required to make formal notification to all parties involved in the investigation. As shareholders we are all involved. You suggested the meeting here instead of at the office. So it isn't like you didn't know what was coming — you've known for some time about the investigation. So forgive me, but I fail to see why you're so upset... "

Unable to control himself, Ronald exploded off the desk, took the two steps to her chair, leaned close to her face.

"You fail to see... you fail to see why I'm upset? Well, little sister, I'm more than bloody upset. I'm looking at losing everything that matters to me! And it *is* absolutely your fault."

Jeff had observed many powerful men backed in a corner with disastrous results. Afraid of what Ronald might do or say, he tried again to intervene, using his best counseling voice.

"Rachel, please, it might help Ronald if you took this more seriously, if you just try to *hear* what he is saying... "

She laughed. It was a mistake, but she preferred Ronald's bullying to Jeff's hypocrisy. "Oh, please, Jeff," Rachel said. "I'm not having trouble hearing him. My cats can probably hear him. I think his argument is specious and I'm having trouble understanding how the financial improprieties of the company, as laid out by Agent Arnheim, are in any way my fault. It's not my lifestyle in question by the government. I don't take million dollar salaries and millions more in benefits like you two... "

"Lifestyle!" Ronald interrupted, red blotches appearing on his face. "Lifestyle! Who's talking about lifestyle? Near as I can tell, mine hasn't changed in years. Yet here we are with an investigation so serious the lawyers are taking turns having nervous breakdowns. So don't talk to me about my lifestyle. That isn't the point!"

"Of course it's the point," Rachel answered, keeping her voice even. "I know what inurement means, Ronald. And it appears the government thinks your salary and benefits meet the legal benchmark of excessive compensation. The cars, planes, mansions. Not good for the head of what is, at least in name, a Christian ministry. You too, Jeff; I'm sorry for Ellie and the kids, but you and Ronald are going to be forced to answer for what is at the very least unwise, unethical, and maybe even criminal practice. Over the last ten years, bottom line is you have raised money through donations, then used those contributions, often given by people of humble means, in ways that created your own personal wealth. That's fraud. Who knows when or if the IRS would have come after you without a Phil Grant, but I'm sure it didn't hurt that you have painted a target on your own back by being so political. I'm sorry for the mess but I don't see how this can be construed as *my* fault. I haven't ever had anything to do with running the company."

Jeff disliked his sister on so many levels. Most of all he hated her ability to remain calm, condescending, and above the emotional fray in a crisis. With no hint of a counseling voice he snapped.

"Now you're calling us criminals? Is that what you've been telling Agent Arnheim? You're spending time with the person investigating our family and you can't imagine why we think it's your fault. Really, Rachel, this is unbelievable. Even for you. I saw it too, how you looked at each other. It was disgusting."

She took a deep breath. Adjusted her countenance to the least offensive expression possible and tried again.

"Yes, Jeff. I smiled at him. As I have explained to everyone multiple times. I do know Agent Arnheim, as a friend. He nodded a greeting to me as he left the room, I responded with a smile. Turns out we enjoy each other. So, yes, I have seen him several times since he first came to me for professional advice."

"Yeah," Ronald snorted. "And you're saying he was attracted to you on a purely physical basis and just couldn't stay away. I don't want to be unkind, but you are not in the same league as his real girlfriend."

"I know," she replied quickly this time, an edge creeping into her voice. "You were kind enough to point that out the first time we discussed this."

"Seems it didn't get through to you, though. Do you ever stop to think, when you are spending those 'enjoyable' times together, that Agent Arnheim might just be passing along the information you give him to his girlfriend in the administration? Our enemies. My God, Rachel do you actually think he's interested in *you*?"

Old familiar blows. And truth be told, Ronald had a point. She would have reasoned exactly the same way in his shoes. Still, Rachel had no intention of letting her brother see how much the blows hurt.

Usually more observer than participant when his siblings fought, Jeff now watched what was happening with growing fear. Making Rachel angry, as Ronald was doing, might be fun, but it was also dangerous. He couldn't exert control over her, like he did his wife, and it rankled, but he didn't want this meeting to get out of hand. Jeff was afraid of what Ronald might say if Rachel pushed him over the edge; his life and career were on the line, as party to the second blackmail payment, and minimally a co-conspirator on the first. Jeff tried again to lower the temperature.

"Look Rachel, Ron absolutely shouldn't say these things. It isn't fair and I'm sure he doesn't really mean them to be so insulting. But if you could try and understand how upset he is. How we are... you've always been critical of the family, but this... this is more like... well, more like treason. Enoch Arnheim is the enemy and you're his friend. What do you expect us to think? The least you can do is promise not to see him again and tell us what you've told him."

The winter sun was fading fast and the snow was really beginning to fall in earnest. Rachel wanted nothing more than to escape the room and start walking home through the snowy woods. Instead she took a deep breath and said slowly, as though speaking to a child or a foreigner.

"Well, I have told him where and how his parents should travel in Russia while looking for long-lost relatives. I actually gave him a history lesson about Great Falls once, including our colorful moment in the history of Russian–American relations. One time I told him... "

"Shut up, Rachel. Do you think we care about your stupid conversations with this man! You know exactly what we mean," Jeff said. "What have you told him about us? About the business?"

"Nothing relevant to the investigation. And as strange as it may seem to you, I do have a life outside the family and he is a part of that life. We are friends."

Her brothers did not look convinced.

"But," she went on, "he did tell me the investigation started with a letter from your contest winner, a Mr. Phil Grant from Minnesota. Mr. Grant came, he saw, and he wrote a detailed letter about his concerns. You probably treated Mr. Grant like some kind of a peon. "

"A peon!" Jeff exploded. "We treated him like an honored guest, including an expensive weekend in Washington, D.C., introduced him to all the important people at our gala... and this is how he thanks us."

Rachel remembered Ellie telling her how embarrassed she had been for Phil Grant at the reception, and Jeff's treatment of him in the receiving line. Her brother really was clueless.

"Exactly my point, dear brother, you thought of him as a country bumpkin who should be happy to rub shoulders with you and all the other Christian celebrities. He may not have been such a simpleton after all. It's possible the man was actually sad to see a ministry he had invested good money in over the years not be up to his expectations, but rather a very powerful, and very political, media empire making a few people very wealthy while throwing marginal help to a few needy souls. Occasionally. And let's at least be honest with each other. Remember, I grew up in this house too. WOWL should be registered as a PAC, truth be told, which would be fine as long as you don't try to fool the Phil Grants of this world. Maybe Mr. Grant resented being treated like a stupid-Christian-pet-trick, I don't know. One might. But once again, hardly my fault that the man saw, analyzed, and then wrote his conclusions to the IRS. They, not being stupid either, decided to pursue such an inviting target. So please let's get this one point straight. I've spent a little time with the man, not the IRS agent. And as a woman, certainly not as a traitor."

Without taking so much as a deep breath she went on.

"And if you have nothing to hide, then nothing will be found. And all of this will go away after a few news cycles." Rachel had warned Ronald about Eric's past, but she wasn't about to discuss it once again with Jeff in the room. In fact, utterly finished with this discussion, Rachel stood to go. As she did, a vase filled with water and fresh cut flowers sailed near her head and smashed into the wall.

"Does the name Cricket Hartford mean anything to you?"

Shocked at the flying vase and the question, Rachel paused, one arm through her coat sleeve. Aware on some subliminal level that the real reason for her brother's almost irrational anger was about to be revealed and that it didn't have anything to do with how she had looked at Enoch during the family meeting. She braced for it. Someone from Eric's past had surfaced, just as she had feared, to consequences she could only imagine and didn't want to know about.

Jeff tried to stop his brother.

"Hey, man, don't do this. It'll only make things worse."

Past reason, the senior Lorten charged on.

"I'm waiting, Rachel. You seem to know everything. So, tell me this: do you know a woman by the name of Cricket Hartford?"

She collapsed back into the chair, her coat half on.

Satisfied he had finally wiped the smug smile off her sister's face, Ronald continued.

"I'll take that as a 'no.' Okay, let me tell you about her."

Ronald had wanted to do this for months. He felt happier than he had all day.

"I'll try to stick to the relevant facts. Eric had an affair with Ms. Hartford, and due to his previous promiscuity, he passed along the HIV virus to her. Seems not just homosexuals can get it, unless he was both, who knows — but when a blood test revealed the virus in Ms. Hartford only days after Eric was killed, she was understandably upset and came to me demanding compensation. You might call it blackmail but I felt in many ways she was justified in asking for some financial help, given what Eric had done to her. But the real reason I gave into her demand was to protect you from the scandal. And, I admit, it was also to protect the company from fallout from gossip about Eric. So, I risked everything so you wouldn't have to endure the humiliation of having your husband's affairs splashed all over the news, and yet somehow I don't think you are going to thank me. Then, and the irony of this is killing me, you came to warn me about Eric's past possibly coming up in an IRS investigation. Well, believe me, dear sister. It had already come to my attention."

Rachel wanted to scream and cry and beg him to stop.

But she didn't. And he didn't stop.

"So... I actually found a way to solve Ms. Hartford's problem, protect you and the company from your useless husband, and do good at the same time. I did that. Do you hear me, Rachel? I did all that. And now because you couldn't keep your husband satisfied, and became friends with the enemy, it could all come tumbling down."

"Ah," she said, the light dawning. "The Awareness Campaign."

"Yes. The Awareness Campaign. It worked as a way to hide the payments and protect the company. And great good came of it. I was there, I saw those kids, so don't sneer at me, little sister. All these months I've had to live with the knowledge that what I did was technically... wrong...

wrong and yet right, but with the threat of exposure hanging over my head. And then this IRS investigation comes along at what couldn't be a worse moment, putting the company and all of us at risk while you are merrily going along 'enjoying time' with the investigator. God forbid that you should actually think of the family instead of hiding out over in that horrible little carriage house, condescending as ever to the rest of us. Well, I can't say I totally blame Eric for straying, not if you treated him the way you treat us. And to think I actually felt sorry for you when he died. Poor grieving widow. Ha! Well, when I think of what I've been through while you are, at least figuratively, 'sleeping with the enemy', I swear, Rachel, I could... " Afraid he might throw something else, Ronald turned so he couldn't see his sister's face seemingly unmoved by his words or revelations. His sentence and his anger trickled out and died in a sigh of self-pity.

So it was true, Rachel thought. Eric's unfaithfulness was no longer hidden in her whimsical little box under the floor in her house, but about to spill out into the public domain — front page of the *Washington Post*. It was the smoking gun she had feared might exist and tried to prevent Enoch from finding. Now she might as well know it all. Prodding Ronald was the surest way to get it.

"You know, Ronald, I don't know if it's your narcissism or your victimhood that offends me more. But if you succumbed to blackmail by this, this Cricket person, I'm quite, quite sure you didn't do so for my benefit."

The enjoyment of throwing the name Cricket Hartford in his sister's face was fading.

"Damn you, Rachel. Can't you see the cultural wars are real and what we do is important to the country? All you can think about is your own feelings for a man who is using you to get at us."

"Oh do shut up, Ronald. Please," Jeff pleaded.

There was a momentary lull. Not a comfortable one, but a moment of quiet.

"I should have known. The Awareness Campaign was so out of character for you. And to think, I was proud of the company there for a moment. Who did you use to help you hide the payments to the mistress, Ronald? Clearly not Jeff, he doesn't have the nerve. Martha? Poor Martha, I bet she doesn't even know she's been used. Did Ms. Hartford come to the office to shake you down? Cricket Hartford? That might be an alias, Ronald, did you think of that? Who names a child Cricket? Anyway, can Martha connect her to you? Or did Cricket track you down at a CITMAC meeting... speaking of which, they won't be thrilled to have a new president under indictment. I don't suppose there were any other blackmail payments needing to be covered up? And no, I'm not worried about you saving the country. It will survive without the likes of you and your political machine. But I am worried about us. All of us."

Since no one threw anything else at her, she went on.

"Do let's try to be honest for a moment. You didn't put the company and your political power at risk for me, but we do have a mutual interest in limiting the damage. It must be perfectly clear, even to you guys, that the government still doesn't know about Cricket what's-her-name — which, if they did, they would be a using as a major full-blown-page-one scandal. And forget the IRS. Blackmail makes it a case for the CID, so Agent Arnheim is a small threat by comparison. For me it's a matter of privacy. For you, well... it could be a great deal more."

Jeff knew Rachel didn't care about the company, or most of the family. As a last resort he tried appealing to what did matter to her.

"Look, Rachel, think about what such a scandal would mean to Ellie and the kids. You need to help us stop the government finding out about this. You've admitted to being friends with this IRS investigator, so maybe you could use your influence with him."

Her laugh was genuine. It bubbled up from a deep well of emotion and release; the irony was delicious.

"Please guys, don't look at me like that. Surely you see the humor in what Jeff just suggested. But how lovely the thought that we should work together, won't Mother be pleased?"

Ronald was now on his feet striding about the small space.

"Cut the crap, Rachel. I don't see the humor, but I do see Jeff's point. You seem to be friends with this guy, for whatever reason. It might be a good idea if you remain 'friends' with him. But try to remember it's in your own best interest, as well as ours, to keep me informed of what you hear."

"You mean pass along the pillow talk?" she suggested.

Utterly sick to death of the ludicrous conversation and reeling from what it had revealed, Rachel stood up, hoping her legs wouldn't give way.

Snow was covering the ground and falling in big wet flakes as she started walking home on the little path through the woods.

CHAPTER 30

WIT'S END ANTIQUES

There are no unsacred places; there are only
sacred places and desecrated places.

—*Wendell Berry*

STRETCH LEDUC WAS IN HIS LATE FORTIES, MEDIUM HEIGHT AND build, with glasses and pattern balding. A middle-aged white guy in a suit. Rachel had picked him from a short list of private investigators because his name made her smile on a day she needed a smile. The man stood behind the desk when she entered his modest office off 11th Street. He shook her hand and motioned to the chair across from his desk. She sat.

Mr. Stretch Leduc was not out of central casting. The office was neat, he wasn't hung over, and didn't have bad breath from stakeouts.

"Take your time," he said.

Mr. Leduc pushed a folder across the desk to Rachel. "I think you'll find what you need is all there."

Rachel kept her face impassive as she saw a picture of her husband's mistress for the first time. She skimmed through the extensive information about Cricket Hartford, including current address and phone number.

"Wow, that was fast," Ellie said when Rachel described what the private investigator had found. "So, did you call him Stretch?"

Rachel giggled and handed Ellie the file. "No, we were not on a first-name basis. And as I don't expect to hire a private investigator again, I kept it formal."

"Wow," Ellie said again, looking through the material. "Cricket Hartford is beautiful. Eric had good taste. I guess. But I don't envy her life. It looks like she held a series of low-level government jobs, secured for her by 'friends', as Stretch so delicately puts it. I wonder where Eric met her?"

"No idea and don't intend to ask. I already know too much."

"And yet you're going to meet this person who slept with your husband. It doesn't make sense, Rachel. It's going to be harder than you think. Please let me go with you."

"Thanks, but no," Rachel said, shaking her head. "I have to do this alone for lots of reasons, most of all because she is more likely to open up just to me. Two against one might feel threatening."

"And you hope to gain what? Other than satisfying your curiosity?"

There was a moment of silence before Rachel answered.

"I admit to a little curiosity but that isn't why I'm going. I really have to know more about the blackmail."

"And use that information how?"

"I don't know for sure, but I can't just sit back and wait for all this mess to show up on the front page of the *Post*."

Ellie was quiet. Rachel waited.

"Okay, you're probably right, and it will save me lying to my husband. He keeps asking me what I know... what you are saying, what you're doing. He has even tried a new approach, sweetness and light," she smirked. "So I know he's desperate."

"Sorry," Rachel said. "I've made a terrible mess for everyone. I wish I could go back in time and keep walking when I first saw Eric by the Horse Fountain in Salzburg."

"Don't be silly. It's not your fault. Just do be careful, please."

Rachel laughed.

"I don't think she's dangerous."

"I mean emotionally. Be careful *emotionally*. This isn't going to be as easy as you seem to think."

Rachel drove west along US Route 50 toward the Blue Ridge Mountains. Trappers and traders had traveled that same road, slogging through mud and snow when it was known as the Pike and connected the western wilderness, via Ashby Gap, to the Chesapeake Bay. Back before America was America. The old trail was soaked with blood from northern boys and southern sons. Despoliation, development, and sprawl had claimed the past up to Gilbert's Corner. But at the little town of Aldie fields and farms, sunken roads, and stonewalls remained as if locked out of time, looking much as they did during the war that divided the states and nearly destroyed the Union.

Old families with means, and new money, looking for a place to show it off, had protected a little pocket of countryside, keeping out developers and even the threat of a Walt Disney theme park. People who made their money spoiling other parts of the country came to the Middleburg region to enjoy it out of sight from the middle-class sprawl of cookie-cutter homes, strip malls, Walmarts, and Olive Garden Restaurants. And a few ordinary people somehow found a little niche in the quiet corners of the protected beauty.

Rachel knew the road. Her mother had insisted on riding lessons for Rachel in a never-ending quest of trying to interest her teenage daughter in something other than books. Not a natural rider, Rachel's seat was wobbly and unbalanced; she felt less graceful on the horse than off. And, unlike most young girls, Rachel hadn't bonded emotionally with the horses. She never felt the need to nuzzle a soft horsey nose or whisper her troubles to the highly strung thoroughbreds. Rachel remembered her first (and last) ride in a foxhunt. It had been a crisp fall day with riders in their pinks sitting on perfectly groomed horses. Certain she looked fat in her riding breeches and certain she would be dumped at the first fence, Rachel had waited nervously at the back of the field while the Episcopalian priest performed a liturgy for the hunt.

"Bless, O Lord, rider and horse, and the hounds that
run in their running, and shield them from danger to life and limb.
May thy children who ride, and thy creatures who carry, come to the close of the
day unhurt and give thanks to thee with grateful hearts.
Bless those over whose lands we hunt, and grant that no
deed or omission of ours may cause them hurt or trouble.
Bless the foxes who partake in the chase, that they may run straight and true and
may they find their destiny in thee.
Bless the hounds to our use and their joyful part in thy creation.

Bless the fox? More like curse the fox, she thought with empathy. Wit's End Art & Antique Shop was tucked away one block south of main, facing an open field. Rachel tentatively opened the door and stepped in, wondering if she would recognize the owner. It was more art gallery than antique shop — filled with light and polished brass, without a hint of old dust.

Considering retreat, Rachel was inching toward the door when Cricket Hartford appeared, looking more at home with the lovely objects of art than Rachel ever could.

"You are Eric's wife," Cricket said without any hint of drama. "I wondered if you'd come one day."

There was a moment of uncertainty and silence, Cricket wondered why Eric had been unfaithful to such a dynamic woman. Rachel was not at all surprised that he had chosen such a beautiful one.

Riding a roller coaster of emotions about Eric's unknown mistress since Ronald threw the name in her face, Rachel had felt anger, fear, disgust, and contempt. But now face to face with a human being, those emotions gave way to simple understanding.

"Let's go someplace where we can talk," Cricket said, taking charge of the moment. "It's not that cold... would a walk be okay? There's a wood near here, with a bench where we can sit and talk. I'll lock the shop and we can walk together."

Rachel was wearing Levis, boots, and a warm jacket. Cricket pulled on boots, a black pea coat over her sweater, wrapped a scarf around her neck, and led the way.

"A pileated woodpecker lives here," Cricket offered, looking up at a partially dead tree. "We might see him. And a herd of white-tailed deer. The occasional hawk hunts from the high branches of that very old oak. It's a lovely, quiet place. I like to come here, winter and summer. I grew up in the Shenandoah Valley and I've always missed it. Or at least the idea of it."

Nothing in Rachel's imagination had prepared her for a conversation about the wonders of nature with this woman who had more or less slept her way through the different government agencies, if Leduc's research was to be believed. She was beautiful, that was no surprise, but the Wendell Berry part was unexpected. As was the warm welcome.

The hawk didn't appear and neither did the woodpecker, but the woods were filled with life. Not unlike the woods outside Rachel's carriage house. Cardinals darted in and out of the branches, startlingly red against the winter browns. Squirrels ran along the crumbling dry stonewall sagging with creepers and the weight of time.

They walked for several minutes in silence until they came to the bench in the woods. Cricket wiped off dead leaves and a trace of snow, then motioned Rachel to sit. The antiviral meds were effective but not without side effects. Cold seemed to bother her more. She still worried about dying.

"I'm sorry," Cricket spoke first. "I'm really very sorry."

"For what, precisely?" Rachel asked, surprised, wondering if the woman was sorry for blackmailing her brother or sleeping with her husband.

"Well, I'm not very sorry I asked Ronald for money, unless it sends me to prison — maybe not even then. These have been the best months of my life here in the country. For the first time I have been financially independent. And, well, personally independent too. But, I am sorry I slept with your husband. I've thought about how many women I have wronged over the years; you can probably surmise Eric wasn't the first married man I had an affair with. I'm not going to find each wife and apologize but, well, I am sorry and I'm glad to be able to tell you that. I don't expect you to forgive me but... "

"Hmm," Rachel broke in, getting more and more uncomfortable. "I don't think you really need my forgiveness, but I readily give it and accept your apology. Kind of you to think I do actually, but you didn't cause Eric to be unfaithful... he clearly managed that pretty well before you came along. You were more or less the last in the queue, as it were. My brothers think it's my fault, of course, and my mother would agree with them. The wonder for them was always why Eric married me in the first place and so it came as no surprise that I couldn't hold on to him. What a quaint idea. But never mind all that," Rachel laughed nervously. "I haven't come to talk about your relationship with my husband."

Cricket stared. Utterly baffled.

"What have you come to talk about, then? I don't understand how you can be so calm about this," she said. "I slept with your husband, often, for over two years. I was with him the day he died. I have gone over this, over and over in my mind, and... " She turned away, unable to understand how a wronged wife could offer forgiveness so easily. "Aren't you angry?" she added.

Rachel smiled. "Oh, I'm angry at a number of people, starting with myself but not particularly at you. And I'm sorry you're sick. It's not like I need to or can make amends for what he did. Oh my, this is getting weird. Maybe it would be better if I told you why I'm here. I'm not comfortable talking about my non-marriage and certainly not with you."

Cricket stood up and walked a little way along the path, then came back and sat down like someone who had made up her mind.

"Before you tell me why you've come, I have something I want to say to you. I knew Eric was married. He didn't talk about you, but I knew. I had been having relationships with married men for so long I forgot to feel guilty and rationalized that those men would all carry on pretty much the same with or without me. Anyway, I told myself the wives were probably glad to have their husbands out of the house for awhile. And, trust me, some of the men I've known, I'm sure of it. But unlike the men who blamed their wives for not understanding them or some other equally lame excuse, Eric never said anything negative about you. Then, he started cooling off. Not calling as often. Or staying as long. We were together on the night he died. He called me from the DMV, lamenting the terrible time he was having. I invited him over and he came. After we made love he said it would be the last time, that he had decided to work on his marriage. He refused to stay the night, you know, Eric was coming home to you when he was killed."

"Okay," Rachel snapped. "I don't want to know about your last moments together. Or your impression of his intentions about our marriage. But I am curious as to why you would choose such a self-destructive life. Clearly you're bright and I presume you have skills, so why let men use you like that?"

Cricket shivered. Confused by this strange woman who had been Eric's wife.

"It's a fair question but I'm not sure I can explain. I've asked myself the same thing over the years. I don't know really, maybe I think it was just too easy. I didn't study in high school, I was too lazy to finish college and I kept getting jobs, promotions even, that I didn't deserve. Not that I was all that happy but," she thought for a moment. "... and I was beginning to want a change when Eric came along. He was like... like high school. I fell in love with him. And he dated me. He didn't give me a job or money or even particularly expensive gifts. He just wanted to spend time with me. And we had fun together. But I knew it was over before that last night. I recognized the signs, and when he said he wanted to make his marriage work I believed him."

"Thanks, but you shouldn't have. Eric was on the brink of moving from being a radio personality to a television personality. He couldn't afford to jeopardize that with a scandal; breaking up with you had nothing at all to do with our marriage. You probably meant more to him than I ever did."

Cricket was stunned.

"How *can* you say that, don't you even care? He was the most attractive man, the kindest, most amazing man I've ever known. I think the blackmail was more about how angry I was with him for rejecting me. I wanted someone to pay. I was furious with Eric when I found out about the HIV and then I saw all those pictures of your rich, pious family... I was scared and mad and wanted revenge. And I wanted the money, needed it to change my life, but now that I have my beautiful house and shop and... " she lifted her arms as though in prayer. "I find that all I really want is Eric."

Tears were running down Cricket's lovely cheeks. Rachel was embarrassed and had no idea how she was supposed to comfort her husband's grieving mistress. And she was afraid she would burst out in hysterical laughter at the absurdity of the situation if she tried. So Rachel waited for Cricket's emotion to spend itself... gazing at the sky, searching for the hawk or woodpecker, hoping she would think of a suitable way back to the reason she came.

"Haven't you ever wondered why?" Cricket asked when she had her emotions under control. "He was your husband for God's sake. Don't you want to know why?"

"I know why," Rachel said simply. "But I'm not here about Eric. I mean not specifically about him. Please listen, I feel guilty as well. And that's why, well, one reason why, it's easy to accept your apology and offer forgiveness. I married someone I didn't love. I stood before God in a sacred ceremony and took a vow to love my husband till death do us part. And I didn't even love him then! Not that day standing with him in a beautiful Austrian church and most certainly not in sickness and in health. I knew it was a lie and I did it anyway, so both of us could use forgiveness. But from God, not from each other."

Cricket had dried her tears. She looked stunned. "You didn't love him... so why did you marry him? I'm sure you could have married a great many other men."

"I doubt it, but thanks for the compliment, if it is a compliment. Look, it's complicated. But the point is I was wrong to marry Eric and a great many people have been hurt because of it. So just accept the fact that I don't blame you for what happened with my husband. But please, now you have to listen to me. Something has happened. Things have changed. My family clearly tried to hide the payments to you, successfully, for a time. But there has been, what you might, call a complication. An irate donor filed a complaint about WOWL, Inc. last year and the IRS started an investigation. So far it appears they haven't found out about the money paid to you but it's possible they will."

Cricket shivered again, from fear as well as from cold. Wary and embarrassed at her emotional outburst, she continued with more caution.

"Possible? Likely? And why are you telling me?"

"Like I said, it's complicated. But, I might be in a position to help mitigate some of the damage to you and to my family. However, I'm not exactly on friendly terms with my brothers. They don't confide and I want to ask you some questions."

"So if they didn't confide, how did you find out? And how did you find me? My name was kept out of all the transactions, at WOWL and the church records, for that matter. Your brother made sure of that. So if you know all that already, what is it you want from me?"

Cricket's voice had taken on a sharp edge. No longer focused on her guilt and grief, she had just realized that this walk in the woods might have something to do with her survival.

Rachel was stunned by what Cricket had just revealed with that one tiny word. Church. Rachel tried to keep her voice neutral, to keep Cricket talking. So my lousy brother, she thought, not only compromised the family business but his church as well. Ronald must have used Leif Ohlsson to pull that one off, and she desperately needed to know *how*.

Looking up at the turkey vulture soaring overhead and keeping her voice as even as possible, Rachel said not altogether truthfully, "I know Ronald used the Washington Bible Church and the Awareness Campaign to hide payments, but I am not at all certain how he did it. Especially in the case of the church. And, as I said, I may be in a position to help if you give me a few more details."

"Look," Cricket said warily. "I said I'm sorry about what happened with Eric but that doesn't mean I'm going to tell you about the 'arrangements' I made with your brother. Let him tell you."

"We're not exactly close, remember."

"Still, if you really are 'in a position to help', I can't see him not telling you what you need to know. Your brother must have told you my name, a rather substantial detail, since no one else knows it." With the possible exception of Martha, the obsequious secretary, she thought but did not add.

The sun was beginning to set. Cricket shivered again, pulling the scarf over her head.

"Why are you so keen to help out anyway? Not for your brother, it seems, and surely not for me."

"My privacy and reputation," Rachel said firmly and without hesitation. "Which might not sound like much to you, and it's true that you and Ronald have a great deal more to lose than I do, but just trust me when I say it matters enough."

Cricket did not look convinced.

"Look," Rachel went on. "I understand your hesitation to talk to me but I am giving you something as well. I am giving you a heads up that the IRS is now investigating WOWL and that puts your arrangements with Ronald at risk of being discovered. Once the press learns about this, which they will now very soon, there might be other women from Eric's past who decide to come forward for their fifteen minutes of fame... "

"Hey, wait a minute," Cricket interrupted hotly. "I clearly don't want even one minute of fame."

"Obviously, I wasn't suggesting you do. But I assume you don't want to go to prison either, so please listen to me. An investigation of the Lorten family empire will be big news. It just might cause some woman, or women, to step forward and tell their sordid stories. Then the proverbial snowball will keep getting bigger, and the IRS will only be too happy to add sexual scandal to financial scandal. That trail will lead to you. So I am, admittedly for my own reasons, saying I might be able to prevent that from happening. But, in order to do so, I need to know more than my brother is willing to tell me."

"Okay," Cricket said. "Let's say I believe you. And don't get me wrong, I am grateful you came to warn me. But I don't see how either one of us can stop the Feds from finding out what they are going to find out. Still, if you think you can help please tell me how. I'm willing to listen."

Trying to remain as truthful as possible and still get what she wanted, Rachel went on.

"Well, first of all I'm not promising I can prevent this already underway financial investigation from leading to the blackmail payments. But if I can convince Ronald, with a little of my own 'blackmail,' that it would be in his best interest to cooperate with the IRS. He could pay a fine and settle and end it before they dig deeper. He could then spin the whole thing to his base as a witch-hunt by his political enemies, and maybe even do himself some political good while protecting us from much, much worse. And protecting you from, let's face it, criminal charges. I would suggest, by the way, worst case scenario, you might also want to accept a plea right away as well to save you, save us all, the circus of a trial. It would lessen any prison time for you, and I'm sure given your current health condition, that is vital for you so you can... "

"What? Die in peace?"

"Yes. Can you? Die in peace, I mean?"

Cricket chose not to answer that question; she had actually been asking herself the same thing now that the virus was active. But she was through answering Rachel Lorten-Kissane's questions.

Aware she had learned more than Cricket realized, and having satisfied a measure of curiosity, Rachel was also ready to end the conversation.

"I'll walk back alone if you don't mind," she said, standing. "But think about what I've said. If you are willing to tell me more it might prove helpful to both of us." Rachel handed Cricket a business card with her office address and telephone number.

The pileated woodpecker finally swooped in with his dipping flight and settled on the dead beech tree near the bench. Cricket didn't bother to look at the rare and beautiful bird. Devastated at the news the company was under investigation and that her freedom was now threatened, she slumped on the bench. The woodpecker proceeded to strike his bony beak against the dead wood, creating a pile of sawdust on the forest floor. He worked with force and precision until some internal signal alerted the bird and, with a cry, he lifted off on majestic wings and soon was out of sight.

"It came through the Deacon's Fund," she said to Rachel's retreating back.

Rachel turned and stood there for a moment in the silence and the beauty. She gave a quick nod of her head to Cricket, thanking her for the important information she had just shared. Then, as Rachel walked back through the woods, away from her husband's mistress (who had loved him much more than she ever could) she finally wept at all the brokenness, spoken and unspoken, they had brought into that peaceful, beautiful, place.

CHAPTER 31

ELLIE GOES TO CHURCH

Trying very hard, Hell has totally failed in the least
understanding of the mystery of love.

—C.S. Lewis

"LIFE IS SO UNFAIR," RACHEL MOANED, WATCHING ELLIE EAT A disgusting hot dog purchased from a street vendor. It was slathered with pickles, mustard, and sauerkraut.

"You're just jealous," Ellie laughed, wiping mustard from the corner of her mouth and finishing off a bag of chips.

"Yes, I am very jealous. You eat that... that thing filled with who-knows-what and never gain a pound. While I, on the other hand... "

She finished her healthy brown bag lunch of veggies and hummus and got back to the point.

Sitting on the grass with the dome of the Capitol Building gleaming behind them in the afternoon sunlight, Ellie had just listened to her usually wise and careful friend make a most outlandish suggestion.

Sweaty bureaucrats jogged by; most of the men turned to stare at Ellie.

"Please," Rachel implored her friend. "You know I can't just saunter into the church office and check the files."

319

"Like I can?"

"Yes, like you can. It'll be easy."

"So let me get this right. You're suggesting I basically sneak into the records room at church to read through the 'confidential' minutes of the Deacon's Board for the last few months."

"Well, not so much sneak as just walk in and ask your friend Wendy to show you."

"You know sometimes, Rachel, I wonder about you!"

"Please, Ellie. It's important. For all of us. I need to know enough to convince Ronald he absolutely can't fight this case."

They dropped their trash in a dumpster near the bronze stegosaurus by the Smithsonian Museum of National History and kept walking.

"Okay, I do understand, Rachel," Ellie said, getting in her car parked on Constitution Avenue. "But I don't like using Wendy like this. She's a friend and a really nice person. It seems like a betrayal of her trust."

Rachel dropped her eyes, knowing her friend was right.

"Oh, don't look so miserable, Rachel. I'll do it," Ellie snapped.

"I am sorry to ask. But it's important to all of us. Just tell her your family gave some money and you want to check the records. That is more or less true, she will let a Lorten look at the files. Look for a Deacon's Fund contribution during that time period that is much larger than most. It clearly won't say Cricket Hartford. Look for some obviously made-up name."

"You mean that sounds more made-up than Cricket Hartford?"

"This isn't funny. It will stand out I'm sure, by its size and, who knows, my brother might be dumb enough to suggest it is assistance to some victim of HIV."

"What if Leif Ohlsson happens to wander in while I'm reading from the Deacon's file and asks what on earth am I doing?"

"I don't think the big man deigns to mix with the workers in the Administration Building, but if he does, just show a little leg!"

Ellie growled.

Rachel laughed and reminded her to call as soon as she escaped with the information.

Ellie drove into the sprawling complex at the Washington Bible Church as people were returning from lunch. It was a maze of utilitarian buildings on the outside; little distinguished the sanctuary from parking garage. No soaring architecture was deemed necessary for this seeker-friendly church. No arches or stained glass windows to scare off the uninitiated. Architecture had been divorced from theology and replaced with a 'if you build it, and provide easy parking, they will come' philosophy of evangelism, which seemed to be working, as the parking garage was full every Sunday.

Ellie parked behind the administration building and stepped into a small reception area. The polite receptionist did not recognize her but, in a chirpy voice, put in a call to Wendy Bradley.

Nerves on edge, Ellie focused on the large poster hanging behind the receptionist while she waited. It showed a fit young woman in spandex exercise outfit announcing the Faith & Fitness Aerobics Classes starting up next month in the church gym. The caption read, "Bod by God."

"That seems a little redundant doesn't it?" Ellie asked rhetorically to no one in particular.

"Excuse me," the receptionist said in a much less chirpy voice. "I'm sure I don't know what you mean."

Don't make a scene, Ellie said to herself as she followed Wendy back to her desk. Focus.

Ellie volunteered on several boards at the church. There were things she didn't like about the Sunday morning service but, unlike Rachel, those things didn't keep her from worshipping at WBC and enjoying the fellowship of small groups, including a women's Bible Study on Thursday mornings where she had gotten to know Wendy Bradley.

For her part, Wendy was very surprised to see Ellie Lorten and even more surprised by her request, but still she was a member of the church and a Lorten. It must be okay.

Organized in files by month, Wendy showed Ellie the relevant time period and left her to pursue whatever she was looking for in the Deacon's Committee file.

Wendy was not completely comfortable with Ellie's request, and she most certainly hoped that no one from the pastoral staff would drop in while Ellie Lorten had access to confidential church records. Still, Wendy reasoned, the Lortens practically built the church. And Ellie never took advantage of her special status as part of such a famous and important family.

Ellie read quickly through the minutes of the first meeting in October, scrolling through the electronic copies. Nothing unusual stood out. There were two unscheduled meetings called in mid-October to consider emergency needs, but nothing big enough to be the blackmail payment, also she couldn't find minutes for the second meeting in October.

She rushed on, getting more nervous every minute.

November turned up nothing of interest either, so she scrolled back through October. Minutes from the second scheduled meeting of the month were definitely missing.

"Wendy?" Ellie asked, wishing she didn't have to but now actually more curious. "Could you take a look here? Some October minutes seem to be missing. You said the church also keeps hard copies for five years. Could I see those?"

"Sure," Wendy said trying not to be more concerned. "But you must be mistaken. Let me see."

She took a seat in front of the computer. Her fingers flew across the keyboard, opening and closing files, checking, scrolling, and checking again. "Well, that is odd. Okay, let's get it from the file room. I will have to retype them into the computer anyway."

But there was no hard copy in the filing cabinet.

Feeling guilty for having used her friend and wondering what Wendy would do with the knowledge that a file was missing, Ellie rushed to her car. Her hands were shaking as she pulled onto Route 7 in the direction of Tyson's Corner. She was in a hurry to find a place where she could pull over and call Rachel.

It was late afternoon when Berta wiped bagel dough from her hands before answering the phone. She was making the last batch of the day and her feet were killing her. The bagel maker sat down on the tall stool by the phone and listened to what seemed to be a very strange request.

When Rachel Lorten-Kissane finished speaking, Berta sat quietly for a moment before replying.

"You are right in your assumption that Lewis is an old-fashioned man. He does still take the minutes by hand during the meeting. Later on he puts them on the computer and they are printed off and used for distribution at the next meeting and stored electronically. What happens to his handwritten copies is a question I can't answer. However, why don't you come to the house around 7:00 pm this evening and ask Lewis yourself?"

Ronald was at the funeral of Dr. Wilbur Culberson when he received a rare communication from his sister. Demanding, in the form of a text, a meeting for the next day. Martha had been out of the office for a few days taking care of her mother since the eminent theologian's death. Lorten had planned on firing his secretary when Dr. Culberson inconveniently died. Now he would have to put it off for some time or risk looking heartless. Still, she had become a liability and would have to go.

Ronald swore under his breath at his sister's message, then made for the back of the church where mourners were paying their respects. "Please accept my deepest sympathy and that of the entire Lorten family," he said to Mrs. Culberson. "I know how much you and Martha will miss him, as will the greater evangelical community."

Fortunately, Martha was surrounded by others so his greeting to her was mercifully short, and he made his way out of the church, calling Rachel as he got into his car.

"So what couldn't wait?" he growled when Rachel answered. "I was at Culberson's funeral."

"How nice of you to support your secretary. He was a great man and will be missed."

"Rachel, you did not call me to talk about the death of a theologian. Get on with it."

"No, you're right, nothing so unimportant as that. I am calling to tell you that I have reason to believe the IRS might be willing to settle the case at this point. You need to agree! If you don't, this investigation will get even more dangerous."

"Did your boyfriend tell you that?"

She ignored the dig.

"Ronald. Listen. To. Me. I have met Cricket Hartford. And I know about, not just the Awareness Campaign, but your use of the Deacon's Fund to funnel a second payment to her."

He took the cell phone from his ear and hit the steering wheel with it.

"Damn you, Rachel," he said over and over until he calmed down enough to speak.

"Well, I hope you enjoyed meeting your husband's mistress. What a sick thing to do. But no matter what she might have told you there is no record of any payment through the Deacon's Fund, so you are guessing, and no reason why the Feds would find that or the one to Wharton & Wharton Consulting during the Campaign. So I've decided to take my chances with the IRS. Go tell that to the Agent Arnheim."

"Actually Ronald, there is a record, and it shows that a $100,000 anonymous gift was designated for an AIDS charity out in Loudoun County."

She didn't tell him that the record she spoke of was Lewis's slightly hard-to-read notes taken at the meeting, not the official record. But they were damning nonetheless.

"It is all out there, Ronald. Just waiting for the Feds to find it. Real people, like your secretary Martha, who must have met Cricket when she came to the office. She could, and probably would, connect Cricket to you. As will the the money trail to the fictional consulting firm and now the minutes of the Deacon's meeting. So, calm down and do a risk analysis. You'll see I'm right. Please don't expose all of us to scandal and ruin just because you can't bear to lose."

Rachel didn't know when her brother hung up. Or if he had heard her through his hate.

CHAPTER 32

Cover Up

I have become a brother to jackals and a companion of owls.

—Job 30:29

Pippin, who could sleep through Beethoven's fifth played at concert level with full surround-sound and not flick a whisker, was awake and on full alert at the sound of Enoch's car coming down the drive. It was well into the night when the cat heard the car and went from deep sleep to guard cat in seconds. Gray hair standing straight along his short back, he issued a series of low growls before giving up his post and disappearing under the bed.

Rachel heard the sound of the approaching car as well and felt a similar measure of alarm — not because the sound was unknown, but because it was unexpected. The distinctive whine of the sport's car engine was unmistakable. She walked out on the deck, gripped the rail, and watched the low-slung headlights flicker through the trees as the car made its way down her very private, wooded lane until it rolled to a stop at the front door.

Enoch had never come uninvited or unannounced and she knew the reason for such a late-night visit, either as friend or IRS agent, would not be a casual one. Fear outweighed expectation as she waited.

He took long strides across the short distance from car to the front door, hard leather soles noisily striking the gravel. Rachel remained on the deck, clutching the rail while he made his way towards her.

They stood close together in silence for several long minutes staring out into the night. And then taking her by the hand, Enoch led Rachel to the swing.

"I think you better tell me why you've come," she said in a small voice.

He shuddered.

"I'm cold," he said. "Okay if we go inside?"

She took a safe seat across the room from him and managed a weak smile of encouragement.

"You know I wouldn't bother you, Rachel, coming without an invitation. Not without a very good reason."

She tensed. Waiting for the worst.

Enoch stopped and looked at the woman whose company he had come to enjoy. His late-night visit to warn her about the news that would break tomorrow was highly unorthodox and definitely unwise both personally and professionally. But he had pondered the alternatives and in the end decided to make what might be his last trip to the carriage house and tell her the bad news in person.

"I've just come from a very long meeting with your brother and his lawyers," Enoch began. "It looks like the case has been settled. Ronald has agreed to plead to certain counts of financial malfeasance, which will involve hefty fines and a flurry of publicity. He will most likely be able to turn it to his political advantage by making the IRS the enemy of conservative Christians. However, initially his guilty plea will hit the news like a bomb after weeks of denials and non-denial denials. It will be front page tomorrow morning and I didn't want you to read the news in the *Post*. In fact, you might want to stay out of D.C. tomorrow. Lorten family members will be prey for the press."

Rachel had no idea if her face reflected the relief she felt. This was exactly what she had hoped for, worked for and, in weak moments, begged God for. She looked around her house, her place, and knew now life could go on as she had hoped. Ronald, despite her worst fears to the contrary, had listened to her and taken her advice. Relief flooded her heart.

"Thank you for telling me, Enoch," Rachel mumbled, eyes lowered so he wouldn't see how glad she was for this news. "It sounds like you have achieved a fair settlement. And while it's kind of you to come and warn me I'm not too sure why you did."

"I don't think you realize what a firestorm will be unleashed tomorrow. So don't thank me. Before this is over I'm sure you'll wish we had never met."

Rachel was pretty sure he was wrong about that.

"My brother is not an easy man. I'm a little surprised, actually, that he agreed to plead."

"I was too," Enoch replied. "I went back and forth with my boss thinking there was more out there to be discovered. Some will see it as a slap on the wrist. But my instinct was to get what we could, save the taxpayers any more expense. In the end, my arugument won. But I'm not here to talk about your brother. At the very least I owe you a heads up about tomorrow and I'm so sorry, Rachel, for the unwanted and undeserved attention this is going to bring down on your head."

Rachel realized full well what it would be like. The press hordes would be back, but this time without the pity for the widow they tried to show when Eric was killed. There would be none of that this time. All Lortens would be painted with the same brush as corrupt, rich, right-wing hypocrites. Rachel did not care in the least about her brother's political downfall, but she did care about family members who would be hurt in the scrum. Ellie, Justin, and Sally. Even her mother didn't deserve what was coming. Her world would be shattered.

"So what does it mean, actually? How bad is it?" she asked.

"The fines will be huge, but nothing the company can't absorb. And you know your brother. He might even be able to convince his donors and constituents, most of them anyway, that the government is piling on Christians and conservatives again. Still, it will hurt him. He might lose the presidency of CITMAC and I can't see him running for the president of the U.S. Not this time around anyway. The lawyers seemed relieved, to be honest, and Ronald didn't fight as hard as I expected."

No, Rachel thought. He had reason not to.

She was trying to think fast and be careful when all she wanted to do was tell Enoch how much she was going to miss him now that the reason for seeing each other had come to an end.

"So the ink isn't even dry on the deal and the *Post* already has the story. That's seems fast... did you leak it?"

"I did," he agreed, miserably. "But it wasn't like the news could be delayed for more than a day at the most and I owed a favor to Tom Willis at the *Post*. That's why I wanted to tell you tonight. I am sorry, Rachel, I know how much you hate publicity."

"I'll be okay. It was kind of you to come and I think I will work from home for a few days."

Enoch's second call had been to Laura. Right after he gave the story to a very pleased and pleasantly surprised Tom Willis. Enoch wanted Laura to be first to alert a grateful White House. Funny, he thought, in the end the case will probably help Laura's career more than mine.

Rachel sat quietly, staring at the detailed patterns of the carpet that covered the small metal box beneath Enoch's feet. Lewis had given her his notes from the October Deacon's Meeting. She put them in with the Inova medical report and Cricket Hartford's name, address, and a brief outline of her admission to Rachel of the blackmail and the cover-up. It held all the evidence Enoch would need to tear up the current plea agreement and pursue criminal charges against her brothers.

Cover-up. Now *she* was a part of it.

There were so many reasons to remain quiet and only one good one not to... the truth.

Trying to silence the quiet voice inside her, Rachel suggested coffee.

"It's the least I can do. I don't want you falling asleep on the way home."

He ground the Kenyan beans, she boiled water for the French press. While they chatted about safe things, the room filled with the satisfying aroma. He told her about his recent visit to see the now rundown farmhouse where Khrushchev once stayed. Rachel found a few slightly leftover sugar cookies that Sally and Ellie had given her last week. She put cookies, napkins, (she knew he didn't take sugar or milk either) and filled mugs on a tray and carried it back upstairs to the comfortable window seats in her library.

A great horned owl flew by, swooping past the window in the moonlight like some kind of omen.

"So," Rachel said, wishing Enoch would go but wanting him to stay. "Whatever you owed Tom Willis must be paid up now. This story won't just have legs, it'll have wings."

Enoch chuckled. "Yeah, you could say he was grateful. Funny thing though, he asked if this was the whole story or if I had given the more salacious information to someone else. The cagey old reporter went on about it until, actually, I began to wonder. I have to admit it made me a little uncomfortable, but what could he know that I don't know?"

He hadn't really meant it as a question, but it immediately sounded like one to both of them.

To speak or not to speak! That was *her* question. She knew which was nobler but she also knew which was infinitely easier. No one in her family would ever, ever forgive her if she actually did the very thing they were already sure she was doing, namely giving negative information about the family to Enoch.

The smart option was to finish her coffee, stay quiet, and take a long trip until the media got bored with the story and moved on to another. Rachel could ride out the storm and then resume life here in her beautiful house. Maybe run into Enoch occasionally in D.C.

A heavy weight settled on Rachel. The taste of the coffee was suddenly bitter in her mouth. She put her cup back on the tray and sighed.

"I have become a brother to jackals and a companion of owls," she said with great sadness.

"Excuse me? I have no idea what you are talking about."

"It's a quote from the Old Testament, book of Job. Imagery of a spiritual wasteland."

Enoch's Old Testament wasn't as good as it should be, and he had no idea where she was going with that obscure reference, and misunderstanding her misery, he apologized again.

"I know Rachel, I'm so sorry. I wish I could go back and bury this case. Your brother deserves this but you did nothing wrong and this is going to hurt you too. The press can be vicious. And, well, one of the reasons I drove out is because it might be best if we don't see each other for a while and I didn't want you to misunderstand if I seem to be avoiding you. In the short term, the case may be over, but our friendship doesn't need to be."

But it was, of course, and they both knew it.

She sighed again. More deeply than before.

"What *is* wrong?" he asked sensing there was something more.

"I keep thinking about my nephew, Justin," she tried to explain, "He reminds me of me at his age. He is all idealism and existential questions, along with some real ones about the family business. Now this. I wonder how it will affect him. And the sad thing is Justin thinks I'm the honest one, the 'moral' one in the family. I think I'm guilty of fostering that impression, of course. I like his trust. Now, I'm worried about what all this will do to him."

"Oh, he'll be fine," Enoch said, greatly relieved that the fear he saw in her eyes wasn't something more troubling. "Kids bounce back. And I don't see how this will make him respect *you* less. You didn't have anything to do with it. Anyway, he's probably so focused on girls right now he won't even notice."

Enoch stood to go. "It's getting late, Rachel. Tomorrow, oops — it's already tomorrow, and it is going to be a very long day. Just keep your head down for a while. When this is all over we can go back to Great Falls for tea on the rocks. What do you say?"

Rachel remained seated. "Wait, please," she said in a very small voice. "It isn't over."

He reached down and took her hand as if to pull her up. "I know. It isn't over. I'll be busy for awhile but... "

She withdrew her hand.

"No, Enoch. I mean the investigation isn't over."

He froze.

She stood up and moved across the room. Kneeling down, she lifted the edge of the carpet, pressed a joint in the floor and took out the small metal box

"Here," she said handing him the manila folder.

"Rachel?"

She was sitting now on the floor by her hiding place. Looking down into the emptiness.

"Rachel?"

Enoch sat down next to her. The folder unopened.

"What is this?"

"Oh dear," she sighed. "My family, and a great many other people, are never going to forgive me for what I am about to do."

He waited.

"My husband," she began in a shaky voice, "had multiple affairs. He contracted HIV and passed it along to the last woman he was sleeping with. She learned this disturbing fact in a routine blood test soon after he was killed. Furious and scared, she went to Ronald and demanded payment for silence. Ronald paid. I don't know exactly how, but he passed what was a substantial amount of money from the company, and through the company, to her. I saw the beautiful place it purchased. Then, for reasons I'm not exactly sure of, a second, smaller payment was made using a different entity, namely the Washington Bible Church Deacon's Fund. I think you'll find that the designated gift from an anonymous donor to an AIDS charity was actually from my brother, and it went to a woman by the name of Cricket Hartford. We met and, strangely enough, I rather liked her. We took a walk in the woods out near Middleburg, did a little bird watching, and talked about my husband."

Enoch sat very still. The implications of what Rachel was telling him were so enormous he could hardly breathe. He said nothing, afraid to break the flow of her story.

Somewhere nearby the owl screeched. Rachel shivered but went on.

"The official, signed, copy of the meeting minutes went missing from the church office," she explained without revealing how she knew this or any other of the salient points.

"What you have in that envelope is Eric's medical report from the Inova Medical Center. Popular Christian celebrities really shouldn't have HIV. You also have a handwritten draft of the minutes of the Deacon's meeting in question. The clerk of the Deacon's Board is a good man.

He didn't know about the fraud, and I doubt if any of the other men did either. But the pastor knew. He took the money from Ronald and passed it through the church. The rest, well, it doesn't matter. You can suss out the details. That's your job. The point is, crimes have been committed."

Crimes have indeed been committed, Enoch thought, shocked, and excited by the revelations.

"I wanted to keep it hidden," Rachel went on, feeling very tired now. "I have hoped and prayed and schemed so that Ronald would do exactly what you came tonight to tell me he's going to do. I was thrilled. Investigation over, WOWL pleads, pays the fines, the case goes away. I go on with my life. I have been so afraid that you would stumble onto the facts... oh sorry, I don't mean to suggest any lack of competence on your part," she smiled at him.

"I want to go on living in this place. I love it here. But in the end, my own personal peace and prosperity just isn't worth covering up a crime. No one will thank me, except maybe you. Certain liberal press. And the administration. Not my family and certainly not the thousands of good people who attend Washington Bible Church and follow their charismatic pastor, Leif Ohlsson."

Enoch had learned to like Rachel Lorten-Kissane. He had enjoyed her company. But truth be told, he had continued seeing her mostly because of the case. At least that's what he had continued to tell himself.

When he finally spoke, it sounded more like a lawyer than he intended.

"Are you aware of the implications of what you have just done?" he asked, tapping the still-unopened folder on his knee. "Not only will this scandal be spread all over the press, but other women may come forward to tell their sordid stories about your husband. Your name will be dragged through the mud in a sin, sex, and hypocrisy scandal of mammoth proportions."

Even as he stated the facts he was struck by how terrible it would be for her.

"God, Rachel, I'm so sorry. It's going to be awful."

She laughed. Not a very happy laugh.

"I know. I have considered all that. Rather obsessively, actually. Why do you think I've tried so hard to ensure that you never found out? It seemed rotten timing that Phil Grant came along just when he did."

"So," Enoch said putting together more of the pieces, "we've been using each other. At least in the beginning. You wanted to know what I was finding out and try and focus my attention on the purely financial issues and away from your husband. But," he hesitated remembering. "But sometimes you hinted at something else. Like the day we picnicked at the Falls. Every time I mentioned your husband, your face changed. And the whole weird cenotaph thing — that's what this was about. Oh no, what about your own health? How long have you known all this? Is it possible you were infected?"

He was slowly realizing the enormous implications for her.

She ignored the last part of his question, but carried on explaining now that the floodgates were open.

"I learned about Eric's lifestyle shortly after the funeral when the Organ Donor Unit of the hospital called to inform me he had HIV. They were just telling me for my own protection, they said. And for the protection of any future partners I might have. Oh, how I hated the smug little toad giving me all the dreadful information, even thought I knew it wasn't his fault really... just doing his job and following procedure. Giving me a string of loathsome bureaucratic euphemisms," she shuddered. "I hated it."

Enoch moved to comfort her. He sat beside her and put his arm around her shoulder. "Oh God, Rachel. I'm sorry. I'm so sorry."

It was the wee hours of the next day before she walked Enoch to his car.

"What you've done is amazing, and very brave," he told her again. "And I know this seems impossible now, but someday your family may see, well, they may see this differently."

Rachel didn't think that was very likely.

"I don't feel brave at all. How could I have lived with the alternative? Actually, I'm beginning to feel a stirring of relief already. Like a weight has been lifted."

He kissed the top of her head and tightened his arms around her.

"Will you really leave this place? Oh, dear Rachel... oh my, I don't want to do this to you."

They had touched before over the months. A brief hug hello or good-bye on the street or at her door. Lingering touch of hands longer than required when moving from car to curb or in and out of doors. His hand resting a little longer than necessary on her knee to make a point in conversation. Fleeting touches quickly withdrawn.

But now he kissed her. A goodbye kiss and an acknowledgement of what had been and might have been.

The beginning and the end all in one night, she thought miserably, watching him drive away.

Rachel stood watching the car until she could no longer hear the whine of the Austin-Healey engine or see the headlamps scatter light through the trees. Then she walked back inside and looked around, seeing her creation through such different eyes. I could have gained the whole world, and lost my own soul, she thought, knowing it would not have been worth it. But wishing for it anyway.

She hadn't answered his question about leaving. Her plan had been to run away immediately if the scandal exploded. She could live in Europe again until things settled down. Be spared the reaction of her family.

Rachel had a book to finish about Eastern Europe and it could be written in the field.

Living well in Europe was an option. Avoiding endless stories in the press and the looks of pity from strangers. That had been her plan. But now she knew she wouldn't go. Not now. When I leave, she thought, it will be because I have something to go to, not run from.

CHAPTER 33

THE BEGINNING

Faith without works is no faith at all but a simple lack of obedience to God.

—*Dietrich Bonhoeffer*

RACHEL PLANTED TOMATOES, CUCUMBERS, DILL, ROSEMARY, and thyme. She turned over the soil to drown out the sound of the scandal. It shattered what was left of the Lorten family, rumbled through the nation's capital spreading joy and sorrow in equal measure.

The political left celebrated.

The right lamented.

The president was re-elected despite new scandals.

No one thanked Rachel for staying, nor seemed particularly glad for her support during the dark days of the trial. Cricket agreed to a plea and disappeared. Even Ellie, suffering Jeff's fury for her own small role and "treasonous" friendship with his sister, wondered if it had had to be, and what good could come of exposing the rot for everyone to see.

The story was told in dry legal terms by the lawyers and in scandalous color by the tabloids. Cable channels carried new revelations and announced them breathlessly as 'breaking news' every day.

The press found the carriage house and sent reporters to Rachel's door. They terrified the cats and trampled the garden.

But she stayed. She stayed until the trial was over and she finally had something to go to, not run from.

* * * * *

It was a pleasure to walk through the old streets of Sarajevo. The city provided its own kind of privacy to Rachel, utterly unlike the dense woods around her carriage house and far more impenetrable. She set out for work on a Monday morning in May, two years after leaving the United States, expecting that day to be like all others, without grand expectations or inner fears. Justin would be arriving soon to spend another summer working with her as an intern. Rachel smiled as she walked, content for the day and what it offered.

Driving rain overnight had scrubbed the Hapsburg-era structures clean and exposed pockmarks left from ancient wars and more recent conflicts. There were scars that could be seen and others hidden in human hearts. Few had healed, but hope, along with pollen, was in the air these days in Bosnia.

Rachel offered a cheery hello as she passed a street sweeper clearing away mud and wet litter from the storm. The bent figure didn't reply. She kept her head and back bowed down, pushing debris with a broom made of twigs. Street sweepers were as ubiquitous as the ever-present pigeons. Part of the cityscape.

She liked the pigeons despite having received more than one direct hit from a low-flying bird. They perched on window ledges, statues, and monuments. They gathered on city streets eating crumbs dropped by generous or careless humans. A pair of pigeons came to preen and coo on Rachel's window ledge every morning and evening.

The only other wildlife she encountered on a regular basis happened to be much less welcome. Cockroaches infested the old buildings and while

Rachel could understand they should be admired as a species (for sheer survivability) the particular family group of prehistoric bugs living in her building were gigantic shelled creatures that terrified her when encountered in the dark. An immediate seek and destroy mission undertaken on her first day had proved futile. Despite a well thought out battle plan and all available resources, Rachel had succeeded in a high kill ratio, but the insects won the war. They continued to beetle out from unseen cracks, crawl up walls at will, settle, and raise families in her kitchen cabinets.

She missed her cats. However, Rachel knew her cats didn't miss her and would hate living in the city, confined to four walls and two tiny windows. Ellie assured her on a regular basis that the cats were fine.

Rachel's mother blamed her for the collapse of the family and Ronald's ruin. Alice Lorten lived alone now in the family mansion with her servants and her anger. The rest of the family, if not fine, were at least surviving. Spared a prison sentence but unable to face life in D.C. after the fall, Jeff had joined Ellie and the kids in Indiana where they kept a second home on a lake near Ellie's parents. A less pompous, if not much kinder, husband, it seemed to Rachel, reading between the lines of Ellie's letters. Jeff was writing a new book entitled *How To Get Back on the Tightrope*. Having fallen off, as it were, he was using *repentance* as a comeback, a tried and true strategy in Washington D.C. It was one sure to sell books and re-open the corridors of power to Jeff's brand of spiritual support and counseling.

Some indefinable essence marking Americans abroad gave Rachel away as a foreigner, but her Serbo-Croatian was unaccented and flawless. Talking to locals provided insight into the emerging country and she enjoyed their different perspectives, often stopping to chat with people in shops and cafes in the neighborhood. Everyone was eager to engage in conversation about the United States, even those who resented its cultural and economic reach. Here, in this old city far from Washington, Rachel felt safe from prying eyes and dangerous questions. Sarajevo had worse secrets than her own. She had dropped Lorten from her hyphenated name and was known in the office only as Rachel Kissane.

Juggling a large set of keys with a hot cup of tea purchased at the corner kiosk, Rachel opened the office door and let the stale weekend air escape. Local directors, Ratko Loveric and his wife Milina, were in Lausanne at a conference and she was looking forward to a quiet morning catching up on the mail.

The Justice Center had been expanded, in part with assets from the breakup of WOWL, with Rachel directing the model and other smaller facilities spread across Eastern Europe as it fought the seemingly unstoppable trafficking in vulnerable human lives. But Rachel knew it wasn't about winning the war, but about waging the battle. Girls and boys were still being abducted and evil still found a way. God still called his people to bind up the brokenhearted and lift the burden from the heavy laden.

She stored her sandwich in the small refrigerator tucked in a tiny kitchen alcove, also equipped with an electric teakettle and microwave. Eating the delicious but greasy cevapcici, available on every street corner, was a temptation better avoided if she was going to keep off unwanted pounds.

Sipping the hot sweet tea, Rachel went through the morning mail and gave a little sigh of disappointment not to find a letter from Ellie. Sometimes, despite Rachel's explicit instructions to the contrary, her friend wrote and enclosed clippings from the *Washington Post* about the new IRS Commissioner, Enoch Arnheim.

Although there was continuing estrangement from most of her family, Rachel was beginning to feel the first stirrings of a desire to return home. Her blood tests continued to show no trace of HIV. Maybe life could go on.

Distracted by thoughts of home, Rachel nearly missed the last envelope, tossing it, along with the junk mail, into the dustbin. As the letter sailed through the air she glimpsed a distinctive postmark.

Virginia State Correctional Institution, Jarrad, VA, with "Ronald Lorten" written in familiar script under the stamped return.

Her brother had made it very clear to Rachel that he neither wanted nor expected to hear from her while in prison. Ronald blamed her for the five-year prison sentence and nothing she could ever say would change that. So, not wanting to upset Ronald further, Rachel had honored her brother's request, until three weeks ago when a compelling reason to write to him had walked through her office door.

It had been an ordinary day. Martha Culberson, who had looked after her mother until she passed, was now settled as Rachel's assistant, enjoying her first experience abroad and seemingly happy to be working with another Lorten.

"Rachel," Martha said, interrupting what was usually time set aside for her to work on scholarly pursuits, "I have some visitors to see you. These two young ladies would like to meet the sister of Ronald Lorten."

Surprised and not at all pleased at Martha's mentioning the family connection, Rachel managed a smile and motioned the girls to take the two chairs facing the desk. Martha stood, hands clasped in front of her, with a 'don't worry this is worth it' smile on her face.

"My name is Raluca," a cheery voice said in broken English. "And this is my very best friend in the world, Nadia. I am sorry I didn't come before, to pay my respects and thank you. But, I didn't know Ronald Lorten had a sister in Bosnia."

Taken aback and not at all certain what on earth the young woman could mean by 'paying her respects', Rachel didn't reply. She waited for an explanation, a quizzical look on her face.

The Romanian girls were both neatly dressed. They had on jeans and what looked like matching shirts with cotton sweaters and comfortable tennis shoes. Rachel thought she had seen the girl called Nadia at the after-care center, but she did not recognize the confident, bold young woman who had just addressed her as Mrs. Lorten. The silence grew uncomfortable before it was broken by the same eager, but now nervous, voice.

"Well, like I said, I'm sorry to bother you but I just learned from this nice woman," she nodded at Martha, "that you are the sister of Ronald Lorten. I had no idea Mr. Lorten's sister was here, in Bosnia," she said again, "or I would have come to meet you the last time I visited Nadia. It is such a big honor for us, for me, to meet you. You have no idea."

No, Rachel thought. I most certainly do not have any idea what you are talking about. She glanced at Martha for enlightenment. Martha said nothing, just nodded at the girl to go on.

The story of Ronald Lorten's crimes and incarceration was unknown to all except the senior staff. None of the young people who worked at the Justice Center had ever heard his name, let alone understood the part he played in building it... or the scandal that sent him to prison. There was enough everyday drama in the ministry and lives of the victims that no one could be bothered to talk about something that happened in far-off America by people they had never heard of. Except, it seems, for the young Romanian woman looking at her with something like awe *because* she was the sister of Ronald Lorten. This was a first for Rachel and now she was curious.

"Martha, why don't you make tea for all of us and bring sweets for the girls. This might take some time."

Actually, it took no time at all to tell of the brief encounter Nadia had with Ronald Lorten over three years ago.

Nadia did not say anything as her friend related the story. But she did look at Rachel, and as she did, she smiled.

That night, Rachel had written to her brother. It took most of the night. Trained to use words, she had never tried harder to use them more effectively. What Ronald had done had saved a life. It was his private, and redemptive, act of mercy. She was humbled. Rachel wanted him to know that this morning while sitting in an office an ocean away from his prison cell in rural Virginia, she was very proud to be known as the 'sister of Ronald Lorten.'

Now, only three weeks later, Rachel had a reply from her brother. The letter was still lying unopened on her desk at the end of the day, mocking her fear. What if he spewed more of the hate she had heard from him during the trial? And afterwards when he was on his way to prison. Her hands were shaking when she finally slit open the envelope and took out a single sheet written in her brother's own hand.

Dear Rachel,

I have read your letter a hundred times. Literally. I do have a fair amount of time to kill, as you might imagine.

I have so many questions about Raluca and Nadia. The memory of my short conversation with that remarkable young woman and my small private gift (we both know the amount of money was not a sacrifice for me) to help her friend is one of the few things that I can remember without shame.

But, first things first.

I want to ask your forgiveness. I don't know if I have the right to do so, but I must.

I have injured so many but you are my sister. Rather than seeing my own failings I put them on you. I blamed you, resented you, and mocked you... when all you did was challenge me to see what I had become. A man hungry for power. Now I have no power, and have been forced to look within.

The prison chaplain encouraged me to read the Psalms, and out of desperation and boredom I began to do so. 'Search me and know me, oh God,' was a very foolish thing to say for a person in my spiritual condition. But I prayed for that and God answered.

Time is a gift, on the outside. Inside, time is a curse. And nighttime is the hardest time of all. I long to sleep and when I can't I return to the Psalms. This one by Solomon, disgraced king, dysfunctional family man — a man I could identify with — broke through the hardness of my heart.

'Except the Lord shall build the house,
the builder builds in vain.

Unless the Lord watches over the city, the
watchmen stands guard in vain.

In vain you rise early and stay up late, toiling for

Food to eat — but he gives his loved ones sleep.'

I did far worse than labor in vain on my own house, I built a house of false ministry at WOWL. In my hubris, I tried to build a house of the Lord, without the Lord, and put money from the faithful in my own pockets. I understand (finally) that I deserve far more than the five years I will serve.

I'm sure forgiveness will take time. I can wait. Thank you, Rachel, for hearing me out. When you find it in your heart to write again please tell me more about the Justice Center, your work in it, and most of all about the young girl, Nadia.

Can she speak now? If God reached out to someone like me, I know He cares about and can heal that poor girl's wounds and give her back a voice. I pray that one day God will give you grace to forgive me.

I am your brother,

Ronald

Rachel walked home through the same city streets she had passed on her way to work that morning; now, however, she was utterly unaware of sights and sounds that usually fascinated her. Her mind was on the letter she carried in her hand. She didn't stop to feed the pigeons in the square or greet the old women sweeping the street. Rachel walked with a purpose, composing a reply in her mind. It began:

Dear Ronald,

Nadia Iovan cannot speak yet; but she *has* learned to smile.

346

ABOUT THE AUTHOR

MARY REEVES BELL IS THE AUTHOR OF A HISTORICAL FICTION trilogy for young adults that has also been translated into French and Norwegian. The first of these, *The Secret of the Mezuzah*, was honored by the Anne & Charles Corrin Jury at the Sorbonne for contributing to the remembrance of the Holocaust. Mary has written for Christian publications. She founded and devotes much of her time to a non-profit mercy ministry rescuing at-risk children in Romania. Mary lives with her husband, David, in the beautiful Virginia countryside.